ECUADOR

Also by RS Perry

Off The Edge

Over The Line

Out Of Time

ECUADOR

RS PERRY

ISBN (Trade Paperback) 978-0-9880827-8-6

ISBN (Hardback) 978-0-9880827-7-9
ISBN (Paperback) 978-0-9880827-9-3
ISBN (e Book) 978-0-9880827-6-2

ECUADOR

Paper back, exclusive rights, CA.

Copyright © Jerome Sands, LLC

Published by Penelope Ltd.

My heartfelt appreciation for the time and commitment spent editing to Jenny Lyons and Ethel Beach. And also to Shelly Davis.

The author wishes to thank Joan Oliver for the poem in Chapter 60.

Thank you, Magdalene Pagratis, for cover preparation and formatting – custom-book-tique.com

Back cover: author's photo taken in the Yukon, fall 2018.

To unique people, diverse cultures and their lands.

Prologue

Centro Nacional da Infecção, Rio de Janeiro, December 2000

Mateo and Luiz stood before an old wooden door with dingy, peeling paint. An iron bar with spots of yellow-orange rust crossed the door at waist height. One end of the bar disappeared into a metal slot like a giant deadbolt. An old-fashioned iron padlock secured the other end.

'No one has entered here in a long time. It is a funny old lock,' said Luiz.

'I don't like this place,' said Mateo.

'I wonder where the lock came from? Maybe from Portugal,' said Luiz as he inserted the oversized key he'd been given into the lock.

Mateo lifted his upper left lip, arched his eyebrow, and looked toward Luiz, as if to say, *You think this old lock will open?* Then he thought, *I hope not.* Luiz turned the key. He twisted it, then twisted harder. The key reluctantly turned—grating—and the heavy lock fell open.

'I don't want to go down there,' said Mateo with a shiver. 'These ancient places make me nervous.'

'Why, you believe in ghosts?

'Never mind. Let's see how long this is going to take.'

'First, we see how many samples there are. Then we will know how long it will take.'

'I have to go to my cousin's wedding next week, so I hope to God this doesn't take more than a few days.'

'You have cousins here in Brazil, Mateo, or do you go home?'

'Yes. No, I mean. No cousins here in Rio. I have to go home to Colombia.'

Luiz pulled the iron bar out of the slot and set it against the wall; it rang like a bell as the steel hit the concrete floor. The shrill ringing permeated Mateo's mind, renewing his nervous shivers. Luiz reached into the darkness and around the corner to the wall, pushing his fingers through sticky cobwebs. Eventually, he found the light switch, illuminating gloomy walls.

They stepped through the stale air, down worn, stone stairs, batting clingy cobwebs out of their way to a windowless basement. The walls were covered with years of accumulated grime. Dust clung to gossamer webs. The upright freezers, once shiny white, showed spots of rust, erupting like miniature orange volcanos.

'Hijo de puta,' said Mateo as he counted. 'Eight freezers. Many more than is good, but maybe they are not too full. Just so we're finished before I have to fly home next Wednesday. We could work this weekend?' he said hopefully to Luiz.

'Uh-huh,' said Luiz dismissively.

'Don't you think working this weekend would be a good idea? Get it over with, yes?'

'Maybe you, Mateo, but not me. I have plans.'

Luiz started opening the freezer doors. 'We're in luck. Look at this one on the end. It's almost empty. We can transfer the samples fast from the next one, so they don't thaw. I was afraid we were going to have to bring down boxes and a lot of dry ice to keep them cold while we worked. We'll inventory this one first. After that we can move the next freezer's samples into it. Put on your gloves and move a table in front of the freezer.' He pointed at a rickety table against the wall. 'Clean the top off while I get the computer booted.'

'Let's look in the other freezers.'

'They will be what they are. We have a job to do. Let's get started.'

Mateo unloaded the first freezer's contents, setting several small boxes and Styrofoam containers on the table.

'Tell me what the first box says, then put it back in the freezer. Rápido, so they don't thaw. Going fast should suit your time schedule, too.'

Mateo started reading labels. Some he read with difficulty. Luiz typed them into the computer spreadsheet. Containing only a few samples, the first freezer went quickly. They started on the next, which was packed full. Mateo took out a couple of stacks of small boxes and wire containers holding glass slants, set them on the table, and then closed the freezer door.

'There's hundreds in here. This could take forever. Do you suppose any of these are bad?' asked Mateo.

'I don't think so. My boss said they are old. The big boss told him that many are probably not still alive. He thinks most are samples of plants, mushrooms, and soil bacteria. But he said to be careful as the crazy old professor that collected them could have stored anything. After they have our inventory and see what's here, they will either destroy them or move them to the university microbiology department.'

'*P. Aeruginosa*, 1966,' said Mateo. 'I don't like it down here,' as he scowled at the disintegrating walls. 'There are no windows. I don't feel so good.'

'You want to get sick or are you going to spell the next one for me.'

'Ana…car…dium occi…dentale.' Mateo struggled with both the spelling and pronunciation. 'What's that? It doesn't sound like a plant.'

Luiz rolled his eyes. 'Spell it, don't say it. You're wasting time. And I don't know much more than you. Just be careful not to drop any.'

Chapter 1

For the past three days, Jago's band had moved along the edge of the expansive Río Napo, staying in front of their pursuers.

Jago gambled that the army pursuers would continue to chase his small band in the same way, and not jump ahead to ambush them. If the army leader was skilled, he would lull them into the complacency of the chase. If he was arrogant, he might assume his men could overtake them. Or maybe Jago was wrong, and an ambush was only minutes away. Jago knew, however, that sooner or later this would end. A mental guessing game between him and the army officer who was chasing him further and further south and away from his home country.

Chesswits, he said to himself. While his English was limited, he enjoyed playing word games with himself. He was alive because he was good at reasoning and liked playing games of wit. *But how good is the army commander? Perhaps he is better,* Jago mused, *and he will play a better game than I will.* He sensed he had prolonged the game as long as he could. Spotting two dugouts partially hidden at the bank's side, he made a decision. They passed a narrow disused game track that he would later take after a little misdirection. They boarded the canoes and paddled downstream for a mile.

As they drifted with the murky current, Jago pointed to an overgrown area where the trail veered away from the river. After landing, they set the canoes adrift before ascending the muddy bank, picking their way through the dense growth, and crossing the trail into the jungle. Carlos scooped water from a puddle into his hat and washed away their muddy footprints. He was the last to cross the trail, brushing their tracks away with a handful of long grass.

As they slowly worked their way parallel to the path and back toward the game trail, San broke the silence, whispering to Chico, 'Why not stay in the canoes and get far away?'

Chico made a cut sign across his throat.

San looked irritated and continued anyway. 'I think it is better we stay in the canoes,' he said.

Chico whispered, 'We're sitting ducks in the canoes. Ahora, silencio.'

After moving through the tangled growth, Jago found the little-used game trail near where they had taken the dugouts. Spider webs spanned the little track, glistening silver in thin shafts of the late afternoon light that filtered through the dense canopy.

The webs stretched innocently across the insect superhighway, apparently invisible to the fast-flying speedsters. To the insects' eyes, there were few obstacles to skirt in the relatively uninhabited space above the trail. Whether it was their diminutive cognitive powers or reckless behavior, they raced over, around, and occasionally, into a sticky thread.

Jago reached down to a web and, with a long elegant finger, flicked a filament, sending a vibration along the shimmering thread to its patiently waiting weaver. Camouflaged by its stillness, a large black and red spider gingerly stepped across the web, moving quickly but hesitantly. Jago tickled the thread again, and the spider moved toward the source of the vibrations. Jago smiled, stood, and stepped over the web, continuing methodically ahead.

Jago's pursuer's commander assumed his prey was now lulled into a false sense of security as they progressed along the wide river. Soon, when the helicopter arrived, he would fly men ahead and snare his target in an ambush, just as Jago assumed he might do. A two-pronged ambush: men in front, men behind, and the helicopter with its gunner coming in from the riverside.

Jago wondered, however, why the forces behind them had not set up an ambush immediately. Perhaps the army commander had no transport. They had heard a few boats moving up and down the river, but they observed none with army troops. No helicopters had flown overhead, scouting for his band. This didn't mean, though that the choppers had not flown around them out of hearing range, ferrying troops for an ambush.

In this game of cat and mouse, one would win and the other lose. Jago was not arrogant enough to assume that, while he had evaded his enemies for most of his life, he would always win.

Everyone followed carefully in his footsteps as he walked around, over, and sometimes under the dew-laden webs. The army would have expert trackers. He avoided soft soil and mud, leaving little sign that humans had passed this way. León followed the none-too-intelligent and less-experienced Carlos, making sure he left no sign for others to follow. Jago stopped to watch a slow-moving, eight-inch, brown-colored, hard-shelled turtle, admiring its prehistoric beauty.

Jago was tall at six feet four inches, and thin, with sinewy muscles that looked ropy through his taut caramel-colored skin. A black drooping mustache, together with a few gray hairs and sleepy-dog brown eyes, suggested an amiable character.

'The depression to our left probably leads to a stream. Search and see if you can find a place for us to stay for a few days,' he whispered. Chico was smart. He had been with Jago since he was old enough to carry a weapon. He could be relied on to choose a good overnight spot.

Chico, mature for his age, shared with Jago a caution that had kept them alive through the years and out of the clutches of the government troops. San did not share their caution. 'Why don't we keep going? I don't think they will catch us,' said the fifteen-year-old.

Jago held up his hand, silencing him before turning to his sometime lover. 'Cherry, go back along the river and make sure our army friends don't notice our little subterfuge when they pass.'

Cherry, wearing bandoleers crisscrossing a tan shirt and amplifying her breasts, turned to leave, giving the young San a look that suggested exactly what she thought of him.

Jago, ever the patient teacher, explained to San what he didn't need to explain to the others. 'They pursued us long enough to think we will keep running along the river in front of them. They will soon call additional troops in ahead of our route, or perhaps send men by boat or plane ahead of our path to set an ambush. Their commander possibly will try to catch up with us, push us into the ambush, and his trackers will see the place where we took the dugouts and assume we are on the river. It would be very lucky for them to find us camped here.' Then he added, 'as long as we are careful to leave no sign for their trackers and keep quiet.'

Jago assumed his role as leader naturally and with a dedication to instruct and pass on knowledge, both about war and peace.

'I see,' said San, 'it is smart thing to do but still we must have luck.'

'Our lives are decided by judgment and luck,' responded Jago.

A bird-like whistle, blending with the jungle sounds, came from the direction of the river. Cherry was sending a note of caution, not danger. Jago motioned the others to fade into the jungle.

After ten minutes, another whistle twittered through the green understory, and the men reappeared. None were concerned, as it was the way they spent their days, cautiously moving in and out of the shadows.

'Good place with water,' said León as he, too, appeared from the dense jungle understory.

'Show the others. Set up a guard. I'll wait for Cherry, and we will be along just after dark.'

Jago whistled his unique birdcall. Several minutes later, Cherry silently and slowly walked off the trail to Jago, her white teeth showing in the fading early evening light. Except for a small scar below her right eye, her shoulder-length black hair and an unblemished light-coffee complexion suggested she was younger than her twenty-nine years.

She liked and respected Jago, just as he did her. They had known each other since she was thirteen years old. He had been her first lover one year later. They had never belonged to each other and had only made love infrequently over the years. Occasionally, they embraced each other. She could not say she loved him other than in a paternal way, but she would willingly give her life for him. He had been the only family she had after hers was killed, and she was abandoned in an army camp as a blossoming teenager.

They walked indirectly to the camp, approaching from the opposite direction that León had taken earlier. Jago whistled his evening birdcall, alerting them they were arriving. A return whistle indicated the exact direction to their night's resting place.

A smile broke out on Jago's face as he reached out, slapping Lobo on the shoulder. The big man had remained still as they approached, nearly invisible in the dark shadows cast by the last vestiges of twilight filtering through the jungle trees. Lobo was the same size as many of the tree trunks. Jago nearly missed him. As it was, he only sensed Lobo when he was close enough to reach out and touch him.

The three veterans of many battles moved carefully to their small campsite. The ten-foot-by-ten-foot clearing was faintly lit by early stars. They sat on the damp soil by the edge of the trickling water to eat their sparse rations. León, San, Chico, and Carlos were already in their net hammocks around the edge of the clearing, talking softly while they ate.

'We search in the morning and make sure the soldiers have passed,' said Jago as he stood.

Chapter 2

Mateo and Luiz were nearly finished with the second freezer. It had taken them the better part of four hours. Mateo knew that, at this rate, they would not finish in time for him to leave. He estimated it would take until the end of next week. He started to move at a faster pace, which did not accomplish much. Mateo became exasperated when Luiz typed too slowly, and he had to wait.

In Mateo's haste, he dropped a sample. Luckily the Styrofoam container cushioned the fragile glass. Luiz scowled. 'Calm down and pay attention. Most of these are probably harmless, but don't be careless. Some might kill you.'

Mateo ignored the lecture. 'I will have to continue this weekend to have any chance of my family leave. Could you please help me a little?'

'Sorry, my friend, but not a chance. Maybe you can ask Anibal or Fausto? It has to be someone from the lab. You can't bring just anyone down here. It's lunchtime. Let's go.' And he started up the steps.

Mateo frowned and reluctantly followed him. His mind kept going over and over how to get this job done. He was not finding any solutions. He had been given a week off starting Wednesday, but with the condition that they finish the inventory first.

They were sitting outside on a bench eating the lunches they had brought with them. 'I don't see any way to get this done except to work this weekend. I'll find someone to help me, but I need you to leave me with the computer.'

Luiz was getting tired of hearing about Mateo's problem. 'Okay, enough! You can use it this weekend, but it better be in perfect shape on Monday. And you can't miss any samples. If Doctor Santos finds out that we missed any, we'll be out of a job. And spell them correctly. If I say okay for you to work this weekend, don't let me down?'

'Gracias. Muchas gracias.'

'When are you going to learn some Portuguese? Obrigado. Muito obrigado.'

'Muito, muito obrigado.'

'Let's go back. I want to leave early,' said Luiz.

Mateo rolled his eyes. *That's it, then. I'll keep working tonight, too*, he thought. *I have to get ahead of this. I want to go home and to the wedding party.*

Mateo worked until just after midnight and managed to get almost to the end of the third freezer. He was bored, his mind was taking flights of fancy, and he started thinking about just chucking some samples out. He couldn't. Both his cultural indoctrination and upbringing to do the right thing mixed with the thought of doing something which, if he were caught, he would have to pay a penalty. *I like my job. Mierda. I need it. If I can get to the fifth freezer this weekend, then we can finish by Tuesday.*

The next morning, Mateo pulled himself out of bed and walked to work, stopping for a shot of espresso at the Jacaré Café on the way. It was the only place where he could get an espresso that compared to that of his home city of Bogotá. The proprietor knew what he liked and knew his distaste for the sweet cafezinho that Brazilians seemed to like.

Mateo walked along the tree lined Rua Vincente de Sousa as he neared the hospital, then turned right onto Rua Bambina. The beach was not far away. *If only he could spend the day there, instead of in the basement dungeon.* Just thinking about what ghosts might be lurking made him shudder.

By lunchtime, he had efficiently finished the third freezer and was partway through the fourth when he decided to take a break. He had only purchased a Guarana soda at the Jacaré Café. *Now I wish I had bought a lunch,* he mused. Earlier, he had thought missing lunch would help him finish earlier, and at the same time diminish his midsection. Now that he was hungry, he regretted it, even though his mind kept telling him to lose his belly for the wedding. The thought of the girls that would be there finally took his mind off his hunger.

The soda was cool and one of the few things he had learned to like in Brazil. The freezers were good for something—keeping his liquid lunch cold. He sat on the stone steps with the freezers spread before him. He felt he was making good progress, but this freezer was full, and many of the containers were small wire racks holding multiple glass tubes. It would take him many more hours.

He got up and walked to the fifth freezer to see whether it was packed with small or larger containers: all small, just like the one he was working on. *Mierda. Not good at all,* he thought. Still, if I keep working fast, we will be done on Tuesday.

He returned, removing several small boxes and racks and setting them on the table. The small containers and the individual vials were slowing him down, and he struggled with the long and unfamiliar names: *Filoviridae unk, Marburg Marburgvirus (MARV), Staphylococcus aureus, Ebola bundibugyo, Variola major, Rotavirus A, Rotavirus B, Clostridium difficile.* He was happy whenever an easy name came along such as *India 1.* He entered them on the laptop computer, over and over, out of the freezer, letter by letter adding the names into the computer, moving them back to the preceding freezer, getting new boxes and vials, adding them to the computer, and repeating the whole process, hour after hour.

Bored and impatient, he was having a hard time focusing. His thoughts elsewhere, Mateo grabbed an armful of containers and vials. Several fell from his arms to the floor, but only one broke. 'Mierda. No, no, puta madre.' *No one would miss one vial, would they? They hadn't been looked at for many years,* he reasoned. 'Mierda, mierda, mierda.' Mateo took out his handkerchief to protect his fingers from the broken glass, and carefully picked up the pieces. He put them into an empty box, wiped up a tiny drop of goo, and shook the handkerchief. He inspected it and, not seeing any pieces of glass, he returned it to his pocket.

He would have to think about what to do with the broken pieces. One small vial out of hundreds couldn't possibly be missed. He started to feel less guilty. The episode meant two things: there was one less stupid vial to write down, and he was jarred out of his malaise. He was ready to get to the job.

The day continued. He was starting the fifth freezer when his resolve let him down. 'I can't do this anymore,' he mumbled to the freezers. He looked at the small box containing the broken vile and put it in his pocket. He walked up the stairs, replaced the steel bar and the old lock, and then headed toward his studio apartment, knowing tomorrow would be just as boring as today. *But I am a lot closer to getting out of here in time for my flight home.*

As he walked up the Rua Bambina, he saw a refuse container. He looked around and— no one was watching—lifted the lid and threw in the small container with the broken pieces of glass. He wondered if the sample had been valuable. *I should be throwing many more out,* he thought, but he knew he wouldn't. He was not that kind of person. His mother and the church had raised him to follow rules.

Mateo continued walking down the Rua Bambina. He looked back as he turned the corner toward home. He didn't see anyone. Perhaps Monday he and Luiz could finish, and he would be on his way.

Only seconds after he turned the corner, a man emerged from the shadowed alley and went to see what the passerby had thrown into the refuse barrel. He reached in and rummaged around, hoping to find some food. He pulled out a small container. It was too lightweight to hold much food. Maybe some cake crumbs. He opened it and put his fingers inside. He felt broken glass and then something gooey. He touched it to his tongue and then spit. His hope of finding an easy dinner dashed, he sighed and set out down the Rua.

Chapter 3

'W here's Barbara?' asked Jim.

'Ah, um… Doctor Milton's home sick. She asked me to fill in for her, ah with you,' said Nusmen, looking decidedly uncomfortable.

The two men were close to the same height, with Jim's defined muscles giving him the larger, wider presence compared to Nusmen's beanpole body. Jim studied the man for a few seconds— looked at his crazy untamed hair and watched his Adam's apple move up and down as Nusmen kept swallowing.

Then, Colonel Johnson considered the respectful way Nusmen had said Doctor Milton's name and said, 'The general has put a lot of faith in you. I didn't have anything to do with you being appointed the co-director of BWC's laboratory. What I do have is a long history with General Crystal, and I trust his judgment. And Heather always said you were not only exceptionally knowledgeable with botanical studies, but helpful with her field research. I value her opinion too, but I thought you to be…'

As Jim hesitated, Nusmen finished his sentence… 'weird?'

Jim didn't say anything. There were probably several psychological terms to describe Nusmen besides weird. He would bet that Katarina had a mile-long psych profile on him. He would ask her for it some time.

Nusmen continued, 'Well, you were no doubt right and still are. It doesn't mean that I don't love this place, the chance to be here. I'll never forget what the general has done for me. I have even made friends here…uh, maybe a friend, Brad, and I think Doctor Milton likes me, even though she says I am not very good with people, so maybe weird is, …ahh, right. I don't know…I've never paid much attention to what people thought.'

'Maybe one good friend is more important than many. Time to quit chatting and get on with it.' Something Nusmen, the General, and Colonel Johnson had in common: none liked small talk, and while Jim was perhaps coming to a new understanding of Nusmen, he had had enough chitchat. The colonel just didn't like to waste time chatting about unnecessary things that weren't pertinent to the topic at hand. But for a different reason than Nusmen—who didn't know how.

Jim interjected, 'This is a big place, and I only have about an hour left today. It's been a long time since I had a real feel for what goes on here, so stay with your main projects on this level. We won't do the restricted levels today, but you can tell me how everything weaves together as we go along.'

Nusmen looked down at the floor and said, 'Finding a cure for the *Staph aureus*, the one I turned loose. The one they call the Nusbug…'

Jim cut him off. 'I don't care about the past, only the present. Anything else?'

'Well, with the resistant *Staph*, we are in the final tests, a different protocol than just a new antibiotic. We are combining antibiotics with phages. The phages poke a hole through the cell wall, and the antibiotics enter and wreak havoc on the bacteria,' he said with a little regained pride at his new method.

'Both Gram-positive and negative bacteria?'

'I dunno yet. I have only been testing the *Staph*. They get right into the cell wall through the peptidoglycan. Of course, there is only a thin lipid layer in the gram positives. I hope we might be able to penetrate a thicker lipid layer on the gram negatives too.'

'What else?'

'This is peculiar. There are these groups of repeating DNA

sequences.'

'Why is that unexpected when a lot of DNA appears to serve no function?'

'I dunno what it means, but I found the same thing a while back looking at archaea sequences.'

'Go on.'

'We're sequencing the H5 N1 flu virus, the avian coronavirus that emerged in Hong Kong in 1997. I'm trying to work out how someone could re-engineer it.'

'To what end?' asked Jim.

'To make it transmissible from human to human. The problem is still transmission. It's a hundred times deadlier than the 1918 flu. The same thing for other coronaviruses, or dengue, or lassa. A variant could be deadly if it jumped species and was transmittable human to human.'

Jim had to smile, as Nusmen stated the reasons the Biological Warfare Center had been started. In order to prevent pandemics, they needed to create the very organisms that could cause them, understand them, and develop countermeasures to them. As a philosophical problem, Jim had endlessly wrestled with whether what they did was ethical or not. His practical side said that if they didn't pursue this, someone else would. By the same token, his natural distrust of the people running governments caused him concern. What if the wrong people were able to gain control of the BWC? What if one of their creations escaped?

Nusmen, mirroring Jim's thoughts, looked distracted as he mumbled, 'And we have to understand it, so we can fix it before someone turns it into a bioweapon.'

'Our exact purpose for being here. What else?'

'I'm sorry. You already know all this. I'm wasting your time.'

'I want to hear your take on things.'

Nusmen had not intended to mention this, but he couldn't help himself. He became excited and blurted out, 'This one is really cool! If rabies could be made transmissible, either by engineering it, or combining it with something like measles or a flu virus, then it would create Zombies. You know, like the movies. It gets into your brain and messes up your personality and makes you aggressive like dogs when they get it.'

'Combining rabies with other viruses is unfeasible, right?'

Nusmen's eyes twinkled. 'Difficult maybe, but not impossible.'

'Fictitious zombies become a reality. That's pretty freaky, Nusmen.'

'Yeah, like I said, really cool. Okay. On level four, we're working on the current top ten viruses and bacterial resistant bugs: MRSA, *Pseudomonas aeruginosa*, resistant *Neisseria gonorrhoeae*, etc. Also, we have a re-engineered the1918 flu virus, the H5 N1 bird flu, and a Variola major species. The general said the Russians were once working on combining smallpox with another virus to shorten the incubation period. You probably know more about it than me.'

'Doubt it. Too much time spent in admin or the field to keep up as well as I would like with the science. Time is short, so take me through the rest of the lab.' While they walked, Jim said, 'I reviewed your safety inspections. They're first-rate.'

'It's not me. It's Barbara. She is almost fanatical about level three and four protocols.'

They walked for another forty-five minutes, looking at the high throughput genetic analyses, beaker after beaker on shaker platforms, robotic arms moving multiple pipettes up and down, a wide array of mass spectrometers with dozens of tiny acrylic holders, clicking faintly as they stopped and started on conveyors. Machine after machine: High-Performance Liquid Chromatography; electron microscopes, both SEM and TEMs; and the newest addition, a combination Scanning Electron and Transmission Electron Microscope; even an MRI. Much of the lab was automated, seemingly run without human input: hundreds of small lights blinking on and off, leaving a faint blue glow, with only the occasional technician moving, inspecting, and adjusting equipment.

The tour brought Jim more respect for Nusmen. Had he

misjudged him? He had only briefly interacted with him outside the laboratories and hadn't been impressed with what he'd observed in the mountains last fall. When he eventually arrived at the assumption that Nusmen was most likely autistic, Jim's opinion had softened. He would later find out from Katarina that she labeled Nusmen a super-high-functioning Asperger's with typically little or no social skills. But she emphasized that he was not an extreme case and was able, more or less, to temper many emotional reactions. Nevertheless, he found it nearly impossible to mesh with most "normal" people.

What didn't jibe was that Barbara, the BWC's long-term lab manager, decided Nusmen had a heart. *Time would tell,* thought Jim again. *I'll have time to see who he really is.* He would have that time while he replaced the general as the BWC acting director. Jim was determined to keep his new admin role as short-term as possible.

The tour showed him the exponential growth that the lab had gone through. He remembered the past all too well: buildings that housed mainframe computers with humming punch card readers, optical microscopes to observe bacteria, and then, in later years, tedious manual culturing, splicing, and analyzing. *All ancient history now.* The question he wondered most about was, *Who else had this sort of ability? Who was creating and producing a dangerous, infectious virus or bacteria out there?* It was only a matter of time before a terrorist obtained or engineered a deadly microorganism.

The main public biothreat so far had been anthrax. Despite its bad reputation, it was easily treated with antibiotics.

Tomorrow, Jim planned to take a look at the BWC's security as well as one of his favorite areas, the weapons and equipment rooms. He hadn't been there since Najma had killed his long-term friend Sergeant Mason at Jim's and Heather's Eastern Washington ranch. His death had left an empty spot. *Another old friend that was no more,* he thought. After tomorrow, he would fly back to the ranch. He had promised to take Pedro horseback riding along the bottom edge of Wolf Mountain if the snow wasn't too deep.

Chapter 4

Angélica Noboa Perez, hovered over a notebook, counting species of birds on the edge of a small, wet area almost completely covered with large lily pads. A silent Jago, looking bemused, walked up behind her and softly said, 'Please do not make any sudden moves, señorita.'

Unafraid, the feisty Angélica turned and glared at the ruggedly handsome, dark-skinned man causally pointing an AK-47 at her, and said, 'How dare you. Get away from me. Now!'

Jago, somewhat surprised by a fearless response from the short, but not unattractive dark-haired woman standing alone in the jungle, could not help but smile. He looked down at her petite hands, perched on healthy, wide hips. 'Your name, señorita?'

'Kiss my ass.'

'A most generous suggestion; I haven't kissed one for a long while. Is that your desire?'

She turned and started to run, but before she got more than a few feet, strong slender fingers gripped her arm, and the next thing she knew, she was lying on the ground.

'Bastardo.'

Jago was amused. 'A nice little chicken like you must have a family close by. You are not out here alone, I think?'

She was about to say who she was but caught herself just in time.

'You would do yourself a service by answering. I see in your manner that you do not want to answer. Perhaps you have a rich family somewhere, no?'

'What do you want?' she said as she pushed herself up against a tree trunk.

Jago sat down beside her, 'To live a good life and take money to my people, and, for the moment, to escape those who are pursuing us.'

'Us. You are not alone?'

Jago whistled. Within seconds, Lobo, Chico, San, León, Carlos, and Cherry materialized from the jungle, each with a different thought. Jago, curious, wondered who this woman was. Besides drugs, the FARC kidnapped many people, earning high fees before giving captives their freedom. With her expensive hiking clothes, this woman would probably be from a family willing to pay for her freedom.

Cherry looked at the woman, wondering if Jago would sleep with her. Young San, inherently meaner than the rest of the men, and consequently the least liked in the band, leered with desire and fantasized about forcing her legs apart. Women had been too scarce away from their home territory to satiate his teenage hormones.

Lobo caught his intention and motioned for the fifteen-year-old to move towards the edge of the small pond to stand guard. Besides wanting to move him away, he did not think this woman would be out here alone. Although they had neither seen nor heard anyone, others might be close by. He motioned to Carlos, who was only two years older than San, to position in the opposite direction.

'Lobo, you and Cherry see if you can find any soldiers, or where this pretty young thing's home is.' Angélica, thinking about soldiers nearby, almost let out a yell. But something stopped her, and she remained silent.

'If soldiers are after you, perhaps you should run away from here.'

'Being still is sometimes safer than moving. The mantis is invisible as long as he stays motionless.'

Angélica watched a bright yellow-green frog sitting on the side of a small branch ten feet away.

Jago followed her gaze.

'If your sting is sufficient, you can move without such caution,' she countered.

Jago shifted his body and turned his head toward Angélica while moving closer to her. He searched her eyes. She did not pull away and, instead of fear, felt lightheaded. He watched her pupils become larger, a slight movement as she turned toward him, her fingers opening and closing as they massaged her thigh.

He smiled. 'Your name, señorita?... por favor.'

'Angélica Perez,' she answered. She could feel her heart beating faster and could not understand why. After a few seconds, again without understanding why, she whispered her family name, 'Angélica Noboa Perez.'

Chapter 5

From his chair, General Will Crystal contemplated his new oversized office inside the world's most powerful spy agency. He wondered why he had agreed to be here; nevertheless, he had agreed, leaving him no choice but to follow the old military saying that he, Jim, and Brush often used, 'Nothing for it but to do it.'

His intercom buzzed, breaking the silence. 'They're here.' The door opened. The general's inherited PA did not have to ask the general if she could enter. She had quickly learned that the new Director of Central Intelligence did not like to waste words. She remained quiet as Bertrand Gupta, the Director of Intelligence, and Eric Sands, the newly appointed Deputy CIA Director, entered Will Crystal's office.

'Morning, General,' said Bertrand as he moved straight to one of two chairs across from his new boss's desk, followed by Eric, who nodded. Bertrand felt at ease and content. The agency was in capable hands again. After the full story of the terrorist Najma's Guantanamo escape and Sorenson's cover-up had been exposed in the press, the White House had wasted no time in forcing the former politically appointed director, Senator Sorenson, to resign.

The deputy director had just returned from giving the morning briefing to the president. The general loathed giving the briefing and having decided that Eric Sands was the best choice to succeed his intended short tenure as DCI, passed this duty to his deputy. Sands also disliked the briefing task, but having General Crystal as their new director more than compensated for the extra duty. While it had never been mentioned, he knew the general's intention was for him to eventually become the director. General Crystal's true loyalty was not here. It would always be to a different Washington, 2,300 miles west-northwest from where they now sat.

'Good morning, gentlemen. Let's go over the high points,' said the general. All three men had the same morning write-ups. They always met to discuss Eric's presidential briefing after he gave it, not before. After they'd covered all the briefing points, General Crystal asked Eric if he had anything to add.

'One request we are going to have to act on immediately. The VP asked us to research a disappearance in the Amazon,' said Eric. 'An old school chum of his, who as it happens is now the president of Ecuador, has just been informed that his daughter vanished from an ecolodge where she'd been working in the Amazon. We have several assets in northwest South America, especially in Colombia, but this happened in a remote area of the jungle in Ecuador. It is unlikely we will be able to gather much on-site information.'

'If this is a priority, let's bring the BWC in,' said Will. Then he reiterated his position. One that everyone already knew. 'I don't think it is a good idea to start having my people at the BWC start to work with the CIA, even with me here. I want to keep them independent. So, let's get the agency working on this, and I'll ask BWC to see what they can find out on their own. Then, we'll decide how to handle it.'

'Is that a challenge?' asked Eric.

The general thought about the young army hackers sitting at Fort Huachuca and the brilliant older academic IT experts, Misa and Vidya, that he had finally persuaded to move from Fort Huachuca to the BWC. He also knew something that Bertrand and Eric didn't; Vidya had hacked into the CIA's computers without the agency's techs detecting them. *I hope it stays that way.* Then, a thought struck like a thunderbolt. What if the agency had, unbeknownst to him, Misa, or Vidya, hacked BWC's computers?

His mind returned to Eric's question. 'Let's just say it will be interesting to see what each comes up with.'

'The VP was emphatic that he wanted this actioned as soon as possible. I'll bring Eileen and Martin in and get them started on it,' said Eric.

After Bertrand and Eric left, Will called Sheilla. They agreed she would set up a group to look into the woman's disappearance from the ecolodge. Then, lounging back in his oversized director's desk chair, he contemplated his situation as director of the Central Intelligence Agency.

He had agreed to be the new DCI but only until the re-elected president could find the right person to head the agency. The White House realized what a poor choice could mean to the nation, even the world, and this time they would carefully vet their new nomination. In truth, the man currently sitting behind the desk was, and would be, the White House's first choice, just as he was Bertrand Gupta's, but the general intended his replacement to be the thirty-year agency veteran, Eric Sands. The general needed to persuade the president that someone from within the agency was best equipped to run the company, not another outsider.

Many wanted Bertrand Gupta to be the director. But he didn't want the job any more than the general did. Bertrand's expertise was problem-solving and intelligence matters, not interfacing with politicians. And if General Crystal would not remain director, Gupta supported Eric for the permanent job of DCI.

Then his thoughts turned to Jim. The colonel had agreed to head the BWC only as long as he also remained its lead field agent. General Crystal understood, and not only because of their long friendship dating back to Vietnam; the general understood that Colonel James L. Johnson was not yet ready to trade in his Glock for a pencil.

In reality, all these director titles were only a mirage; nothing significant had changed with the BWC. The general remained its de facto director. Jim still ran field operations. The only thing that had really changed was that the general spent time on the East Coast at Langley, and Jim spent more of his downtime at the BWC and less at his ranch. Nevertheless, General Crystal could not help feeling removed from the beating heart of the laboratory he had conceived of and started many years ago. He intended to return as often as he could and would do so tonight.

Chapter 6

Will Crystal was getting used to his shuttle back and forth from one Washington to the other. He elected to take the Citation X as a late-night flight, sleeping on board. In a way, the plane had become his first home. He didn't embrace his quarters at Langley. Nor did he feel his house at Fort Lewis was his home anymore. He had become a transient.

The plane deposited the general at the BWC hangar at zero-six hundred. He walked to his office and then to the conference room. Three men and two women were seated around a shiny mahogany table. Sheilla was conspicuously missing. Mark started to stand, an involuntary response to authority, and then caught himself, hoping the general had not noticed his movement. The general did not like wasting time on formalities.

While taking his seat at the head of the table, General Crystal began talking to the group in a voice that commanded their immediate attention, 'Mark, summarize. I want to make sure we all start out on the same page. We have to get this operation up and running.'

'To recap—the daughter of the Ecuadoran president is missing. Our Vice President Davis is an old friend of the president. With our latest information, she is presumed kidnapped. We have an authenticated ransom letter. A small squad of FARC rebels probably have her. Apparently, the president doesn't trust his military to retrieve his daughter, so he called his old friend Davis. They met in their law school days, roomed together, and he has asked for our government's help in rescuing her.'

There was a knock on the door. Kramer walked in. 'Excuse me, General. The Director of Intelligence is on a secure line for you.'

The general pushed his chair back and walked out.

'What intel makes him suspect the FARC?' asked Bridget, Mark's second in the chain of command.

'We weren't given much of anything else. Just that they believed a FARC rebel band did not head back to their home territory in Colombia. They were in the area where his daughter disappeared, and there is a ransom demand, which appears genuine.'

'How do we know kidnapped? Why not killed?' asked Katarina as she pulled her long blond hair behind her ear, leaving a few wild strands behind.

Mark shook his head. 'I don't know why they are saying kidnapped, other than the rebels are famous for kidnapping and ransom. She would be a prize. Maybe the CIA has some evidence they haven't told us about. When the general returns, he'll give us the latest.'

Mark pulled out several folders and handed them around. 'Sheilla gave me a list of questions to answer before the meeting. Number one on her list was that very question. As you can see, I tried to collect everything I could, and it is listed for you along with several other items that might be useful. Read through it and talk to me later before our next meeting,' said Mark.

The general walked back in. 'Let's continue. Katarina has worked up detailed profiles on the daughter and the president. We'll integrate the profiles with what the agency postulates. The FARC sometimes cross over the Colombian border into Ecuador. If our information is correct, they did not go back north this time. Rather, they continued south, further toward the Ecuador-Peru border. If they have Angélica Noboa Perez, our best chance of finding her is finding them. If they are not holding her, we have to start over.'

Katarina said in a soft voice, 'I was just wondering if perhaps the

Ecuadorans or Colombians had someone on the inside with the FARC rebels?'

'I was going to say not likely,' said the general, 'but on second thought, it's worth looking into. Money trumps ideology; maybe they have a paid informant.'

The general looked at Fred, who was the quietest of the analysts, never adding much but by far his most computer-savvy person—at least until Misa and Vidya joined the BWC. 'What progress have we made?'

'Some, sir. Misa and Vidya had no trouble getting into the Ecuadoran government computers. So far, they've found nothing interesting.' He looked

down at a printed page, 'unless you count a government as interesting. I quote Misa, who says the Ecuadoran government seems to be screwing over their citizens at every turn, especially their indigenous tribes.'

'Stay with it. Expand it to Columbia and the FARC. Make it a priority,' said General Crystal.

Due to the unique skill set that Misa and Vidya possessed, the general allowed them to work rather than attend meetings, as was their preference. They both seemed to abhor meetings and felt most comfortable nestled in their computer rooms—ones built specifically for them and based on their design. The general knew their value and allowed Fred, his old head of computing, to be their liaison. The general had offered them carte blanche to entice them to the BWC from Fort Huachuca.

Misa and Vidya's two close friends were young hackers that chose the army over jail, the only alternative the government had offered them. The group of four that made up what had become known as the Wolf Pack, and more recently the Wolf Warriors, had been together at Fort Huachuca and were now separated by hundreds of miles. Using a virtual reality program of their own design, however, Colonel Jake Montgomery and Sergeant First Class Jason Lyle worked just as closely with their old comrades as before. It was as if they were still a team in the underground Strategic Air Command facility at Fort Huachuca. The general was pleased that he had plugged a weakness in his computer group.

Fred was not jealous of the pair. He understood that they far surpassed any ability he would ever have. He was content just to be in their shadow and to represent them and their findings. In fact, he was more than content. Being part of their team made him feel special and, in a strange way, complete. He felt that a sliver of their brilliance passed through him.

Mark waited to make sure the general was finished and said, 'It is going to be tough locating the FARC in endless miles of dense jungle.'

'Let's follow up on Katarina's FARC idea,' said the general. 'Do any government agencies have anyone feeding them information from inside the FARC?'

'Fred,' continued Mark, 'pick someone to check on FARC moles and then work on locating the kidnappers along with the Ecuadoran army. Use the intel maps from Bethesda. Formulate some likely routes. Do a time analysis—how would they travel and how far could they go? Look for computer intercepts about any incursions or unexplained firefights. Put it together and then go to satellite to see if you can find out where this group might be in those thousands of square miles of the upper Amazon. They could even be moving by boat. Explore all possibilities.'

'Mark, keep Sheilla in the loop but with abbreviated summaries,' said General Crystal. 'She's working on another project for the next few days with Bridget. Katarina will stand in for her as we work through this.'

'General,' said Mark, 'I would like to add that Fred should try to locate any Colombian troops as well as the Ecuadoran army and their recent movements. We'll need to start keeping track of them. The FARC won't be any closer than they have to from the army, but you might get a sense whether the army is chasing after them again and whether they have crossed back into Colombia.'

General Crystal nodded and started to move his chair back.

'Worth a consideration.' Then he stopped and turned to the only non-operation person at the table, Sergeant Mason's replacement, Sergeant First Class Williston. His skin reflected the light like mahogany shoe polish. He had close-cropped, curly hair, graying at the temples. The forearms of his green army dress uniform had a dense covering of several gold slashes, marking his years in service. A memory jumped into the general's mind, a flashback to Vietnam with Mason, Jim, and Brush.

The general continued looking at Sergeant Williston. 'Start setting up transport for Jim, Brush, and Glenda. Lay out the equipment you think they will want.'

'Yes, sir. I've got a good idea of what that is, after reviewing Sergeant Mason's records. He left detailed notes.'

'Good,' said General Crystal as he stood.

'Do you plan on sending support with them?' asked Williston.

The general turned. 'SOCOM already moved Neilly's Special Forces team to a training base in Peru.'

Williston nodded. Neilly's team was as good as it gets, as had been explained to him by the BWC's own special response team. They were legendary in their past support of the BWC. Even with Jim's and Brush's capabilities, the new Special Operations Forces sergeant knew that everyone needs good backup.

The general noticed a small hand raised. 'SOCOM, general?' asked Katarina. The BWC's profiler never stopped being amazed at the jargon, which until recently was outside her realm.

'Special Operations Command,' replied the general. 'Mark, I want you to have a meeting to assess where we are. Start at sixteen hundred. I won't be here. Afterwards, brief me in my office. Not later than seventeen hundred.' He scanned the group as they rose from the chairs, and seeing no one had any more questions, walked out the door.

Chapter 7

Shuskin previously spent his winters in missions in Vancouver and sometimes Seattle. He had never wanted to stray far from his summer mountain home. Many others migrated south to warmer weather. Shuskin had been more than willing to trade the warmth of California for the damp winters of Seattle to be close to his favorite place on Earth, the Cascade Mountains of Washington State.

It was cold at Wolf Canyon Ranch. The same cold he had escaped when he went to the cities on the west side. But here he had a home. A warm place to stay. He felt safe; he wasn't being abused as he'd been in the missions.

At this moment, he was in a place he had never expected to be: a dentist's office. He looked in the dentist's mirror and hardly recognized himself. His teeth gleamed white, and even more surprising, all of them were there. The dentist and Heather both seemed to relish the transformation in the old vagrant. He had put twelve crowns on Shuskin's top teeth but decided to leave the bottom ones alone. He cleaned them up, bleached them, and repaired cavities. But the lower teeth needed braces to straighten them.

'Bob,' said Heather, 'I'm impressed with the result. Wow! Maybe later it will be worth the effort to have him wear braces on his lower teeth. I think Shuskin has endured enough for a while.'

'They don't have to be the old type with wires and all. He could wear the clear covers. It's the latest system. They're a lot easier to deal with.'

Heather looked at Shuskin, who looked down and shook his head. He didn't know what to think of his new smile. He let the dentist work on him out of thanks and deference to Heather, not because he cared what his teeth looked like. Nonetheless, something inside him felt pleased that people, including the dentist, cared about him. For the time being, though, Heather was right; he had had enough.

He looked up at them both with a shy smile.

'Come on, Shuskin. Let's see a big smile.'

Shuskin hardly knew how, but he attempted a grin. Heather exclaimed, 'Man oh man, you look wonderful. Handsome really.'

Bob looked at her, wondering if she was serious. Handsome. *Is she kidding?* Heather returned his look with a pleased smile. Then she looked at Shuskin whose face had a tinge of pink. *Was he blushing,* she wondered? 'Okay, we're out of here. You ready, Shuskin?' The old man nodded at her, happy to leave.

'First, we'll pick up Pedro from his tutor and then get an ice cream cone in Winthrop.' At this Shuskin smiled for real. The things that Heather was doing for him made him feel cared for. The mission staff said they cared, but it had never felt as though they had.

Had he lost his freedom? Or was freedom a delusion for vagrants, or for anyone? Still, he was feeling the pressure of being a certain kind of person, acting and looking in ways he hadn't cared about. But he didn't miss the winters and the religious missions— sleeping on the sidewalks, tolerating the gospel, and putting up with the occasional beatings. And he loved his new friend, Pedro.

Often, repellent memory shards cut into his thoughts, like the hundreds of transients that slept on the sidewalks on Hastings Street to the east of the Gaslight District of Vancouver. He preferred Vancouver to Seattle. He would rather sleep outside than inside on cots doled out by missionaries whose only interest, he thought, was to steal his soul. While the mission was warmer, it was a stagnant, smelly prison. The streets were colder, wetter, and more dangerous. Even so, he felt freer there, always dreaming about the return of summer when he could go back to the mountains to breathe fresh air in a place with no people.

He knew that Heather loved the mountains too, and that added to his feelings for her. He was not sure what he would do when summer returned. Would he leave for his old existence in the mountains? Would he return to Heather when winter approached? Would she let him? He had almost as many questions as Heather who rattled them off one after another without a pause.

Heather was all smiles. Jim would arrive in three hours. Heather had to encourage and almost drag Shuskin into town unless they went for ice cream. She was determined to introduce him to the local market store. Shuskin did things for Heather, went along with Heather's whims where he would have gone silent and refused if anyone else had asked him. Anyone else, that is, except Pedro.

The boy's simple openness had enthralled the ex-vagrant. A new experience since he had never spent time around a youngster. Although the boy did occasionally push Shuskin to play with him. Shuskin felt little threat from Pedro's demands. Not like he did when adults bossed him around in the city or at the missions; telling him what to do, how to behave, and what to believe. Shuskin accepted that this was different.

Shuskin's need for freedom was now starting to be replaced with a caring he'd lost many years ago. He had latched on to Nusmen because few people had ever been kind to him before.

Underneath, Nusmen was not callous or uncaring. He simply didn't understand how to deal with people, let alone someone like Shuskin. Still, he provided food and clothes for the old man when he had found him hiding at a trailhead in Heather's truck. That was as far as it went. Nusmen could provide nothing emotionally. Heather had stepped in with all the emotion Shuskin had missed in his life. Despite being half his age, she nevertheless became a mother figure for him. Shuskin still was grateful for Nusmen's kindness, but the feelings he had for Heather and Pedro were of a different caliber.

Heather gave him a home, a reason for being, comfort and care.

She accomplished what the homeless missions intended but never delivered. Some truly cared for the street people; others purported that they cared by satisfying their own needs.

Still, Shuskin was confused by his feelings. Like Nusmen, he had never fit in with society. From an early age, he had abhorred authority, with understandable reasons—a mother who beat him, just as she had allowed any of her male friends to do. He had run away at fourteen. His education limited to street learning, survival was all he knew.

Eventually he had found solace in the mountains, away from people and the anxiety they produced in him. He had learned a different kind of survival. He learned enough wilderness survival skills to get by in the summer. Little by little, he learned a few things he could eat and not eat, but mainly he scrounged leftover food and supplies from horse camps. Hikers with their scanty rations left little.

Jim scared him, even though he had always been kind. Shuskin could see that the colonel and Heather cared deeply for each other. Yet his aversion to people sometimes became activated when dealing with Nusmen, a sort of friend, a colonel, a mother figure, and a small boy.

***

The clouds suddenly parted just above Coyote Ridge as Jim's Seneca descended at over 200 miles per hour into the ranch valley. Heather smiled. Pedro jumped up and down with delight. Old Man Shuskin shivered involuntarily and slightly ducked as if the plane hundreds of feet overhead might shake loose his new teeth.

Pedro ran over to Shuskin and wrapped his arms around him.

As quickly as it appeared, the plane disappeared down the canyon, tipping wings from side to side as Heather waved with both arms. The sound dropped from a higher frequency to a lower tone as the plane picked up speed and moved away.

Pedro looked up at Shuskin, sensing his fear and said, 'Doppler shift.' The strange word distracted Shuskin from his fear. Pedro said,

'The plane sound. It's different when coming at us and then going away. I learn from Dad.'

Shuskin had never known the open love of a child. That hug and a small voice saying words he didn't understand caused him to know he could never desert him. The decision was made; it was now beyond his control. He would go to the mountains with his new family, not on his own.

Heather turned to Shuskin. 'You and Pedro take care of each other. I have to hurry.'

'Mama, I want to go too.'

'You watch out for Shuskin and Bluebell's baby. She could have it at any moment. Keep a good eye on her. She needs you.'

***

The drive was shorter to the small Twisp Airport than to the larger Methow Valley State Airport. Heather drove fast up Beaver Creek Road, knowing she should have left earlier. There was only the occasional car, as usual, on Highway 20 to Airport Road. She smiled as she approached the airport. *I'm not late. Timed it just right.* The plane was taxiing toward the hangar. She was so excited that she drove through a small ditch at the end of the runway, over a hard mound of snow, up onto the runway, and sped toward Jim.

The props slowed to a stop as she pulled the parking brake on her dirt-, mud-, and salt-encrusted Volvo 240 station wagon. The burgundy color peeked through, mainly around the door handles where the winter grime had been rubbed off. She sprinted to the plane's right side just as the door opened and Jim stepped out on the wing above her. He jumped down. For a moment they just stood inches apart, both smiling. He took her shoulders in his hands and placed his forehead against hers. They looked into each other's eyes, blurry from the close distance, and rotated their heads, back and forth, in opposite directions as endorphins eased their time apart.

Heather pulled her head back and said, 'This looks so dangerous, baby.'

'I have to admit it isn't the best idea to land and take off here even without the snow or ice, but I wanted to have Albert check some things on the engine.'

'What if you hit the snowbank?'

'Not a good idea. No such thing as a fender bender on planes.'

'Why don't you get them to plow it better?'

'Only high wings here and I don't land very often. There's still about a foot clearance from the wingtips to the snowbank.'

'A whole twelve inches, huh? You kill yourself, lover, and I'll never forgive you.'

'Let's go home. Albert will tow it inside, and I'll leave it here until I go back to the west side.'

'I wish you never had to. At least with your new position, you can come back and forth. That is, until you get some sort of mission.' Heather puffed out her cheeks, and then she sighed.

Jim looked at Heather and almost risked saying what was on his mind. 'I'm enjoying coming up to speed in the labs, but I would rather be here with you...' *or out in the field*, he thought. *Not good. Tell her your real thoughts.* He took courage and for once said something he never would have risked previously, 'Or out on a mission.'

Heather started to scowl before she realized that this is what she'd always wanted from Jim—the truth. It hurt that he placed her equal to missions. *Or did he?* she wondered. *No, he loved her but needed his missions, too. They weren't equal; they were different. It was part of who he was,* she thought.

***

Shuskin stood next to Pedro in the dirt road, now only partly covered with packed snow. They were standing outside his new home, the old homesteader's cabin that Jim had once stayed in. Pedro smiled up at Shuskin. They watched a puff of dust rise when Heather's Volvo hit a dry spot, as she drove fast over the speedway. The ranch environment sandwiched between two mountains was unique in that, for most of the winter, the sky was blue, and the sun melted the snow's surface, leaving a frozen crust on the fields. The road was different. Once a small patch of road was exposed through the packed snow, the heated soil captured the sun's warming rays, causing the surrounding snow and ice to retreat, and exposing wider areas of dirt.

'Soon Dad home,' said Pedro.

Moments later, the Volvo wagon appeared over the rise and followed the curved road in between the wood rail fences and around the crystalline snow-covered field in front of the cabin.

Surrounded by brilliant reflective snow, small patches of dormant grass absorbed more heat on warmer days like today. The exposed grass, which enjoyed the momentary exposure to the light and warmth, paid a price when the weather turned cold. Without its protective snow blanket, the bitter temperatures wreaked havoc on the grass, turning the blades wind-bitten brown. The occasional stubborn yellow aspen leaf pried loose from a branch would dance and skitter on top of the snow crust.

'Dad, Dad,' yelled Pedro as he ran toward the side of the car as Jim got out. He was so excited running that in a flash, his feet went up in the air, and he hit hard on the hard-packed road.

Jim reached down to comfort him. But instead of shedding tears, the intrepid Pedro grinned and then giggled. 'You okay?' asked Heather as she came around the front of the car in a hurry and slid her way to them.

'Maybe sore bottom.' Pedro started to giggle, and then they all did.

'Shuskin, climb in. We're going to have some snacks at the house and watch the sun go down. Lola has made your favorite stew. After dinner, I'll drive you back down.' Shuskin's face lit up at the sound of Lola's beer stew.

'I walk back,' he said. 'Nice out. You stay with your family.'

'Hold up there, bud. You're family now too. Come on. Give Jim a big smile and show him your new choppers.'

Shuskin looked down embarrassed; he couldn't do it. Jim would eventually see the teeth created with care by Heather's dentist friend.

Pedro stood impatiently for some attention. 'Dad, Dad. Carry me on your shoulders.'

Jim smiled, reached down with two hands around Pedro's body, and lifted him level with his face. 'Okay, big guy. A hug first.'

Pedro, grinning from atop Jim's shoulders, looked down and over the wood rail fence at Pipestone, his dad's favorite llama. The extra-tall human apparition caused Pipey to fold his ears back. Timidly, he relaxed at the sight of such a tall person, raised his face to Jim's face, and they exchanged breaths. All the time, his eyes were keeping Pedro under scrutiny.

***

'Time to eat,' said Heather.

"How long you stay?' asked Lola as she placed plates on the table.

'Two days,' responded Jim.

Lola clucked, 'You need stay longer.'

'What do you say we go skiing tomorrow at the Loup Loup?'

'Pedro has been cross-country skiing almost every day,' said Heather. 'I think he is ready for a little downhill.'

Pedro grinned alternately at Jim and then Heather. 'It's a deal then,' said Jim. 'We'll go around ten, so the snow has a chance to soften.'

Heather and Pedro nodded. Lola just shook her head. 'Muy loco. Pay money to slide down hill in cold.'

The next morning, they drove down the ranch road, along Beaver Creek road, and left up Highway 20. The Loup Loup ski area was only a mile as a crow flies from the back of the ranch. The driving distance was closer to seven miles.

Pedro took to downhill skiing as if he was meant for it. Fearlessness helped, along with the advantage of not much mass or distance to fall, which he did over and over, always laughing and smiling no matter how scary looking his tumbles.

'I think we have another skier in the family,' said Heather. 'I love it that we have a ski hill so close to the ranch. Aren't we lucky?'

It brought back a good feeling for Heather, reminding her of their ski trips to Canada. It seemed a long time ago now. Maybe going to the Loup Loup had been a portent of good things to come.

Returning to a warm house always felt especially luxurious after a day of skiing. The woodstove radiated heat, and the oversized fireplace burned brightly. Lola was happy cooking. Pedro and Heather were happy to be together. Shuskin had never known this sort of secure feeling. He, too, was happy, but also something inside agitated him. As he had learned throughout his life, things going this well always end.

Chapter 8

Jim pushed hard on both foot brakes, holding the plane stationary at the end of the runway as he brought the engine rpms up. As he lifted his feet, the 400-horsepower twin-engine leapt forward and picked up speed quickly. The small rural airport runway was barely long enough for the Piper Seneca's take off. Once the run was started, there could be no errors, either mechanical or human. Jim observed the other end of the runway as it rapidly approached. Power lines hung in a deadly snare, only feet from the end.

He looked straight ahead, concentrating on centering the low-wing plane between the unforgiving snowbanks, mere inches from his wingtips. Small ice patches glistened on the blacktop. His eyes flicked at the gauges. Both manifold pressures held. He had passed the point of no return. He was now going too fast to stop on the runway. It was now a full commitment. He would either fly or crash.

Heather disliked flying. She shook her head whenever Jim flew in and out of the Twisp Municipal airport, especially in the mid-winter. She worried that, one day, he would kill himself. All the other planes that used the airport were single-engine high-wing Cessnas. Their wings were much higher than the top of the plowed banks. The Piper's wings were lower than the snowbanks. It was a tight fit without room for error. Hitting the wing tip on the hard snow mounds would not only be expensive, but probably irreparable, and most likely deadly. Jim concentrated on keeping the plane centered between the snowbanks as they blurred by.

It was crazy using this short field. It was one of the reasons he had built a larger hangar at the mile-long, hundred-foot-wide Methow Valley State Airport. He wondered if one day he would cross the line here at Twisp. One small error or lapse in judgment would be all that it would take.

Just past the halfway point, Jim applied slight backpressure on the yoke as Eight-Four Charlie neared its takeoff speed. More backpressure and 200 feet before the end of the runway, the plane sprung aloft. He immediately retracted the landing gear and lowered the nose to gain speed. Jim watched the power lines become invisible below him as he soared into the early morning sky. Today, he had survived to fly again.

He engaged the autopilot. Reduced manifold pressure. Adjusted the climb rate, beginning his ascent to 10,000 feet. The mountains spread out in front of him as far as he could see. Most of the way to the army field south of Tacoma was mountain wilderness. Sandwiched between the mountains and Puget Sound, a thin strip of coastal land held most of the state's humanity.

There was no radio communication from other pilots. 'Twisp traffic, Seneca Eight-Four-Charlie departing runway twenty-eight for southwest departure.' There was no response, which didn't mean there were no other aircraft. Planes whose radios were not working, kit planes not required to have a radio, or a stray military jet practice-strafing the town could all be out there.

Mountain snows fed the Twisp River, winding below him. It languidly snaked its way south down the valley. The valley was laden with seas of mist. He gained altitude as the foothills fell away, and the taller Cascades rose majestically, shrouded with white in the western sky.

He looked north toward Oval Lake, thinking of the many times he and Heather had hiked to the lakes. Then Pedro's image emerged in his mind, the smiling boy who seemed so happy. Jim still marveled at his newly adopted son's ability to embrace the present, dismissing the pain of his early Mexican childhood.

He watched the fifty-mile-long Lake Chelan as it appeared far below the Oval Lake mountain ridge. His mind drifted to Najma, wondering if she were alive or dead. He grimaced. Alive, but where? They had heard nothing, nor detected any of her perverse-style killings. She was resourceful, but without backing such as she had had in Mexico, she would find it almost impossible to move easily in a world where she remained a top wanted criminal on the FBI's list.

Sheilla, Fred, and occasionally the full Wolf Pack spent time looking for Najma's killing signature. They found nothing and looked less as the months passed. No one was certain whether she were alive or dead. As time went on, she would be less likely to signal her whereabouts. She was a psychopath with a unique set of survival skills, a sixth sense keeping her out of reach of her pursuers. The FBI had all but stopped searching. The agents in charge asserted that if she were alive, they would have found her. Therefore, they concluded, she had crawled into a hole and died.

Jim, of course, didn't know which one: alive or dead. However, his well-developed sixth sense shouted alive, and sooner or later she would emerge. There was a high probability of a future battle. Knowing where to find him, she would have the advantage. Would she use that knowledge to terminate him, or would she ultimately challenge him to prove she was the better of the two?

Chapter 9

Jim, accompanied by Captain Kramer and Major Brush McGuire, took the elevator up two levels from the laboratory and office on underground Level LG3 to LG1, the weapons floor. As the elevator door opened, Sergeant First Class Williston, wearing dress greens, snapped a salute which, to an observer, might seem incongruous, as Colonel Johnson was dressed casually in chino slacks and a light blue shirt. Standing at attention behind SFC Williston and his eight-member logistics team were the full BWC complement of three special response teams and two HazMat teams—in all, fifty-seven men and women.

Jim returned the salute and said, 'At ease.' He looked with some pride at the soldiers and civilians under the BWC's command. For a moment he studied the new weapons room sergeant who had recently replaced his old friend, Master Sergeant Mason. *Tough job filling Mason's shoes,* he thought.

'You all know the importance of our mission. There is nothing I have to say about why we are here that you don't already know. What is different today from yesterday is that genetic engineering developments are proceeding at an explosive pace.

'With the gains in molecular biology, it becomes increasingly easy for groups, even with limited resources, to set up labs to produce lethal pathogens. We all know that governments, including right here in our facility, experiment daily with deadly viruses and bacteria. With the ease and speed this can be done, terrorists become more of a threat than ever before. The tools are available to create new and terrible doomsday diseases. This isn't anything you haven't already considered. What I want to emphasize is that we are going to be tested. On our watch, the probability of a major and deadly event that will change the world as we know it is approaching near certainty.

'One day, and maybe soon, we will face a major bio-event. The potential death toll from a naturally mutated disease outbreak, or a manufactured one could be in the hundreds of millions. Until that happens, we will likely face repeated, containable outbreaks, whether something like Ebola, or bird flu, or maybe a terrorist release of a modified anthrax.

'The outbreaks, whether caused by rogue individuals, governments, or natural causes, will keep us on our toes. Eventually containment won't be good enough. The last line of defense will be the researchers, here in our labs, finding a solution.

'You all have a wide variety of specialized skills as does our logistic group.' Jim looked directly at Sergeant First Class Williston and his team. 'Sergeant Williston's credentials and past performance are superb. And while we will all miss Master Sergeant Mason, we have a good man in Sergeant First Class Williston.'

SFC Williston nodded at Jim with a look that conveyed his understanding of the high requirements the BWC placed on his abilities. While he directly commanded only six men and two women, dozens were at his disposal in an emergency. Keeping the BWC's equipment in perfect condition and the supplies organized for a wide variety of worldwide missions, ready at a moment's notice, was his remit. Minutes and seconds mattered in a lethal outbreak, whether natural or engineered.

'Most of us have worked together for many years. You have my respect, our respect,' as he looked at Major McGuire, 'and General Crystal's. While we won't be seeing as much of him for the next several months, make no mistake. His home is here, and he will be with us, or available to us, whenever needed.'

***

The general's intercom buzzed.

His PA said, 'I have Katarina holding on the secure line.'

General Crystal picked up the phone. 'There's something I need right away. I want you to do profiles on a Gustavo Noboa, the president of Ecuador, and his daughter, Angélica Perez Noboa. Do briefs on the rest of his family and key people in his administration including his military officers.'

'How much time do I have?'

'The rest of the day.'

'I'll do my best, sir.'

'Use who you need. Fred, Misa, and Vidya can research for you. I want to know in particular if there is any reason someone surrounding President Noboa would want to pressure him by hurting or kidnapping his daughter.'

***

Jim spent the rest of the day observing, inspecting equipment, talking to and assessing the staff. Their new sergeant, Williston, earned high marks. He took his job seriously and knew the equipment. Nevertheless, it would take a long time, if ever, to find the understanding that Jim had had with Sergeant Mason. The kind that can only be developed over long years.

The sergeant, Jim, and Brush had spent a good two hours together inspecting a variety of weapons. In some cases, Jim would quickly reduce a weapon to its components, inspect it, and nod his approval. The storage rooms were neatly stacked with dozens of ten-foot-by-ten-foot containers, all pre-packed for various missions. Williston could load a plane with enough equipment in minutes to support a wide variety of missions: orange containers for HazMat teams; olive drab ones for the special response teams; and numbered white containers for a wide variety of bio responses.

Brush ran his fingers over the black polymer of the bat wings, just one of the exotic pieces of equipment they had used. More to the point, one that he had tested with his usual nonchalance—a previously untested experimental piece of equipment—and he had survived. He fondly remembered the descent he and Jim had made into Mexico. Neilly's Special Forces had gone on to develop newer versions; then they donated the older model to the BWC and promised them the latest model when they finished testing. *Would they ever have occasion to use it again,* wondered Brush.

***

There was one remaining area to inspect with Nusmen. Jim felt the last two days had been worthwhile, renewing his familiarity with the labs, the systems, the projects, and the people.

Nusmen opened a door. A slight puff of air touched them as they walked through the opening, and the door closed behind them. They removed their clothes and put on a soft suit much like children wear to bed. Nothing was left exposed other than their faces. The material was fine and thin, covering their hands.

Nusmen nodded at Jim, and they each opened their door. Inside each compartment were identical lightweight white suits with re-breathers on the back, allowing the wearer to move about in the small compartment. They donned the suits and looked at each other through the glass that separated their small compartments.

The system was newly installed. Jim had read the manual the night before that contained both the instructions and the logic behind the high-security labs. The idea was to keep people in separate, contained areas in case of contamination and to enshroud them in a soft, thin undergarment and a flexible, sealed outer shell.

Jim nodded at Nusmen, and they opened another door into another small compartment. They closed that door and pushed a button on the wall to start up pumps to reduce the air pressure inside, making it difficult for a microbe to escape if a breach occurred. With the outer door sealed, the room glowed blue from UV lights, an environment lethal to most microbes. Several panels with LED lights added their colors to the mix and signified, among other things, various levels of alert.

'Are you comfortable?' asked Nusmen. 'Any questions about the new system?'

'None,' said Jim.

'Okay, let's move up to the compartment and insert our arms into the gloves.'

They both looked through the glass into the small, contained area on the other side and slipped their arms into sleeves, allowing them to manipulate Petri dishes and wire loops, the tools of the microbiologist.

The compartments they were in only controlled one level-four microorganism at a time. Today, Nusmen had arranged for it to be a lethal *Esherichia coli* strain. Bacteria, viruses, fungi, and prions lived in their individual sealed areas. They could be stored at various temperature levels, incubated, and manipulated in several ways.

'These rooms are only for basic handling and culturing. We have, as I'm sure you know, several different ways of testing microbes. Starting here with basic studies, and at the other extreme, tissue and live animal studies. I doubt I like those any better than you do.'

'No, I don't like it at all. It has to stop. We need another, better way to test. I try to rationalize it as a necessity,' added Jim. 'Soon, I hope, we will find artificial ways to handle it. I'm at least glad that we only use living organisms when no other way can be found.'

Heather and Jim had discussed this on many occasions. Heather had been involved in many animal rights organizations, some of which bordered on violence and violent confrontation. They never argued about it, as Jim was simply in her camp and had always searched for better alternative methods. Anyone that did not have a similar, compassionate view had a short employment at the BWC.

While it was still deemed necessary to use a living, breathing animal in rare instances, it was only allowed after a panel met and approved procedures after exhaustively looking for alternatives. To the laboratory's credit, a small group of dedicated scientists worked to develop experimental procedures to address alternative methods for testing the effects of organisms and treatments on biological entities. They had moved the testing procedures light years ahead by artificially growing tissue that could be used as an alternative.

'As it is,' said Nusmen, 'we only test inoculations on animals when we are as certain as we can be that they are not harmful to them. Most everything else we can accomplish, as well or better, in the lab. Remember when we used to put bacteria into PCRs, onto culture plates, into ovens, isolate them, break the DNA with enzymes and insert new sequences, etc., etc., etc., ad infinitum—all by hand? Totally automated now. Even though I see it change daily, the progress is still really amazing,' said Nusmen as he deftly lifted a lid off a Petri dish, waited a second for the red-hot glowing wire loop to cool, lowered it into the white slimy *staph*, then closed the lid with the dexterity of someone who had done this hundreds of times. He then opened another lid and quickly streaked the loop back and forth across the agar. 'Want to try one?'

Jim did not say anything. He was thinking about the old procedures Nusmen had described as being part of the past, but he was still performing them in the present.

Then Nusmen explained why he used the old procedure that Jim remembered from his days as a student. 'I just do it sometimes to compare results with the automated systems. Instead of only experiencing them through looking at the computer data, I still like to experience their color and textures. I like knowing our bugs personally.'

He is a character, thought Jim, and then answered Nusmen's question. 'I remember our old lab procedures all too well. Time is short, and I'm here to observe. Let's get on with it and into the other sections. I want you to tell me about each of the high-security microbes.'

They moved to different cubicles over the next two hours and discussed MRSA, variations of the 1918 flu virus, and Nusmen's special favorite, H5N1.

'Someday, one of these little beauties is going to mutate all on its own and kill millions,' said Nusmen.

'Which one do you think?'

'If natural mutation, my money is on the H5s. Some lab kook, maybe…' Jim looked at Nusmen. Nusmen looked back, wondering if Jim thought he was a kook. 'Hard to say, but something I think a lot about. Endless possibilities. Combining Ebola with Variola, so it infects faster without the incubation period. My best guess, and the simplest to perform, is probably a variant of flu, like the 1918. Rumors were the Russians were trying that,' added Nusmen. 'And combining Ebola with smallpox.'

Jim didn't say what he knew about the Russians as he wanted Nusmen to have an open mind when he approached his research. 'There are still ongoing discussions at the World Health Organization about destroying the last remaining samples of Variola major here and in Russia,' said Jim.

'That's stupid. We need it to test, to get a full sequence, and see how someone might combine it. Besides, the Russians will never get rid of it anyway. No matter what they say.'

'That's why we still have it and will likely keep it. So, are you close to combining it with any other viruses?'

'Doctors Willis and Margot work on it daily, trying different avenues as well as being in charge of increasing our vaccine supplies. If we aren't successful here, then that makes me believe the Russians haven't been either, despite the rumors.'

Jim knew a little more than he was willing to share with Nusmen. Not that Nusmen wasn't cleared for the information; however, Jim didn't see a reason to tell Nusmen the CIA had evidence that the Russians' experiments had failed. Jim wanted the BWC to keep pushing the fringes. He didn't want the Russians' failure, if true, to affect the lab staff trying to combine it. They might still find a way and then—the important part—figure out how to neutralize it. 'Smallpox—Variola— was never a big issue in the modern-day Americas like it was in other parts of the world, and because it was eliminated, people don't care about it any longer. They felt a false sense of security from past pandemics.'

'Except for us,' said Nusmen. 'It would be a big mistake not to completely understand a virus that was that lethal.'

Jim turned to Nusmen. 'I agree. There is a lot we need to find out—host specificity, resistance to vaccines and drugs, virulence factors.'

Despite his past fears, Nusmen was starting to feel comfortable, even starting to like, Colonel Johnson. He wasn't like other bureaucrats and academics. He was a generalist but possessed specific knowledge in several areas. Nusmen was likewise intrigued by the great historical killers of millions. The orthopoxvirus was not very interesting to most people, especially since humans had come close to causing its extinction. Nevertheless, it remained the greatest killer of all time. Jumping new boundaries, tweaking its interactions with immune systems, and above all, speeding up its incubation period was the stuff that Nusmen thrived on.

'No one knows how many that flu virus killed. The figure could be as many as seventy million,' said Jim.

After nodding agreement, Nusmen continued, 'Whatever that number for the flu virus, orthopoxvirus—*Variola major*—killed more over the years. So many they didn't even name babies until after they'd survived it. Like as many as 500 million.'

'Not many people even know about that history. Not at all on Americans' radar,' said Jim. 'I know a bit because it was a pet interest of my advisor James Taylor when I was a grad student.'

Nusmen lurched inside with thoughts of the University of Washington and all the trouble he had caused from not getting accepted as a grad student, and at the same time getting dumped by his girlfriend professor. He was able to accept the rejection now and to live with it because it had led to his confinement at BWC and his eventual elevation to joint lab manager. The knot inside unwound, and he smiled at his good fortune.

'I remember JT,' said Nusmen with his head down.

'You have to get over it. Make up for that lapse in judgement and find a cure for that strain. The last time I talked to JT, he said much the same. He's currently on sabbatical in the Australian outback northeast of Perth, searching for the oldest organic carbon in a place called the

North Pole.'

'Wow. Would you tell me what he finds?'

'I will. Anything more you want to add?'

Nusmen's thoughts shifted back to smallpox. 'Of course, its big problem was the long incubation period. Shorten it and it would be very deadly, even now. That was its demise, an example of an unsuccessful evolutionary trait, and it's cool to look at, being so freaking big for a virus,' he said, his voice rose as a crescendo. 'Almost the size of a small bacteria...,' Suddenly, his voice trailed off to inaudible as it dawned on him, he was saying things that the colonel not only knew, but was an expert in.

From the last two days, Jim could sense Nusmen's excitement about everything virus, bacteria, archaea, and prion and encouraged his enthusiasm. 'But it isn't in the general population anymore,' said the colonel, thinking how far away he had strayed from his original laboratory research to being an administrator and field agent. He was at the BWC to stop lethal outbreaks: Ebola, Hemorrhagic fevers, Variola, or any killer virus that either jumped species or was created by terrorists. Fortunately, there were not many such outbreaks requiring his attention. Consequently, he had become something between of an enforcer, assassin, facilitator—a hired gun for the government.

Nusmen realized he was talking to the Colonel as if he were a grade-schooler, but he couldn't stop. 'Avian flus are going to be, at some point, dangerously lethal; sooner or later one of them will jump species and mutate, becoming highly transmissible.'

'Maybe. One day, what we discover here will save millions of lives.'

'Never really thought about it. I think I would like that. Me in the lab and you in the field.'

Jim let Nusmen's statement slide without comment. Its familiarity caught him a little off guard. *But I have to remember to take into account his personality quirks. His value trumps his personality.*

Chapter 10

Bertrand sat at his desk, wondering why the world held little intrigue today—an anomaly, not a usual day. The only real issue on his desk was the vice president's request for a status report about the daughter of his old Yale school friend, President Noboa.

He rehashed what they knew. From all reports he had received so far, the daughter and the father were not close. But the reports contained little real information about what might have caused her disappearance. This was the first instance, as far as he could remember, where the agency needed assets in the western Amazon.

A soft knock on the door broke through Bertrand's thoughts. The door opened and Martin Pearson, his Deputy Director of Intelligence, walked in.

'Good morning, Bertrand,' Martin said, with what Bertrand could only discern was a look that conveyed sincerity. *After so many years of Martin's smart-ass jokes and calling me Bertie, it's still hard to digest the fact that Martin has changed,* mused Bertrand.

'I'm sorry,' said Martin. 'You look like you are thinking about something. I hope I didn't interrupt.'

'No Martin, you didn't interrupt anything. Sit down. What have you found out?'

'Maybe the first shred of something tenuous, at best. One of our informants with the FARC rebels in Colombia reported the Ecuadoran army was chasing a handful of their rebels south.' Martin looked at where his missing thumb had been, a habit he could not shake whenever rebels were discussed. It didn't matter who the rebels or rebel types were—FARC, Al-Qaeda, or the Siastra cartel.

When the facts emerged about how the cartel and Najma had fooled Martin, he was not blamed. Trick or no, he had survived cartel capture and a face to face encounter with the terrorist Najma. His reputation changed overnight, and to this day, remained intact: a CIA hero who'd been tortured and who had escaped. The respect he currently enjoyed had more to do with his changed personality than with his disfigurements. He came back from Mexico to Virginia without his right thumb and left ear. His ear had been fixed with skillful plastic surgery, and although the thumb could have been repaired, he chose not to. For Martin, its absence had become a badge of honor. Other parts of his anatomy had been subjected to Najma's knife. It was still questioned by CIA staff how much of his penis was or was not missing. After all, their business was finding out facts, and the mystery haunted them.

'Why not the Colombian Army?' asked Bertrand.

'Good question,' replied Martin. 'Jurisdiction?' Bertrand shook his head a little, still having a hard time adjusting to the new, always courteous and serious person Martin had become. 'The Colombians had set up an ambush for what it called an extremist FARC faction. They were engaged in a shootout with them when a group escaped the ambush and went south across the border. It's a small group, but led by a seasoned fighter named Jago, the man the ambush was set up to kill or capture. Our estimates put them in the vicinity of, uh.' Martin looked down at his papers. 'Uh Angélica, the missing daughter's ecolodge.'

'The FARC make money from kidnapping.'

'Yep,' answered Martin. 'We're focusing on intercepting any communication. If there is a ransom demand, we should have something soon.'

After Martin left, Bertrand sat for a minute, assimilating the little they knew.

He then called the general and quickly filled him in on what Martin had found out.

'Call the VP. Give him an update and I'll give him a brief in a few hours,' said General Crystal.

Bertrand called the VP and explained what they had found so far.

'What is your confidence level, Bertrand?'

'The conclusion seems reasonable. Even so, let's wait until we have more pieces of the story. We can start planning a course of action if the information holds up. We can always adapt with better data.'

'The FARC. I've been calling them that for so long, I've forgotten if it stands for something?'

Bertrand never got into a discussion without thoroughly researching any details associated with a problem. 'The acronym stands for the Revolutionary Armed Forces of Colombia.'

'Well shoot, that doesn't add up. RAFC, not FARC?'

'In Spanish, it's Fuerzas Armadas Revolucionarias de Colombia.'

'Noboa was my roommate and friend for a long while, but I never learned his language.'

'The general said he will brief you shortly,' said Bertrand.

'One more question,' said the VP. 'If the FARC ran into his daughter Angélica, would they kill her? Or, uh, maybe worse?'

'The probability is they would kidnap her. SOP for them.'

'If that is the case, what would you suggest we do?'

'I don't know, sir. If the data supports the hypothesis, then the general will likely have a plan by the time he talks to you.'

'I don't want to wait; have Will come over right away,' Bertrand hung up the phone and called General Crystal back.

'General, he wants you now. I'll call you if we find out anything new before you get there, although that isn't likely.'

***

The general walked into the vice president's office. Vice President Davis stood and walked around his desk, shook hands with General Crystal and motioned to two lounge chairs in front of the fireplace.

'Good morning, sir.'

The VP rubbed his eyes and yawned. 'Sorry, Will. Late night last night. Since we were elected, I have never had a good night's sleep. Constant phone calls. Like being on call as a physician, I imagine.'

'I can still remember those days. A long time ago but hard to forget. You have my sympathy, sir.'

'I just received a call from Gustavo, President Noboa. He received a ransom demand. A copy should be arriving as we speak. I arranged for him to send the original to the FBI. The demand is for ten million U.S. dollars. The FBI will let you know as soon as forensics learns anything. There was apparently a fingerprint in a small blotch of blood. We assume the print and blood is Angélica's.'

'How did the letter get delivered?' asked the general, feeling a little awkward as the CIA or the BWC should have had this information. He should not be hearing it from the VEEP.

There was a knock on the door. A woman walked to the vice president and gave him a file, followed by a man who brought in a silver serving tray and asked if the general would like his usual.

'Yes, black, please.'

'It was in an envelope from the lodge where she was volunteering. It was dropped off in person at the gate of the presidential palace. The delivery person disappeared. Will, I can tell, for once, someone else knew something before you did. If it makes you feel any better, my friend only called three minutes before you arrived.'

The VP handed Will the file. Inside was a copy of a scrap of paper addressed to President Noboa. "We have your daughter, pretty little Angel she is. Ten million U.S. dollars if you want to see her alive and with all her body parts still attached. That money should be no problem as you have stolen far more from your people." On the upper right-hand corner was a stain with what appeared to be a fingerprint.

Will's cell phone rang. 'Crystal.'

'The FBI sent a copy of a ransom note,' Bertrand informed him. 'It appears authentic and similar to past ransom demands from the rebels. However, nothing useful yet from our sources in the FARC or the Colombian military. Only that there are no new hostages at their main base camp, which makes it all the more plausible that it's the group being pursued by the army.'

'Keep me up to date, director. Day or night.'

'Understood.'

'General, you look healthy. I would ask you about the family, but you never seem to have had one.'

'Maybe it is one of those things I am starting to regret,' said Will.

'Never too late,' added the VP.

They studied each other for a moment. The general waited.

'I want to let you know more about my relationship with the Noboa family. This is about someone I have come to consider just as much my family as my own. You already know I have a special relationship with Noboa from our Yale days.'

Will waited for more, as this was not new information.

'He and I were roommates. Then he was the chancellor of the University of Guayaquil. He did a short stint teaching law at Yale as a visiting academic, and we continued our friendship. Good friends, I might add. It's why he asked us for help. I want the best people to try and find her.'

Chapter 11

Yellow light filtered through the canopy, streaking downwards in isolated shafts. Angélica's black hair, similar to Cherry's, just touched her shoulders and, with her dark brown eyes, she became part of the heavy jungle's shadowed mosaic.

'I want to be away from here,' she said, gazing up at Jago. She admired his taut, sinewy muscles and his drooping mustache with its few scattered gray hairs. His long dark hair was pulled into a ponytail, bound with a butterfly-blue cord. The battle-worn survivor, now thirty-six years old, had found his home with the FARC as a seventeen-year-old teenager, after the Colombian Army had killed his family— a past trauma he shared with many other rebels, including those within his group. He had been eleven years younger than Angélica's twenty-eight years.

Jago smiled at his new woman. Naively opinionated. A flower blooming in a world she did not yet comprehend. 'Lobo and Cherry will return soon with the status of our pursuers.'

She stood hands on full hips, as she often did and looked up at her new lover. By nature, she was argumentative, defensive, and normally very vocal, but less so with Jago, although he had no way of knowing this. Her dark brown eyes softened. 'I only worry because my papá has ways to find us, and he might send more military to rescue me,' she said. 'We have been here for days, and our position might become known. They will be looking for me.'

'A chance we will have to take, Angel,' the name Jago had

decided to call her, 'unless you want to go back to your papá now?'
He thought it unnecessary to tell her that San had taken some of her
clothes and spread blood on them, leaving one piece by the edge of
the river on the opposite side of the compound, throwing others in
the water. With luck, the ones in the river would be caught on a snag
or washed ashore, throwing off the searchers.

He knew she would not leave him. The privileged girl in a
woman's body had quickly fallen in love with him, or at least with the
image of a charismatic leader of a rebel band. He knew she did not
want to leave. For his part, he was not in love. She was attractive
enough and having her in his bed was pleasant. That was all.

'You did not answer my question, Angel. It would solve that
problem if you went back to your papá.'

At times, she questioned her sanity for so willingly abandoning
her volunteer position with Save the Amazon. She had left her life in
Quito to do something worthwhile, to give back something to this
Earth. Like so many who had been sheltered from the ugly daily
survival of most of the world's people, she shunned her upper-class
life, dressing the part of her chosen conservationist identity, in the
certainty she would make a valuable contribution.

She reached up and punched him playfully in the arm. 'You
know I'm never going to go back. My father will pay, and it will help
your people.'

'That would not be acceptable. When people pay, we return our
hostages. It is our way. Otherwise, this arrangement, this game we
have developed, would not work. It is a comfortable relationship
based on certain assurances and expectations.'

He looked down from his twelve-inch height advantage at her
light brown unblemished face, much lighter than Cherry's darker skin.
Besides their shared black hair, both women had the same thick dark
eyebrows.

Years ago, he had objected to the idea of kidnapping. But they
always needed money—his band needed money. The government
troops in Colombia were constantly harassing them, causing

disruptions in their other sources of revenue: drugs and mining.

He had been forced to the Río Napo after a large CIA-sponsored attack, coordinated with the military, separated him from the main FARC force. The Americans had always been a thorn in their side. Complicit in the drug trade, the Americans had a relationship with the army, thus becoming enemies of the rebels.

The rebels' revenue in the past derived mostly from the drug trade. However, the competition had grown fierce. Not only the cartels, but now the army and the Americans were involved. The FARC would still have been able to generate an adequate income from growing and processing drugs, if only the army had not seemed to be one step ahead of them.

At this moment, drugs were far removed from Jago's thoughts and concerns. His foremost task was simply to escape and survive his pursuers. He knew through long experience not to return north too hastily. However, this new opportunity had presented itself in the form of a woman. Potential ransom money for a president's daughter. Perhaps a great deal of money. He would head south, away from Colombia, and arrange to exchange her for the ransom.

Angélica, like so many sheltered rich girls, started with high ideals. For two years, she refused to fly, citing gross polluting of the atmosphere. She tried being vegetarian. Next, meditation, but found it boring. She started training to become a nun; demonstrated against big oil companies; and lately, she had joined a group trying to save the rainforest's birds, eventually volunteering at their remote base sixty miles downriver from the frontier town of Coca.

She'd found herself bored there, too, and had hated to wake up early in the morning. She couldn't see the value of documenting and counting birds. Like her other attempts at personal protest, she'd realized that volunteering as a conservationist was not what she wanted. Angélica felt almost as empty and purposeless as she had felt at home. Now, in a few brief moments of time, she felt she was doing something worthwhile, something valuable, by being part of a rebel family.

Possibly, it was nothing more than rebellion against her privileged past, or against her parents. Whatever it was, the emptiness had been replaced with feelings of attraction for Jago, along with a sense of belonging to a fight for what she believed to be a just cause. Certain that this cause was different from her previously adopted causes, she vowed to fully embrace this one. She would truly commit. This was what she had been searching for, had always wanted. The band accepted her, and Jago loved her, making her feel warm and protected.

There were exceptions: Cherry made her uncomfortable with her unbuttoned tan shirt, crisscrossed bandoleers over her breasts, cocoa skin, and a look that said she was "all woman."

On the other hand, she liked broad, muscular, six feet tall Lobo. The men respected him, but there was no doubt Jago was their leader. Fighting was second nature to Lobo and the others; Jago gave them purpose and direction.

San frightened Angélica a little with his toothless grin. He leered, but his ability beyond the menacing looks had long ago been impaired. San had once assumed that Cherry would be pleased to have a younger man. That she would spread her legs for him whenever he wished. His first attempt to force her to have sex had resulted in a broken nose—still bent to one side—the loss of several teeth, and testicles that would likely never perform as intended.

***

The whoosh-whoosh of a helicopter beat the air. Jago listened with interest as it landed not far from their position and in the direction of the lodge where Angel had, not many days ago, spent her nights in relative comfort.

'From its direction, it is landing near your lodge. Saving the Amazon, no?'

'It is not my lodge,' she said defiantly.

'It is late in the day. If the helicopter does not take off soon, they will wait until morning.'

Pensively, she looked up at him and asked, 'What difference does it make?' Jago shrugged and walked away.

Angélica reflected on her recent past at the lodge, and in Quito, flying in her father's helicopters, but she could find no inklings of regret for that life. Jago had become her Robin Hood. She blocked any thought of delusion. Instead, she rationalized he was a reprieve from the privileged life that had been dictated by her father and expected of her by her family. Living with this man, free, wild, and rough, excited her.

Chapter 12

Jago, whose flying skills were minimal at best, felt fortunate to have autorotated the helicopter to a small clearing in the jungle. After shredding some leaves and branches, it hit with a bang. He couldn't tell at first if anything was seriously damaged. The struts were bent. Then, he saw the tail rotor damage. *A dead bird that will decay in the jungle,* he thought.

He searched the fuselage until he discovered the emergency locator transmitter and disconnected it. Still, someone might have picked up the ELT signal. They walked rapidly through as many vines and branches as they could before joining a small overgrown trail along the river.

***

The general's thoughts turned to Vice President Davis' request for Colonel Johnson to find and retrieve the president's missing daughter. The general had always been careful not to agree to send them on missions with unacceptable risks. Within reason, he now had to be just as careful not to refuse the White House. A fine line he had so far been able to walk.

Even though the request could have been made to Jim directly, as acting head of the BWC, the vice president, adept as to how politics functioned, understood that his request should be to the general and not directly to the BWC. The general was pleased that Davis was still acknowledging him as the head of the Biological Warfare Center.

As was his habit, the general considered options, even though he would comply with the VP's request. Who else should he send? As he pondered the permutations, he knew the best choice, besides Jim and Brush, was Neilly's Special Forces and, of course, Glenda Rose Stuart. That settled, he turned his thoughts to the situation.

The vice president of the U.S. and the president of Ecuador had not only been friends since their university days, but their families had visited each other in their respective countries. The VP had been shocked and personally saddened when he heard that Angélica had disappeared and presumably been captured by rebels. He had always been fond of Angélica, a strong-willed girl with beauty and charm, who had grown into a conscientious young woman, full of idealism. The VP wondered why President Noboa did not trust his military with his daughter's well-being.

The general decided he would talk to Jim and Barbara Milton about the lab's status and needs. Bertrand and Eric would discuss with him the problems in the world. Then he would need to spend the rest of the day working on a particularly sensitive issue in Afghanistan before getting a summary from Mark at 17:00.

***

Mark sat proudly at the head of the table. Never before had the general, the colonel, or Sheilla let him chair what he considered an important planning session.

'Let's first review your additional findings. Give us a summary of the profiles you've worked up, Katarina.'

'Right, let's see. Each of you has a detailed written profile, the longest for the daughter, full name Angélica Noboa Perez, and for the father, Gustavo Noboa. I've started on the FARC, but I will need more time. Like so many rebel groups, they started with a charismatic leader with a purpose, who later became shaped by changes in ideologies, and more importantly, in tactics. They finance themselves cultivating the cocaine near the Colombia and Ecuador border. That apparently was not something that was in their original game plan. Now, it is their major source of revenue. They are well-equipped, well-funded, and well-prepared with a depth of survival skills developed over the years.'

'They obviously kidnap people too,' said Fred.

'Yes, besides drugs, they specialize in kidnapping corporate employees, and if they are lucky, ones that allow for large ransom demands, such as executives of natural resource companies, primarily captured over the border in Ecuador. This appears to be more than just for money. There is a faction that is not only against capitalism, but also the exploitation of resources in the jungle. I would like Fred to help in researching them.'

'No problem,' said Fred.

Katarina continued, 'Noboa is a politician and lawyer. His portrait suggests a man that is out of step with time. White chin beard, a legal technocrat, an icon—not a president. Ironically, he has the support of the indigenous people. He seems to have little understanding of finances. He is not well-liked by the armed forces. Oddly though, there has not been an attempt at a takeover or a coup, and he seems strangely insulated from them. This strikes me as odd since he seems so weak, and the military is so well-funded and strong.'

'He doesn't sound like a typical lawyer,' said Mark.

'He isn't. He's an academic and never practiced or sat for the bar exam.'

'Silver spoon type,' mused Mark. 'Sorry to interrupt, Katarina, please continue.'

'He has little imagination. Just like you implied, Mark, he comes from a sheltered life in academia. Rule of law over individual rights, except his own. In short, a bit of a pompous ass. Cares for his daughter, our subject, Angélica; rules the rest of his family with a strong hand. Not loved. He is intelligent, as evidenced by his year at Yale, where he was respected. He was Chancellor of the University of Guayaquil before moving into politics. It was an appointed position, not earned, but received reasonable recognition for his management of it.'

Sheilla walked in and asked, 'Any insight into why Noboa wants American involvement?' Mark slumped a little in his seat, seeing his control of the meeting slipping away.

'There was a news story,' said Katarina, 'indicating he has had a falling out with the military commander. If that is true, he most likely doesn't trust the military. I am still researching the profile on the commander. It is as possible as not that the military is involved with her disappearance.'

'Makes sense,' said Sheilla. 'I've only been able to scan your profiles, but nice work, Katarina, Mark, and all of you. If you think I can help, don't hesitate to ask. I want to keep our guys and gals out of harm's way. That is, as usual, nothing new there. This has all the elements for disaster: unknown location, unknown people, questionable request and motive, animosity among the military, experienced rebels, and drug cartels. This is not a good mix from my perspective, and far from straightforward.' Sheilla looked at Mark, smiled, and then turned to leave.

Mark visibly sat taller and relaxed, seeing that she was not going to stay. 'Thanks, Sheilla,' he said, and he meant it. For a moment, he had thought she was going to come in and take over. 'Katarina, are you ready to start on Angélica?'

'Sure. An interesting, immature woman from what I can tell. Self-esteem issues, but I think there is an underlying strength waiting to break free. She is outspoken, an environmentalist. Upbringing from a domineering male and perhaps from a bossy mother. Throughout her past, she's started on crusades and then dropped them. Anti-plane pollution. Embraced religion once. Likes men but does not like to relinquish control to them. She is intelligent. Subject to group or personal pressure. The type of personality that joins cults and can be manipulated by strong personalities, although she would deny it. My surmise is she has diminished self-esteem, caused both by her father and pushy mother. She doesn't care about money. Her need to feel dominant over men is not about power, rather a product of low self-esteem. She does not accept criticism well and always wants to feel she is right.'

'If her mother was like mine, I can sympathize with her repressed feelings,' said Bridget.

'When we have a few minutes, I would like to hear more about that,' said Katarina.

Bridget looked a little embarrassed. She immediately realized her comment about her personal life added nothing to the mission issues they were discussing. She looked sideways at Katarina and said, 'Sure, when we have time.'

'Others,' continued Katarina, 'I have scant information at this point. The head of the conservation camp where she was working is a strong manipulative personality, just as I suspect the rebel leaders or military commanders are. As a hostage, if she is one, there are several possibilities. If the FARC have her, she could be forced into servitude or sexually abused, or possibly brainwashed into accepting it as her new norm and join their cause. Of course, she may have been killed, but I view that as unlikely.'

Fred added, 'If her captors know who she is, they would keep her safe and as a hostage for more ransom. Wouldn't they?'

Katarina hesitated for a moment and then said, 'Probably they would. Their past behavior suggests they do not harm captives, and when a ransom is paid, they return them. They could also use her as a bargaining chip for safe conduct back to Colombia. It is hard to say. As they are not short of funds, they might decide a political statement of not returning her or even killing her might bring more benefit.

'Which would you speculate, Katarina?' asked Mark.

'Without knowing who the FARC members are, there is no way to surmise the outcome or make an educated guess. Not at this point. The circumstances of her capture combined with the personalities of her captors leave too many other possibilities, besides the ones I mentioned.'

'Okay. Thank you. Let's move next to the FARC group and Fred's impossible mission. But with Misa and Vidya, maybe you can find a way to narrow down which FARC rebels are involved and where they are.'

'We're giving it our best and making some headway,' said Fred, thinking he was ultra-glad for their help. 'Bridget, could you dim the lights, please?'

Bridget lifted her ultra-slim body, topped with a dark pixie haircut, and stood carefully on her unstable foot. Everyone watched her move to the light switch and Fred immediately regretted asking her. Bridget moved slowly but with no concern for those watching, half pulling, half dragging the right foot she had damaged two years ago in a car accident. No one understood why she wouldn't have an operation to reconstruct the damage. They all watched her move in slow motion.

Bridget had shared her fear of doing the reconstructive surgery with no one. She just hadn't been able to work up the courage to have it done. She would eventually.

'Thanks, Bridget.' Fred clicked the icon on his computer screen labeled "Jungle Bunny," slightly embarrassed that he had not changed it to something less flippant. A satellite view of the Amazon appeared with lines depicting the country borders from Peru to Columbia.

'Thousands of square miles, separated by wide rivers, descend the eastern slopes of the Andes and end in heavily forested jungle,' Fred said, pointing out the locations. 'To the south, the Río Santiago, and to the north, the Río Napo. The daughter worked at a combined ecolodge research facility, here, next to the Río Napo, about sixty miles south of the frontier town of Coca. Rebel sightings are mostly near this area, closer to Columbia and normally way north of the town of Coca. It is uncharacteristic for them to venture far south of the border into Ecuador. Three days ago, during a military operation near the ecolodge, a helicopter was stolen after a skirmish with the army. The military reports, the ones I was able to view on their computers, said it was a FARC unit that captured it. Of course, the military reports might not be true. The military is more criminal in this area and might have sold the helicopter and then said it was stolen.'

'If the rebels did end up with the chopper, they could have gone a long way from the camp and probably back to Colombia,' added Bridget.

'True, except that an abandoned Huey helicopter was reported to the University of South Carolina by their cultural anthropology team, doing studies near the Río Santiago, here,' Fred answered as he pointed with his laser light.

'That far south?' asked Mark. 'It doesn't make sense. Why not fly back toward their home turf in Colombia if they took it?'

'I have no idea at this point, but I'll keep trying to piece things together. I want to see if I can find out which FARC members might have been in that area. Then Katarina can profile them, and maybe we can gain some insight into what they might do.'

'How did they get a ransom notice to the father? asked Fred.

'I don't have any idea. Perhaps in the morning, the FBI or the CIA will have some information. Anyone have anything else to add?'

When no one answered, Fred stood and turned on the light switch.

'Tomorrow morning, we meet here again at eight.' Mark brought the meeting to a close, thinking to himself that it had gone well.

***

Mark could hear the general talking long before he got to the office door. As he got closer, he recognized the voice of Captain Russell Kramer. He liked Kramer, but he always felt inhibited around him. Kramer wasn't the only intelligent person around; he was just a different sort from Sheilla, and completely different from the operation field staff like Jim. Sheilla was outgoing and quizzical, while Jim was contemplative and cerebral. Both were problem solvers.

Kramer was quick-witted. The type of person that aced tests and won at "Jeopardy." His intelligence allowed him to be a first-class intel analyst, and like most of the analysts, he had never had any field experience until a few months ago in Cuba.

Mark wanted to like Kramer because they were both military brats and office jockeys. They shared the same light brown skin. Kramer's from his black father and white German mother. Mark's brown skin was from generations of Filipinos, Africans, and Asians melting into the same color pot.

'Mark, sit and bring us up to date.'

'Yes, sir, General… Captain Kramer, sir.'

The three talked for over an hour. The general and Kramer asked pointed questions. The helicopter found camouflaged by cut foliage near the side of the Río Santiago matched the one allegedly stolen by the FARC. It seemed probable that the FARC were still in this area. Of course, Angélica, the daughter of the president of Ecuador, might not be with them. She might have been killed or even escorted to Colombia by the rebels.

'The only way they could have moved far was by boat or another helicopter,' said Russ Kramer. 'I'll check satellite images for boat traffic when we adjourn. Why did they crash land and abandon the bird? It would be more valuable to them working. They could have set it down and camouflaged it till they needed it again.'

'Good point, and I don't have any idea yet,' answered Mark.

'Well, gentlemen,' said General Crystal. 'Maybe, a big maybe, we have pinned this down to a few hundred square miles from several thousand. That is, if the helicopter was stolen by the FARC and if they have the daughter. That makes sense, and it's our best lead. I want an update brief at nine.'

After Kramer and Mark closed the door, the general pushed his intercom. 'Ask Sheilla to come to my office.'

'Sheilla, are you okay? You look tired,' he said, as she came into the office without her usual bounce.

'Just tired. Too many options to consider.'

'It's always the way,' added Will, 'until we find something that quantum jumps us forward.'

The general's PA placed a coffee next to Sheilla.

'Thanks, Marsha.'

Sheilla anticipated the general's next question. 'There really is nothing more. I think our best hope is having Fred, Misa, and Vidya intercept military or FARC transmissions. They are monitoring the army's calls but have not learned anything useful. The FARC have some unique encryption. They are working on breaking it.'

The general considered that his BWC computer group might be duplicating the work of the CIA. For a moment, he wondered which tech group was better. Then he decided not to mention it to either and see how things played out.

Chapter 13

Lobo's long experience and logical thinking, aided by his size and strength, meant that he naturally assumed the second-in-command position. According to Jago, few men could best him in a fight,

While his intelligence was average, he exhibited a unique awareness of situations, especially when engaging government forces. He could predict how and where the army would choose to fight. While the men respected Lobo, there was no doubt Jago was their leader. The odds of winning firefights improved with Lobo's instincts; Jago gave them purpose and direction.

Lobo stood in direct contrast to his best friend, the diminutive, salsa-dancing Chico. The small Cuban's mother was a local Indian and his father a Cuban, sent to the north of Colombia to advise and control the shipment of drugs from Colombia to Cuba that eventually ended up in the United States. His father disappeared when Chico was six years old. No one knew whether he had been killed or had merely returned to his native country. Chico had never known anything but the FARC. His mother, who cooked and performed other menial tasks for them, and the rebel forces had become Chico's only family. Jago had become a father figure to him. As a small child, the undersized Cuban had been bullied by larger boys until Jago intervened and became his protector.

San never stopped teasing the smaller Cuban about his size. Over time, the incessant teasing turned more and more mean-spirited, a teasing which inflated San's ego with little effect on the smarter Chico.

San was the youngest and, besides having low self-worth, he was cruel. Chico found San's insults tiring. With his superior intelligence, he understood the reason San acted the part of a bully.

For the most part, the band lived both the way they wanted and the way that was forced on them. They fought and killed; they stole and kidnapped, mostly executives but sometimes tourists. Some of them farmed, and others processed drugs. They were not saints; however, Jago and the others thought of themselves as civil. San was the exception. He stepped on lizards and pulled the wings off butterflies. Jago tolerated him only because he was a willing fighter.

Cherry was born in Bogotá on July 21st. The date became famous as it was alleged that a young girl had thrown a cherry bomb into a small fireworks factory, igniting the factory into a conflagration, shooting fireworks in all directions. After someone noticed her birth date years later, Cherry was anointed with the name "Cherry Bomb," not only because of her birth date but also because, in every sense of the word, she was viewed as a bombshell. She stood a curvaceous five feet four inches tall.

At thirteen, she had been abandoned and left as a farm helper in the mountains north of Bogotá. Her growing breasts and comely look started to cause her attention she didn't want. A drunken army soldier grabbed her one night, raped her, and took her back to his camp for several days, where she was raped and molested by other soldiers. Shortly after her first week of being brutalized, Cherry took a gun from a passed-out soldier and killed him and then three others. She escaped into the mountains, finding a home with the rebels, and met Jago. He was not like the soldiers. He did not try to molest her but simply befriended her. Later, they had made love on a few occasions. While sleeping with Jago had been okay, Cherry had found that she had become disinterested in sex. In her own way she loved Jago. She remained completely loyal to him. She would die for him, and the others did not doubt Jago would die for Cherry, or indeed for any of them. Jago had the respect of everyone in their small band, except for San, who had no respect for anyone.

***

'Good morning, General, everyone.' The faith the general and Sheilla had placed in him yesterday continued to add to Mark's self-esteem. A person as strong-minded as the general was hard to feel equal to. Yet Mark, along with everyone else, thought the world of General Crystal. He was loud and sometimes short and, to some, a bit gruff. Even with his abrupt manner, there were few people who didn't either like or respect the man.

'The ransom demand has now been judged authentic by both the FBI and the CIA.' The general placed a copy on the table.

'That's something,' said Mark.

'All we have is a piece of paper. Kidnapping, or maybe not…someone wants us to assume so,' said the general. Without compelling data, he was not easily convinced 'This note is possibly a subterfuge.'

'From who?' asked Mark.

'The military for one. By having her alive, rather than dead, they buy time to plan a coup.'

'That's why it's important,' added Fred, 'to monitor the Ecuadoran army's communication. Vidya broke their encryption, and there is some talk of a takeover of the government.'

'Just a few minutes ago, I received word from a group of researchers in the Aguaruna area that an indigenous woman gave them a scarf she found on a trail. Apparently, she thought it belonged to one of the women researchers. It had Angie written on the size tag,' said Mark.

'What's the status of the scarf?'

'It's still with the Carolina scientists.'

'Mark, get in contact with them and see if they can take a picture of the scarf and get that picture to us. I'll see if the family can verify it's hers. Then have them send it to the FBI and get something of hers from Quito or the ecolodge for DNA comparison.'

'The scarf, if it's hers, strongly suggests the president's daughter is in the area of the downed helicopter and adds strength to the kidnapping hypothesis. Let's get it identified first. See if you can find out anything else from the Carolinians and find a way to keep in contact with them. They are the best source of information we have for the area. Focus your satellite reconnaissance there. Let's assume Perez's daughter is not far away. Anything to add?' asked the general.

'I've some additional profiles worked up on the FARC and the military commanders in that area,' said Katarina.

'Send copies to everyone and keep them in the mission book. Captain Kramer, get Sheilla and Jim, then meet me in thirty minutes in my office. In the meantime, work with Mark.'

***

'Ben, how would you like to ride to Seattle with me?' asked Heather.

'What for? I mean sure, but….'

'I'm going to visit Nusmen.'

'Nusmen is nuts.'

'No, he isn't. He's just different. But you can't go where Nusmen works anyway. How about it? Want to ride over with me?'

'You bet. Sounds like fun.'

'Good, then. I talked to my old schoolmate, Doctor Dakine. You met her about a year ago, remember?'

'Hard to forget her and that couple of days with terrorists shooting at us in the mountains.'

'And she said maybe you would like to go sailing with her?'

'Wow. Yeah.'

'You talk to Loretta and make sure it's okay for you to go, and then go check on Betty Lou. Make sure she is all right. When you do, ask if there is anything we can bring back from the city. I'm worried about her ever since Duane died.'

'She's okay. I mean she misses him.' Tears welled up in his eyes as he turned away from Heather.

Heather put her arms around him.

'I know, Ben. I loved the old guy too.'

'I'm okay.'

'On the way over, I want you to give me a full report on how she's doing. It must be hard to lose your partner after being married all those years. And for you, it was like losing a father.'

***

Brush sat with Fred in the conference room studying topo maps of the region of Ecuador where the helicopter had been found. Mark had given him the mission book, and Fred was briefing him on the area.

Brush scanned the maps. He spotted a small tepui and wondered what they were like on top. *Would it be like in the movie "Arachnophobia"?* It wasn't as tall as those in Venezuela, although it might still be a good vantage point. *It could be a good place to land a chopper,* he considered.

'I'm going to take the stereo maps down to my office.'

Fred looked perplexed. 'What for?'

Brush shook his head and said, 'Kids.' Then he grabbed the old stereo maps and walked down the hall. He hadn't expected there would be stereo maps for Ecuador, but it was not for him to reason why. He arranged the maps and peered through oculars, shifted them, and the maps jumped into 3D. *The old ways are the best ways,* he mused. Even as he thought it, he knew it wasn't true. The stereoscope might be fun for him, but there was nothing like the detail that the satellites provided.

He studied every inch of the area for more than an hour. He found a way to climb up and down the tepui. It rose about a thousand feet, and there appeared to be no way anyone could get to the top by casual walking. He started thinking that this might be a good idea. A little climbing to the top, and no one could likely follow them; or easier, they could land on top with a chopper. *A bird perch to recon the area. Not bad,* he thought. *And I get to be on a tepui.*

Chapter 14

Glenda walked into the room and looked curiously at the maps spread on top of the table. Brush looked up and smiled.

'What's up? What's our general trying to get you to do?' asked Glenda.

'Not me, us.'

'Well then, from the looks of the maps, we're headed south,' said Glenda.

'Take a look at the mission book I left in the small briefing room. Then we can discuss it.'

Glenda smiled. 'You mean this mission book?'

Brush rolled his eyes. 'Yes, my beautiful teaser.'

'I read it an hour ago. It seems that you forgot that I'm an equal in this unit.'

'You're more than equal, baby. I just didn't know you had a copy yet.'

'All right, you. Slipped your way out of that one.'

'Slipping and sliding with you makes me feel like a lucky guy.'

Glenda gave him a cuff on the shoulder, then leaned over, kissed his head, and whispered in his ear, 'I know.'

'See anything on those old 3D maps?'

'Not you, too. I like them. And, I found an interesting tepui. I didn't know there were any outside the Venezuelan Amazon.'

'In Peru or Ecuador?'

'Near the border. Right where the east slope of the Andes

meets the Amazon.'

***

Fred walked into the room with Brush and Glenda. He was elated that his team had found their target in such a huge remote area. He turned with a big grin and said, 'They're in Peru. Jim, Kramer, Sheilla, and the general will meet us in the briefing room, with, ah, some more modern satellite data.'

'He can't help himself,' said Brush while looking at Glenda.

A few minutes later, a world map appeared on the screen. Fred clicked the keyboard, the image zoomed to South America, and eventually Ecuador and Peru. The countries were cut in two by a strip of cordillera that separated the Amazon basin from the Pacific Ocean. On the Amazon side of the Andes, dozens of large rivers covered much of a vast central area of South America. The Amazon was nearly the size of the United States, seven million square kilometers. Fred clicked, zooming in closer and closer to a small tip of Ecuador that protruded into the Peruvian Amazon. 'Just north of this lobe.'

'Shift northeast a touch, eh. Stop. That's my tepui.'

Brush turned and looked at Fred. Shortcut hair, the shaved line along his neck, neat sideburns. Very well-groomed, soft-looking hands. No color to his skin, since he rarely went outside. 'Fred, you need to get out more. Why not go on an adventure and visit a tepui?'

'If I had a clue what one was.'

'You can look it up. A tabletop mountain.'

'Yeah, right. Sounds exciting. Look, you want me to show you where the lost girl is?'

'Whenever you're ready.'

The door opened, and the general walked in, followed by Jim and the others.

Fred zoomed the image back out, so everyone could get a good perspective on the area's location, then zoomed back in until the topography along a river came into view. Rectangles stretched for hundreds of meters along the river's edge. 'Gold miners,' said Fred.

'I've printed out hard copies of information.' He pointed to a two-inch stack of papers in the middle of the table.

'It is just luck that the North Carolina researchers found the chopper and scarf and then heard rumors that a band of rebels was in the area. We searched and spotted the group here,' he pointed. 'Also, several indigenous groups both here and here. We are compiling information on the different tribes. I should have briefing materials ready in about an hour. The Indians, by the way, generally don't speak Spanish. They speak Aguaruna. I think that is how to say it.'

'Well done,' said Sheilla.

'Fine work,' added General Crystal. 'I have other business in the morning. Let's meet again here at noon. We should have a reasonably complete picture by then.' He stood and walked toward the door, followed by everyone except Brush and Fred.

***

'Fred, give me the exact coordinates for the rebels, tribes, miners, and military,' said Brush.

'You going to go back to that antique machine? Okay, don't hit me or anything. I just thought that I could show you how to use this computer sat system if you wanted. We import and store not only the maps from Bethesda, several universities, and energy companies, but we also get rapid access to satellite data.'

Fred hit some keys, and a printer ejected a paper. 'I printed the military coordinates, too, in case you need them.'

Brush rose, put a firm hand on Fred's shoulder, nodded, took the printed page with the coordinates, and walked out.

***

Jim went straight to his office, picked up the phone, and called Sergeant Williston. 'We ready to go?'

'Everything I think you will want is loaded and packed. I can have it on the plane in fifteen minutes when you give me the order.'

Jim hesitated for a second, 'Load it up.' *Williston ran a tight ship,* Jim thought to himself, confirming the opinion he already had of their new logistics sergeant. Time would tell if he was as good as his predecessor Mason had been. So far, Jim had no complaints.

Jim dialed Heather's cell phone. 'Hey, how are things at the ranch?'

'The usual. Rudolph is sick. I think the females were picking on him since he dropped his antlers. Not sure why he got sick, though. Maybe stress, but I'm trying something new. The reindeer don't seem to be able to handle antibiotics. I think it kills their stomach flora. So, I am intubating him with yogurt every few hours to replace the good stomach bugs. What's up with you? When will you be back?'

'Not sure. I might have to go away for a few days. Later tomorrow or the next day.'

Heather's stomach tightened a little. Then she bit her lip and managed to get out, 'A mission?'

'Yes.'

'I want to see you. I was going to ask you if I could come to the labs tomorrow. Remember you said you would give me a tour since I have clearance, and I want to know more about what you do. I asked Ben if he would ride over with me. Maria Dakine is going to take him sailing.'

'Winter sailing?'

'It's supposed to be sunny tomorrow, and it would only be for a few hours.'

'What about Pedro?'

'He'll be fine with Shuskin and Lo.'

'What about the feeding and the reindeer?'

'If you can believe this, Shuskin is turning into a pretty good hand. But he won't have anything to do with vet stuff, like sticking a tube down Rudy's throat. He's capable of taking care of the feeding and seems to like it. I think he feels more comfortable with animals than most people. I don't ask him to do anything. He seems to want to.'

'If you're sure he'll do it. That is a bit of luck, having him to back us and Ben up when needed. But what about intubating Rudolph?'

'This one will really floor you… Pedro.'

'He's a bit young, huh? It's pretty easy even for us to get the tube in the lungs by mistake.'

'He's going to be six in a few days, and he seems to take to it. He's done it several times now. He knows how to insert the tube and to listen for breathing before he connects the liquid. He is very cautious. He knows how terrible it would be if he aspirated him.'

'Suppose you are right about trusting him. I just don't want him to accidentally kill Rudy. It would be hard on him. He's been around enough death for his age.'

'Speaking of age, he knows you will miss his birthday. I told him we would do both his and yours together after you return.'

'I hate to miss it.'

'Reality, Jim.'

'What time are you going to leave to drive over?'

'Pretty early. Around six or seven.'

'I'll talk to the general.'

'He said it was okay before, and said you were in charge of the labs now anyway, so it was up to you.'

'True. See you tomorrow around midday. I have a meeting at noon, so I'll have Doctor Milton or Nusmen meet you if you get here before I'm out. Drive safe.'

'Love you, Jim Johnson. Thanks for this.' Heather was happy that she was going to see Jim, and she did want to know more about the labs. She always had. It was a part of his life that maybe now she could enter. Then her mind flipped abruptly to his leaving. Going away again. *A mission? No doubt. Dangerous? No doubt. Shit,* she thought, *I have to come to terms with this. I have to. He's letting me in. I have to accept being in his life.*

Jim picked up the pager they used to communicate inside the BWC. There was a sticker on it that still said "BWL." Because of the expansion of their remit over the last few years, the labs had been rebranded the Biological Warfare Center, that is, to those who knew of its existence. Some were still getting used to the name. Everyone acknowledged that these were far more than just laboratories and center was better. It felt appropriate to replace the "L" with the "C." He pushed the four-digit code for Brush.

Brush called seconds later, and Jim asked, 'Whatcha up to?'

'Going over maps.' Brush looked at Glenda. 'Glenda suggested we go out and get some chow tonight.'

'Let's go tomorrow evening. Heather will be here, and I want to go over the mission book tonight.'

'She's coming here, eh?'

'She's trying to understand what we do better, and the general invited her. Her clearance is still active.'

'Let's take her to SA if we go. She can get us up to speed on the jungle plants.'

'I think it's a big enough step coming to the lab. We've never discussed what goes on here before.'

'You making progress, buddy.'

'Trying my best.'

'Okay, what did you interrupt me about?'

'Let's talk for a few minutes before the three of us talk to Sheilla. I have a feeling this is going to be a go. She'll be mission leader. I want to make sure we're all on the same page.'

'Do you think Williston will have all the gear we want?'

'He seems pretty tight, and I told him to load it. He's read Mason's notes and gave me a quick rundown of what he put together. Sounded like he's overdone it if anything. So, I don't think we'll come up wanting, unless you want something special?'

'Nope. Be in your office in ten, give or take a few,' he said as he looked at Glenda. Brush put down the phone and moved over to her.

'Hey, buster, I know that look. Give or take a few minutes isn't long enough!'

'We could see.'

'Later. We have all night alone.'

Chapter 15

Mateo saw himself floating above a river, passing close to a wall, surrounded by blue-green parrots. First one parrot, followed by dozens, opened their azure-tipped wings, highlighted in the middle with a red brushstroke. His eyes fixed on the axel of a Ferris wheel. The wall of birds turned at first slowly, then sped up, turning into a blur. The image transitioned to green dresses as the dancers stopped. A white wedding cake rose toward a blue sky. Tower bells tolled, penetrating his dream and his sleepy haze. The bells become louder, then real as he awoke.

Startled and angry with himself, Mateo bolted upright only to have his worst fear realized. *I slept through the wedding* was his first thought before he realized the bells tolled for mass. The clock said noon. 'Stupid. Stupid.' *I'm okay, it doesn't matter. I will work later, faster. It will be okay. No church today. No time.* He had planned on going to the nine o'clock mass before continuing the inventory.

He dressed. Sleepy-eyed, he walked to his depressing basement dungeon. The day dragged on. He was becoming impatient, wanting to get this over. Then his resolve weakened. *I have done enough. Louis will be surprised at how far I got,* he thought. *We can finish on Monday. Tuesday at latest.* He had cataloged five freezers already. Surely with Louis on Monday, they would be able to go faster than he had been able to. *I'll be able to leave on Wednesday. Of that I am certain.* His feelings of gloom changed to those of confidence as he assessed the row of refrigerators.

He had permission to leave early on Tuesday if he and Louis were finished. In any event, he had Tuesday as a buffer. His flight would leave minutes after six a.m. on Wednesday. Oversleeping this morning gave him an idea. *I will sleep Tuesday afternoon and evening and stay up the rest of the night. I won't miss my flight.*

He latched the old lock on the basement door, happy that he wouldn't have to pass through this door, at worst, maybe two more times. *I worried needlessly.* With a smile and humming a tune, he walked light-footedly down the rua, past an alley, watched only by an unseen vagrant hidden in the shadows.

***

Heather stamped her boots on the snow-covered ground. The burgundy Volvo puffed vapor into the cold air as its engine warmed. The stars shone brilliantly as she marveled at the density of the Milky Way. The white snow reflected the intense starlight, preventing darkness, even on this moonless night.

She hustled back into the house and looked into Pedro's room. Even with Lola clanking about in the kitchen, he didn't stir. Lola had insisted on getting up at four to make breakfast and to pack an oversized lunch for Heather's and Ben's trip.

Lola handed Heather a rather heavy, used green plastic REI bag with their lunches inside. *My life really has changed,* thought Heather. She smiled at Lola and leaned over and kissed her on the top of her head. Lola felt the importance of what Heather had just conveyed. Lola's life had changed, just as had Heather's, both in completely different ways: one losing a child, the other gaining one; the near enslavement in Mexico, exchanged for the warmth Lola felt here in the cold mountains. She looked up, smiled, and wrapped her arms around Heather, nestling her head momentarily on Heather's chest, then pulled away nodding. Feelings that required no words. 'Be safe, roads no good, make señor Johnson eat plenty, no worry about here. I take good care of Pedro,' and then she scrunched up her lip, a mannerism acquired from Heather, and added, 'the old man too.'

87

'Ben, let's get a move on. Let's go hit the ice- and snow-covered roads. The mountains will be beautiful at sunrise. The car should be warm by now, and Lola made us lunch.'

Ben rubbed his eyes and got up. He had fallen asleep on the couch. Heather quietly opened the door to Pedro's room, gave him a soft kiss, and backed out.

***

Sheilla was the last to enter the conference room at noon. She added a stack of tabbed maps and papers on the conference table.

'Bring us up to date,' said Jim.

Colonel Johnson sat at the head of the table with the general to his left, and Brush next to Glenda on his right. Sheilla was at the opposite end with Katarina and Bridgette on her right and Mark and Fred on her left. Williston sat between Glenda and Fred. Kramer was positioned on the opposite side between the general and Bridgette. With his other duties, the general knew he couldn't directly supervise the mission and reluctantly relinquished control. He would back them up with his CIA resources only if it became absolutely necessary.

It was an odd situation to be in. He had never trusted the CIA to be involved in their missions. Nor any outside agency. The BWC controlled its own destiny, never involving other agencies. Now he sat at the head of that untrusted agency. His instincts and beliefs had been long ingrained in his psyche. It was difficult to shake them. *Does it matter? Other things to worry about.*

'The mission,' said Sheilla, 'seemingly is simple —retrieve Noboa's daughter. Neilly's group are in place at an old training base on the east side of the Andes.'

Fred tapped his computer keys, and the map appeared on the big screen, marking the camp's location.

'The downed helicopter is here,' said Fred as he highlighted the Colombian Huey's crash site. 'The FARC, we believe, are here. Why they have stopped close to the gold mining area is a mystery.'

'I think the answer to that is gold,' said Brush.

'That's probably it.' Fred continued, 'Misa and Vidya are monitoring the army's communications. They have heard nothing from the rebels. I assume they are not using a radio or phone to talk to anyone. General Crystal will coordinate with the CIA. Colonel, would you explain the plan?'

'We fly to Cuenca tonight and arrive early morning. We hook up with Neilly there. We head to a forward base, called Toucan, and fine-tune the mission. Head to the area where the pres's daughter is being held and retrieve her. The details are in the mission book.'

'I'll review all docs and any new materials you send me on the flight to Cuenca. Secure satellite communications to the situation room here and with the SF. Even so, follow our usual protocol and only use code names on the air, but only during missions. We know all the players except for the rebels. We have gathered a lot of useful data since yesterday,' he said as he glanced at the stacks of paper on the conference tabletop. 'Because the request is from the vice president, there is no shortage of support available. Marcus,' Jim looked at Master Sergeant Williston, who looked up, surprised to hear someone using his first name at an official meeting, 'has been coordinating logistics and equipment with Glenda and Neilly. We have air and watercraft on-site in Ecuador.' Williston nodded.

'Brush has given me a run-down of the topography. Mark has briefed me on the army presence, indigenous population, and the miners. Glenda will work with Katarina and Kramer from the training base. The general has put Kramer in direct contact with his lead intelligence analyst, Martin Pearson.'

'The man of fame who survived Najma in Mexico?' asked Fred.

'The very same. Pearson has suggested that it might be useful for Katarina to liaise with an FBI profiler, Doctor Sigger. Anyone have anything to add?'

'Departure time?' asked General Crystal.

'Zero five Zulu,' responded Jim. The general, Jim, Brush, Glenda, and Williston got up, and left Sheilla and the rest to an extended meeting.

Katarina looked at her watch. 'That's nine tonight. Right? Eight hours behind jolly old England.'

'Yep. Same as GMT time,' said Fred.

***

Sheilla looked around the room. 'We'll be here for the duration of the mission. Fred, Misa, and Vidya will monitor rebel, military, and government communications and computers. Our two juniors, the other half of the old Wolf Pack team at Huachuca, are going to be standing by to assist with any computer issues and to monitor our secure communications.'

'More like the Wolf Pups now that Misa and Vidya are here,' said Fred in a rare attempt at light humor.' Sheilla's mouth hung open for a fraction of a second as she looked at Fred, then quickly smiled at him before continuing.

'Brad, the drone operator from our "Over the Line" mission into Mexico, along with two drones, is flying to Ecuador from Fort Huachuca as we speak. He'll link up with Major Neilly.'

'Why doesn't he control the drones from Huachuca?' asked Kramer.

'Something about testing their new portable control system. Katarina, run us through all the players' profiles.'

***

Jim and Brush walked to Jim's office after the briefing. Brush smiled. 'Sounds like fun: rebels, miners, mountains and jungle, a nutsy rich enviro girl, head-shrinking natives, two countries' armies, and we can't drink the water 'cause it's full of lead, arsenic, and mercury.'

'We couldn't drink it anyway. Full of microbes we can do without,' added Jim.

'Parasites are your department. All in all, a piece of cake, eh?'

'Truth is, Brush, I'm looking forward to it. It's been a while since we've been in the field. After all the admin around here, it will be a relief. I'll tell Heather when she gets here that we'll get back way

90

before Christmas for sure. I don't want her to worry about that, and I don't want to miss Christmas with everyone, especially Pedro.'

'I think we'll get back a lot sooner than Christmas, buddy. Plenty of time, no matter what happens.'

'Yep. We'll hustle out of here tonight and not mess around getting back when we're wrapped up. Otherwise, the mission dictates the time frame.'

'What do you figure that will be?'

'I can't see it being less than a week. A day with Neilly, a day or two days to get in, and at least another two days to recon with drones and Neilly's watchers. Nice to have both.'

'Sort of think visiting a tepui is out. Kinda like me wanting to get to Alaska. I got close to it, but never seemed to get there.'

'You did get to Alaska eventually, and with Glenda.'

'True. It was a long time coming though. I might then get to a tepui sometime too.'

'We ready?' asked Jim.

'Williston's finished loading the plane. Sheilla will be adding to your homework,' Jim laughed. Brush would sleep like a baby on the plane while he'd spend most of the night reading. Then he wondered if having Glenda on board would change that. Brush continued, 'The pilots have a flight plan, and the plane's good to go.'

'Okay. I'm going to call Heather. Her ETA is 1300. I'll be her tour guide.'

'You are progressing, buddy.'

'I'll show her my quarters.'

'Good idea, pal. Your mind is in the right place.'

'Occasionally it's in the same place where yours is twenty-four seven.'

'I'm a happy Canuck.'

'You always have been, but Glenda is special.'

'No argument there.'

'After I tell Heather we're leaving on a mission tonight, I might show her our weapons room. Then, let Nusmen take over and show her anything she wants to see before we head out for dinner.'

'Nusmen?'

'Remember, they are old friends, have botany interests. It will be good to have Heather know what we do here. At least, I hope it will be.'

'You never talked about much with her, did you?'

'Classified, and now she has clearance, a temporary one, and …'

'And you are turning a new leaf. About time you let her into your life.'

'Yeah, something like that.'

'Like I said, about time.'

'Spect you're right about that. Let's do dinner at the O club at 1800.'

Chapter 16

Heather laughed out loud. Ben had gone gaga over Maria's thirty-seven-foot Fisher motor sailboat. She explained it wasn't perhaps the fastest sailboat, just the most seaworthy, and to her, beautiful. If they wanted, it could take them anywhere in the world. The three of them spent a wonderful two hours talking while they ate lunch. Maria proceeded to tell Ben more about their old college shenanigans than Heather wanted him to know. She had had her life before Jim. Probably Ben would also have some less-than-dignified times ahead as the seasons added to his years.

They left Heather on the dock as the prop of the North Star churned the cold waters of Puget Sound. Heather was glad that she had brought Ben and that she had had some time with Maria.

She turned off I-5 into the entrance to Fort Lewis. She gave her name to the military policeman at the gate. He turned, waving to a sedan waiting just past the entrance booth.

'Please follow the car, ma'am.' They drove past an area with World War II vintage houses and several warehouse structures made out of wood. Nothing modern, nor architecturally pleasing. The olive drab army vehicle pulled into a large parking area and stopped in front of a more modern brick building. A sign told her they had reached the Fourteenth Strategic Signal Core Command. The MP motioned her into the parking spot painted, "Command Parking." This doesn't seem right, she thought. Then she saw Jim standing at the entrance.

With long strides, he walked toward the burgundy Volvo as she unhooked her seatbelt, stepped out, and locked the car. She wondered if it was really necessary to lock a car on a base and especially after she observed that the front of the building had several large cameras. Jim gave her a kiss and hooked her arm through his. Another smartly dressed MP clicked his heels and saluted as the door opened.

Inside, there was a front counter with a long wall separating a large open desk area with several halls behind leading into the building's depths. Jim's workplace was not at all as she'd imagined. *I guess secret agents still need to have an office somewhere. But where is "Q," and all his special gadgets,* she wondered.

'I guess I should have brought you here sooner; but even for me, it would have been difficult to get you clearance. Now that you were inadvertently mixed up in the Mexico adventure and have clearance....' He looked at her to see if he had crossed a boundary, wondering if he shouldn't have brought up Mexico. He didn't see any adverse reaction to his bringing up what had been a major shock to her, not to mention watching her friends die at the hands of the cartel and Najma. It pleased him that he could be himself talking to her.

'This is a large office but not quite what I expected, Jim.'

Jim smiled, looking forward to her surprise when she saw the full extent of the BWC. They walked through the halls, stopping at an obscure door with no labels. Jim swiped a card and the door opened. Inside, there was a person at a desk, and more cameras mounted on the wall above. Another door opened, and they stood in front of an elevator. Jim swiped his card again. The elevator door opened, and he depressed the minus one button. He stood for a few seconds looking into a glass mirror. The elevator started down. Heather scrunched up her lip and nose. *Descending,* she thought, *more than one floor.*

'Either you have very tall ceilings, or are we going down more than one floor? And what's with that mirror?'

Jim just smiled, enjoying this. 'We're going to level minus four where my office is and the main labs. The mirror has a video camera with facial recognition.'

Okay, this is getting to be more interesting, she thought. 'I've never heard of facial recognition.'

The door opened. They walked down a small hall with dark mirrors on both sides and through a door that automatically opened. Heather's jaw dropped open when she saw lab benches and equipment extending into the distance. She looked up, and there were yet more labs behind glass walls on a mezzanine floor.

'Oh, my. I had no idea. This is gihugeic. Two floors tall and the offices above. Wait, you said floor minus four?'

'There are five underground floors. The offices up top we use, of course, but they are there as cover for what we really do and so people don't wonder about staff coming and going. We have hundreds of people, and we need cover for them coming and going. Behind the offices is the hangar. Let's take a short look at the whole place so you can get your bearings. It will take a few minutes. Each floor is about 500,000 square feet. It's about sixty acres total. Then there are annexes to HazMat; your friend Doctor Dakine is headquartered there. Our storerooms....' He couldn't quite bring himself to say weapons rooms and ordnance bunkers. *Be honest. Be yourself. Don't hold back if you want a complete relationship with her.*

'You got to be kidding. I never imagined that any laboratory could be this big.'

'Let's look around the labs here first. The secure level labs are below. There's no reason to go in them. We have up to level four security for the dangerous bugs.'

'I guess I should have known. You mean like MRSA and that sort?'

'Yep and including most everything you can think of.'

'Jeez, I thought CDC did all that? It's dangerous, isn't it? Why do you have them?'

'They have high-level labs, and so do we. Just like us, they have layers of redundant safety features. We need to understand how to counter them if a population becomes exposed.'

They walked down a central hall as Heather scanned left and right. Lab bench upon lab bench. Areas with jiggling vials, moving along on miniature metal conveyor lines. Seemingly endless mass spectrometers, with tubes running in all directions. Lights blinked at every turn. Then they walked down a hall with glass sides. Behind them, row upon row of computer banks.

'Jesus, Jim. How much computing power do you have?'

He cracked open a door and smiled at her. 'Let me introduce you to our resident IT types.' Inside, several dozen men and women were sitting at desks. Most had multiple screens perched at the back of their desks. Fred walked over.

'Heather, meet Fred. He's in charge of computing.'

'I'm pleased to finally meet you,' said Fred. 'I know all about you, of course, from the Arizona/Mexico, ah problem. I know, it turned out well for most of us. Just not all.'

'Nope, it didn't turn out well for everyone,' said Heather as she remembered her friend dying in front of her at the hands of Najma and the Mexican cartel.

Fred looked down, wondering whether she thought they had failed her. Then he looked up and said, 'Jim flatters me. I was in charge here, and I still am in many ways, as a manager. But there are two people who are really at the head our computer group.' Fred knocked on a door and walked into a dimly lit room. Large screens were on the walls with only two desks, both having several monitors each.

The lights raised a little, and Heather jumped with delight. Misa leaped out of her chair and gave Heather a long hug. 'Wow, wow. I never expected to see you. I was about to tell Fred to take a hike for barging in on us.' Fred rolled his eyes. 'We don't talk much face to face. We communicate using a topic-oriented program. Usually, no one comes in here.'

Seconds later, Vidya enveloped Heather in another hug.

'When you were at the ranch, I thought you had come up from Fort Huachuca to visit.'

'We did, but it was to stay up here. We couldn't say anything to you. It was classified, sorry. We both kind of like being up north. Even if we rarely go outside.'

'I understand. The distance from the Mexican border makes me feel safer too. I have a security clearance. Why couldn't you tell me?'

'It was critical-sensitive, or special access only,' added Jim.

The three nodded, so happy to see each other they didn't care about past security protocols.

'You want some tea?' asked Misa.

Heather looked at Jim. 'Sure, I'd like that. Do we have time?'

'We do, if Misa does.'

They walked into a kitchen and dining area at the back of the computer room. It felt more homey than institutional.

'Nice kitchen.'

'Mikey, you make us some tea. I'll show Heather around. I'll have green tea. Heather, what do you want?'

'Jeez. Knock it off Vid. You know I hate that nickname.'

'Just teasing. I do like it. I think it's special.'

'How about some Market Spice?' asked Heather.

'You got it,' said Misa, scowling at Vidya.

Jim had never seen the quarters that the general had built for the two recruits. Vidya opened a door, and they entered a living room. 'Misa calls it a sitting room.' It wasn't huge, but there were separate bedrooms, full bathrooms, and an exercise room.

'Do you really live here? You don't have a place outside?' asked Heather.

'This is our home. Each room is fully wired and has workstations. Sometimes, I like to use a laptop and just sit around when I don't need bandwidth. I can transfer data to any computer using a thumb drive.'

'What's that?'

'It's like a mini hard drive that plugs into the USB on computers. They're so useful. You'll hear about them soon enough as they are going to be sold to the public this year.'

They sat in the kitchen, chatting happily. 'I'm starting to like it here,' said Heather. 'It's nice to know you two are so close by. You are welcome at the ranch anytime.'

'Thanks. We'd like that sometime. Most days we are occupied and challenged here. It's exciting and doesn't leave us much time. We'll make it happen, soon.' Then she added, 'It's safe here.'

'I felt totally safe in the mountains before Najma too, so I understand how you feel down here, where no one can get to you. What do you work on?'

Misa, with her high cheek bones and pert dark blond hair, looked at Jim. She was unsure of what she could say. He nodded his assent. Heather noticed and felt a warm glow inside.

Before she could answer, Fred said, 'I think you are in the presence of the two best hackers in the world. They can get into anyone's system.'

'Our two kids at Fort Huachuca would disagree with you, Fred,' said Misa.

'But they'd be wrong, in my opinion.'

Jim added, 'We don't think of them as hackers. If they are, they are white hat hackers, maybe sometimes gray hat—helping, not hurting people. After a few more minutes, Jim said, 'Let's get on with our tour. I have meetings before dinner, and you are welcome to come back if you want.'

'Absolutely,' said Misa and Vidya at the same time. 'We can have more tea anytime you want.'

They walked at a fast pace as Jim needed to talk to Heather alone, and they hadn't covered much of the lab yet. 'Let's skip the secure level and go up.'

Heather raised a questioning eyebrow.

'More levels?'

They went back to a different set of elevators, and Jim pushed minus one.

'It's our equipment area. Brush and Glenda might be there unless they are back in our offices looking at maps.'

Heather could sense something coming. It didn't bother her though. She felt that Jim was letting her into his life, and she absolutely loved all the labs. Her mind wandered to the things she could look at in the electron microscopes. And seeing Misa and Vidya here was incredible. They had all shared something that only combatants can. It made her understand Jim's and Brush's relationship—why they were so close.

'I love it here, mister. Thanks for this. I mean it.'

He put his arm around her and gave her a brief kiss just as the elevator door opened. Master Sergeant Williston walked over and introduced himself.

'It is a pleasure to meet you, Ms. Asplund.'

So few people called her by her surname that she was momentarily taken back. 'Heather if you please, Sergeant.'

'Yes, ma'am.'

'Let's do the two-second tour, Sergeant,' said Jim, 'I have a meeting in about twenty minutes.'

'You got it, sir. Mostly what you see are shipping containers that we can load fast into our planes.' Forklifts were loading the containers onto a moving ramp that went up one more story. They ascended on an open-sided elevator to the floor above and into a huge hangar where the containers were being loaded into a jet.

'Jim, you can leave me if you have to go. I'm sure the sergeant can get me back to your office.'

'Except that I was planning on having a little time to talk to you. You're the first meeting.'

'All this stuff is going on a mission?' She raised her eyebrows questioningly again.

'Yes,' was all Jim said.

They went back down via the cargo platform. It was not

normally used as an elevator.

'We have a broad selection of equipment and armaments.' Jim wished he had said weapons. His old compartmentalized thinking had selected the word before he spoke. He continued, 'Explosives and ordnance are down that long hallway. At the opposite end is the special response team's area. Through that door to another building is HazMat.'

'Maria Dakine?'

'That's right. We rarely connect here, though, as they have separate outside entrances for their vehicles. People expect a Hazmat response team to be here. They don't expect that they're connected to us. Doctor Dakine is more than just the HazMat leader; she is part of our bio response group.'

'Amazing. I couldn't have conjured this up in my wildest imagination.'

'Floor two is mechanical systems. Lots of vents and filters and backup power,' Jim explained.

They rode back to Jim's floor and walked along a hall until he opened a door to a functional office. He opened another door into a small sleeping room. It was spartan compared to Misa's and Vidya's quarters.

Heather was now certain Jim was leaving. In the past, it would have driven her to tears. This time, it was not affecting her like it used to. Nonetheless, some anxiety crept into her throat.

'I would have brought this up before,' said Jim. 'But we didn't know for sure until just before you arrived. We're going on a mission,' he hesitated and then thought. *Okay, keep it straight up with her; she has clearance still...* 'to South America. Ecuador. Tonight.'

'Brush and Glenda?' asked Heather.

'Yep. If you want, we're thinking about going to the O club for dinner at 1800.' He almost said 0200 Zulu. Much of his life as a pilot and in the army, he used Greenwich Mean Time. He was used to using GMT or Zulu time at work or for filing flight plans.

'I don't think this mission will be especially dangerous. A

daughter of a South American president has probably been kidnapped.'

'Is that normal? Do you rescue kidnap victims? Why isn't that dangerous?'

'No, it isn't normal. But as it happens, the Ecuadoran president was school buddies with our VP. So, it's a special request. Neilly is onsite, and Brush, Glenda, and I fly there tonight. I doubt we will be gone more than a few days, maybe a week.' And then, since he valued accuracy, he added, 'One never knows, though, how long these things will take. We have to stay loose. There's plenty of time to get back before Christmas. I want to be there with you and Pedro.'

Heather looked at him with glistening eyes. 'I'll never stop worrying about you. You know that. But Jim, we're in a different place now. I can feel it. I trust you. It's important that we share everything.'

In spite of himself, Jim let out an audible sigh, nodded his head, and took her in his arms. 'Thank you, baby. Thank you for being you and for being in my life. Things have changed for us, haven't they? Pedro, Shuskin, Lola, us talking about my work, you being here....'

'Just hold me for a minute, please.' Then she lifted her head, and they touched foreheads, shifting from side to side, she said, 'I love you, Colonel.'

'I love you, too.'

'I know,' said Heather. 'I know.'

Jim looked at his watch. 'I have a final mission briefing with Sheilla in ten minutes.'

'Can I say hi?'

'Sure. Let's go.' Jim stopped at a door, and they peeked in. Brush and Glenda were peering at maps spread over the top of a big table.

Glenda jumped up, 'How are you, girl?' After a long hug, 'You look good.'

Heather looked at Jim, 'I'm very good, actually.'

Jim pointed at his watch. 'We'll meet you in the conference room. Heather wants to say hello to Sheilla, and Barbara is going to meet us there and then show Heather around some more.'

Heather looked at Glenda and then back to Jim, hoping she was not pushing it. 'Can I sit in on your meeting. It would save you telling me what you're going to be doing?'

Glenda gave Jim a look that said, you better make the right choice here. Jim looked at Brush, who cocked an eyebrow, and Jim said simply, 'Okay,' as was his habit when he completely accepted an argument.

Chapter 17

Mateo slumped in his seat as the airplane taxied at Galeão International Airport. *Amazing! I'm going to make the wedding if the plane does not crash.* Then he crossed himself. He didn't like flying. He tried to set his fear aside and think about seeing his family and enjoying the festivities. As much as he disliked flying, he had always liked weddings and the celebrations that followed. Camila, his cousin on his mother's side, would be there along with many other single, pretty girls.

Sophia is marrying an army captain. *My father sounded none too pleased. There will be many military officers. The girls like them. Mierda,* he thought. His thoughts were interrupted when the engines became loud and the plane thrust forward. For seconds, he thought of nothing and gripped the armrests.

The middle-aged woman sitting next to him said, 'You no like to fly, señor?'

He shook his head.

'Do you live in Rio?'

'I work there. I am going home to my cousin's wedding in Colombia.'

'I am señora Acosta. You may call me Leonor.'

'Mateo Mareno Rojoz.'

'Boa sorté!'

'I am feeling lucky to be on the plane and leaving,' he said as he gripped the arm rest. 'Obrigado, I hardly noticed the plane taking off.'

Leonor smiled, pleased she had helped. Mateo laughed at his foolishness. Even so, the laugh vibrated a little nervously.

***

Jim, Brush, Glenda, and Heather walked into the briefing room. Sheilla, Mark, Fred, Kramer, and Katarina were already seated, with a topographical map projected on the large screen.

'Heather is visiting and is going to sit in on the briefing. She has the proper clearances, so you don't need to watch what you say,' said Jim. 'Katarina, I believe you are the only one who has not met Heather?'

'Not formally, but we talked when the Mexico operation was ongoing.'

'It was the same for me until we met earlier,' added Fred. 'Sheilla is going to brief us on the latest information.'

'First, on the left of our viewing screen, let me introduce Martin Pearson, the Director of Intelligence at CIA. Are you hearing me clearly, Mr. Pearson?'

'Loud and clear.'

'This will be the first time we have included someone from the CIA in one of our missions. Mr. Pearson you will be linked to our mission control here.'

'I'm happy to do whatever I can to support the success of your mission. Although we've never met in person, I feel as though I know all of you from previous debriefings or from hearing the general discuss you. I'm pleased to meet you.'

'Mr. Pearson,' said Sheilla.

'Please, please. All of you call me Martin.'

'Martin it is,' said Sheilla. 'Martin has agreed to keep me informed as to what the CIA resources learn that could be useful to us. However, Martin will not disclose details of our mission to them. The general speaks highly of you, Martin, and has asked me to include you in today's mission briefing. Then, Katarina will fill us in on the principal characters. Fred, you run the screens.'

'Will do,' said Fred.

'The principal area is map grid reference 17MRS1039464015.'

Never having heard of the military grid system, Heather barely refrained from blurting out, 'What is that?' Just in time, she realized she was lucky to be here, lucky to be part of Jim's other life, the one she had known so little about. *I'll ask later and not interrupt Sheilla.* '…an isolated area where Peru meets the south Ecuador Amazon. You have several detailed maps in your briefing books. Major Neilly and his special operations team are located here, southeast of Cuenca.' She increased the scale and pointed to an area upslope from the Amazon on the eastern flank of the Andes. 'Their base is 130 kilometers from our projected target area.'

An image of the Ecuadoran president appeared on the screen, and Katarina said, 'Gustavo Noboa, sixty-three years old, born 1937. A technocrat, and in every sense of the word, a bureaucratic leader. Not known for imaginative approaches. Still, he is supported by the indigenous people who live where we will be operating. Many Shuar have fought in the army, mostly against Peru. He has, however, a tenuous relationship with his military. They have little respect for his czar-like style and lack of military experience. As you know, he was educated at Princeton with our Veep. Our information says the military officers make fun of his demeanor and appearance, especially his white goatee. Except for VP Davis, he has few close relationships, even with his family.'

Katarina continued to summarize the president's family, the principal military officers and, at the end, gave a detailed profile and psychological assessment of Angélica Noboa Perez. 'Nickname, which is not often used, is Angel. Born 1972, twenty-eight years old. Five-foot-two inches tall. Not attractive in the conventional sense: wide hips, olive skin, dark eyes as you can see. Very opinionated. She has moved from one cause to the next.' Katarina continued for several minutes, profiling Angélica's personality and relationships.

'I won't go into detail,' said Sheilla, 'about the native population in the area you will be operating in. Briefly, there's more than one group, as they coincide where both Peru's and Ecuador's lower Andes meet the Amazon. I must say, they all are fascinating. You have full briefs in your mission book. The Shuar Indians are interesting and, in the not-too-distant past, were the quintessential Amazon headhunters. You are most likely to encounter them. The other two tribes you might encounter are the Awajún, also called the Aguaruna, who have a reputation as the most skillful warriors. They defended their lands from the Incas and the Spanish. The other tribes are the Wampis communities from Peru. You might also encounter gold miners or oil prospectors.'

Sheilla continued, 'The CIA has prepared a detailed list of plants, insects, reptiles, fish, and animals you may encounter. Martin, do you have anything to add?'

'Only a little. As you pointed out, there are Canadian miners in the area. A rough lot, apparently. We are attempting to insert a Canadian operative. As you know, we have had very few operations and/or contacts in that area. Consequently, we have little information to provide you. We are working, just as your computer team is, to monitor any communications in the area. If we are successful, the operative should be in place in the next three days. His code name will be "Python."'

Jim left the meeting. He planned to read all the documents in detail on the long flight. He motioned to Heather, and they walked out. Heather turned and nodded to those still seated as she followed Jim out.

Jim closed his office door. Heather looked at him and then wrapped her arms tightly around him. 'Thank you,' she whispered.

***

An animated Heather returned with Marsha up the hall. 'She looks quite happy,' commented Glenda.

'Big day for her,' added Brush. 'Next, you'll be taking her along

106

on missions, eh?'

'Wow, wow,' said Heather.

'Sounds like you had a fun day,' said Glenda.

Jim put his arm around her. 'Tell us all about it on the way,' said Jim.

'It's amazing. The labs are huge and the equipment—how many electron microscopes are there? Does Nusmen really live here? Do you want to take my car to dinner?'

Brush rolled his eyes. Glenda chuckled. Jim said, 'We have a car up top waiting. Truthfully, I don't know how many electron microscopes there are. The newest is a scanning transmission that can obtain up to a million magnification.'

'I loved it when you taught me to use the Scanning EM at the university a long time ago. And I have always known about transmission EM, but a Scanning Transmission EM is beyond comprehension. And you said it can capture images at a million magnification. Wow!'

'Remember, sweetie, no discussing the facility or what we do outside the building. We are a very secret facility. To the world, we do not exist.'

'Is it hard to segment your life and keep track of what you can and can't say? All the things you didn't, wouldn't, or couldn't confide in me?'

'We get used to it.'

Jim knew that he was going to have to make sure that Heather understood the costs, both to her and especially to others, for divulging or hinting about the labs or their missions. Frankly, it worried him. It wasn't that he didn't trust her. He needed to make sure she understood the importance of secrecy.

They retraced the way they had entered earlier and got into a green sedan. Jim got in the front. The other three climbed into the back seat. Jim turned toward the rear. 'Heard from Ben or Maria?'

'Not yet. I said I would call this evening. But Maria is taking Ben to some crab place for an early dinner. She wanted to get the boat back before sunset.'

The Officers' Club wasn't busy. The bar was full, but not many were eating yet. Heather felt like a new person. *I'm on the inside,* she thought.

Chapter 18

'Shut-eye time,' said Brush as the Citation X taxied toward the southeast end of the 10,000-foot runway. 'Did you and our fine pilot decide on the route?'

'Straight through. No stops.'

Brush rubbed his chin.

'Piece of cake,' said Jim, knowing what Brush was thinking. Sixty knots, north winds changing to northwest between a huge departing high, and a low coming in.

'Leaves us pressure-sandwiched with a tail-wind highway, eh?'

'Let us know if you want to talk,' said Glenda. 'Anytime. Don't worry about waking us up. I'll come out a couple hours before landing.'

Brush's face said what he thought about her idea.

'No need to do that, honey.'

'Brush needs his beauty sleep, and I need information. We always do it this way,' said Jim.

'Jim will wake us up at the other end.'

'It makes me feel guilty,' said Glenda.

'Yeah, me too.'

'Uh-huh. Pleasant dreams, pal. Get some rest and don't worry, Glenda. I'll be fine.'

Although the distance capability of their plane was extraordinary, it was only slightly longer than their planned flight. Without favorable winds, they all knew they were cutting it close. If their destination had been another 200 miles, they would have had to make a stop. While it was a close call, it was the same choice as on most long-haul flights. The trick was to go as far as you could without running out of fuel. Jim and the pilot had worked on the flight plan and agreed it was doable.

Sergeant Williston and his men had reconfigured the twelve-person plane for two sleeping berths, a table, and comfortable lounge chairs. Jim settled into one of the chairs and picked up the first file. It was a detailed psychological profile of the Ecuadoran army major, the commander of 200 soldiers who operated in the northeast of Ecuador between the Cordillera del Cóndor and the Amazon basin and part of the way south to the Peru border. Katarina had covered many of the facts in the briefing, but this file also contained much more: her assessment of the Ecuadoran army colonel who was in charge of the far southeast.

It did not take long for Jim to understand the probable accuracy of Katarina's summary of the man. He wore the uniform of the government forces and operated without any compassion for the local tribes. Katarina suggested miners and oil drillers were paying for protection. In short, he operated his fiefdom like any other head of a criminal protection racket.

The question was, how much did he work with Angélica's father's approval, and how much outside it? He searched through the files and took out Gustavo Noboa's folder. Law school with the U.S. vice president and, later, Chancellor of Guayaquil University. On the surface, he didn't seem to be the type to work with Colonel Ortega. But then, his insulation in governmental headquarters from what went on in the field might leave him oblivious, or living an alternate reality. Jim pulled out his picture and studied it. White chin beard. Katarina had called him a pompous bureaucrat. But, indigenous people generally supported him. Did he deserve it?

Mark had said most of the tribes were declining in population. The Shuar and others had fought the Spanish Conquistadors successfully. They had survived. While they still embraced their ancient ways, they seemed adept at prodding politicians to preserve their land. Still, their population had declined, and their lands were logged and mined; pipelines leaked oil into their rivers. Miners, both small local operations and larger Canadian and Chinese ones, dumped massive amounts of mercury into the rivers and streams, killing fish and poisoning their children.

The Awajún and Wampis lived in Peru, across an official border that existed only in the minds of politicians. They were less successful in slowing down their government's assistance to the miners than were their Ecuadoran counterparts.

The environment versus money, thought Jim. *Which side was Noboa on, and did it make a difference to his mission?* He closed the file. Then he picked up the file on Angélica Noboa Perez.

Sent to the U.S. for college. Bachelor's degree in social science from Brown University. Satisfactory grades. Opinionated without reasoned knowledge. Started causes with a passion, and then switched to another cause, changing course many times in her twenty-eight years. Neither attractive nor unattractive, dark skin, dark hair, not known to have had any serious relationships. Heterosexual. Katarina felt Angélica wanted to do good. She just didn't know how or where.

He proceeded to read file after file. The ones that he found the most interesting were those on the FARC rebels and the indigenous tribes. The FARC had a lot of bad press, possibly much of it true. Like many movements, it had started with an ideal: farmers banding together against the government. Then the never-ending need for money and supplies eventually changed the dynamics of their cause and method of operation, and they fell out of favor with the people they originally set out to represent.

If Angélica had been taken hostage, how would she respond? Her history suggested that, even though she thought of herself as an independent thinker, she could be manipulated. A persuasive leader potentially would have little trouble in recruiting her to the FARC's cause.

Unfortunately, they had no empirical evidence besides the

scarf. They didn't know who the members of the FARC group were, or even if it was the FARC that had taken her. She had disappeared; the Colombian rebels had been in the area. Analysis of the ransom note supported a FARC origin, if it was real. Katarina suggested in her analysis that the circumstances supported that Angélica Perez was being held by the rebels or had been recruited to their cause. Based on Angélica's personality type, Katarina gave it even odds.

He continued through the stacks of files discussing mining companies and their personnel who used child labor. Then he moved to the reports by the University researchers who had provided vital clues as to the daughter's whereabouts. The topography, although interesting and important, would have to wait until they discussed it with Neilly. At this point, there was no way of knowing whether they had moved from the area where the helicopter had been found.

His last thoughts, seconds after three in the morning, were that the local indigenous people were the answer to finding Angélica. He read the file again on the Aguaruna, the people of the water, who lived in the jungle near Brush's tepuis. As he drifted off to sleep, he formed a mental image of the land that the tribes called the land of rainbows.

***

Angélica peered through the dense foliage at the wide expanse of the Río Santiago. It was about ten in the morning. She looked up and saw a jet thousands of feet above the river, passing east to west. The trail of carbon it spewed into the hazy blue sky disgusted her.

***

The White Citation X braked and turned off onto the taxiway of Cuenca's Mariscal Lamar International Airport. The pilot wished that he could switch the 6,000-foot runway for the 8,300-foot elevation. He would have to keep the weight low to get the plane in

112

the thin air before he ran out of runway. Worse still, it sat on a plateau surrounded by hills. Even though landing would be easier than takeoff, the pilot visibly relaxed as the jet pulled to a stop near a large hangar. Right on cue, three vans pulled onto the tarmac and up to the left side. The plane door opened, and steps settled onto the tarmac.

Jim scanned the area and then trotted down the steps as Major Jasper Neilly exited a van, followed by six members of his special operations team.

'You travel in style, I'll give you that,' said Neilly.

Brush stood on the top step and raised his arms, yawning. 'You got that right. Pretty, isn't she?'

'It always looks a little strange to me,' said Mac. 'Those two high engines, the T-tail, and the pointy nose aimed at the ground.'

Brush stepped onto the tarmac, 'Hey Mac, it's good to see you without a knife stuck in your neck.'

'I'm not sure which one of us looked worse, and that was before the chopper bit the dust.'

'Hands down, Marilyn was the worst, eh? Not sure how she survived,' said Brush.

Glenda walked down the steps and into the conversation. 'Your days of getting banged up are at an end. Mine too.'

'Let's get the gear unloaded, and we can catch up on the road,' said Jim.

As they loaded gear into the vans, Jim said, 'Okay, Mac, tell you what. Someday we'll take a trip in the Citation, and you won't care what it looks like when you're inside.'

With the nine of them, it didn't take long to finish loading. They filled one van with their equipment and pulled out just as a tow truck arrived to back the plane in the hangar. The twenty-million-dollar plane was never left out in the elements any longer than necessary. The vans drove through an open gate and headed east for the sixty-two-kilometer journey. Jim turned around and watched the plane, with the tow truck attached to its front wheel, disappear into its temporary metal den.

Neilly turned to Jim, who was in the first back row seat of the lead van. He looked back at Brush and Glenda in the next row back, 'Brush and I have talked a few times in the past months; he has kept me up to date on your recovery.'

'Compared to Marilyn and Mac, my injuries were minimal,' said Jim. 'How is Marilyn doing?'

'You'll see for yourself in about ninety minutes.' Jim nodded and felt pleased to see the old gang. 'Same team,' continued Neilly, 'Except for one new guy and woman, and two new snipers to keep Roberta company. This'll be her last mission. Having the extra watcher will be training for the new guy, and I was ordered to use all caution for this mission. An extra set of eyes with a long rifle will give us an edge. We had one of the drones up for a test flight earlier today.'

'Anything yet on the location of our target?' asked Jim.

'Nothing precise. BWC has been tracking as best they can, considering the jungle canopy makes seeing anything on the ground with satellite nearly impossible. The drone is better equipped to find them. A computer hotshot wrote a program to try and predict their movement. We'll see. Mid-afternoon, we'll send the drone out for its first official recon. I sent one of the new watchers, Phil Aleski, out two days ago. He is going to where the computer program predicted the rebels would be. He has a lot of experience in long-range recons. Potential problem: there are a bunch of local languages and dialects, and Jean-Paul is the only one that understands them. He speaks a little of the local language, and he's quick on the uptake. By the time we leave, he will be an expert. He's pretty small, so he blends in and won't look intimidating to the Indians. Not like too-tall Mac over there.'

'Major, you just wish you could see things from my vantage point,' said Mac.

'Nope,' said Neilly. 'When I hit the ground, I don't want to be doing it from the stratosphere. I'd break something.'

Neilly went through each of the new member's qualifications for Jim and Brush, ending with Fleur Martinez.

'I thought we might need an extra medic along besides Jeff. There's no shortage of men with guns down here. Not to mention the odd poison-tipped arrow,' said Neilly.

'I like your positive attitude, Jasper,' said Brush.

'Not all of us seem to be as immune from flying projectiles as you, Canucks. I lost more people on our last mission together than I ever have. Two killed and three badly wounded including you, Jim.' Neilly knew Brush was going to get on his case for saying that. He quickly added, 'Don't say anything, McGuire, and don't get what I just said wrong. Like you two are jinxed, or something. You're not, and if I had my choice of working with anyone, it would be with both of you. Just that the missions you get involved in aren't always the safest.'

'Heather said much the same thing,' added Glenda. 'But don't forget, Jasper. This bulletproof Canuck took a bullet six months ago.'

Brush grinned at Neilly.

'So, your luck ran out.'

Brush looked at Glenda and said, 'Doesn't seem so to me.'

Neilly turned away from Brush, shook his head, and then turned to Jim. 'Heather doing okay? We only met those couple of times—I liked her. Count yourself lucky. Having someone waiting at home for us is not normally in the cards. The only one of us that manages a happy home life is Gaston, and I don't know how he does it. Hum, actually I do. It isn't him at all. It's his wife that keeps them together. She's a peach to put up with him being away as much as he is. We don't have the same stand-down time that you three do.'

'Gaston's wife must be unique,' said Jim. 'Has to have lot of faith, waiting for a demolition guy to come home.'

'Yeah,' said Neilly. 'But it's not like he's defusing crushers every day.'

Brush changed the subject. 'What's with this camp?'

'Nice. Not too glamorous enclave with Quonset huts. Perimeter about a half-mile across, including a short-field runway. Not long enough for that shiny jet of yours to land. It's primarily been a Special Forces training center. Close enough to the high mountains and the jungle. CIA used it for some operations way back, but it's military now. Perfect for us as our base.'

'Primarily?' asked Jim.

'Some black ops still get run from here. Mostly drug interdiction operations,' he said, as they drove through a tall gate.

The road was hard-packed red clay. The back two vans stopped outside a rusty metal-roofed building. Their van continued past two more buildings and stopped. 'Chow time, and then we'll get serious,' said Neilly.

As they got out of the van, a tall, dark-haired woman with a long face, a bush hat and BDUs walked out of the mess hall with a big smile, 'Colonel, great to see you looking fit,' said Marilyn.

'You look good too. No lasting damage? Nice camo pattern.'

'Our latest battle dress. Nah, no real damage. You know. The usual. Sometimes, I need some limbering up and get a pain here and there. On the whole, I feel pretty good. I just talked to General Crystal and told him you were only a few klicks out.'

'The general still likes to talk about flying with you. I think if he needed a helicopter pilot, he would try to recruit you.'

'He wouldn't find that too hard. Gets pretty boring sometimes with these jokers.' She gave Neilly a playful punch on the shoulder.

Mac looked up toward the sun and said, 'You can palaver inside.'

'Let's go then, Mac. I'd rather be eating than yakking, eh,' said Brush as he walked onto the porch with Glenda and Mac on their heels.

'That big yellow thing shining on us gives me a homey feeling. It reminds me of being a child on the Sinai,' said Marilyn. 'Not too hot. The temps here are pretty okay at this elevation. Let's go in. I was looking forward to catching up while we eat, unless Neilly wants you before you get your belly full.'

Neilly rarely ate lunch in the mess hall and looked at Jim. 'Meet me back in thirty where the other two vans stopped.'

'You been here before, Mac?' asked Brush, eating some macaroni and cheese. 'Not bad, eh?' He turned to Glenda, who just nodded.

'Chow's decent for sure,' said Mac.

'Glenda, I'm pleased to meet you. I guess you'll be hanging here with me.'

'That's the plan. I'll liaise with BWC, give you some shut-eye time, and, more importantly, I'll be available to rescue this big lug if he needs it.'

'You asked if I'd been here before,' said Mac. 'I have, three or four times. We've had some fun here. We used to get our best camouflage on, and the trick was to follow a course through the jungle without getting busted by the natives. Not many of us succeeded. They are just too good at sensing disturbances in their back yard. But our new guy, Aleski—a Polack who's out on recon now—never used to get caught when we trained with him. He went to another unit, and then Jasper managed to get him assigned to us. Besides being sneaky, he can put one in your eye with his Barrett at over a mile, and I mean consistently.'

Chapter 19

The rebel band encountered no one during the first two days. Even so, Jago had the persistent feeling that they were being watched. They found three dugouts. It was slower paddling against the current, but a welcome reprieve from fighting their way through foliage along the river's edge. Late afternoon on the second day, they heard distant sounds. After hiding the dugouts, they made camp. The next morning, the small group moved cautiously toward the sounds and discovered their source—miners—gold miners.

They backtracked to a slope so they could climb to higher ground above the river. There was a small, steep-sided u-shape-cut that Jago decided would make a secure camp.

After they had made their rudimentary camp, Jago found a position above the mining camp to use as an observation post. On the third day, he was once again at this position a little over a mile away from the gold mining camp. He sat cross-legged with his slender back against a tree, a large rock obscuring everything but the top of his head. San and Chico watched from about twenty yards to his side. Each, with different thoughts: San was enthralled while Chico was angered. Below them, there were multiple trails along the base of the hill. The hill rose behind them, ultimately forming the threshold to the Andes.

Jago moved to the rear, toward their camp. He watched San and Chico, ensuring they observed him leaving. When he was safely out of sight, Jago headed back to their campsite in the steep-sided ravine, more than two miles from the miners and several hundred feet above the river.

Twenty feet above their campsite and on top of the ravine's craggy edges, he looked down at the wide river to their east, giving way to the seemingly never-ending Amazon basin. The only exceptions were two flat-topped monolithic rock outcrops, rising incongruously through the green vegetation to an altitude of almost 6,000 feet.

The wide muddy Río Santiago separated their hill from the thick jungle vegetation. And it wasn't that the tepuis had risen through the jungle. Rather, the hard rock plutons had resisted erosion through hundreds of thousands of years as the jungle moved ever lower, exposing more and more of the resistant rock. The high peaks of the Andes were not far to their west, hidden from view by foothills.

Their camp, snuggled in the base of the small ravine, had few flat spots for sleeping. Pushed in close together, they sat discussing the mining camp.

Jago looked at León. 'The only way we can enter the cave where the gold is stored is to kill the guards at night. León, you will first have to kill the guard above the cave and then take the one on the left. I will kill whoever is on the other side.' León was nearly Jago's age. His weapon of choice was the knife. His proficiency made him extremely valuable at times like these.

'How much gold do you think they have?' asked Chico.

'Chico, you're not going to let the glitter of a little gold make you greedy, are you?'

'Of course, no, Jago. I am curious is all.'

'It has been many days since we arrived; using the soldiers, they have shipped out much gold. Many kilos.'

'Sí, we could support our people for many months,' said Chico, thinking Jago would approve of what he said.

'You see what they do,' said Cherry. 'They mine their gold, using the children, who die young, and babies in the villages down the river are deformed by the poison water. I think we should slowly kill these men before we relieve them of their gold. They are bad hombres.'

Jago sat silent, knowing what had truly roused her anger. They had seen these men taking girls no older than seven or eight into the trees. Some of the young girls looked to be either drunk or drugged, and they kept the men company at night. 'You are right in this, Cherry. They do not deserve to live. But we are only seven, and they are maybe forty. We could kill many, but perhaps we would die too.'

'They anger me,' said Cherry.

'I agree with Cherry,' said Angélica. Cherry shook her head in disgust at their captive.

With her anger boiling below the surface, she turned to Angélica. 'We should cut off your fingers and send them to your papá, little chicky. That is your use to us. What do you know about killing?'

'I see what they do to the pueblos indígenas, the gente, the people. Why don't they fight back?'

Jago spoke quickly to defuse the tension between the two women. 'These Indians are not warriors. I have heard that the Indians in the mountains are, but they have no reason to risk fighting the Canadian and Chinese miners to save the jungle water people. They are all trying to save themselves.'

'How you know there no mountain Indians there?' asked Chico.

'I do not know,' said Jago. 'I am only guessing why their tribe does not come to rescue them.'

'Maybe the mountain people can help us, and then we will go help them,' suggested Angélica.

'Rich girl, you are only going to help the FARC when papá pays.'

Jago interceded again. 'Cherry, tomorrow I want you to take someone and find out where the soldiers' camp is located. Lobo, take Carlos and León and make sure that there is no one else headed to the mine in the direction we came from. From the papers we found in the chopper, this capitán following us is from Colombia. He sounds a persistent man. I don't want him sneaking up behind us.'

San said, 'He couldn't be behind us. We flew many miles.'

Jago was always patient with the less experienced. 'Maybe the colonel could obtain another chopper or boats. We check to be certain, so no one can surprise us, including the Indians whose boats we have taken.'

San realized he had not considered the alternatives. Never wanting to be wrong, he said, 'Yes, but not likely.'

Jago continued, 'Tomorrow night, after we deal with the miners, we make sure we can take the dugouts back down the river without interference. We will steal their gold, five hours after sunset when we are certain there are no soldiers close. The miners will be drunk and passed out as usual.' Jago stood and stretched his six-foot-plus frame. 'Now, I will rest until night. Then Lobo, you and I will observe them and make a plan.'

***

Phil Aleski crested the hill high above the rebels' camp. He found a position where he could observe the mine. The mine was a blight on what would have been a pristine landscape. Red-brown dirt replaced trees and plants after hoses had pumped out thousands of gallons of water, leaving a muddy slurry to cloud the river.

A few feet above the river operation, he saw a cave. *Or is it a mine?* he wondered. The entrance looked to be the center of activity for the male miners. Several stood guard, shouting at the laborers. As he looked more closely, it became apparent that the workers were not adults but children.

Through his high-powered scope, he could see dozens of sparsely clothed workers. He could also see large sluice boxes through which water was loosening gold trapped over tens of thousands of years. It had probably taken millions of years for the gold to make its way from the mountains' veins to the mining camp. Above the sluice boxes, the miners were crushing rocks and, from the coloration, Aleski could tell that they were amalgamating the gold using mercury. *These children will never become adults*, he thought.

From the little Aleski knew about mining, it still looked a bit odd. Two different types of operations were going on at once: the rock was being crushed while the gold was being separated from the river mud.

He started a grid scan of the area surrounding the mine. Something moved three-quarters of a mile down the hill. He couldn't yet tell whether it was an animal, bird, or person. He watched and waited, scanning back and forth close to where the motion had been. An hour later, two natives wearing multi-colored hats and face paint appeared, traversing the hill. They frequently looked back to where he had seen the movement.

He kept watching the Indians while he started a grid search in the area where they had been. Thirty minutes later, he spotted a person holding a rifle stand, stretch, and then settle back behind a boulder above a small ravine. Minutes later, a second man appeared.

The men were dressed like FARC rebels. He pulled out his sat phone.

'Cattail, you read.'

'This is Cattail,' said Mac.

'Two possible tangos north of my position.'

'Confirm two tangos. Cattail out.'

Aleski said, 'Gopher out.'

Mac, toggled his mic and called Neilly.

'Gopher reports possible rebels.'

'Give the coordinates to Knight and get one drone on site. Have him keep it high. I don't want any detection.'

Neilly pulled over a topo map, found the section he was looking for, and then pulled out a smaller-scale map. 'It's sixteen hundred. That gives us almost three hours of light including twilight. Then, we go IR and compare the daylight photos. Knight brought a ton of computer gear for some experimental analysis. Guess we'll soon know how much help it will be. Fort Huachuca is linked in, and he said the drone has the latest high res test cameras.'

Jim leaned over and studied the map with Neilly. 'If this is our target group, then dropping in downriver, rafting up, and landing on this little tributary puts us about two klicks away. Have Knight use the drone to make sure no one is in the vicinity of the tributary and upriver.'

'You're thinking tonight, huh?'

'Why not? Waiting only risks harm for the captive.'

'We're set for nearly every contingency. Command spared no expense on this mission.'

Jim picked up a radio and called Brush. 'Come on over as soon as. We are going in tonight.'

Brad flipped a switch on his computer, 'Specialist Knight. Your drones checked out?'

'Both up at the moment.'

'Check these coordinates.'

'Mac gave them to me.'

'Enough fuel to get there now?'

'Osprey's up with full fuel.'

'Move it over to...'

Brad stopped him. 'ETA twenty minutes, incognito all the way.'

'Good. Keep me up to date.' Then he radioed Mac. 'Tell Gopher the plan, so he can check the area, especially north along the river.'

Jim and Neilly continued studying the maps and discussed options until seventeen hundred when Brad Knight called. 'I've got some new visuals. The targets are in a ravine. Five positives.'

'You run any of the new enhancements you told me about?'

'Yes, sir. Not natives or civilians. Best guess is rebels. All appear armed. I'm working other spectra to see if I can pick them up on daylight IR and manipulate the visible to drop the chlorophyll signatures out. Give me another five minutes.'

'Mac, get Marilyn and Reese to the ops center now. Have everyone else follow in forty minutes.'

Chapter 20

'I would choose to have you with me when I fly home, Leonor,' said Mateo.

'You are a nice boy. God will decide when you die. Not your fears. You have a nice time at your sister's wedding. It is a sacred occasion. Don't pester all the pretty girls, Mateo,' as she waved an arthritic finger at him. 'You will know the right one when she appears.'

Señora Acosta had distracted him for the entire flight, and now that they had landed, taxiing toward the terminal, his mind turned to Camila. *She's so beautiful,* he thought. He pictured her sitting with her two sisters at the funeral of his uncle a year ago. He hadn't been able to stop turning and looking at her.

He could see her smile, white teeth against smooth copper skin, and wavy dark hair. Her sisters were opposites. He pursed his lips as he remembered them. One with short dark hair, and overweight. The other thin, and sharp-featured. He imagined her flying off on a broom.

How could the three sisters be born from the same mother, he wondered. Maybe they had different fathers. That would explain it. When they stood, Camila had been nearly his height, just over 172 centimeters. Her knee-length dress had allowed him to see her thin legs. Somehow, they did not match with her full upper half. All top and no bottom. It didn't matter; she made his heart pound.

The plane stopped, and he stood in the aisle next to the diminutive Leonor. He helped her retrieve her brown cloth bag from the overhead locker. Then he got down his small gray suitcase and his half-full green rucksack. He put the rucksack over his shoulder, trying not to bump anyone in the crowded aisle.

Leonor held his arm as they exited the plane, and slowly climbed down the metal stairs onto the warm tarmac. She wished him well. He said thank you again, and he meant it. She was a very nice lady. Then, walking much faster than she could, he went as directed toward a door with a sign labeled "Migraciones and Vuelos en Conexión Internacional." It felt good to be home, knowing he would soon be with his family.

***

The Huey lifted off its pad. Underneath, cables grew taut. Marilyn expertly shifted sideways, keeping the tension as she lifted a large rubber raft off the ground. She guided the helicopter up at a steep angle into the night sky.

Colonel Johnson, the two majors, McGuire and Neilly, and Neilly's second in command, Master Sergeant Gaston Reese, along with two watchers and four others, sat bathed in the red lights that illuminated the interior. In the dim light, the men were barely visible in their jungle camouflage.

The drones had eventually identified eight people in the ravine. As invisible as Aleski was to human eyes in visible light, he glowed a fuzzy red in the drone's infrared cameras. The new experimental clothes that made them nearly invisible to infrared detectors were not necessary for this operation, and their heat signatures allowed Brad, the other Guardian Angels, and the operations center back at Fort Lewis to see each person's position. Brad reported that Aleski and Gopher had moved to within 500 meters of the ravine.

Glenda sat drinking coffee in the ops center shack, watching the same images as the control center. She understood why she had been assigned her role in this mission. It was one she was good at. Nevertheless, she wished she was in the assault team.

***

Chief Warrant Officer Four Marilyn Cutter flew her Huey over the last ridges of the Cordillera del Cóndor, angled toward the river, and dropped down just over its surface with the trailing raft not more than ten feet above the muddy water. As Marilyn slowed the Huey to a hover, she lowered the raft onto the water's surface. Five thick ropes and the main cable were attached to the chopper. Marilyn watched a video monitor, keeping the raft as steady as she could while the oversized ropes undulated.

Standing out on the helicopter's skids, Gaston, JP, and Brush on one side, their second Guardian Angel, with Roberta on the other, they disappeared down the heavy ropes, landing on the raft's edges. All except Gaston, who hit the outside edge of the raft. He hung on the rope up to his thighs in the water. He started to climb, but before he could, Roberta grabbed his vest and pulled him over the side.

'Still have your feet attached, Gas?' joked Roberta in a low voice.

'Thanks, love. Crocs don't like the taste of me.'

'Yeah, I hear they have keen senses about what tastes good.'

'Yada, yada, but thanks for the tug out.'

They were quickly followed by Jim, Neilly, and the two medics, Fleur and Jeff, and Joe, their heavy weapons expert and back-up demolition to Gaston. Seconds later, the main cable was freed, and the chopper rose, turning back down river and disappearing over the low hills. The ninth man still on board, García, their third guardian angel, pulled in three of the thick ropes and left the other trailing behind. Marilyn, watching her GPS, gained altitude as she flew below a ridge five klicks from the tangos. Peering through her night-vision goggles, she spotted a clear spot in the valley below the ridge and positioned her chopper over it. 'You're good to go. Hell of a long walk,' she said, and García slipped off into the night.

They could not risk the rebels' or the miners' hearing the

helicopter by dropping the third watcher closer. It would take García several hours before he gained a vantage point where he could see both the rebels and the miners.

Gaston restarted the whisper-quiet outboard and began their run up the river toward the grid reference point where they would leave the boat.

'Approaching Rendezvous One,' said Knight, peering at his screen. 'No movement at the camp.'

Gaston pulled into a small tributary, and Roberta jumped out. He let the current pull him back into the river and doubled back downriver just past and below where the rebels, hopefully with their captive, were sleeping in the ravine. It was now midnight. Roberta would work her way up to the hilltop not far from where Jago had watched the miners.

Aleski had both the FARC and the miners in his field of vision. The FARC were quiet, with no firelight seeping from their ravine campsite. In stark contrast, the miners had blazing fires. Aleski was disgusted by what he saw. A drunken man backhanded a young girl who tried to run. She was grabbed by another man. This was a scene straight out of a drunken pirate movie.

He peered through his scope, fine crosshairs sides and top with the man's head sitting on a slightly wider rangefinder bottom post. He put tension on the trigger. He wanted to apply just a little more pressure and help the girl, but he knew he couldn't.

After what he had been watching the men do to a young boy, he couldn't watch what was about to happen to the girl; he guessed her age at not more than eleven or twelve. He slowly positioned his Barrett back toward the rebels and tried hard to forget what he had just been witnessing. *Worse, this is probably a nightly event,* he thought.

This was the first time they had been allowed to take the new experimental night vision goggles with their combined scope on an operation. He had switched them on when watching the miners with their large fires and lights. The dark terrain surrounding the ravine became illuminated in a greenish glow. The field of view was wider than the previous generation NVGs, the contrast better, the distance amazing, and what impressed him the most was the improvement in the depth of field. Their old NVGs rendered the world flat and without depth.

A thousand meters was the limit his scope allowed him to see. The crosshair in his goggles linked to his rifle scope through some new wireless technology. As he moved the rifle, what he would have previously only seen in the scope was also seen in his goggles. He felt somewhat uncomfortable using the new system. *Too complex. Too many things to go wrong,* he thought. He could always revert to just using the Barrett as he always had.

Nudging the thirty-foot raft along, Gaston turned off the main river into a narrow and shallow tributary they called the Little Tigre River. About 100 feet in, he pushed the bow up on a muddy bank. Three jumped out with weapons and packs. Gaston and Fleur stayed in the raft. Gaston cut the motor and handed out the rest of the gear before jumping onto the bank. 'Comm check,' said Neilly. One by one, each clicked their radios.

The three watchers clicked theirs, starting with Gopher, who was the only one in position. Roberta, whose code name for the night was Gold, would be in position long before García, whose code name was Mosquito. 'On the hour, comm checks,' said Neilly.

Heavily loaded, they set off into the dense foliage. They eventually reached the tiny and intermittent trail that the drones had imaged. It occasionally disappeared, hidden below the hillside plants. Neilly and Jim were certain that it would continue to follow a contour line below their targets' camp.

The pace quickened now. Still, they only made a kilometer per hour. Stopping often to listen, Jean-Paul was on point, relying on his natural night vision. Gaston followed with his NVG turned on. JP glanced at his watch and stopped. It was almost zero one hundred. One by one, the pause rippled down the line until they all stopped. Rather than talking on their comms, they used the man in front of them as a clue to move or halt.

Neilly clicked his radio. Two rapid clicks near the raft from Fleur, followed by two slower clicks from Joe, one click from Gopher, three clicks from Gold, and finally four clicks from Mosquito. The six-man column started forward again.

The trail was narrow. The dense foliage an inky haze, with just enough starlight filtering through to sense the trail.

Roberta and García hustled to their assigned positions.

'I like these new goggles. Almost as good as day,' said García.

'I like 'em too. Time to go our separate ways,' said Roberta. Gonna have to hustle.'

***

At zero four hundred, Neilly's comm check showed him that everything was as it should be. The watchers were positioned, and the drones had all the IR signals identified. There was only one rebel out of the ravine, sitting motionless on the ridge.

'Execute,' said Neilly.

Jim and Brush were the only two who stayed together. Each of the other team members had a task. The three watchers were their eyes, complementing the drones, and more importantly, their guardian angels—all three of them were targeting the ravine, although they could not see into it. At least one drone would be overhead at all times. The one uncertainty was the number of warm bodies in the ravine. Corporal Knight thought he had them identified, but more than one could be obscured from his IR sensors by a rock overhang in the steep-sided ravine.

'The lookout above the ravine has been inactive for an hour,' reported Knight.

'Sleeping or practicing meditation,' added Gopher.

'Doubtful any of them have Buddhist tendencies; sleeping is my guess,' added Mosquito.

Jim and Brush moved into the ravine on Aleski's side, with Neilly, Gaston, and Jeff on the opposite side. JP worked his way along the edge of the cleft where San was sleeping. Neilly turned toward Jeff and gave him a hand signal to stop and stay put. His job was to guard their backs in the ravine, just as, after taking out the sleeping guard, it would become JP's.

Neilly took the left side and Gaston the right. They moved cautiously, soundlessly, ghosts in the night, step by step. 'One in a hammock ten meters,' whispered Neilly.

Brush and Jim moved into the ravine and found two more rebels.

JP moved forward, settling his feet slowly, without transferring weight to the forward foot until he assured himself that he could transfer all his weight silently. He was now four meters away and could hear the man snoring softly. Three meters. The small man was slumped with his back against a rock and cushioned with a coat. JP moved in a crouch toward him. With a quick motion, he turned his MP5 and slammed the butt-end into San's forehead. 'Guard neutralized.'

That was the signal for the others to move into the sleeping camp. JP quickly snap-tied the young rebel guard's legs and wrists, pulled a hood over his head, cinched it, and looked into the ravine: no movement. He walked to the side of the small cut that Jim and Brush had entered.

The rebels, sleeping in hammocks within feet of each other, showed no signs of sensing the ops team's presence. Jim moved toward the first hammock, heard snoring, and moved on. Brush stayed to one side, watching the hammock while covering Jim as he moved further into the camp.

Neilly passed one hammock. Jim and Brush proceeded forward while Gaston covered Jasper. Neilly stopped short of two more hammocks. The plan was to locate the president's daughter and protect her. Jim and Neilly planned to move around the camp until they spotted her.

There was little light in the ravine. Without the NVGs, it would be difficult not to accidentally step on or bump into one of the rebels.

Gaston looked away from the hammock. Right at that moment, he heard a voice say softly, 'Silencio, señor. Do not even think of moving or speaking.' Gaston froze and shifted his eyes to the left. He could see a rifle barrel pointed at him and a figure rolling out of the hammock. It was a woman. Gaston had his left hand on the radio switch and depressed it as slowly as he could to let the others overhear. They heard the mic open and stopped moving.

The woman moved out of the hammock cautiously, with the barrel of her gun never straying from Gaston's chest. She moved closer and whispered, 'Lay your weapon on the ground.' Still above the ravine, JP slowly rotated his eyes, trying to find Gaston and his captor.

The luminescent green jungle light shone on the woman's dark skin, but Gaston could tell it was not the president's daughter. She moved closer to him. 'Use your right hand and very slowly remove your headgear. Now put your left hand over your head,' she ordered. The radio clicked off, but the others had heard enough. Neilly stood motionless. He turned his head as far back as he could in Gaston's direction. The two shapes came into view. The woman had her back to him.

The woman pushed the barrel hard into Gaston's chest as she leaned in close and whispered, 'How many are you?'

Gaston didn't answer. He was buying time. Neilly turned and slowly started in Gaston's direction. JP continued to work his way down the hill and was now only six meters away. He considered taking out the rebel woman, but it was not worth the risk. They had not yet located the president's daughter. Jeff moved up the ravine. The GAs watched nervously but could do nothing with everyone hidden from view.

'I'll ask you one more time as I tighten my finger on the trigger. Ten seconds you no answer, I pull trigger. Maybe less if I squeeze too hard.' Cherry could feel him tensing, ready to move, and said, 'Malo, señor.' While she spoke, Neilly had managed to move up to her hammock. JP was within three meters. Neilly flipped both his

IR and laser on and painted a red dot on her nose. JP immediately followed, his laser site illuminating her chest. As she started to move, Gaston said, 'Not an especially good idea.'

Cherry could see a faint glow coming from her nose. Then she saw the red dot hovering over her heart. Gaston risked slowly pushing her rifle barrel sideways. She did not resist. She was a survivor and would not throw her life away cheaply. She stood calmly, as Gaston quickly frisked her and found an old Colt .45 automatic and two knives. At first, she grimaced while he searched her thoroughly. Gaston, always considerate of women, did what he had to and intended nothing unseemly, although even he could not help but notice Cherry's figure. She tensed at first as he touched her, but then she realized he was only doing what any professional would do, nothing more.

She was unaccustomed to respect from men, excluding Jago and perhaps a few others. He took her wrist and, with a strong hand, brought it behind her back. She cooperatively moved her other hand back, knowing it was useless to resist. He walked her to the hammock. She sat on it and then lay on her side as Gaston snap-tied her feet together. 'Ahora, señorita. Cuántos son ustedes?'

She said nothing. Gaston could not help but smile at the cool response of the woman he had just encountered. He wondered what she would be like in sunlight.

'Let's wrap this up,' whispered Neilly. They walked through the camp, finding five more hammocks. Brush walked to the closest one, placed a hand over the man's mouth, and pressed a pistol into his neck. Ignoring Brush's hand on his mouth, the rebel grabbed his other wrist and turned it in hard. Brush grimaced, managed to ignore the pain, lifted his hand off the man's mouth, and without hesitation, brought a clenched fist down like a hammer on his head. The man's grip relaxed.

The team turned on their headlamps. Jeff looked into the face of a woman who squinted and said in English, 'Get the fucking light out of my eyes.' Chico, León, and Jago surrendered, seeing the futility of resisting. The woman in Jago's hammock was the president's daughter.

After the rebels' wrists and ankles were secured, JP went back up the ridge. He pulled San's hood off, cut his leg restraints, and sprinkled water on his face. Following JP's order in fluent Spanish, a groggy San, holding his head, walked down the bank and joined the others with a little prodding. Gaston went back to Cherry, scooped her out of the hammock, and put her down gently next to the others.

Neilly looked at the prisoners. 'Who speaks English?'

No one answered. Neilly looked at the girl next to Jago. 'I know you do. What is your name?' Trying to be a good soldier, Angélica did what she thought Jago would want. She put her chin up and said nothing. Neilly chuckled to himself. *Not kidnapped, obviously.*

'Gaston, you and Jeff take the girl and the kid holding his head down to the end of the ravine. Jim and Brush, see if you can get some answers from the big guy and the little one. I'll take this beanpole. JP, rove between us.'

They all knew the drill. Separate them. Get them to talk. Work back and forth on what they said until the story fragments begin to ring true.

Pretty soon, the groups were out of hearing range of each other. Neilly sat down and looked at his two prisoners. He figured the tall thin guy as the leader. In fluent Spanish, he asked, 'You want to tell me your names, maybe even your real ones?'

Jago noted Neilly's confident manner, his equipment, accent, and the fact that they had been careful not to kill anyone. He surmised correctly that they were American, highly trained, and probably had backup. *Our girl prisoner*, he thought. *A big mistake I make.*

'You're American?' he asked. 'What do you want with us?'

'I want nothing from you, besides answers. Start with your name and where you are from.'

'My name is Gomez, and we're from the other side of the river.'

Neilly decided to get right to it, especially since he was not interested in the FARC per se. He just wanted to make certain he had the right girl and some idea what had happened in case anyone was interested. 'You're from Colombia, you're FARC, you kidnapped the woman, stole a helicopter from the military, and your name is not Gomez,' he stated brusquely.

Neilly didn't know his name, but he was certain that it wasn't Gomez.

Jago opened his eyes, wrinkling his brow. He wanted to ask him how he knew all that. The accuracy and the fact that they had located them in the middle of the night piqued his curiosity. He decided his best avenue was saying the truth, at least as much as he thought appropriate. 'You are right in all that you say, so what difference does my name make?'

'None, really, but you will tell me.' He looked at León. What is your name?'

León looked at Jago, confirming to Neilly that the tall man was the leader. Jago nodded his assent. 'León, señor.'

'And his?'

León hesitated then said. 'He Jago.'

'Either of you want to tell me something I don't already know. Like why you left Colombia?'

Listening, JP looked at Neilly, then toward Mac. 'How about the woman and the teeny-bopper? What're their names?'

Jago had already decided it would be fruitless to withhold their names. 'They are Cherry and San.'

JP went over to Mac and Jeff and listened for a few minutes, but neither the woman nor the teenager would say anything.

'Your leader, Jago? He is talking to us, so why don't you as well?' JP suggested, in fluent Spanish.

He could see surprise registering on the woman's face. 'Unless you want to sit here all night, let's hear it,' he continued. She still didn't say anything.

JP smiled and said, 'Do the names Cherry and San mean anything to you?' San jerked his head toward JP, wondering how he knew this. Jago had talked. *He was a coward to have broken down so easily.*

JP continued fluently, 'You are FARC rebels from Colombia. You kidnapped the woman. How did you all get this far south?'

'We have been walking for months,' Cherry finally replied.

He got right up close to her and clearly said, 'You know we already know, so why keep lying? You stole a helicopter; your boss told us.' Then he slapped San, knowing it would cause a lot of pain to his already throbbing head. 'I'll be back.'

Jeff looked as though he felt sorry for San. 'I'll get you something for pain.'

Jeff pulled a waterproof bag from his pack, selected two pill bottles, and handed San two lorazepams and two ibuprofens, then poured a small cup full of rum. 'You like rum?' Jeff didn't know San had been drinking for years, and rum was what he liked.

San stared at the pills, looked at Jeff, and put them in his mouth, drinking the rum straight down. 'You should feel better in a few minutes, and then maybe you can talk with me,' Jeff offered.

Mac walked to Cherry and San and said kindly in Spanish, 'You know, in our own way, we're rebels too. We work for our government, yes. But we're really outcasts. They need us. They still don't like us. We're too independent. They train us to be that way, and then don't like it when we are.' He got up and walked behind her. He could feel her tense as he cut the plastic wrist restraint.

Cherry rubbed her wrists and then, sensing there was no immediate danger, she relaxed.

'Has Cherry always been your name, or is it a nickname?'

'It is the only name I know.'

'Do you have a last name?'

San was starting to feel the effects of the alcohol and drugs and said cockily, 'It's Bomb. She's a bomb.'

Mac gave Cherry a kind look before giving a less kind one to San. 'What's your last name, peckerhead?'

'I don't have one.' Mac started to reach for San's head. 'Hernandez,' San blurted out, then looked at the ground, feeling ashamed.

'Let me be straight with you. We know how you got here and that you sent a ransom note to President Noboa. So, it would save us all a lot of time if you, San Hernandez, answered my questions.'

JP walked back up and listened to San mumbling on in his slightly intoxicated state. Then he looked at Jeff, who just shrugged. They often used benzodiazepines and alcohol as a sort of truth serum to get people to loosen up. 'Real talker, isn't he?' JP listened for a while and then walked down to the others. Little by little, they all talked. JP worked back and forth until Neilly pulled him over.

'What do you think?'

'They have told us just about all we need to know.'

'Lots they could tell us about their drug business. Someone might be interested in finding out more about those activities.'

'DEA can go get their own information.'

'We'll see what SOC says later.'

Chapter 21

The army officers sat in the front two pews on the right side of the emblematic, gothic El Carmen. Their gold insignias and rainbow medals competed with one of the most ornate chapels in Bogotá. The officers' rigidity and identical blue-green uniforms contrasted with the gaily dressed cousins and friends of the bride, Mateo's sister Sophia, the soon-to-be señora Diaz Rojoz Ramos.

'Mi hija, una señora,' sighed Luciana, squeezing Mateo's arm while smiling broadly. However, Mateo's mother's happiness was not shared by his unsmiling father Juan, who after many arguments with Luciana, had only reluctantly given his permission for the marriage. There was nothing that the young officer had done to anger Juan. He was a wonderful match, as Luciana had never tired of telling him. The young captain was gallant, and his father was a Teniente—a three-star lieutenant general in the Colombian army—and very close to people at the top levels of government.

Sitting here, watching the two rows of upright men, he wondered if indeed he had made the right decision. Not to mention that Capitán Romero Ramos' father had treated Juan disrespectfully. The general viewed Juan's position with the Indigenous Rights charity as a worthless occupation and, more to the point, not the advantageous political alliance he had expected from his son's marriage. In truth, Capitán Ramos' father had been more displeased with the marriage arrangement than had Juan.

Which was one of the reasons the captain had decided to marry her. He had no real feelings for her. He had no feelings for anyone. She was pretty enough and would bear his children. And he realized, since he'd first slept with her, *she really likes fucking me.* His father had wanted him to marry someone more influential, but Romero didn't care about social influence. His life was the army. He had money and power. What did he care about society? Marrying lowly Sophia irritated his father, and that, too, pleased the young Ramos.

Mateo noticed Camila turn slightly, looking toward the rigid military men and giggling with her companions. His heart sank, wondering what chance he would have with her. He put his hand on his mother's, feeling her happiness through their touch. He looked at the wonderful chapel, the bright colors, and the gaiety that filled the air. The party later would be spectacular, with dancing and fireworks. Camila would dance with him and see his worth.

The wedding goers emptied from the church into dozens of cars: chauffeured army sedans for the more important attendees, and private vehicles for the less important attendees. The one exception was the general's private limousine, a long black Mercedes containing the bride and groom. The cars made the long procession from the Iglesia del Carmen to the military air command base known as CATAM, adjacent to the El Dorado International Bogotá Airport.

General Iván Tovar Ramos' high position allowed him to arrange for an elaborate reception party at the airbase. The large hall had hundreds of white flowers strung from the ceiling and placed as centerpieces on the thirty, ten-person tables.

Mateo sat with his family at the table to which they'd been ushered. Walking around the table, he noted that Camila's name was not on any of the place cards. He had not seen Camila since they'd left the church. He scanned the tables, looking for her.

'Are not all the flowers wonderful?' asked Luciana. 'Are you listening to me, Mateo?'

She tugged at his arm as he searched the tables. 'Sí, sí, Mamá. Of course. I was just looking…'

'Your pretty cousin, Camila. I know you are taken with her. I can see her on the left near the dance area, sitting at a table with other girls and a few of the military officers.'

Mateo's heart sank further. It almost made him feel ill. He touched his temple, massaging a pain that seemed to split his head.

'Excuse me.' he mumbled, 'I'll return shortly.' He needed to move from the stifling crowd. His cousin would never be in his grasp. He stood, his back ached, his head ached. He needed air.

As he walked away, he heard his mother say, 'Come back, my son. Are you okay?' He wasn't okay. He had never felt more disappointed. The wonderful party and the festive dresses had all evaporated as a black cloud enveloped him.

Chapter 22

The sky lightened, and the sun painted an orange line on the horizon. A soft breeze rose up the slope from the river, both refreshing and full of humidity. The Americans rearranged the rebels' hammocks, anchoring them to the narrow ravine's rocks, so they were as close to each other as possible. They set out two guards on the end of the ravine and left two watching the captives in their hammocks. Jim and Neilly took the first watch and sat a few meters away, talking softly. Field operations had one thing in common: teams were accustomed to dealing with little, no, or at best, intermittent sleep.

'I don't think they're holding much back,' said Neilly. 'I'm taking a liking to this Jago character.'

'Interesting group. Real tight, and probably because of him. The kid that JP banged doesn't fit with the others. Not everyone's favorite.'

'Definitely not the brightest of the group. If I didn't know better, I would think this band were the good guys. Don't suppose they are typical of the FARC, do you?'

'Hard to say. I wouldn't mind knowing a bit more about the FARC. Interesting how these large groups form and are run. They're self-appointed leaders. Not like Plato's politicians. The leaders set the tone and accumulate like-minded people around them, cultivate the youngsters, and select who will lead. This guy Jago seems pretty self-assured. He could be higher up in the FARC than we think.'

'What d'you think of their plan? Ransom the girl, rob the gold miners, and return as conquering heroes?'

'From what they say, the miners are a blight.'

'If what they say is true. We came after the bad guys, but instead caught the good guys, who are about to take on the bad guys. You wanna try for some shut-eye?'

Jim looked at his watch. 'Let's. Suppose we can do with one guard at each end of the ravine?'

'With the drones and guardian angels watching over us, that's a plan. Go ahead, Jim; I'll work out the rotations.'

Mac watched the rebels, who continued sleeping as the sun rose above the shadowed ravine.

Neilly walked out of sight and hearing range and clicked his radio. After all three watchers acknowledged, Neilly said, 'Anything?'

Mosquito replied, 'Nothing, nada.'

'Gold?'

'I wish I could say the same,' answered Roberta.

'Gopher and I witnessed some ugly crap at the mine.'

'It was all I could do not to do some target practice.'

'We're on the same wavelength.' said Aleski. 'I would have rather missed seeing their party.'

'Where do these guys come from?' added Roberta.

'Mosquito, work your way down to us.'

'Gold needs to stay put. Gopher, adjust your position if you need to compensate for Mosquito leaving.'

'Roger that.'

Even with their latest encrypted communication devices, they naturally fell back into the old ways, using call signs. Especially during an operation, they didn't give any more details than necessary. If by chance anyone was able to break their encryption and overhear, they did not want the snooper to know, for instance, that Mosquito was on their south side. They felt more comfortable accepting the protection of the encryption when not involved in the life-or-death stakes of a battle.

***

The prisoners sat on the ground, eating. The team had removed their restraints; Neilly wanted them relaxed. He posted guards near each end of the ravine. It was doubtful that any of Jago's band were a match for any of his team. Nonetheless, they stayed alert. It was not in their nature to gamble.

The day was warming. The jungle filled with birdcalls and piercing screeches. Accompanying the warmth that enveloped them was a heavy blanket of humidity. Not to mention insects. Protection required long sleeves, hats, even light-weight gloves, and heavy amounts of repellent. The clothes soaked through with perspiration as bodies struggled to regulate their internal temperatures. It was all to no avail. The saturated air prevented evaporation from cooling them.

It was the way of the jungle. The teams were as used to it as was the rebel band.

Jim and Brush had decided to take a look at the mining camp. Neilly observed the FARC rebels. He saw how they related to each other and how they moved. He was sure they were very capable fighters; other than the one kid and the women, they seemed a congenial lot.

Neilly was now certain that Angélica was not a prisoner. She wanted to be with the rebels, or at least with the man they now knew was the leader. Jasper Neilly had been going over ideas all morning. If she had been kidnapped, they would have rescued her, taken the captives back, and turned them over to the government. Now, he would have to take her back against her will. He was not motivated to do anything with Jago, since he had not kidnapped Angélica. Whatever he concluded, Jim would probably concur. They both approached problems using similar logic. Thus, their conclusions often ended up the same.

Perhaps he had formed the wrong impression. Maybe he should turn them over to the government. Or easier, just return the girl to her family and forget the rebels. Case closed. For some reason, he wasn't convinced he should take that action. He decided to talk with Jago and then discuss the options with Jim.

'Did you come down here just to steal the gold?' he asked Jago.

'As I said, we were fleeing the army, and we had the opportunity to borrow one of their helicopters.'

'Who flew it?'

Jago decided to keep the information that he could fly to himself and said, 'Lobo flew it.'

'How did you plan to get the gold back?'

'That is a good question, señor. The helicopter would be a nice way, but I think it is not repairable.'

Neilly turned to Angélica. 'What about your family?'

It was an open question. Neilly wanted to see where she would go with it.

'I spit on them. They're greedy, corrupt, selfish exploiters!'

Neilly asked dozens of questions about the FARC, and he felt that Jago, for the most part, was forthcoming with answers. Even so, he did not discover anything that would help him make a decision.

He turned, hearing someone walking up behind him. 'See anything exciting?'

'Let's talk,' said Jim. They walked a short way up the ravine. 'I wouldn't call it interesting. We watched the mine and didn't like what we saw. They're using kids to work the river. Just before we left, seven young Indian girls, wearing colorful dresses, eight to maybe thirteen years old, were brought in by some soldiers. They walked them into a cave. A few minutes later, the soldiers came out, and one of the older miners gave them a small bag. It looked heavy. Gold payment for the girls most likely.'

'You think they are going to work them?'

'Doubt it. The workers are mostly boys.'

'Hum.'

'Rock, Gold has company,' said Aleski. Neilly's one-word call sign was also half of his nickname—Rock Solid. The nickname didn't come from hard muscles, but from how his men viewed him in battle.

'Rock, two Indians nearly walked on top of me. It seems they liked my vantage point. Dressed real colorful, too.'

'Bring 'em in.'

'Wilco.'

'Let's welcome our visitors and have a chat.'

'Soldiers?'

'Not soldiers. A bit more colorful than army types from what she said.'

They both picked up their MP5s, and stuffed several clips in their shirt pockets, then walked out past the end of the ravine. They were about fifty meters from the ravine entrance when they heard talking and moved out of sight on opposite sides of the trail.

The talking stopped, and a minute later two natives walked between them, followed by Roberta. As soon as they passed, Neilly and Jim came in behind them. Without looking back, Roberta said, 'What's up, guys?'

'That's my line, minus the plural guy part,' said Neilly.

'Right after you called me in, I made a grid scan. I spotted these two double-timing it toward my position. For a minute, I thought they had spotted me and were coming to attack, but there was no way they could have seen me. They just about fell into my arms. Can't understand a thing they say.'

'JP, your skills needed pronto,' said Neilly into his mic.

They had started walking back toward the ravine when JP jogged up to them. He looked at the Indians with their red and yellow feather headbands, two dark red stripes on each cheek, coarse fabric skirts, no shirts, and long blowpipes. He greeted them first in Spanish. Nothing. Then he switched to Jivaroan, which was not his best language. The two Indians spoke rapidly, JP nodded, said a few things. 'They are speaking a little fast for me. These two are Shuar, a sub-tribe of the Jivaro. Soldiers abducted their children. I think they were going to the same lookout position you picked to watch for the children.'

'Ask them if they were young girls and what they were wearing,' said Jim.

'They were wearing dresses in bright plain colors, not patterned.'

'They're the ones we saw at the mine. JP, ask if these two are alone, or if there are more of them?'

JP asked them and then said, 'They won't say.'

'Tell them we have seen where their children have been taken,' said Jim. 'Then ask them again if there are other warriors or just themselves?'

The two Shuar men studied JP first and then Jim. They seemed to arrive at a conclusion. They conversed with JP for a minute, 'They said their names are Pwanchir Pacheco and Pempeyo Quishpe. This time, they said others are coming after sunset.'

JP continued to ask questions and translate their answers as they walked back into the camp.

Neilly called Gaston and Brush over and filled them in.

'You planning on doing a good deed, eh?' asked Brush. He didn't need to ask. He knew Jim still had nightmares about two young girls and their mother dying in Vietnam. He blamed their deaths on himself.

'It's well outside our mission,' said Gaston.

Neilly picked up his sat phone. 'Knight, I want a drone on site as quick as you can, area north and northwest of us. Tell me as soon as you spot any humans, and have General Crystal call me.' He turned to the others, 'When he does, Jim, you present our case. The way I see things, Roberta and Aleski both said the miners were scum. You said as much, and it appears that they paid soldiers to kidnap these girls. Our mission, Gaston, is to repatriate a kidnapped young Ecuadoran woman. In this case, we are going to extend our rescue to more young Ecuadoran women.'

'I see your point, boss. Well, more or less anyway,' replied Gaston. 'What's your idea?'

'Let's talk it out. We use the rebels, but we don't mix with them. I like them, but we don't know if we can trust them. Until we do know, we don't. The drone locates the warm bodies in the mining camp. The miners won't be expecting anyone. We should be able to take them by surprise without any shooting, rescue the girls, and Jago gets a portion of the gold.'

'I've taken a liking to Jago and a couple of the others. It doesn't bother me to work with them. But we'd be better off on our own. Why trust them in a fight?'

'Mostly because I'd rather know exactly where they are, observe them in action. They might be helpful.'

'Neilly, you keep your team separate, and Brush and I'll approach with the FARC in two separate groups so we can keep an eye on them,' said Jim.

'Shit boss. Between the rebels and the Indians, too many variables. Don't forget the army is out there somewhere close. Makes it risky with so many unknowns,' Gaston persisted.

'Point taken.'

'More manageable doing what Jim just said,' added Brush.

'Still risky,' replied Gaston.

'All right,' said Neilly, 'Let's sit down with the maps and work something out that makes sense.' Neilly motioned for Jean-Paul. 'Get anything else from our two guests that you can. What were they planning to do, and how many of them are there?'

Pwanchir turned to JP, saying a few words.

'Besides the group coming our way tonight, there's a larger group tomorrow.'

'Okay, same question. How many?'

'I'll ask, but the language doesn't have words for most numbers. Sometimes they use Spanish for larger numbers.' JP tried Spanish and then the little Quechua he knew. After a moment, he gave up. The only answer he could get was *many coming*.

'So, we don't know how many "many" is, meaning we need to get this over with before they do arrive. Having them bust in will complicate things, like Gaston said. What was the other language you used?'

'I tried Quechua. These two don't speak it.'

'Gaston, bring Jago over. JP, come back and fill me in if you get anything else useful.' Then Neilly said, 'We stay quiet about our assets. No need yet for Jago to know about the drones, raft, or communication links.' Neilly did not have to mention their Guardian Angels. They never disclosed them to anyone. He didn't need to say anything at all. Nevertheless, it was part of his nature to make sure there was no doubt in anyone's mind about their plan.

Neilly said, 'Before Jago gets here, we use the raft to go upriver and flank them. Main approach from this side. Leave Roberta and Aleski where they are. Put García on the other side with the raft group. Marilyn in the air on standby.'

Besides the onsite support, Toucan and the BWC were there to help if they needed any support or information.

Jim nodded, 'Seems reasonable. I'll fill the general in when he calls.'

Gaston, Neilly, and Jago sat down. Neilly told Jago about the girls and about the Shuar Indians. It was obvious that Jago didn't like what they said about the young girls. Neilly looked at Jago and then Gaston, 'It seems we're all on the same page.'

'Any objections, anyone?' asked Neilly.

'What if the rest of the Shuar get here before we hit the miners, eh?'

'I don't think we want that. We have to go in earlier, not long after sunset. I would have preferred the middle of the night. Jago, you have an opinion?'

'You're going to let us go, or take us back to Colombia? And what about Angel?'

'If everything goes well tonight, you take whatever gold you can carry and go where you want. We'll give the Shuar the rest. A fair share. You want to take Angélica back to Colombia with you?' Neilly wanted to see what Jago would say.

'No. I think, after seeing blood flow tonight, she will change her mind and want to go back to her papá.'

Neilly felt that Jago was sincere. 'This will be a joint operation, you and us. You good with that?'

Jago looked pleased. While the Americans were being nice, he was still skeptical about their intentions. He would find out soon enough. 'Sí, señor. Muy bueno.'

'We split into three teams. Jago, your group with Brush and Jim will be the right flank assault. We'll send two of ours in on the left flank along the river. They can work up to the high ground above the mine.' He decided not to mention Fleur or the raft at the river. I'll draw their attention up the middle, a frontal assault with JP and the two Shuar. Hopefully, we will just walk in without a fight.'

'Anyone else? Objections? Let's go over the details.' The sat phone rang. 'You want to bring the general in on the plan, Jim?'

'Yep.' Jim stood and walked out of hearing distance.

Those present in the Ops room at the Biological Warfare Center listened, but kept their presence secret.

When Jim was out of hearing distance, he said, 'Here's the new situation.'

'Our original plan was to leave after dark tonight with our target. Then two Shuar Indians showed up and told us about the kidnapping of the young girls. Earlier, we observed seven of them passed to the miners. They were taken by soldiers from their school, then apparently sold to the miners for gold. The two Shuar were going to recon for a larger rescue element arriving in a few hours.'

General Crystal knew Jim would do damn well what he thought best, no matter what he said or ordered. After so many years, they both trusted each other, and Jim was on the ground. The man in the field rule. His opinion was superior. There were children at risk. He knew Jim would make it his mission to rescue them. Adapting to field situations was exactly what made Jim the valuable field operative that he was. Independent thinkers might seem uncontrollable to some commanders. That was not the case with General Crystal.

Chapter 23

Tethered to the rich earth, the green foliage reluctantly released the afternoon heat as the sky dimmed. The humid blanket kept the sun-warmed air from slipping into the clear sky. The daily pattern of afternoon showers had not materialized. The Amazon rain was like a warm shower. Rather than a hindrance, it was a welcome relief for the special operations and the smaller BWC group.

Gaston took the same trail that the team had used last night to approach the ravine. García followed several meters behind him, with his Barrett sniper rifle gently cradled as if it were a newborn baby. To García, his rifle was the center of his life. Nothing was more important. He spent countless hours firing thousands of rounds of ammunition, cleaning, disassembling and reassembling, and sometimes just watching it. As a child in Texas, he had had a small stuffed lion that he carried everywhere; as an adult, the Barrett held the same place in his heart. At the age of twenty-five, García felt as though a part of him was missing when he was forced to part with his Barrett sniper rifle, either at home or off base.

Jeff followed at the rear. He radioed Fleur, 'ETA twenty minutes.'

'Site secure,' responded Fleur.

They walked rapidly, staying alert. No matter how well the NVGs had allowed them to see the previous night, daylight was better. The same path they had traversed last night seemed shorter in the dim but still visible conditions. '200 meters,' said Jeff softly.

Remaining alert, and separated by several meters, they approached the raft and scanned the area.

Minutes later, the foliage parted, and Fleur, with her face painted in shades of green and sprouting plants in her hat and clothes, stepped onto the edge of the muddy bank. She removed most of the plants. Gaston plucked a few remaining pieces of greenery from the back of her shirt. 'Ten minutes, and we shove off,' said Gaston.

'Any extra pearls of wisdom?' asked Fleur.

Gaston said, 'No, but let's go over our approach.' He quickly repeated the overall attack plan and their role. 'We head to the opposite side of the river, about a klick near the mine, and then turn back 200 meters to this side channel.' He pointed at the GPS. 'You, Jeff, and I will stay low, just along the river, and García will make the hill, 150 meters above the mine. We need to be in position at twenty hundred hours.' Gaston waited until she acknowledged.

'Roberta and Phil Aleski have high ground cover positions. Roberta is closer and near the river, about 600 meters from the mine. Aleski is west, much further out but with a higher overlook, close to 1500 meters. Group Alpha: Rock, JP, and the two Indians—frontal assault, as close to the river as they can get, but where they can still ford the shallow water of the tributary. Group B: Colonel Johnson and Major McGuire will attack about 100 meters up the tributary with the FARC.'

'The rebels are our best friends now? And we've adopted two Indians,' Fleur said incredulously.

'Seems so. The chopper will arrive at twenty-ten, staying out of the miners' hearing range unless we call for support. She has an Apache backing her up, about a mile to her east. The FARC probably assume García is a sniper, but they won't expect two more. The miners are pretty lit up with their fires and lights. Gopher says he can hear a generator running.'

'So, we can break some twigs on our approach,' said Fleur.

'Yeah, noise probably not a big issue, and a good thing too as we need to hustle.'

'Bravo one and two, moving,' said Jim. Clicks came back from the boat, the watchers, and Neilly.

The starlight shimmered on the tributary. The half-moon added more light than Neilly would have liked. He watched the shadowy figures to his west head out with Jim and Jago in the lead, and beyond them the other half with Brush. He looked in all directions and started moving toward the mine.

Angélica tried to stifle her fear. She pushed it down, wanting to be fearless. Her pulse increased. She felt tingly vibrations inside. She had wanted to be up front by Jago's side, but he made her stay second from the rear with Chico. Chico would make sure she kept her head down.

Ten meters up the tributary, past Jim and Jago, Brush walked along behind Cherry. Lobo was in the lead. Brush would have preferred leading, but he was uncomfortable having Cherry and the big guy behind him. As they moved, Cherry turned and smiled at Brush.

She is an ultra-attractive woman, thought Brush. Her raven black hair, barely visible in the low light, glistened brightly in his mind. The outline of a beret that she had put on for the attack, handsomely settled on her head. Brush remembered her large black eyes, olive drab pants, and her shirt filled with full magazines for her AK-47, which could not hide her figure, even in the moonlight. To a man like Brush, there was something abnormally attractive and exotic about a beautiful, competent woman who was also a rebel and a soldier. A year ago, Brush would have been thinking of a way to spend a few extra days with the rebel band and Cherry. Now, he surprised himself by not having to fight an impulse to sleep with her; he had no wish to be with anyone other than Glenda Rose Stuart. *Amazing I'm thinking like that*, he thought.

The plan was to move in from three directions, catching the miners unaware, inebriated, off guard, and hopefully unarmed. Roberta and Aleski were keeping the teams apprised of events at the miners' camp. Brad was monitoring and controlling the drone, and Marilyn was in the air, hovering just out of sight and sound.

***

Mateo walked out into the cool night air. His disappointment over Camila had produced a pounding headache. He had so wanted to dance with her. To feel her presence up close, the way he had dreamed of so many times. But it was not to be. He started walking, hoping to make himself feel better. Instead, he felt worse. Dizzy. He touched his forehead. It felt hot.

He looked for a cab, but of course, there were none on the airfield. He spotted a military police car parked on the side of the road and headed toward it. The closer he got, the weaker he became. His back hurt, and then, suddenly, his mind ceased to process, and he collapsed onto the pavement.

There were flashing lights and sirens and people dressed in white. He was in a bed. *A hospital. What am I doing here?* He remembered walking and how upset the military men had made him. They had stolen Camila's attentions. *Why wouldn't she like them? I have nothing to offer her or anyone else.*

Chapter 24

General Crystal, Sheilla, Fred, Bridget, and Captain Kramer were leaning forward in their chairs, watching live aerial video of the operation. The audio was relayed via satellite. Misa and Vidya said that, although they thought the audio was secure, there were some changes in NSA's monitoring capability. They decided it was safer not to transmit video other than from the drone. Everything radiating heat showed up on the large monitor from the drone's IR cameras: the Special Forces and FARC rebels in green, the raft and helicopters in blue. Glenda and Mac watched the same drone images at Toucan. Glenda couldn't take her eyes from the moving green smears that she knew were Brush and Jim with the FARC.

'Their plan seems solid. Highly trained. Overwhelming force. We shouldn't have casualties,' said Kramer whose field experience was limited to one brief operation in Cuba. He wanted to be more involved in the operations as well as in the intelligence side.

'Doesn't matter,' responded the general. 'No battles ever go as expected. They always have to adapt to a changing dynamic. Every change leads to another change. Their ability to make instant choices that don't lead to disaster is what separates them from failure.'

'Fred, any problems with the new satellite secure comm links?' asked Sheilla.

'None.'

'Worked great for us in Cuba,' added Glenda.

'Did you have our team, or our friends in Huachuca check them for security?'

'Oh yeah, and I got a dressing down from Colonel Jake Montgomery about doubting them,' Fred laughed. 'I said the NSA and CIA have some of the best people.' He said, 'You think, huh? Forget it, no one can eavesdrop on our comm.'

***

It was nearing twenty hundred. The FARC with Jim and Brush, separated by several meters, and Neilly's group were in position, separated by a little more than 100 meters. Everything was going according to plan. Abruptly, the relative silence was broken by a long rattle of automatic weapon fire, followed by a short three-round burst. Gaston had been fired on by a miner, inexperienced enough to fire on full auto. The short three-round bursts from Gaston or Fleur had silenced the shooter.

Jim glanced at Jago, who hadn't moved, but stared in the direction of the shots, and then slowly scanned the areas in front of them. Jim observed Jago's movements and reactions with increasing respect. However, he had no intention of letting him out of his sight; trust took a lot more than a day's casual acquaintance to build.

'Bravos, hold,' ordered Neilly. 'Mosquito, position?'

García answered, 'In position, but no visibility on Bravo groups.'

'Roberta, you have eyes on both Bravos?'

'Limited,' responded Roberta.

'Gopher, anyone see the shooter?' Neilly looked at a dim screen he was holding. Through Knight at Toucan, the drones were relaying to him the same infrared images received by the command center at the Biological Warfare Center. There was a general shift in the fuzzy green images toward Gaston and Fleur. Neilly held his position and watched, waiting for his two Guardian Angels to confirm the movement. He assumed any armed miners would move in Gaston's direction. The infrared device showed him how close the miners' positions were to Gaston and Fleur, but it could not tell him who was armed or with what. His GAs could if there was enough light, and if they had a line of sight.

'You have four armed Tangos just outside the cave entrance and three moving toward Bravo,' said Roberta.

'Gopher confirms, and one tango climbing above the mine opening with a larger weapon, possibly an M-60.'

Neilly had not expected many weapons, let alone an M-60. 'Gopher, terminate the heavy weapon above the mine. Bravo two, flank the cave entrance. Three minutes and Alpha moves up. Cleared to fire.' Neilly had not set out to kill the miners. Things never went as planned. Now that the miners were alerted and heavily armed, he had no choice; his mindset shifted to protecting his men.

***

The mine boss, Jackson, was a big man with red bushy hair and beard. He stood six feet four inches. He had learned early in his life that size matters. He had grown up in Canada's Northwest Territories on a cattle ranch, and had left at seventeen to work in a copper mine in his neighboring province—British Columbia. Jackson's father had bullied him. His over-sized son had not inherited many brain cells. He did inherit his average-sized father's mean streak and learned to use his size to get what he wanted. No one knew where he'd got his large frame, certainly not from his tiny Inuit mother.

Like his father, Jackson had slapped his mother around when he felt like it. Jackson's mother had dark bruises under one eye or the other for most of her marriage, and varying degrees of bruises on her body. She never complained. Jackson misinterpreted this as acceptance. In reality, his mother hated every minute that her son and husband were home and relished every minute she had alone. She would have happily left but for the fact that she had nowhere to go. Jackson considered his mother, along with all women, an inferior species, whose only worth was subjugating themselves to the whims of men.

Jackson's meanness and misogynistic views grew worse with age, and they flourished with his autocratic rule over the natives in

Ecuador. He treated the Indians and his men with disdain, ruling them with barbaric brutality. Underneath, he despised anyone not "white" like himself.

Nevertheless, an "inferior" native woman had serviced him until a month ago. He had tired of her and now found that he liked young virgin girls. He laughed when they writhed in pain under his massive body.

***

General Crystal, Sheilla, Fred, Kramer, Mac, Knight, and Glenda listened without talking. Like Neilly, they had expected little or no resistance. They all stared at the screen that marked the IR images and the flashes from the firing. Fleur, Joe, and Gaston in one cluster, Jim, Brush, and the rebels in another. Neilly's group blurred as they moved forward. Distant stationary green blotches showed the three Guardian Angels: Aleski, Roberta, and García.

Glenda whispered, 'Keep your luck, Brush. There's no Najma in this lot.'

Aleski sighted on the miner with the machine gun perched over the mine entrance. He adjusted his aim to account for the light breeze, squeezed the trigger and watched, counting to two before the man's head erupted in the firelit darkness. He smiled. *Nice of them to provide a little firelight for me. Better than the green of this new NVG.* Jim, Brush, Jago, Lobo, and Cherry fanned out, with Lobo only a few meters away from Jim. They moved through the shallow water and then along the edge of the hill toward the cave. The rippled water reflected the moonlight as they rushed across. In crossing, their only protection was to remain unseen. Ribbons of firelight streamed across the slow-moving water.

Chico trailed several meters behind Cherry and watched toward their rear. San was slightly behind, protecting their right flank. If either Chico or San, or any of the rebel band, had known that the Americans had snipers as backup, they would have been surprised. If they'd known the full extent of their backup, they would have been awed. It was a different reality, beyond their comprehension: the watchers, the control center monitoring, IR images, drones, and gunships. The FARC had always been traditional guerrilla fighters. Their only backup was reinforcement from their comrades.

Roberta eliminated one more of the armed miners who had moved into the rocks outside the cave entrance. Neither she nor Aleski had a clear shot at the other two. They watched Bravo one and two converge at the bottom of the small hill below the mine entrance and then move toward the mine opening.

'Bravo, you have two tangos out of my sight above you in the rocks,' said Roberta.

Jim motioned to stay low as he moved toward the mine opening. He assumed the miners would have taken a shot at him if they could see him.

It was not the case for San as he looked at his chest and his shirt turning red. 'I'm shot,' he said in surprise as he crumpled to the ground. The GAs had been watching as best they could in the shadows. García saw him go down. 'B group has a man down,' he said. 'I caught the muzzle flash, twenty mikes in front of the cave, not more than five mikes in front of the center assault team A.'

Everyone else scanned for the invisible shooter who was too far away from the camp light and fires for them to see. There was too much light to effectively use night vision. The man was obviously hidden from the IR on the drone. The watchers could not find him. Jim moved up the hill into the rocks and looked down from his ten-foot elevation advantage. Suddenly, he saw movement next to a large rock. A shadow emerged from the overhang. As the hazy shadow became the shape of a man, he raised and fired a three-shot burst. His silenced MP5 didn't make a lot of noise, and the flash was suppressed. Nevertheless, switching position, he moved down the hill and took three strides toward the mine before stopping.

'Moving,' said Neilly. They raced across the shallow water, directly at the mine. Firing erupted everywhere. The Guardian Angels spotted the miners as they foolishly exposed themselves, firing long bursts on automatic. Both the rebels and Americans used the miners' reloading time to their advantage. As suddenly as gunfire had erupted, it stopped. The Americans and the snipers were deadly accurate and only fired when they had a target. Five of the miners were dead within seconds.

What Neilly had not anticipated was the miners' distrust of the soldiers. The soldiers knew they had gold and where the miners kept it, a knowledge gained when they sold them the village girls. Neither the miners nor the army were the brightest lot. The miners thought they might attack. The army thought the miners would not expect them. Instead of getting drunk as was their norm, the miners had set up an ambush. Colonel Ortega approved the captain's plan to steal the gold sometime in the next few days.

Neilly and Jim had been caught off guard, making wrong assumptions too. The miners, were sober, ready, and waiting, but for a different army. For the inexperienced miners, the cost would be dear. They were no match for either the SF or the FARC. They may well have lost against the army as well, but it might have been a decent fight. Their M-60 might have brought a victory against the army. It had been no more than a minor impediment for the combined assault team.

If Jim and Neilly had been wrong in their assessment, the mine boss's assumption that his ambush would be successful against the army proved to be a far more costly mistake. He had left fighting to them while he attended to his business.

JP, followed by the two Shuar, went to the cave's entrance, quickly examining the miners to see if they were dead or wounded. All were dead. Jim heard the communication and, knowing that the seven girls were in the cave and no threats were outside, he raced the few meters along the hill, stopping short of the cave edge.

'No tangos visible in the cave,' reported Roberta. Jim said, 'Hold position at the entrance and cover me.' In three quick leaps, Jim ran straight into the cave and to the far side, just as Brush, Cherry, and Jago moved to the side where Jim had been.

'You drew no fire with that move, buddy,' said Brush, going into the cave in a crouch as bullets ricocheted off the cave entrance near Jim. 'Okay, I take it back. They're on the slow side.'

Brush assumed that anyone inside would be looking at Jim's side if they saw him dart across the cave entrance. He moved to his left, saw the shooter, and quickly placed a three-round burst into the man's chest.

Jim covered the inside of the cave on one side, and Brush on the opposite. Jago and Cherry, followed by Lobo, crouched low, running straight into the cave past Brush. There were no further shots. Jago and Cherry went over to the miner Brush had shot and saw three bloodstains not more than three centimeters apart, directly in the middle of the man's chest. They exchanged a quick look, then Cherry turned around and looked at Brush with what could only be described as admiration, infused with the desire that battles can bring.

They continued to work their way another twenty meters into the cave as it became taller and wider. Jim, had become more comfortable with the rebels and their leader and no longer felt edgy with Jago behind him. Jim looked into the cave's inner chamber. Brush and Cherry were close behind. They looked to Jim's side and saw a shadow.

'Company on your side,' said Brush. Cherry darted around Brush into the cave. Jim used the distraction, stepped inside the entrance, and shot a miner before the man could fire at Cherry.

'I'm not sure if she gambled on taking him out by herself, or decided she could trust us to take him out before she got shot, eh. Pretty gutsy,' Brush said with respect. 'Using the same methods you did earlier.'

Glenda pursed her lips, as she and Mac listened and watched their screens. *Gutsy woman, huh. I think I better take a little trip to the jungle, my hero.*

'What she?' asked Heather.

Everyone turned toward the door.

'Wondered where you were,' said Sheilla.

'I was working with Nus. How could something be going on so soon? They're already in a fight? Why didn't someone tell me? Can't be already, can they? They're still just getting organized, right?'

No one said anything as Katarina looked at Sheilla. 'Fred, pull a chair up for Heather.' No one answered her questions, and they returned to the screens. Heather got the message and focused on the monitors. She elbowed Fred and whispered, 'Which one is Jim?'

'The first green dot in the center.' Fred was shy, and especially so with pushy women like Heather. He turned away from her and back to his computer. He rapidly tapped on his keyboard. Like Heather, Glenda intimidated him, which is why Fred preferred to talk to Specialist Marcus Gordon at Fort Huachuca.

'Hey, Marcus. It's Fred.'

'Yeah, I see that. Your ID comes up on my screen. How are things up north?'

'Not too bad. Sheilla's worried about our sat communications. She heard something about activity on the sun and wanted to see if you had it covered?'

'Misa has been following it, not us.'

Moments later a cheerful Misa said, 'Looks like it might be something to worry about. The sun activity is picking up, and scientists are predicting the largest solar flares on record in the next few days.'

'Meaning?'

'They could obliterate our sat communication.'

'What do I tell Sheilla?'

'Tell her it probably won't happen. No worries yet, but we are monitoring.'

'Thanks, guys and girls.'

'Maybe you should say women, Fred.'

'Yeah. It's just a saying. Okay, sorry. I'll let her know.' *I can't ever say the right thing around women,* he thought to himself.

Fred, however, had an abiding respect for Sheilla. For some reason, he didn't mind her telling him what to do. She always seemed to be right about things. But then, so were Glenda and Misha. *What's the difference?* he wondered.

'Make sure you keep me informed. Lost communications would be the next thing to a disaster,' replied Sheilla.

Chapter 25

Firelight danced on the cave walls. Jim and Jago peered into a small area carved out of the main cave. A dozen boys and girls were kneeling and lying on the dirt floor, holding their hands out, begging them not to shoot.

'Fleur, see if any of them need medical, and JP, interpret and cover her,' said Neilly.

Brush and Cherry peered around the edge of another similar room where miners had dug with their picks over many years, hoping to hit a gold vein in the hard rock. Suddenly, rock chips flew off the entrance. 'I'll be damned,' said Brush.

Oh, no, Glenda said to herself. She knew how Brush would understate things. Then, they heard a woman's voice in Brush's mic.

'A lot of blood on your cheek, lover, but no serious, I think.'

Glenda's cheeks turned red, and she clenched her jaw. Then, they heard Jim say, 'Not too bad. Seems your lucky streak is ending, though. Besides bullets, now you're catching rock chips, partner.'

Glenda whispered, 'Mr. Canuck, I'm going to cause you more pain than you ever thought possible if you let anything else happen to you, or even think about being cozy with that woman.'

Jago went to the far side of the cave and moved in cautiously. He could see a man inside, holding a young girl. Five other girls were huddled off to the side on the floor crying.

'One oversized carrot-topped-miner behind a naked tiny girl.'

Neilly looked at Jim, exposing himself for a fraction of a second. The man expended a full clip on automatic at Neilly who shook his head at the man's ignorance. Cherry went low around the entrance, keeping her rifle sighted on the man.

'He's empty, no,' she said, and grinned as the man tried to insert the clip. It was a ridiculous sight. His large hairy arm held a girl that seemed more like a doll while he fumbled with his M-16. The man was three times the size of his hostage. Jim stepped around the corner on the other side from Cherry and saw the big man frantically trying to insert a new clip while using the young girl as a shield. Behind him, he saw something that appalled him. Lying on the dirt was a torn yellow dress and a naked girl, no more than ten or eleven. Her body was covered with long red welts. A whip, slightly longer than a riding crop, lay in the dirt. Out of his side vision, he saw the other young girls huddled together.

The man's large, bearded head towered over his hostage, as he still tried to insert the magazine. Jim aimed for the man's head, then moved his MP5 a few inches to the left, and squeezed the trigger. Part of the man's ear disappeared in a spurt of blood. The big man dropped his gun and howled. The young hostage collapsed onto the cave floor.

Cherry rushed over to the naked girl and tenderly covered her as best she could with the torn dress. Then she stood, spit on the bearded man and, without any hesitation, slammed the butt of her rifle into his groin. 'Why you no kill this freak, señor?' Cherry pointed her gun at his stomach.

The big man managed to stand.

'I'm not sure I have a good answer for you. Maybe we let our new Shuar friends deal with him.'

'Sí. Está bien.' Easing the pressure on her trigger, she helped the girl up and moved her over to the others.

Jim moved toward the oversized red-headed bully, his walk graceful: a cat stalking its prey. He looked into the man's face, then at the young girl, who had been beaten and was crying. Then he regarded the other girls who would have been subjected to the same brutality. His mind flashed to the two young Vietnamese girls he blamed himself for getting killed. With the arrival of Pedro, those images had started to disappear. Now, they reappeared with a vengeance.

His eyes narrowed as he stared at the grotesque head, several inches above his own. He could feel the big man tensing for an attack. *Stupid,* Jim thought. He moved his MP5 toward the man's massive head and, without regret or remorse, squeezed the trigger.

A hole appeared in the center of the man's head at the bridge of his nose. Blood and bits of bones sprayed the cave wall behind him. The man seemed frozen for what seemed a long time. In reality, it was less than a second. With a blank stare, he collapsed like a falling tree.

'Señor,' shouted Cherry. 'You tease me.' Then she laughed and looked at Jago, who shrugged, then at Brush, looking for an explanation. Brush didn't offer her one, even though he knew full well what had motivated Jim to terminate the man.

'What happened?' demanded Heather. 'What is going on?'

Sheilla held her finger to her lips. 'We have weak audio inside the cave. I'll fill you in as soon as this is over.'

For a few seconds, the cave was silent. Almost in unison, the young girls crossed themselves. The crying stopped.

Brush walked up to Jim and looked him in the eye. 'Sort of glad we don't have video.'

'Hum,' said Jim, 'JP, bring the two Shuar in.'

Neilly said, 'Dragonfly, my position now. See if the girls need assistance.' The two Shuar Indians rushed through the cave, shouting and running to the girls. Neilly did not have to tell the rest of the team to make sure the cave contained no other surprises. One by one they called in: 'secure.'

Pwanchir and Pempeyo quickly conversed with the girls and then walked to the red-haired giant. Pempeyo shook a small pouch over him, shouting something unintelligible to most of those in the cave.

'JP, tell them that our medic will be here in a few seconds to take care of the girls.'

Glenda desperately wanted to say to Brush, 'You better tell me why she called you lover.' But she stopped herself, not wanting to sound like a jealous woman, although that is exactly how she was feeling.

Knight sat just beyond Glenda and Mac in the rustic metal-sided hut at Toucan's forward base, monitoring the situation from the drone's camera. The old shack seemed incongruous with all its exotic electronic equipment. Marilyn's helicopter and all the friendlies around the mine had been identified on his monitors. As he watched, two new heat signatures, moving toward the mine, entered the area on the edge of his drone's camera coverage. He depressed his talk switch, but instead of talking to Jim and Neilly, he yelped as a harsh static erupted in his ear. 'Shit, what the hell was that?' He turned the volume down and again depressed his talk switch. 'Base, you read me? Rock, you read me?' His only response was hissing and crackling.

Chapter 26

In the field, in the operations room, and at Toucan, the interference crackled in their headsets. Realizing they were without communication, Jim looked at Brush, 'Grab some warm bodies, and make sure the cave entrance is secure.'

'I'll go,' said Cherry.

'Fleur, are the girls okay to move?'

'The one that was whipped is bleeding, but she will be okay, physically at least. JP talked to the others. It seems that the bearded freak tore off their clothes just to look at them and then started to whip this one.'

Jim looked at the dead man with the dark hole in his massive forehead, and wished he could bring him back to make him die a more painful death. 'JP, tell them they are safe, and we are going to take them out of here and get them back to their village.'

***

Just off the Rua Bambina, two tourists bent over a feverish vagrant, groaning on the concrete. His unbuttoned shirt exposed his emaciated chest. His skin hung loosely from his torso. 'He needs a doctor.' Two men and a young woman, curious about what was going on, joined the Austrian couple.

Moira, the woman tourist, stood and asked, 'Do you speak English?' One of the young men answered, 'Little.'

'German, perhaps?' They all shook their heads, no. Moira pantomimed holding a phone, and pretended to dial as she pointed at the man on the ground and said, 'Doctor.' The young man nodded and pulled out a cell phone and called for an ambulance.

The young woman, Estela, took off her lightweight coat, bent over the man, and covered him. Shortly, an ambulance, sirens blaring, stopped in the alley. Bento started to thrash around, throwing off the young woman's coat. Sirens were not an encouraging sound to the street people of Rio de Janeiro; they usually meant police.

'No, Adriano. I don't want the coat back. Cover him,' shouted Estela.

Two medics from the ambulance rushed over and shone a light on Bento. One spoke into his walkie-talkie. 'Male, it is difficult to say, late forties, conscious, incoherent.' He held his hand to the man's dirt-smudged forehead, 'and he is burning up.'

'They will cover him now,' said Adriano. 'Here. Take your coat.' Estela huffily grabbed it between two fingers but did not put it on. She turned and stormed off down the street with Adriano and the other man, rushing to catch up with her.

'It's soiled, and I never liked it. I certainly don't like it now.' She walked to a refuse container and threw it in.

'Your sister's got a temper,' said Renato.

'She's always had one. This is not it. This is her nice side, Adriano.'

Gloria had been watching from across the street and started to run as fast as she could. She saw the person throw a coat in the trash, and she wanted it. Out of her peripheral vision, she saw another person coming up the street. *Mierda. It's that scummy Ros. She's going to get to it first.*

Using her cane, Gloria hobbled as fast as she could. She was right though; Ros would beat her to the coat.

'It's mine, Ros.'

'I got it first, and never call me Ros. It's Rosana.'

Gloria came up to Rosana as she was putting on the coat and, without hesitation, hit her on top of the head with her cane.

Rosana's knees buckled, but she didn't fall. Gloria grabbed the loose sleeve of the coat and was trying to pull it off the other arm, when Rosana shrieked and grabbed her hair.

'Bitch. Hitting me.' They struggled for a moment before the older, weaker Gloria gave in and slumped to the ground, exhausted. Rosana kicked her once and then looked admiringly at her new coat. Smirking, she looked down at Gloria, took the coat, and held it to her face. It smelled good.

***

Hugging the girls, Pwanchir and Pempeyo looked up at JP as he spoke to them. They all slowly got up with a mixture of smiles and tears. Jim reached down for one of the girl's small hands and started to walk back to the cave entrance. She looked up at him with trusting eyes, squeezing his hand as they walked.

As they passed by a small room chiseled from the rock on the side of the main cave, Jago stepped out and put a heavy bag on a pile of other bags sitting on the dirt floor. For a second, he nervously looked at Jim. They exchanged looks, and Jim said, 'Pretty heavy. I don't think I would be trying to carry too much back to Colombia and,' he added as he looked directly at Jago, 'a fair amount goes to the girls' village.'

'Sí. There is plenty,' replied Jago as the diminutive Carlos added more of the small, heavy pouches to the pile with a thunk.

Roberta, García, and Aleski all grimaced from the static and realized that their communication was out. Aleski was the first to hear the helicopter approaching from the west behind him.

The other two guardian angels swiveled their night vision goggles in the direction of the approaching helicopter. Aleski realized that there were two birds. It had been so long since any of them had been without comm, that it took a few seconds to sink in that they would have to make their own decisions. As the first helicopter passed his position, Aleski noted that it was marked with the Ecuadoran flag and another flag he did not recognize.

168

Moments later, Brush and Cherry heard the approaching helicopters. 'I'll be right back, beautiful,' Brush told her.

Cherry looked at Major McGuire with her large, alluring eyes. She saw the effect on him. *A very attractive woman,* thought Brush. Then he shook his head. Flirting with attractive women was in his past. *I've gotta watch what I say,* he mumbled to himself as he turned and trotted back into the cave. Fifty feet inside, he bumped into Jim, JP, Fleur, and the Shuar girls.

'We've got company. Two choppers moving straight in.'

'JP, Fleur, keep them here. If you hear shots, move them back to a safe place, and one of you get Neilly.' Jim and Brush raced back to the cave entrance. Just as they arrived, one of the two Hueys flared and slid to a stop not more than fifty meters away. The other hovered 300 meters away, shining a searchlight on the cave entrance.

The silence that had followed the shooting disappeared with the sound of helicopter blades beating the night air. Seconds later, shots erupted outside the cave where Chico was tearfully going through San's meager belongings. He had never liked San; however, they'd shared a bond in age and time. In his emotional state, Chico assumed the helicopters were the enemy and opened fire on them.

The searchlight moved over the ground to his position. With the blinding light gone, Jim darted out of the cave and expended several short bursts aimed at the helicopter's searchlight. The GAs needed nothing further. The door gunner on the hovering chopper opened up on Chico's position, while a dozen soldiers poured out of the helicopter on the ground. Only moments before, they had communications to the BWC, Fort Huachuca, and Camp Toucan. With the comms down and no warning about the incoming helicopters, the night became chaos.

Jim dove back into the cave just as the Huey's door gunner moved his fire back to the cave entrance. Stone chips and bullets ricocheted off the walls as Jim, Brush, and Cherry hugged the cave wall. The soldiers on the ground rushed toward the cave entrance, firing automatic weapons. Neilly, Gaston, Jago, and Carlos rushed back toward Jim and the cave entrance.

Captain Alvarez's twelve-member army squad rushed the cave, assuming only a few miners guarded the gold.

Jim heard crackling sounds, and then the static diminished.

'Bird one, if you can hear me. Two army choppers, one in the air positioned on the riverside, both with door gunners. The second hovering in front of the cave.'

'One minute out,' said Marilyn as she dipped the nose and pushed the cyclic forward.

From the co-pilot's seat of the hovering chopper, Alvarez watched his men below move toward the cave entrance. He had allowed his men to capture the schoolgirls to find out where the miners kept their gold and how much they had. His men reported that the miners had many bags of gold. He expected them to be drunk and busy with the young girls. They would be no match for his soldiers and weapons.

He sat relaxed, thinking about how rich he was going to be. As he watched, first one man and then another dropped, but he could see no reason why. Then he saw one of their heads explode. He started to look around the camp but saw nothing. He couldn't see any muzzle flashes outside the cave entrance. *Who was killing them? These were stupid miners, no?* As he continued to search the area, he was perplexed. *How were they killing his men?* In his confused mental state, he didn't see or hear Marilyn, followed by the Apache, flying in high, and behind him, from the riverside.

His door gunner continued to fire at the cave entrance. Alvarez watched in amazement as more of his men fell to the ground. There were only four soldiers left, and they started to run back toward their helicopter.

As she banked off to her right, Marilyn said, 'Bird two, she's all yours.' The Apache's front pilot looked through his sight at the pilot's side of Captain Alvarez's helicopter and squeezed the trigger of his M230 front mounted chain gun. The twenty-millimeter rounds tore through the roof of Alvarez's helicopter, through the pilot, and out the front. A stunned Captain Alvarez found himself looking at the scene below. Alvarez shouted, 'Vámanos!' He was seconds too late as the burst struck from the Apache.

Instead of the rapid departure he had expected from his order, the helicopter started to drift. He looked up and over at the holes in the roof above the pilot, the shattered console and windscreen, then at the shredded pilot slumped forward in this seat, a mass of blood and raw flesh. The helicopter's nose turned down, and Captain Alvarez watched the ground come racing at him. As the nose crumpled toward him, he registered a last thought. *The miners tricked me.*

Roberta watched the other chopper's movement as it lifted and turned its nose toward her. She could only see a fuzzy form inside, dimly lit with the chopper's gauges. She caressed the trigger as she moved the crosshair to where she sensed his head would be, letting her subconscious guide her as the tension increased, her mind, finger, and trigger acting in unison. As she looked through the scope, the crosshair jumped.

She started to count and, before she got to two, she said "Bam" as her bullet found its mark. The helicopter settled to the ground in slow motion, turning ninety degrees as the tail rotor pushed it sideways on its skids. Amazingly, the skids did not catch on anything, and it stayed upright. One of the four remaining soldiers threw down his assault rifle with his hands in the air and turned around from the cave, as if it made a difference which way he faced. The others went prone on the ground and started to fire at the cave entrance. They were easy targets for the three watchers who, from their elevated position, easily eliminated them.

Jim, Neilly, Brush, Cherry, Jago, and the Shuar Indians with the seven girls all stood at the cave entrance. The two Shuar Indians talked rapidly, and the girls pointed at the soldier, standing with his arms up. Pempeyo raised his blowpipe, but before he could send a dart, the soldier wildly swatted the air. He began to stumble and fell to his knees as several Shuar in their colored headdresses rushed toward him out of the darkness. They had recognized him as one of the soldiers who had taken the tribe's daughters. His last blurry vision was of birds—yellow, blue, and red—fluttering above him.

'Um, seems there are dozens of new IR signals. Did I miss something with the communication down?' Brad asked Knight. 'Everything okay?'

'Brad, you could say you missed something, but so did I,' said Knight. 'All my electronics went on the fritz.'

'Report,' commanded Neilly. Everyone, starting with the snipers, reported in one by one.

'Shit, I lost a drone. Lost control, and it's gone,' Knight reported.

Jim, Pempeyo, and Pwanchir walked out to the soldier. Jim knelt and looked at the dozens of wood darts, protruding from his head and neck. The main part of the Shuar tribe had arrived at the camp just as the shooting stopped. The man with his arms raised in front of the helicopter's lights was recognized as one of the girls' capturers. Nearly every warrior wanted to punish the man for what he had done, and they blew dozens of poison-tipped darts at him.

Jim turned toward Neilly and was shocked to see Cherry kneeling over Brush, holding his shoulders as Brush's body convulsed. 'Jeff!' yelled Jim, nodding toward Brush. He didn't want to say anything as he knew Glenda was listening.

Jeff pulled out a dart from Brush's neck. 'JP, bring a Shuar over pronto. We need to know right away what they are tipped with, and how much it takes to kill someone Brush's weight.'

Glenda couldn't help herself as she said out loud, 'Oh, no, you big lug! What did you do?'

Fleur trotted up. 'The soldier's dead. Maybe one dart isn't enough to kill, but the dozen or so sticking out of him were sure enough. The soldier didn't last more than a couple of minutes. He convulsed, and his heart stopped. I'm not sure, but I think they are getting ready to do some surgery on his head.'

JP and Pempeyo hurried to Jim. 'Bad news,' JP interpreted. 'One dart can kill him.' Pempeyo tugged on JP's arm and hurried him to a Shuar with a different style headdress.

Glenda tried to control herself and keep radio silence. Mac saw how agitated she was. 'Knight, now that we have comm back, ask them if anyone spotted the drone going down. It would be a mistake to leave it.'

'It's in the jungle or the river. Not much danger of anyone getting ahold of it. But I'll ask.'

Mac looked at Glenda and said to Knight, 'Ask them, and ask for causality status too.'

Glenda let out a small puff of air and nodded her thanks to Mac.

'Anyone see Knight's toy?' No one responded. The drone had crashed miles away during the loss of communication. Reluctantly, Neilly added that the major was injured.

'Damn it, damn it! You dumb Canuck.' *I knew this was going to happen. Maybe I bring him bad luck*, she thought. She pounded her fist on the table. 'Come on, Brush. One little dart isn't going to kill you. Please, don't let it.'

Mac said over the radio, 'Keep us informed of changes,' reminding everyone that Glenda was listening.

'Understood, out.'

'Get Doctor Dakine on comm,' boomed the general.

Heather was relieved in one sense and upset in another. She had become best friends with Glenda. As much as she liked Brush, she had been afraid it was Jim who was injured. In the confusion, she had not heard that Brush was hit with the dart. She felt relief, followed by guilt for feeling that way.

Sheilla and Fred were searching on their computers. Fred sent an urgent message to everyone in the computer group to research poisons. They didn't have enough information yet. Doctor Dakine said, 'What's up?'

'Emergency situation. Major McGuire has been hit with a

poison dart.'

'I'm going to need more than that.'

'We're trying to find out.'

'Okay, I have the doc patched in, and I'm trying to identify what poison they used,' said Fred. Sheilla was typing frantically on her keyboard, too.

Fred shook his head as he read. 'Could be curare or several other poisons. Sheilla. JP, you have to get one of the Indians to tell you what it is.'

Chapter 27

'He's nicely dressed. Hair is long. I don't think he's military. Hands too soft, unless he's an officer. I wonder why he has no identification.'

'I do not know,' said Doctor Salvatore Pazano, a major in the air force and the on-duty emergency doctor at the airbase infirmary.

'I heard there is a large special party. Maybe this man is from there.'

'I'll ask the MPs to wait. I want to question them more about the circumstances. Ask them about this party and advise me. This man has a very high temperature.'

'Perhaps a flu?'

Doctor Pazano placed a gloved finger against Mateo's lips, and spread them, and inserted a wooden tongue depressor. Then, he leaned in closer. 'He has spots in his mouth and on his tongue. Look! See there.'

'And on his throat too. It looks raw.'

'Go talk to the guards. Get them to find out who this man is and find out who the lab technician on duty is. I want complete blood tests and cultures.' He continued to examine Mateo. 'This, I think, is a virus,' Doctor Pazano said to Mateo. 'I think, señor, you are very sick, and your temperature needs bringing down.'

The doctor and his nursing staff added a saline drip and inserted a catheter. Blood samples were drawn while the doctor examined the patient's legs and torso. Then, he made a phone call.

'Tell the MPs at the gate that I have asked a doctor here to consult. I encountered him at a symposium at the university. He's a virologist, very famous, I think—Doctor Viktor Ivanov.'

'A Russian?'

'Yes. I think perhaps he had much trouble in his home country. I don't know why.'

A captain, escorted by two military police, walked into the room.

The doctor turned as a man said, 'It is a reception for Teniente General Ivár Tomar Ramos.'

'He is army. Not air force? Why have this ah, party here?'

'What is the problem, Doctor?' the captain asked somewhat scornfully, ignoring the question.

'My rank is major, Captain. And the problem is we do not know who this man is. We need to find someone that knows him. He is seriously ill. If we do not bring his temperature down, he could die. I add for you that I had your general as a patient many years ago.'

'I do not know him.' The captain looked at Mateo's clothes, laid on a chair. 'Perhaps he's from the reception.'

'Go inquire,' said Doctor Pazano more as an order than a request. He did not like the young captain's demeanor. 'It is possible this is something contagious. Do you have any medical people at this wedding?'

'Sí, General Ramos has his personal doctor with him.'

'Mierda,' said Major Pazano. And then sarcastically. 'Very efficient of you not to bring the doctor to the infirmary.'

The captain turned and walked out.

'Arrogant young officer, don't you think?' said Doctor Pazano.

***

Pempeyo excitedly talked to a man covered with geometrical patterns. JP interrupted Pempeyo and talked rapidly to the man who folded his arms and said bluntly that he had no interest in the white man. When Pempeyo told him that the white man had helped rescue the girls, the richly decorated man, wearing a colorful headband of woven toucan and parrot feathers, shrugged and followed them over to where Brush lay.

As they walked, JP listened to Pempeyo and turned to the others when they arrived. 'He is the shaman and prepared the poison for the darts. He said it is very strong because of the nature of the crime the men committed.'

'Get some specifics, JP.'

The shaman listened. He said nothing while JP pointed at Brush and raised his voice. 'Big secret, but he finally said it's a small amount of poison made from a vine that they use on monkeys and from the frog colored like gold.'

'You got that, Doc, Fred?'

'The poison from a vine is probably curare. Describe the symptoms,' said Doctor Dakine.

'He's alternating between rigid and convulsions.'

'Golden tree frog, *Phyllobates terribilis*. The most poisonous type, alkaloid poison,' shouted Sheilla, who was now frantically typing and reading her monitor.

Doctor Dakine flipped pages in a small book with tiny print and stopped at Batrachotoxins. She listened to Jeff while quickly reading the small print, squinting through her reading glasses.

'Muscle contraction, convulsions, and now he is salivating.'

'Damn. There is no antidote or treatment. Blocks the sodium channels open. Jeez.'

'Do you have digitalis? Since sodium channel blockers are contraindicated.'

'He is starting to fibrillate.'

Glenda couldn't believe what she was hearing. She raised her head and held her forehead with her hand. Tears rolled down her anguished face as she gulped for oxygen, trying to control herself.

'His heart is going to stop,' said Dakine. 'Defib, now.' Dakine stared ahead, trying to think of anything that Jeff could do. She sighed heavily, knowing there was nothing anyone could do.

The shaman looked at the girls and then held out a small pouch and knelt over Brush. He opened the pouch and dipped his finger inside, extracting a small amount of brownish-green paste.

The shaman pushed it up Brush's nose, first on one side and then the other.

'The shaman is putting something up his nose,' said Jeff more to himself than the others.

'Putting what up his nose?' asked Dakine.

'It's some goop, brown-green stuff from a pouch.'

'Let him, Jeff. I've got nothing to offer from here. We've nothing to lose.'

'Charging the defib.'

The shaman bent over Brush and started to chant softly while placing his hand on Brush's chest just over his heart.

He turned to JP and shook his head as Brush went completely still.

'Everyone, stand back.' Jeff ripped Brush's shirt open and placed the black paddles on his chest, sending a high voltage jolt through his body. 'Defibbing,' he said to no one in particular. 'Nothing.' He waited and hit him again and placed his stethoscope on Brush. 'I have a heartbeat. Faint, but it's there.'

'We've opened video,' said Knight.

Glenda stared at the monitor, wishing she could close her eyes and suddenly appear next to her man. She held her hand over her mouth and involuntarily shook, seeing him lying in the dirt, his face bleeding from the rock chips, and brown-green goop in his nose.

The shaman stared at the paddles in Jeff's hands. He stood erect and pulled out a long knife, causing Jim and the others to tense. The shaman said something to JP, turned, and walked back to the dead soldier.

JP let out a breath, 'He said, white man will be okay, and now he has to take the head of the enemy.'

'I'm not going to stop him,' said Neilly.

Katarina looked at Sheilla and said, 'They still shrink heads? I thought that was ancient history.'

'It seems they still do.'

'Maybe they are putting them up on spikes or something,' suggested Fred.

Pempeyo talked to JP for a minute. 'He says it's an old custom, no longer performed. However, this is a special situation. They will shrink this enemy head.'

'Shrink whose head?' A faint whisper drifted up to their ears. All eyes turned to Brush. His eyes were open, and his chest was rising.

'Don't try to move, McGuire,' said Jeff letting out a sigh. 'It's not your head, so no worries.'

Heather, relieved for Glenda, jumped up and whooped. General Crystal, contrary to his normally unemotional character, stood and high-fived her and said, 'A poison dart, who would have figured?'

'Jeff, you bring a sample of that paste back,' commanded Dakine.

'You bet, as long as I can get him to give me some without having to donate my head.'

***

'Now, I'm all ears. What happened to our comm?' asked the general.

'Eleven-year cycle for the sun's geomagnetic storms. Our communication satellites are in high geosynchronous orbit, and the storms caused by coronal mass ejections bombarded our satellites with high-energy particles…' Misa began.

The general said, 'Hum, I want to know all the details, but later.'

'Sure, General. It's an interesting phenomenon.'

***

Neilly was organizing the cleanup and exit operation. 'Marilyn, set the chopper down. I want to get McGuire back as soon as possible.'

'You want to scuttle the raft?' asked Gaston.

'You and Fleur take it back to the drop off point. Marilyn can come back and pick you up. JP, disable the ELTs on the two choppers, and then find out the Indians' intentions.'

Angélica was standing next to Jago at the cave entrance when Pwanchir walked out, gripping the red hair of the beheaded miner. He walked to Jago and Angélica and held it up, blood still dripping from the red beard. Jago smiled and patted the dead man's cheek. Angélica looked horrified. She turned around, gagging. Lobo and the other men were bringing out the gold pouches with smiles. Everyone looked happy, except for the president's daughter whose rebel fantasy vanished in the gruesome reality of a severed head.

'We take the army helicopter?' asked Jago.

'All yours,' said Jim. 'Windscreen has a hole.' Jago shrugged.

Jim reached in a rucksack and took out a plastic mug with duct tape wrapped around it. He pulled off three inches and rolled it around a shell casing, passing it to Jago. Then he passed Jago the rest of the duct tape.

'Should stop the draft from the bigger ones,' saidJim as he looked at the holes in the windscreen.

'Pretty exotic,' said Neilly. 'And, if that doesn't work, give this stick of gum a chew. It should fix one of the smaller ones.'

Cherry had not left Brush's side for a second. She propped his head up on her coat, stroked his hair, and looked down at him with her gleaming black eyes.

Brush smiled up at her, thinking again that if he didn't love Glenda, this would be one interesting woman to get to know. As they looked at each other, Cherry sensed that despite her attraction to this man, she would never possess him. For a moment, it made her sad as she watched Brush being carried over and loaded on Marilyn's helicopter. She walked over and kissed Brush on the lips. It wasn't a kiss that longed for a future. It was a short goodbye kiss. All Brush could do was smile at her as she turned and walked back to the cave entrance.

'Let's get what's left of these bodies into the cave. Set some explosives,' said Neilly. 'Looks like the Indians are leaving.'

The Shuar walked off in a line without saying goodbye.

Seventeen of the warriors carried heads, which only a short while ago had sat atop the soldiers' and miners' bodies. The shaman held Alvarez's head. He led the procession out of the camp and up along the tributary river. At the end of the procession were the young girls. One turned back, smiled, and waved at Jim.

The chaos turned once again to silence and order as the bodies were moved into the cave. Jean-Paul, Fleur, and Lobo pulled in two at a time, dragging them by their feet while Carlos and Chico dragged one man together. Angélica stared at the grotesque headless figures being pulled through the dirt, leaving bloody trails. She hugged Jago, closed her eyes for a second before holding his gaze for several seconds. Then she squeezed his arm and turned. She slowly walked to Jim and Neilly, as Jago knew she would.

Chapter 28

Knight said he had approximately thirty minutes' worth of fuel in the remaining drone. 'I need to start it back pronto.'

'Keep the backup helicopter here to cover us as long as it has enough fuel,' said Neilly. By nature, Neilly was cautious. He never gave away an advantage. It appeared that their mission was nearly accomplished, but he would keep the Apache attack helicopter on site as long as possible.

Jago looked admiringly at the formidable Apache helicopter as it circled several hundred feet above them. Then he noticed something very high up moving off to the northwest. *Spy plane,* he wondered. *Or just a high-flying aircraft.* He didn't believe in coincidences. The Americans had this backup all the time. He wondered what else they might have. It caused him to think that while the FARC guerrillas were expert ground fighters, they were no match for the resources and sophistication that the Americans possessed.

'Everyone, police the brass. We'll dump it from the air. Gaston, are the charges ready?'

'Two minutes,' replied Gaston.

Jago walked over to Jim. 'Maybe you visit us in Colombia sometime. I hope your friend will be okay.'

'I hope so too. Sorry about your man,' said Jim. Jago shrugged, put a hand on Jim's shoulder, and walked back to the Huey, loaded with the miners' gold and his band, but now minus San. JP had asked the Shuar not to take his head. Without ceremony or much sign of grief from the FARC, Lobo and Cherry carried his body, with his head attached, into the cave.

'If the Earth is still around and archeologists are still doing what they do now, what will they make of a dig at this site?' asked Fleur. 'A bunch of skul-less skeletons with only one still attached. I expect it will take a lot of head-scratching to come to a conclusion that explains it.'

Jago started the Huey; Marilyn had left hers running in case she needed to get airborne in a hurry. Neilly nodded at Jago. He twirled his hand, and the team, minus Fleur and Gaston, loaded into the Huey. Brush lifted his head from the stretcher and waved at Colonel Alvarez's ex-army helicopter. In the dim light, he saw an arm wave back. *'What a woman, eh?'*

With a slow, syncopated beat of the blades, the two Hueys rose into the dark air. García was moving toward the raft to rendezvous with Gaston and Fleur, who had walked 200 meters before turning back to watch the cave. 'Fire in the hole, boys and girls,' said Gaston. A muffled boom followed by billowing dust. The cave glowed with a warm red-yellow light. Perhaps one day, archaeologists would excavate the cave. The headless bodies would add to the legends of the fierce warriors: the Shuar headhunters of the Amazon.

***

'I'll call the vice president and ask him to let Noboa know we have his daughter and to arrange for a handoff. Sheilla, you and Kramer meet me in the conference room in ten minutes. Have Fred get Glenda up live.'

The president was in the middle of a state dinner, so the general decided to call the secretary of state's office and got Maeve. 'Good news. Angélica Noboa is on her way to Camp Toucan, unharmed.'

'I'm not surprised, Will. Expected that your boys wouldn't have any trouble retrieving her.'

The general chuckled.

'Guess it wasn't all that easy, huh, Will?'

'Let's say it got a little interesting.'

'Anything that will come back and bite us?'

'Maybe, if anyone knew who was down there. But I think that is unlikely.'

Anyone else other than the savvy assistant to Arthur Willis would have been certain there was going to be trouble. But with General Crystal, Maeve knew that unlikely meant exactly that.

Will continued, 'Maeve, you want to take care of letting VPOTUS know?' 'Sure, general. I'll have Arthur pass it on. It will be a pleasure for him to pass on some good news.'

'Thanks, Maeve.' He hung up the phone, walked over to the cabinet to grab a bottle of single malt scotch and three glasses, and crossed the hall to the conference room.

'What you say, Kramer? How about a celebration drink? Sheilla?'

'I better not until everyone is back at Toucan,' said Sheilla. 'Oh, all right. A small one.'

He poured two large and one small glass.

'To everyone being safe. Everyone from BWC that is.'

Sheilla met the general's eyes and held his gaze for a few seconds, looked down, shook her head, then looked up with a smile. 'Is it always going to be like this, General?'

'I hope so. To successful missions.'

***

Angélica sat next to Jim on the Huey. Marilyn announced, 'We're going to fuel up at Toucan, and then we'll take you back to Cuenca.'

Angélica looked up at Jim and saw what she had seen in Jago. 'I have learned some things, señor. One, women can be as strong as men,' as she nodded toward Marilyn and thought of Cherry.

Jim continued to look at her, wondering if the events of a couple of weeks were enough to change the way she would judge the world. Then, he said, 'Women can be stronger than men, or less strong, as they choose. The choice is based on knowledge, not desire.'

'I will try,' said Angel, sensing that something inside her had changed.

184

***

Cherry reached into the front of the Huey and squeezed Jago's arm. 'Where are we going?' Jago looked at the fuel gauge and said, 'Not far, my pet. Perhaps another forty minutes. We will follow the river as far as we can. Enough fuel, and we could be home by morning. But as it is, it will be many weeks, I think.'

'How much of the gold did you give the Indians?'

'Not so much. Maybe half.'

'That is more than a little. You are kind.'

Jago smiled to himself. 'The norteamericanos were attractive, no? Especially the Canadian?'

'It is true I liked the man named for a plant. But it was only a dream. You are not a dream, and you are here.'

Jago turned and looked at her. 'Seeing the respect the Canadian had for you made me realize that sometimes we fail to see the truth when we are so close to it. Perhaps, Cherry, dreams become reality. If we want them to.'

***

As soon as Glenda heard the unmistakable beat of the Huey's blades, she rushed outside. A military doctor from Manta stood beside her. Inside, he had set up a rustic but sophisticated hospital room to take care of Brush. Jeff and Fleur would act as assistants, if needed.

After the Huey settled to the ground, Jim and Jeff lifted Brush's stretcher, while Fleur fussed with the IV. 'You try to get up again, Major,' said Fleur, 'and we'll drug you up so you won't see anything for two days.'

'Okay, okay, eh.' He was already grinning from ear to ear, seeing Glenda Rose Stuart rushing over.

She didn't say anything, just held his arm, and looked into his eyes, shaking her head. Brush grinned. 'Nice to see you, beautiful.'

'The one thing I can say is that you're not boring, Brush. You're the first person I ever met that almost bought it from a poison dart.'

'Let's get him inside. This guy's not getting any lighter while we stand here.'

The doctor hooked up another IV and did an exam. 'I'm going to be really curious to hear what the antidote was. Everything appears normal. About all we can do is run some tests, monitor you, and flush out any remaining toxins. If all is fine tomorrow, I'll fly back with the pilots to Manta. Ask your Doctor Dakine to please let me know what the witch doctor placed up your nose. I, too, am curious.'

'I'll let her know,' said Brush. 'I feel fine. How about we make a deal? Dump that liter of fluids in me, and I'll march back over in the morning for a check-up, eh?'

'I'll think about it. Right now, we're going to take blood, and I need a urine sample as soon as you can. We'll do another tomorrow. I want to see what's in your system as soon as. We'll see how it changes after a day.'

'You going to keep me company, honey?' asked Brush.

'What, you want me to hold the cup for you?'

'Fine with me, if that's what you want.'

Glenda gave him a friendly punch.

'I'm going to debrief the general and see about returning our kidnap victim,' said Jim as he walked out.

***

'I hope this doesn't come back to haunt us,' said General Crystal.

'The site is pretty sanitized. No army or miners survived. No one to talk except the president's daughter, the FARC rebels, or the Shuar.'

'Not exactly a short list.'

'The wild card is the daughter. The FARC won't get back to their home for weeks. I don't think the Shuar are much interested in talking to anyone. I'll have a better opinion of Angélica after I hear what she has to say when we take her back.

'The two choppers of this Captain Alvarez?'

'FARC took one, and the other crashed next to a rock outcrop. The site is remote, and its emergency locator is disabled. How did you identify the person in charge as Captain Alvarez?'

'The two Wolf Warriors at Huachuca dug into the army computers. With that info and the communications they had monitored, they determined his identity. I'll have Katarina give you a full profile brief tomorrow. We'll continue to monitor comms to see what, if anything, is said about their two missing choppers.'

'Let me know.'

'What's your assessment of the rebels?' asked Will.

'Seasoned and savvy. Not sure if they are generally representative of the FARC. I would rather be on their side than against them. I liked the ones I got to know.'

'You okay with Brush's prognosis?'

'Seems so. I'll have the data sent to Maria, along with the second set of blood samples.'

'She's excited about the toxin and the antidote, and now Nusmen is touting the same thing. There could be some useful biochemical information come out of all this. I'm sending them both to you. I'll be here tomorrow when you take the daughter back. Keep me informed.'

Marilyn waved as the Huey and the Blackhawk took off to drop Jim and Angélica at Cuenca for their flight to Quito. She turned to Neilly. 'I don't like it when there is no whirlybird sitting close to where I am.'

Chapter 29

The sleek Citation stopped near a military hangar at Aérea Mariscal Sucre, northeast of Quito. Four silver Toyota Land Cruisers sat waiting. Noboa, accompanied by several uniformed men, including General Mancuso, stood in front of the cars. Angélica was the first to go down the stairs. Her father walked briskly to the stairs. He kissed her on each cheek.

'I was very worried about you, my child. I'm happy you are back with us.'

'I'm glad to be home, Papá.'

Jim had followed her down the steps and stood a few feet away.

'Please meet Colonel Jim Johnson, the one I told you about on the phone.'

'I am pleased to meet you, Colonel Johnson. Your vice president, my old school chum, has told me a great deal about you. Please come and ride with us.'

'Papá, you normally take a helicopter to the palace?'

'Today, I wanted to spend time with you and hear all about your adventures.'

The feelings they expressed to each other had changed. Something was missing between father and daughter. The tension that both had felt most of their lives was no longer present. Noboa had been genuinely worried about Angélica. Just how worried had surprised him. For her part, she had been transformed by her recent experiences. It didn't mean she would give up on trying to preserve the world from corruption and destruction of the environment. Instead of acting the spoiled child, however, she realized she had the power to make a difference.

During the fifty-minute drive back to the Palacio de Carondelet, she told her father everything, including her affair with Jago. Everything, that is, except what happened with the miners. At one point, she could see her father was uncomfortable with her mention of Jago. Instead of chastising him, she touched his arm, looked him in the eye, and said almost maternally, 'Papá, you should not be surprised that your daughter of twenty-eight years has an interest in men. Perhaps you will be comforted to know that I have had little interest in the past. After my experiences in the jungle, I have learned that there are some truly worthy men, such as our colonel here.' She winked at Colonel Johnson. 'My future will hopefully be one of being your confidante. And, if I am lucky, I will find such a man. A man worthy of fathering your grandchildren.'

Jim had been relieved that she had said nothing of their encounter with the army. Neither had she gone into detail about the miners. She kept that part of her narrative short and only mentioned rescuing the girls and their happy return to the Shuar. Angélica knew that telling the whole story would be a poor move at this moment. Soon, however, she would have to spin the tale to suit the facts that would become known about the miners and the missing army forces.

President Noboa had never heard his opinionated, and oftentimes argumentative daughter talk to him this way. In the past, she had taken what he saw as foolish positions. He now felt comforted. In another way, he felt her newfound strength. He was uncertain how to accept it. *Perhaps I am tiring of ruling,* he pondered. *Perhaps, I need comfort and a soft chair.*

There were many people to greet them. Eventually, they arrived at their residence where a celebratory dinner had been prepared. It was a gala affair, one Angélica would have scorned in her past. But she had changed and now graciously assumed her role as the center of attention, with mealtime discussions revealing a humility that endeared her to all present. To all except her older sister, who was jealous of the attention Angélica received. So jealous, in fact, that several times she pressed her long nails into her wrists to keep from yelling out.

After the dinner, Angélica walked with Jim to her father's study. 'Perhaps before my father arrives, we can discuss your thoughts on how best to present the full story. I see no need to hurry, but an explanation will have to be provided before long.'

'Your father will be here shortly, and we may not want to have our discussion interrupted. Maybe we can find some time in the morning to discuss it.'

'You are right, of course. Now, I will leave you with him to perform your male rituals like smoking a cigar and sipping brandy.'

'Perhaps you should stay, and I'll leave. I have the distinct feeling that someone new might be wearing the pants in this family.'

'There will be plenty of time for me.'

Angélica turned as her father walked up, kissed him and laughed as she said goodnight and walked to her room.

***

'I talked to my father this morning. He wants to do something for the tribe who helped us. I convinced him that their biggest problems are not food or bringing them our culture, but rather protection of their lands from mining, logging, and petroleum exploration. We are going to find a way to safeguard the Jivaro lands, including Kichwa people's lands on the other side of the river. If we approach it the right way, I think we can gain support from various international and local groups, both with publicity and money.'

Jim noted she had said, 'we have decided.' *Interesting change from the profile that Katarina had worked up not so many days ago,* he thought.

'I convinced him that I should go to the Shuar to discuss what, if anything, besides control of their lands, they would find useful. They have an elected official that works with the government, but I have a feeling he is only concerned about his self-interest, not theirs. I don't propose involving him at this stage.'

Jim waited for her to finish.

'Would you, your partner, Major McGuire, and the interpreter JP be willing to go with me?'

***

'This is exciting. I've always had a fantasy about the Amazon since I was a kid,' said Glenda. 'And I hope it is not a fantasy to keep you away from poison darts or, I might add, rebel women.'

'I don't mind you watching out for me. I like it.'

'I got to talk to Angélica a little last night. She's not at all what I expected.'

'Approaching the landing zone. Good thing it's not a smallish LZ with the load we're carrying,' said Marilyn.'

Knight had liaised most of the morning with the BWC, searching for the best place to land close to the Shuar. The closest open spot had been relatively easy to locate with the drone.

It was a small clearing made by an oil exploration company. Marilyn, with Jim backing her up, had staunchly refused to allow the Ecuadoran army pilot to co-pilot. Marilyn didn't like to fly with anyone she didn't personally approve of. Jim, for his part, did not want the military to know where they were going, or what they were doing with Angélica.

The SF team all had overlapping skills. One of Mac's was that of backup chopper pilot, and his flight training had primarily been flying Blackhawks. The one that they were currently setting down in the jungle clearing was an S-70, only slightly different from the UH-60 he was most familiar with. Of the total of thirteen on board, there were four capable of flying the helicopter in an emergency.

Of the eleven passengers, there was one even more excited than Glenda—Nusmen, who was accompanying Doctor Dakine. As soon as the general authorized the expedition, he consulted with both of them about the antidote used on Brush. The discussion eventually led to several possible other plants and fungal derivatives that could be useful to the BWC. By the end of the discussion, General Crystal decided there were merits in sending both Nusmen and Doctor Dakine on the

191

expedition.

'Nus, I'm going to go too,' said Heather when she heard. 'It's the trip of a lifetime. I want those plants just as much as you do.'

'I guarantee, he won't let you go.'

'You need a skilled botanical assistant. It makes sense. I'll talk to him.'

Heather knocked on the general's door.

'But, Will, I know the plants as well as Nusmen.'

'There seems to be one thing, young lady, that you don't understand about the army. Generals make decisions, and all those under them accept those decisions. I have my reasons. No more questions. Out with you, or I'll terminate your security clearance, which I probably should already have done.'

Heather badly wanted to go to the Amazon, both to see Jim, and to collect the exotic plants that she and Nusmen had often discussed around a campfire when they worked for the Forest Service. It was not going to happen, and she understood she was pushing her luck. She produced a smile and said, 'Thank you, sir,' without sarcasm, and left his office. She realized he had only allowed her to be here because her security clearance had not been pulled after Fort Huachuca and the mess with the cartel, and also as a favor to Jim.

'Marsha, could you do me a favor and ask General Crystal if it would be okay if I stay at the lab and monitor them when they go back to the Amazon? Maybe when you think the time is right.'

'It should be fine. Don't worry. I'll take care of it.'

'Thank you. Much appreciated.'

***

The helicopter touched down. 'Same call names,' said Jim. Roberta and García exited opposite sides and disappeared into the surrounding forest. Marilyn busied herself with shutting down the helicopter while Mac carefully did a walkabout in the clearing. He headed up the path toward the Shuar village, placing listening devices along the path. Then, he walked in the other direction and did the same.

JP took the lead, followed by Fleur. Angélica was behind Fleur, and followed by Jeff, Nusmen, and Doctor Dakine. Jim brought up the rear with Brush and Glenda in front of him.

***

Mac listened intently with his headphones on. The procession of the president's daughter, a doctor, and three of his team came through loud and clear. With the two watchers looking out for them, the listening devices functioning, and the comms working fine, he and Marilyn could rest easy in the chopper until the group returned.

***

'The jungle isn't as thick as I thought it would be,' said Doctor Dakine.

'The soils are not very nutritious, and the tall trees block out the light, so the understory is often not as dense as we remember from Tarzan movies,' said Nusmen.

'Bet this will surprise you; I have the full set of Johnny Weissmuller's Tarzan series.'

Brush laughed, 'I wouldn't have thought that would be your sort of thing, Doc.'

'It happens to be the way I relax. *Journey to the Center of the Earth* and *Lost World.* That sort of thing. Everyone gets killed in action movies. They give me anxiety. I like lightweight, make-believe films. Maybe I see enough death as a doc, and don't want to see it in books and movies.'

'Working in the lab relaxes me,' said Nusmen.

'I'm not surprised,' said Dakine. 'You're not normal.'

'That's true,' added Brush. 'He's a prize winner though, eh?'

'Look at that,' said Nusmen, stepping several yards off the trail.

'It is pretty' said Dakine. 'What is it? What's it good for?'

'It belongs to the violet family. A flowering vine, *Drymonia gesneraceae.*'

'So freaking unique. Yellow and pink.' Nusmen threw his pack down and started to collect a piece of the vine with a flower.

Jim walked over to him. 'Nusmen, you can't have us stopping today. We need to get to the village, and then you can work out a way to start collecting samples.'

'But it's important, Colonel. You never know the value. I could spend months collecting here. The biodiversity is incredible.'

'Nevertheless, we move on now. And no, I can't leave you to catch up. You're too valuable.'

Nusmen slung his pack over his shoulder, wearing a pout that evolved to a quizzical look. 'What do you mean, too valuable?'

'You're one of the brightest people in the lab, and I can't let anything happen to you.'

Nusmen stared at him. Jim gave him a hand motion to move. Nusmen did, but his perplexed look turned to a slight smile as what the colonel had just said sank in. *Valuable. I'm valuable.*

'The village is about two kilometers ahead,' said Jeff, studying his GPS.

'Is the shaman the one you are going to talk to, Miss Noboa?'

'Knock off the formality. We know each other well enough by now.'

'Pleased to, ma'am, Angélica.'

'The shaman is respected and might be a good choice. There is no tribal leader, per se, with the Shuar. So I plan to talk to as large a group as possible. Unfortunately, there is no real equality; men have the power.'

JP turned toward the back. 'The good news is, almost everyone will be in the village. Either gardening or shrinking heads.'

'I'm kind of happy that we have four women in this group. Almost equal,' said Doctor Dakine.

'Maybe that will give the women some sense of power,' said Glenda. 'What's your pitch going to be, Angélica?'

'In the past, I've had a strong opinion about everything right and wrong… I'm not sure. I will try to listen to what they have to say, and perhaps something can be figured out.'

Chapter 30

'We're close' said Jean-Paul. 'We follow the plan. I go in and try to find the two P's.'

'Who?' asked Maria.

'Oh, yeah. You don't know them. Pwanchir and Pempeyo, our special Shuar friends.'

'Got it. Heard them mentioned at the mine.'

'I think that Angélica should consider talking to them first,' said Jean-Paul. 'Pwanchir is the more talkative one, and I think he would be more useful for advice than going to the shaman, at least at first.'

He looked back at Angel as he spoke. She considered for a minute. 'I think you're right.'

JP made a fist, signaling for them to stop. They had decided earlier that he should enter the village alone. It might be a shock if all of them stormed in at the same time.

The trail widened as it approached an open expanse with the village houses and gardens. It looked both sleepy and busy at the same time. There was no frantic activity. After a couple of seconds, no one paid any attention to the American walking amongst their homes. Then there was a yell as a young girl ran toward JP. It was one of the rescued schoolgirls. JP let out a sigh of relief. The villagers would see him as a friend and not as an intruder.

JP picked up the young girl who giggled delightedly. He set her down, and she took his hand and started dragging him toward an oval-shaped structure with a palm-leaved roof and woven stick walls. She was taking him to her home to meet her mother and father.

Both parents had heard her excited yelling. Her mother got up from the garden plot alongside their home, and the father stopped repairs to the outside of the house. Six others came out of the house. JP asked her how many lived here. She said, 'Many.' He rolled his eyes at himself for forgetting they had no use for numbers. A quick peek inside, and he saw at least a dozen bamboo sleeping mats.

JP wondered how they could be so friendly toward him, a white person. After all, from the time of the Spanish Conquistadors, so much harm had been inflicted on them by Western culture. It was a given that the children would be friendly. However, everyone else seemed friendly too. He knew how social they were as a group; his language tutor at Toucan, several years ago, had told him tales.

JP was often asked why he had wanted to learn something as obscure as Shuar and Quechua. It was nothing more than curiosity on his part. He had a facility for languages and was always curious. His language teacher was a cook and sometime consultant to the Special Forces at Toucan. Shuar was added to his more than sixteen languages. If he didn't know a language, he could listen, try a few words, and would soon be able to get along in basic conversation.

While musical and mathematical savants were generally well-known, polyglots, or as in JP's case, hyperpolyglots were less well-known. Several years ago, others of the team read *The Sparrow*, with its multi-language, space-travelling priest. Then they discovered the feted Cardinal Giuseppe Caspar Mezzofanti who reportedly spoke more than sixty languages.

For years, his team members teased him, calling him Caspar, emphasizing the 'par.' In the Amazon, having a brain able to put together the way a language was constructed so fast was very valuable to the team. Eventually, the team quit teasing him and started to respect his unique skill.

Tshui pulled him along toward another palm-leaf topped oval shaped home. As they neared, two more of the young girls came running with big grins and grabbed his hands. After a few moments, JP inquired as to the whereabouts of Pwanchir and Pempeyo. Tshui pointed toward a hut several hundred yards away. As she pointed, she started tugging at his hand, walking in that direction. More of the Shuar started to cluster around JP and the girls as they walked, smiling at the tall man and accepting him as a guest in their village.

Chapter 31

Tshui and the teenage girls led JP to the far end of the village, stopping several feet away from where Pwanchir stood, watching a pot boil. As soon as he saw JP, he shyly grinned and motioned them over.

'Dinner?' asked JP.

'Food for my dead relatives' souls.'

'Ah, I see.'

JP looked in the pot but could not see anything through the vapor and bubbling liquid.

'Apach man,' said Pwanchir.

JP nodded, understanding that it was one of the soldiers' and not one of the miners' heads that was boiling. Apach was the Shuar word for a Spanish-speaking person.

Pempeyo walked up, grinning, and nodded to JP.

Pwanchir said, 'Pempeyo took the skulls to have the ants clean.'

They talked over the boiling pot for a while. The villagers seemed proud as Pwanchir explained the ancient Tsantsa ritual to JP. They had removed the tissue covering the skull by making an incision in the back, separating the tissue from the bone. The bone was set aside. Then they poked two holes in through the lips, and inserted bamboo stakes. The boiling would shrink the tissue. He had to be careful to boil for only the correct amount of time. He pointed to a tree, saying that when the sun touched the treetop, he would remove the head.

JP leaned forward, actually very interested. He had always wondered how the Shuar shrunk a head with the skull. The answer was obvious. *Duh*, it was shrunk without the skull. A bit less exotic or mysterious, perhaps.

'My friends are waiting on the trail. The tall blue-eyed man and the stocky one, along with some others.'

Pwanchir, who in the past was the shy one of the two, now spoke rapidly as Pempeyo returned. The girls started to run off toward the trail with Pempeyo close behind.

JP said, 'Lots of little visitors on the way.'

Seconds later, the patter of running feet grew louder. The girls, with Pempeyo not far behind, abruptly stopped. The size of the group surprised the young girls. Jim stepped in front, walking toward them. Tshui overcame her surprise and ran to him. She hugged him for several seconds, stepped back, looked up happily, and held out her hand. They walked hand in hand toward the other girls. Jim waved for everyone to follow.

By the time they arrived in the village, Doctor Dakine was holding a small hand, Glenda holding another. Brush carried a beaming little girl on his shoulder. Angélica held a small hand in each of hers. Nusmen walked in back, stopping every few feet to examine something and then hurrying to catch up before he was yelled at.

Glenda looked at the little girl, smiling up at her. 'Mister, I didn't think anything was missing in my life.'

'They're cute. There's no doubt about it,' replied Brush.

'Don't worry, big guy. I'm not ready to have a family. Maybe never. I like things like they are now. But I love holding this little hand, I admit it.'

The afternoon turned out to be educational. The Shuar were very social and seemed willing to share whatever they had with their visitors. They visited the Catholic school the girls had been kidnapped from. It was at the far end of the village, past Pempeyo's and Pwanchir's house. Surprisingly, there was no Catholic teacher.

A village woman, who had stayed for some months in the city, taught the children what she could about the outside world. The school was in session only one day a week.

A bigger surprise, however, was that just inside the door hung two shrunken heads. Small and black. 'Why are they here? asked Glenda. JP translated the question.

'The word they say, muisak, is what we might call soul. They believe that the soul of the victim is contained in the shrunken head. These heads belonged to the two Jesuit men that were here long ago.'

'But they are very dark-skinned,' added Maria Dakine. Then, asking multiple questions very much like her friend Heather, 'Why is it called a Catholic school? Why no full-time teacher?'

JP asked Pempeyo about the heads and why they were black. Then, he translated, 'He'll explain why they are black when we are back at his hut.'

As he gazed off into the foliage, Pempeyo told JP about a missionary they called Sally. 'She was evil and suddenly disappeared one day.' Pempeyo did not offer any further explanations. *I think I'll keep my eyes open for a woman's head hanging about,* thought JP, *just out of curiosity.* Later, he couldn't be certain, but he spotted what might have been a blackened shrunken head that appeared to belong to a female, hanging from the edge of the shaman's hut. It was mixed in with several other pint-sized heads and colorful artifacts.

'Pempeyo says we go back to his home, and he will describe Tsantsa to you. The head he and Pwanchir are working on is ready to be removed from the pot. He says, though, that these two heads are from white people. The best I can understand is that the faces are covered with charcoal and baked. I'm not at all sure how one bakes charcoal.'

Nusmen interjected, 'We need to find the shaman and find out what the goo is made from.' JP translated the question.

'Pempeyo says the shaman is performing a ritual in his home.'

'Can we go there?'

'He says no one can enter. He will come out when he is ready.'

'Jeez, tell him it is urgent. We need to see what plants they use for different drugs.'

'He said no one can disturb him. If you do, you will get very sick or maybe die from tsentsak. He is a powerful Quechua shaman.'

Pempeyo nodded to an old woman to come over.

'He says that medicine is known by all villagers. This old woman knows more than most.'

JP talked to the woman for some time. 'She will get several of the women to collect the plants they use and bring them to her house. Then, they will show you how they prepare them. What I suggest is that you collect and explore for a while and, when they are ready, I'll translate for you. I will find you someone to go along as a guide to help you.'

'Doctor, you want to go alone exploring, or with me collecting, and see what we can find?'

'Together, Nusmen,' responded Maria emphatically. 'I'm not going out on my own. Wait. I am more interested in the head shrinking, and I don't know much about the plants and fungus. I think I'll stay in the village. Someone else want to assist our resident...,' she almost said maniac, and then thought better of it and instead said, 'scientist.'

No one volunteered.

'It's why we are here. It's important,' said Nusmen wondering why anyone in their right mind would not want to collect plants, fungus, slime, and algae with him.

'It is one of the reasons we are here. Your reason. Not the only reason. You go ahead. You have a radio. Call if you have any trouble.' Jim added with a stern look, 'Serious trouble.'

Pempeyo brought an older woman over and introduced her to Nusmen. She grinned at him.

'She will keep you safe,' said JP.

Pempeyo motioned for JP and the others to follow him.

Pwanchir pulled the head out of the pot. It looked like a deflated football. It was less than half the size of a normal head. He let it cool, holding it on a stick before giving it to Pempeyo who cradled it lovingly in his hand for a while before turning it inside out.

'I'm going to look around,' said Angélica. 'This is too… not my thing.'

JP looked at Pempeyo and hunched his shoulders up. Doctor Dakine bent over, scrutinizing the head in Pempeyo's hands. Pempeyo managed to turn it inside out, all the while making sounds like, um, yes, and good.

'Thinking about trying this when you get home, Doctor?' asked Glenda. 'An ex-boyfriend, perhaps?'

'Ah, no time for boyfriends,' she said, continuing to inspect the head.

Everyone broke out laughing.

'It's just that it is fascinating. I wonder if we could take one with us?'

JP said, 'You think? I'll see if I can find a way to ask before we leave.'

Pempeyo was now scraping remnants of flesh. When he was finished, he turned it right side out and stitched them back together where the incision had been made to remove it from the skull.

After a long while, Pempeyo held it up and admired it. The eye sockets were sewn up. Two pegs were sticking through the lips.

'Fascinating,' said Maria.

Pempeyo was pleased with the white woman witch doctor's interest in his project. He scooped up several stones and sand with a wooden spoon from another pot on a fire. He filled the head with them and carefully set it down.

'He says that the hot stones will shrink the head more and cure the skin. It will have to set for some time. Should we walk around the village, and let our Angel ask some questions? Where did she go, anyway?'

It was decided that Pempeyo would give them a tour and then collect a group to talk to Angélica. They found her sitting on the ground with a group of women. JP sat down. 'Might as well start with this group.'

'I guess,' said Glenda. 'I am going to research the Shuar when we get back. This is not at all what I expected. Peaceful village life. Men and women all working around the village and in their gardens. It seems every house has a garden. I thought, now I see it as sexist, that the women would be cooking and the men out with bows, hunting for game and fighting their enemies.'

'Pempeyo says they eat very little meat from hunting. The majority of their food is yucca and plantain. Chicken sometimes, along with the occasional monkey. This village is old, and they plan to move to a new location. He says they stay for many seasons and then move. It is up to the shaman to decide.'

'Not the fierce headhunting, male-dominated warriors that we are told tales about,' said Maria as if to confirm to herself just how wrong her perception had been.

'I think,' said JP, 'they can be fierce warriors. We got a taste of that at the mine. Mostly, though, they live peacefully and like to be left alone.'

During their walkabout, the process of shrinking heads was in various states throughout the village. Pempeyo looked at Glenda's hair and pointed.

'Seems that the redheaded miner's head is over yonder,' said Brush.

Pempeyo collected more villagers, adding them to the group. Angélica talked for over two hours about the government, soldiers, miners, tourists, and oil explorers. Jim asked several questions too. When the group broke up, Jim asked, 'What are your conclusions, Miss Noboa?'

'First, Colonel Johnson,' she said rather playfully, 'I appreciate your helping the discussion along. And now, if you please, you will call me Angélica.'

Jim didn't say anything but gave a small smile and almost imperceptibly, nodded.

Angélica smiled back. 'To me, there is only one conclusion we can make. They don't need or want us here. Especially not the army, miners, or oil people. What they need, I think, is to have complete control over their lands. The problem is that they already have a designated area. The government, however, owns the land, which means they can lease it to miners, loggers, whoever. What I think is that maybe the land should be titled to them, and then, perhaps, others couldn't take whatever they wanted. Otherwise, the only thing that might be of value to them are tools like axes and— my father would have a fit with this suggestion—some functional, modern rifles for hunting.'

'You think getting the land deeded is something you could get your father to do?' asked Jim.

'I will have to think about how.'

'Not too sure about the better rifles idea or providing them with any of the other tech stuff. It might be better to leave them be, to hunt as they do now,' said Jim. 'Our culture is going to catch up with them fast enough in any event.'

'They use ancient rifles now.'

'Shotguns might be more useful for them and more acceptable to your father,' added Jim.

'I have a thought,' said Glenda. 'What we are talking about is politics. It seems to me that this is something that the general might discuss with the VP to see what could be worked out. What do you think, Jim?'

'General might try to influence him or some group to pressure your government, but I don't have a clue if the VP or anyone else in Washington would give a hoot about the Indians. The mining and petroleum lobbyists will oppose it. Suppose it depends on your father convincing the VP.'

***

'This is very social,' whispered Glenda. 'I think I counted fourteen in the house. And I think that sound I hear is someone trying to increase the size of the village.'

'Does sound like it. You think we should…?'

'Not a chance, buster. Keep your Canadian hormones to yourself.'

'Pempeyo said that all the families sleep together like this.'

'Cozy. Just a little hard to get used to.'

'I wonder how everyone else is doing?'

'They have all tucked in for the night. All except one. Nusmen was so fired up after he came back with his guide, that he kept the women, men, and JP talking. I think the villagers were just too nice to tell him to shut up and go to bed.'

'I think maybe they have a plan, though,' said Brush. 'The last I saw, Nusmen was slurring his words and laughing like a wild man as the women giggled and decorated his face with some reddish paint.'

'I think you are right about them having a plan. What did JP call it, manioc? A beer. Getting him to pass out was probably the only way to get some peace for the night. I'm going to try to sleep. A year ago, sitting in an FBI office, who would have thought I would be out here and with you. Life will never be dull, will it? I think that beer is affecting me too. Sweet dreams, honey.'

Chapter 32

'For some reason, this intelligence caught my attention. Quite likely, for no other reason than our involvement in rescuing the woman in South America. It is only a rumor and needs more facts to measure its substance. Perhaps, your men can question the FARC to see if they can add any insight?'

'Too late, Bertrand. The rebels have broken contact and left for home. It seems that our boys liked them. What was it you heard?'

'A curious bit of information, General. While we were monitoring the Ecuadoran and Colombian military to keep abreast of anything that might have affected the rescue op, we overheard chatter about a missing army squad that operates in the area where your team was.'

'You want to know?' asked the general, holding Bertrand in a steady gaze.

'I was curious, as I mentioned… I think you have assuaged my curiosity.'

'Just to resolve a little of your curiosity—I did hear something along the same lines; an Ecuadoran army unit kidnapped several young Indian girls, after which the girls were returned, and the unit disappeared.'

'Curiosity resolved,' said Bertrand. 'Do you need anything for the oversight testimony tomorrow?'

'I don't believe so. From what I hear, it will just be the usual about the lack of transparency in our disclosures, and about us wasting the taxpayers' money.'

'They say it for their constituents' benefit. Beyond the rhetoric, most of them understand that what we do is necessary for national security.'

***

Jim studied Tshui's face. She had a wonderful smile, with a slight gap between her two front teeth. Black hair hung straight, reaching past her shoulders. A red headband, decorated with light-colored seeds, kept the sleek black hair to the side of her face. Her cheeks, with the same reddish designs that Nusmen now had, puffed out when she smiled. The bridge of her nose and chin had small dabs of red, which contrasted with her cobalt-blue dress. She wore a necklace of what appeared to be snail shells strung on a cord.

Jim wanted Tshui's image to mask his memories of the girls' faces he had not been able to rescue so long ago in Vietnam. The images of the two who died with their mother haunted him. He still saw it all vividly—his hand stretched out toward the girls, their eyes looking to him with both fear and trust. Their eyes changed as they were riddled with bullets. It was a long time ago. He hoped that Tshui's smiling face and those of the other six girls they had rescued would once and for all supplant the images of the past.

He bent over and kissed her on the forehead. With difficulty, he turned and walked away. After several yards, he turned. She still hadn't moved. Raising her hand in a wave, she watched her new friend walk into the jungle. *I would like to bring Pedro here sometime*, he said to himself.

***

The Huey settled softly into the grass at Camp Toucan. It had been a peaceful flight over winding rivers, hills, and lush jungle. They gained altitude as the ground rose below them. The lush plant growth changed to savannah as they passed above cloud forests and eventually to the camp, which was barren and devoid of plants inside its perimeter fence.

A shirtless Nusmen stepped out gingerly, his head throbbing from his overindulgence in the manioc beer. His wild night had, however, born fruit. The plant and fungus ingredients of the antidote had been revealed to him. The shaman, as it turned out, also enjoyed the chichi, the Shuar name for their home-brewed beer made from manioc. Combined with his apparent feeling of affinity for the wild-haired Nusmen, the shaman had accepted him as an equal. It had helped that Nusmen knew about plants and fungi. The evening ended with the shaman providing sample materials for the antidote along with a comprehensive recipe and several other concoctions he used to treat his people.

An inebriated Nusmen had desperately wanted to give his new shaman brother something in return. His gifts included variously colored Sharpie marking pens, his hat, shirt, and belt. Fortunately, he had passed out before throwing in his shoes and pants.

Jim went directly to the comm center and had Mac place a call to Heather. He was anxious to get home, to the ranch, to her and Pedro. Heather, to Jim's surprise, was still at the BWC. She assured him Pedro was being well looked after by Lola and Shuskin. Roy was coming up daily to make sure the feeding was being done right and also to give Pedro riding lessons on their small mare. Blacky, as Pedro called her, was gentle and only about twelve hands high; not much taller than a pony, she was the perfect horse for him.

Jim's main question for Heather: did she trust Shuskin with that much responsibility? Heather said she did. 'Also, I'm more comfortable with them having each other for company.' The old man had a heart of gold, she said, underneath his anti-social veneer, and he had really taken to Pedro.

But does he have the judgment? Jim wondered.

***

'Nusmen, it looks like you are going to have to get used to those red decorations on your face,' said Brush. 'I thought it was paint until

JP talked to the women, who looked very pleased with themselves and informed him it was permanent.'

'Looks very attractive,' said Glenda, trying to keep a straight face.

'Huh, oh yeah. I have to analyze the dye, and then I can figure out what will neutralize it.'

For a second, everyone was stunned around the table. Then Glenda started to laugh. 'Nusmen, you do have a unique outlook on life.' The rest couldn't contain themselves, and they all burst out laughing.

'Here's to our very own shaman,' said Marilyn, holding up her wine glass; beer and wine glasses clinked as everyone toasted Nusmen.

'Why are you toasting? I didn't do anything. Oh, I see. I guess I did get the formula,' he said, looking quizzically at them.

'So, what's our plan tomorrow?' asked Mac, looking at Neilly.

'We'll take our plane with the drone back to Fort Huachuca. Then, we're off to home for a week's stand-down.'

'Thank God for that,' said Gaston.

'I'm not sure how Jenny puts up with it. You're seldom there for her and your three kids,' said Mac. 'I can't find a woman who will do that.'

'She has good taste and knows I'm worth it.'

He had barely got that out, when García poured a bucket of water over him. 'I think you need to have that ego cooled down a bit, Sergeant.'

For the next hour, the dinner deteriorated into crazy partying. The Special Forces unit was happy. No injuries. Everyone was happy except Nusmen, who, moments later, looking pale, ran outside and didn't return.

The SF team had not expected to have things turn out this way. They had gotten used to the idea that when Jim and Brush were involved, a mission could become deadly. In the end, they all agreed Glenda Rose Stuart must be the mitigating factor that had changed their fate.

Chapter 33

'Wake up, buddy.'

'What's up, Mac?'

'You are, Colonel. General Crystal is on a secure line.'

Jim looked at his watch, zero-six hundred.

'Morning, Will.'

'Morning depends on what part of the world you're in.'

'True enough.'

'Assume you are all rested up after a couple hours sleep. The sergeant said everyone partied last night.'

'What's up?'

'Hospital doc in Rio de Janeiro called WHO, claiming he has a patient with smallpox.'

'Are we talking major or minor?'

'Good question. WHO contacted one of their staff near Rio. He doesn't believe it. He said the guy is ignorant of the differences in chickenpox, or just a misdiagnosis for monkeypox or Meningococcemia. CIA monitored the calls and sent them up to Bertrand. The WHO doc was dismissive. We need to take a look. The doctor that called it in sounded rational and knowledgeable about the differences between Variola minor and major. He worked in an eradication team back in the '70s. He should know what he is talking about. As unlikely as it is, if it proves to be smallpox, we need to make sure it's an isolated instance and find the source.'

Jim looked at his watch again. It was now twelve past six. 'If we leave in the next few minutes, we should be able to be in Rio by noon.'

'Keep me posted.'

'Mac. Wake up Marilyn, Doctor Dakine, Brush, and Glenda. Tell Marilyn to get the chopper fired up to take us to Cuenca. Have the others meet me in the canteen.'

Nusmen was already up and sitting in the canteen with small plastic collecting bags holding several plant samples spread out on a table. His hair looked wilder than usual, if that was possible. Wild and uncombed. Combined with his beanstalk body, bobbing Adam's apple and, the latest addition, his face decorations, he really did look like a vagrant rather than the research scientist he was. He had missed a buttonhole, his shirt hung lopsided, and it looked like his thin waist could barely hold up his drooping tan pants. They hung low, allowing the bottoms to fold on top of his bare feet.

As the group walked in, Jim grabbed a cup of coffee and a muffin. 'You're not eating these muffins, Nusmen? They're okay, but not quite up to Mazama muffins.'

'Huh. Oh yeah. I didn't see them.'

Jim looked at the others. 'Fifteen minutes, and we're out of here.'

Nusmen looked over and started to pick up his samples.

'Not you, Nusmen.'

'I want to go back to the lab. Why not me?'

'We're not going back to the lab. We're going to Brazil.'

Nusmen looked perplexed, as he often did.

'You will fly back with Neilly and the drone tomorrow to Fort Huachuca. From there, you can get a military transport to Fort Lewis.'

'Why can't I go straight back in the jet?'

'The jet will be in Rio de Janeiro for one reason. You can't fly commercial with your samples. You go to Huachuca.'

Brush looked at Glenda and started to chuckle. 'Fill us in, Jim.'

'We're going to check out what might be smallpox.'

Nusmen, who had been sulking like a child, jumped up. 'Not possible. It couldn't be. It's eradicated.'

'That's probably true, but the general feels it's worth looking into.' Jim looked at Maria. 'Your Bio HazMat team is already on their way. We'll hook up with them at the Rio Jobin Airport.'

'He obviously thinks it's serious, then? Accident of terrorism?'

'No idea. He thinks the doctor reporting it knows what he's talking about. Has to take it seriously. We'll find out if it is Variola major and, if so, where it came from.'

'What about WHO?'

'The doc reported it. The WHO rep in San Paulo blew it off. He'll arrive in Rio later today.'

Marilyn walked in, grabbed a muffin, and poured some coffee in a thermos. 'Ready when you are.'

***

A little over five hours later, the plane landed at Antonio Carlos Jobin International Airport, popularly known by its original name, Galeão International Airport. The steps descended, and Colonel Johnson, Major McGuire, Glenda Rose Stuart, and Doctor Maria Dakine walked down into the warmth rising from the tarmac.

Maria's hair was pulled back into a ponytail. From a distance, her hair appeared blond. But on closer inspection it was brown streaked with gray. She walked away from her Amazon adventure friends and toward her Bio HazMat team. 'Hey, you guys. When did you arrive?'

'About two hours ago.'

'Okay, let's get this show on the road. The BWC faxed me the latest just before we landed.' The HazMat team climbed into the waiting van. Jim, Brush, and Glenda climbed into a Toyota Land Cruiser. Two motorcycle police escorts turned on their sirens and flashers. The Toyota followed close behind with the white van in the rear.

Maria put a small earpiece in one ear, clipped a small mic on her collar, and said, 'Can you all hear me?'

'Loud and clear,' responded Jim, Brush, and Glenda, one by one. 'I want everyone in on the discussion. If this is serious, we won't have time to repeat things, and I want everyone on the same page,' said Doctor Dakine.

With their motorcycle escort, they rapidly bullied their way through the twelve miles of streets to Hospital Municipal Souza Aguiar.

'I don't think we can assume, Doctor Dakine, that this is Variola, either major or minor, ma'am,' said the twenty-six-year-old, five-foot six-inch, bronze-skinned team's disease specialist, Trisha Marshall.

'Trisha, we are not formal in our group. Call me Maria and with your permission,' she said with a mischievous smile, 'I'll call you Trisha. We haven't worked together since you replaced Adam. I know, however, your credentials and the recommendation that you received from your mentor. I have the highest respect for Doctor Ward at the School of Hygiene and Tropical Medicine in London who unequivocally recommended you. I spent two months working with him at Scripps Institute once. He was very good. I developed a lot of respect for him,' said Maria.

'Of course, we can't assume anything,' interjected the team's virologist, Geoffrey. 'The hospital is not generally well-equipped. It has a functional Transmission Electron Microscope but no Scanning scope. We collect a sample, and we'll soon have a positive ID. SEM would be quicker, but I can make a positive ID with the TEM.'

Doctor Dakine turned to Geoffrey. 'How fast can you get a sample prepared and loaded?'

'I'll collect a sample when you start the clinical. Maybe ninety minutes, barring any problems with their equipment, we'll have an answer. It's been a long time since I used a glass knife instead of a diamond knife.' His voice lowered, while his mind pulled memories from his early student days. 'It's a public hospital, and they don't have the latest and greatest.'

'Colonel Johnson will be present at the clinical. She turned to Corporal Mendez, 'Quick as you can, make sure you round up all those that have been in contact with the patient and use the police to detain them until we have an answer.

'Yes, ma'am.'

'Who's in charge?' asked Geoffrey. 'You as our team leader, or Colonel Johnson, or the general?'

Maria laughed. 'Geoffrey, and you too, Trisha, are both new to working in the field. While the general is our ultimate authority, if you have brains in your noggin, you'll quickly realize that Colonel Johnson has the general's full confidence. He runs all field operations, not to mention he is the BWC's acting director and a specialist in pathogens. In other words, he is your bosses' boss. You will also notice that the colonel is not autocratic. Do your jobs, speak your mind, and we'll all work well together. To answer your question, I'm in charge of our team, and there is a chain of command.'

'I just didn't know when it came to clinical...,' stammered Geoffrey.

'Forget it. We have things to discuss. Let's go over what we know. The doctor that called WHO is Doctor Miguel Iniz. They directed him to their local rep for this area, Doctor Wolfgang Krumbine, who is, I believe, a German microbiologist by training. Doctor Iniz is certain of his diagnosis, and the WHO rep, Krumbine, says *Variola major* is clearly a misdiagnosis, so he is not concerned. The male patient is thought to be out of work, from a remote area of the Pantanal, and living on the streets. Krumbine asserts the man might have chickenpox, a *Herpesvirus simiri,* or even a HIV-1, the main virus of AIDS that's jumped species from a monkey with simian immunodeficiency, SIM, or a monkeypox that leaped the species barrier, which in itself would be interesting, however improbable. Or, he suggests, it is more likely to be a Herpes—*Meningococcemia.'*

'Other than herpes, the others are remote possibilities, to say the least. But as we discovered with HIV-1, the virus resides comfortably in primates, and when it jumps species to humans, it becomes aggressive in its new host. It killed close to thirty-two million, which is pretty aggressive. Doctor Krumbine will arrive at sixteen hundred. We should have it identified by then, so not much use in speculating until Geoffrey scopes it out. General Crystal's opinion is that this Doc Iniz is credible. He worked on the eradication with the World Health Organization in the '70s. We assume it is serious until we have evidence to the contrary.'

'Maybe a stupid question. Why didn't this Iniz use the TEM to ID it?' asked Brush.

'The only operator they have is on vacation.'

'Along the same lines, why isn't WHO taking his opinion seriously?' added Glenda.

'Might be their rep Krumbine isn't. There was a history of infighting all through the eradication program,' said Maria. 'I sat in on one of the never-ending debates on whether to destroy it. The fight still goes on with one side saying it has research value, and we have no right to facilitate an extinction of a species; the other side argues we have its DNA sequenced, so there is no need to keep the whole virus.'

Maria picked up the report that had been provided by Doctor Iniz.

'Okay. The patient, male, mid-forties presented with a rash with pustules, moderate temperature, often incoherent, complained of back pain. They have done cultures and found *Bartonella henselae*, which if you are not up on it, is the main bacterial causal agent of Bartonellosis in humans. There was no evidence of *Neisseria*, the cause of Meningococcemia, in the cultures that the WHO doc suggested as a possible cause. Of course, we'll double-check everything during our workup. The man is a mess. Sores, fleas, a tapeworm, oral cavity carcinoma, jaundice. No telling what else is going on inside his body.'

'There isn't room for much else,' said Trisha attempting to add a little humor.

Maria continued, 'Geoffrey brought along our latest and greatest optical scope, but still the resolution is only to three microns. Variola is nearly that big, and while not likely, it's possible that a strain could push over three microns.'

'I'll do a quick exam in the optical scope first,' said Geoffrey. If it's abnormally large, and we can see it, we can assume it's VAR. Then I'll get a positive ID in the transmission microscope.'

'That,' said Maria, 'and I can also do limited immunoprecipitation tests. Hopefully, that will give us a clear ID fast. If we ID it as VAR major, we'll need to send samples back to BWC right away, and, by protocol, also to the CDC as soon as possible.'

'What else do you want me to focus on?' asked Trisha.

'See what other bugs you can identify in the optical scope, and Sunita, start interviewing and compile a list of everyone exposed, so we can start vaccinating if the ID is positive. Have Mendez get the names of the people he is detaining.'

'What's the time limit from exposure to when a vaccine works?' asked Glenda, admiring Maria's knowledge and quick-talking style.

'That's the virus's weakness and our good fortune. Typically, from exposure to about the ninth or tenth day, when there is the first sign of a rash. With a vaccine, it is pretty easy to contain with the long incubation period, and the reason it was eradicated, or we thought it was. Historically, why it killed so many, hundreds of millions of people, was because vaccination had not been discovered. They didn't even bother to name babies, way back when, until after they survived. Those that did survive were disfigured for life.'

'It's a big stretch that it's smallpox, isn't it, Doctor?' asked Glenda.

'Of course, it is highly unlikely. There have been a couple of cases through the years after the eradication in 1977. Lax lab protocols. Allegedly, there are only two places that have stocks. The CDC and the Russians' facility at Zagorst. The CDC has over 400 strains suspended in liquid nitrogen at minus ninety-four degrees Fahrenheit. I had the pleasure of seeing them a long time ago.'

'The Russians tried to weaponize it, didn't they?' asked Geoffrey.

'The Russians experimented and produced large quantities of Variola major. They even successfully tested bomblets, with smallpox delivered by rockets. The general sent us a full history if you are interested in reading it.'

Jim added. 'Only two official stocks of smallpox, yet we have samples at BWC, which makes two official and one unofficial. No telling how many other governments or labs have secret or unofficial stockpiles.'

Chapter 34

Cherry held the cyclic in her left hand. The chopper flew level above the wide river then started to slow. 'Edge the stick forward,' Jago said, tapping the airspeed indicator.

'Very easy. Many people can fly this,' said Cherry.

'We have to do this fast,' Jago said, 'I have the controls. That means you let go inmediatamente, cariño.'

Jago slowed the forward motion until the helicopter was motionless. 'Now, Cherry, cariño, you say *I have the controls*, and I let go, and you hover, no?'

'I have them.'

Jago let go.

'Sí, easy as I say.'

The Huey held steady for about two seconds before starting to move slightly to one side. Cherry overcorrected, and then it moved too far to the right. She jerked the cyclic back to the left. Within seconds, it was lurching out of control.

'I have the controls.' Jago smiled as he stabilized the chopper, pushing the cyclic forward and resuming their forward speed. 'Easy, no?'

'Sí, easy for you.'

'How you learn to do this?'

'Long time ago a friend taught me, like I am teaching you. He was killed and I had to fly the helicopter many miles to get home.'

'Then you will teach me when we return to bring this helicopter home. It is harder than I thought.'

'Do not feel bad. No one hovers without practice. We need to find a small open place not far from the river. I think we not crash land again. It is valuable to us. In the future, we will bring fuel and take it home.'

'We take the gold with us?' asked Cherry.

'It is too heavy to carry and leaves us vulnerable. We can't move fast or react fast weighed down. We hide it a little way from our helicóptero, corazón.'

***

'The Veep is happy, I hear. The daughter of his friend is tucked away safe in Quito' said Martin. 'Your boys ever fail?'

'Nobody's perfect, Martin,' said General Crystal. 'But I have faith in them. This mission, though, turned out to be easy. The FARC were the good guys, and she was in no real danger. They will be a good contact if we are ever in need of information from that part of the world. I'll have Colonel Johnson brief you.'

'As you asked, we're tracking them on sat,' said Martin. 'They parked the chopper in the jungle and are moving north along the edge of the river.'

'Are they likely to encounter the military?'

'Not for 100 miles or so.'

Bertrand sat shuffling through several papers. 'I can't get a story put together about what the big happening is with the Colombian Army. It bothers me. There are rumblings there, and they fit a story someway or other. Our contacts can't learn anything. It's means something is happening. I want to know what it is. Anything new with the report of possible smallpox?'

'The BWC team and a Bio HazMat just arrived at the hospital. It's a low probability that it will turn out to be Variola major.'

'We've just about finished a profile on Iniz,' said Martin. 'Everything so far in his background supports him as knowledgeable and credible.'

'It's easy to confuse smallpox, especially since not many have firsthand experience with it anymore. Iniz, however, has experience, so it is possible he is right. We'll soon know.'

***

'When are we going back?' whined Nusmen.

Neilly looked at Marilyn and shook his head. Without answering, he turned and walked away.

'What's his problem?' asked Nusmen.

Marilyn chuckled. 'I am supposing, Nus, it's you. You need to chill. My bird is ready to fly. The trucks are on the road back and will get to the airport about the same time we do. It won't be long now.'

'But I have to get back right away.'

'Look, bud. Go play with your samples or whatever and keep quiet. Otherwise, you'll piss everyone off, and they'll leave you here to fend for yourself. They want to get back, too. So, enough already. Just think, will ya? We can't leave the airport until the trucks get there.'

Eight plus hours later, the huge Globemaster III touched down at Libby Field at Fort Huachuca, Arizona.

Nusmen walked up to Neilly, 'Why don't you take me back to the lab? I have important things to work on.'

Neilly and Mac looked at each other and couldn't contain themselves. They used to think Nusmen was weird. The current thinking, however, tended toward serious social problems.

'Mac, get Marilyn to see if she can rustle up transport for our ruffle-topped twig before he either blows away in this desert wind or drives us all nuts.'

'He's strange, all right. Looks like I used to picture Ichabod Crane as a kid. Supposed to be brilliant, though.'

'Yeah, single-focused on his projects…Personality could use a little work. Well, he is sort of humorous, if you view it the right way. Let's get the drone unloaded; I want to get out of here and back to home base too. We'll let Knight worry about the paperwork for the one sprouting plants in the jungle.'

'Okay, boss.'

Nusmen was feeling happier by the minute. The general's jet whisked him directly to Fort Lewis. He couldn't help smiling to himself. *I'm the lab manager. Well, Barbara is really. I'm sitting here on a private jet with a bag full of rare medicinal plants from the world's last and largest biodiversity laboratory.*

Nusmen walked as fast as he could, dragging two rolling olive drab army duffel bags full of samples. If he had flown commercial, the U.S. border protection would have been overjoyed to intercept them, thinking they were protecting the world, or at least the U.S., from dangers of the exotic natural world. He descended in the elevator, making a face at the camera. As he got out of the elevator, he turned serious, 'Where's Heather?' he demanded from the first person he saw.

'Heather who?' asked the man, backing away.

Then he saw his friend, Brad.

'Nus, returned from his adventures in the outside world.'

'Where's Heather?'

'I think she left right after you did.'

'No matter. Come with me and help me get these sorted. They're important. Some need to get in the freezers ASAP.'

'I can't, dude, I'm in the middle of a splicing experiment.'

'But I need help.'

'What's on your face. War paint?'

'Huh, what?'

'Cute, Nus. I'm headed to area thirty-one. Gotta go.'

'Try to find somebody for me.'

'You should have called Doctor Milton on your way back if you needed help.'

'I didn't think.'

'As I said, I gotta go. Put your stuff down and page her. She'll know who's available. Sayonara.'

It took Nusmen until six in the morning to sort the samples. Separating them, freezing some, and preparing others for various analyses: it would take him hours more before he had samples in the mass specs, high-performance liquid chromatography, Fourier transform infrared, and small bits separated for DNA analysis. That he might be tired never crossed his mind. In his excitement, he focused only on what he was doing; he forgot about the other experiments he had been working on, as well about eating and sleeping.

He went to his room, satisfied that the samples were safely stored and being analyzed. He decided to lie down. Seconds later, he bolted up. Barbara was usually in by now. He ran a few steps and slowed to a walk, afraid he would run into her and get chastised for running again.

'Barbara, what's the status of the phage experiments?'

'I thought you had forgotten all about them. Sit down. This is going to take a while.'

'I want to hear, but the FTIR samples will be finished in a few minutes. We don't have the data analyses working just right yet.'

'I'll have a tech look at them. Sit still and pay attention until I'm finished.'

Nusmen knew he was stuck, even though he did want to hear. He bit his lip, fidgeted, and rapidly tapped his foot.

Barbara squinted her eyes and stared at him until he gave in and became still.

Chapter 35

The silver Peugeot van and the white Toyota Land Cruiser pulled through the open gate and stopped at the entrance under a sign that read Hospital Municipal Souza Aguiar.

'I don't know why I expected this hospital to look old,' said Glenda. It's architecturally modern yet weatherworn.'

'A big box with colored stripes,' said Brush.

'Let's hop to it,' said Doctor Dakine, tumbling out of the van, almost falling onto the concrete. She made a characteristic lopsided grin and turned to the two corporals who had come with the team. 'Bring the two large red bags and follow us.'

'Interesting tumble. She's sorta cute,' said Brush.

'Un-huh,' said Glenda as she shook her head, 'I like her. Seems like she knows what she is talking about. A down to earth, quiet, authoritative woman. Not a snooty doc.'

'Fits right in.'

They walked rapidly through the white-tiled entrance and were met by Doctor Iniz.

He was tall and thin with wiry dark hair, tinged, here and there, with gray. His complexion was light and golden.

'Nice to have all of you here. Follow me.' He turned and set off at a fast pace. Maria, who was in the habit of walking fast herself, almost had to jog to keep up with his long strides.

'He is very bad. It is smallpox, I am certain.'

'We'll see. What's his condition?'

'Critical. Fever has gone down.'

'Regardless of what he has, we need to start collecting patient contact information. Will you introduce my epidemiologist, Sunita, to your staff, so she can start that process?'

They stopped at a nurse's station, and Iniz introduced Sunita to the staff assembled, including a male nurse who would direct Geoffrey to the TEM for analysis.

'Let's suit up and see our patient,' said Maria.

Trisha opened a small rolling suitcase and passed around gowns, gloves, and masks. When everyone was ready, they walked down a once white, polished stone corridor with white tiled walls to a double door where a uniformed guard stood, holding an army assault rifle. They opened the doors and went down another short corridor. A handwritten name was posted on the door: "Pan." Below that was another sign in red letters labeled "Quarantine."

'That his last name?' asked Doctor Dakine.

'We don't know his name, so we had to come up with something. Everyone got tired of referring to him as the patient.'

While they fussed with their gowns and face masks, Brush asked, 'What's the deal with the name they are calling this guy?'

'Pan is the Greek god of the wild. Del Fauno in my language, but much shorter or usually abbreviated as Pan.' He opened the door and walked to the curtains shrouding the patient's bed and pulled them back.

Geoffrey, Trisha, and Maria followed Doctor Iniz to the side of the patient's bed. Geoffrey opened a hard-plastic container and pulled out two test tubes from their slots. 'Doctor, if I may, I am not here for the clinical discussion. I need to take this to your electron microscopy facility after I look in the optical scope.'

'Certainly. Please procced.'

Geoffrey used a curette to collect a sample from an oozing pustule on the patient's forearm and placed it into one of the test tubes. Then he repeated the process. Pan's forearms and face were barely visible beneath the pustules and forming scabs. Geoffrey nodded, and said, 'I'll have a result as quick as I can.' He handed one of the tubes to Trisha. At the door, he dropped his gown, hat, and mask in a foot-operated bin, turned back to the group, nodded, and walked out to where a man wearing a name tag that read Gomez was waiting.

'He smells awful,' said Glenda.

'Yes, typical,' said Doctor Iniz.

'I have only seen pictures,' said Maria, 'but this looks to be a pox.'

Gomez led Trisha and Geoffrey back down the hall and, just before the double door with its guard, he turned into a small room with three tables.

'It is probably alastram, Variola minor, but... antigenically indistinguishable from major,' said Trisha as she lifted a box containing the heavy Leitz optical microscope onto a table that had been set per their earlier request. 'I'll take a quick look and then prepare the slides as you pass me samples.'

Looking at Doctor Iniz, Maria said, 'I've read the reports you sent. But tell me everything from the beginning.'

'Ten days ago, emergency services responded to a call concerning a comatose man in an alley.'

'Is the location name in your report?' asked Jim.

'It's in an orange binder at the nurses' station.'

'Thank you. Please continue.'

'He was brought to our emergency room at ten twenty-six p.m., Saturday the fifteenth. He was incoherent. The medics said he seemed to be in pain. He kept holding his back with one hand and his head with the other. He appeared to be having back spasms. His temperature was thirty-nine and has since dropped to just below thirty-eight. That is approximately 102 to just below 100 in your country.'

Maria didn't comment.

He continued, 'His blood pressure was 143 over 95. Blood and culture tests are in the report.'

'Have you tried to locate any friends or relatives?'

'He was out of work and lived on the street. The police took his fingerprints and found no record of the man. Local police are interviewing transients in the area.'

'Doubt if that will do much good. It's like asking the enemy for information,' said Brush.

'To continue, he had a rash that three days ago evolved to papulovesicles, and then to the raised red pustules you see now, that are starting to form scabs.' He passed a clipboard to Doctor Dakine. 'Here are the complete records. I instructed everyone to keep detailed notes and leave nothing out.'

'We'll do a complete exam when you're finished.'

Doctor Iniz nodded.

'I can see there is ocular damage. I would like to start him on cidofovir.'

'We have been washing his eyes and were not able to prevent further damage. What is this drug you wish to try?'

'It's an antiviral used for cytomegalovirus retinitis, primarily for AIDS. It might help. Your diagnosis then, Doctor Iniz?'

'I have seen it before. I am confident that it is something we should not be seeing, Variola major. The "Angel of Death" as we called it. My fear is it is a new strain or a new recombinant virus. One that has jumped species, possibly.'

His voice turned low, and he spoke so softly they barely heard, 'or maybe somehow from the Vektor Institute.'

'What did you say, Doctor? I didn't hear that,' said Maria.

When there was no response, Glenda said, 'I think he said Vector.'

'The Vektor Institute in Novorsibirsk, Russia.' said Jim.

Doctor Iniz jerked his head and looked at Jim and said a barely audible, 'Yes.'

Jim sensed there was much more to Doctor Iniz's history with WHO. They needed to have a much deeper discussion.

'Sorry. Discúlpeme. It is a long personal story from my early days in Puerto Rico and the effort to rid the world of smallpox. I continue. We don't know his time from exposure to the rash. Thus, we have no idea if it exhibits the typical ten plus or minus days. If it is shorter, of course, that creates a greater risk.'

'If the patient, Pan,' interjected Maria, 'had an advanced rash on admission, as you say, we have no idea of the incubation period. It could be fulminating, or, as I remember, it has been called sledgehammer smallpox. We need to determine his history before admission.'

'Have you inoculated anyone?'

'We have no vaccine. The World Health Organization has stocks in Sao Paulo. Doctor Krumbine said it was unnecessary to bring them with him today.'

'It could be smallpox. My opinion is we have more than sufficient evidence to begin inoculating those exposed, especially those we can determine were the first exposed. Doctor, if you agree, we begin immediately. We have a small supply with us. Sunita should have an initial list compiled soon. We can start with the staff.'

'You know my diagnosis was and is smallpox, and I agree we should begin inoculating immediately.'

'One further question,' said Maria. 'It would be very useful to have a room that we can filter and negatively pressurize. Can you assign someone in authority to see if a suitable room can be found?'

'Yes, if you'll excuse me, I'll go check for such a room now.'

Jim, followed by Brush and Glenda, turned and left with Doctor Iniz. Outside the room, Jim asked him, 'Can you find a small-statured male we can borrow as an interpreter?'

The doctor raised his eyebrows in confusion, 'Sim. Sorry. It is sometimes difficult not to answer in Portuguese. So, yes, it is possible. Why?'

'We don't want to intimidate people on the street.'

'I shall try to find such a person and send him back to the nurses' station.'

'Quickly, Doctor. We will want to start immediately.'

Doctor Iniz started to say something. Instead, he turned away.

'You were about to say something, Doctor, about the Vektor Institute. 'Perhaps we can have a discussion later?'

Doctor Iniz turned and held out his hand, 'Doctor Miguel Iniz, and you are?'

'Doctor James Johnson.'

'I see. You are the colonel that the general in Washington said would be arriving.' Then he turned and walked rapidly down the hall toward the swinging doors.

'What's the plan, then?' asked Brush.

'We see who he finds for us, and scruff him up some, so he blends in with the street people,' said Jim. 'He questions them, says he has money for anyone with information, and brings them to us. If this is V. major, we'll have a leg up on finding out where it came from and who else was exposed. We need someone fluent in Portuguese that they will accept. Mostly I want to look around the area and start getting an image of what might have happened.'

'I'll call Sheilla and ask her to assess the area,' said. Glenda. 'Do we get the police into the area to prevent the transients from leaving, Colonel?'

'Not yet. Not until we know what it is for sure. We keep a low profile until we find some answers. If Doctor Dakine's team says Variola major, we change our approach. If it is smallpox, there'll be a lot more people arriving,' said Jim. 'Their mission will be the control of its spread. Ours will be to locate the source.'

'I'm starting to like this,' said Glenda. 'The containment is up to them. We play detectives, looking for bad players. I like investigations. They're what I trained for.'

'WHO will send a small army, and many will be good at their jobs. But they will also get in our way with too many rules and procedures. I want to track down the source before they get here. Let's get our translator and get to where Pan was picked up. Brush, make sure he looks his part. Glenda, could you get the info that the doc said was at the desk about where Pan was picked up? And call Sheilla. I'll fill the general in and meet you at the Land Cruiser, fifteen minutes. I need to call Heather too.'

'Say hi for me,' said Glenda.

Chapter 36

'Will, it's a pox. We'll know which one shortly. Symptoms suggest it's aggressive, so it seems probable it's V. major. Everything's in motion. The WHO rep, Doctor Krumbine, sounds arrogant.'

'Katarina can work up profiles,' said the general. 'The other likely players, too.'

'I'd like Krumbine's background before he arrives.'

'Anything else?'

'Sunita has a secure fax hookup to BWC. Corporal Mendez will send hard copies. Glenda is talking to Sheilla, too.'

'Sheilla will be the main contact. CIA will back up BWC. I'll liaise with World Health if needed. We'll be ahead of them, however, if this materializes. We operate courteous but independent. Need anything else, let me know.'

Before the general could hang up, Jim said, 'One more thing. See if you can get any briefs the agency has on smallpox rumors with any governments. Especially Russia. The Vektor Institute in particular.'

'Anything else?'

'Talk later, Will.' They had worked together long enough that Jim did not have to say he would keep the general informed of important developments. They both knew what they needed to do, and neither liked repeating the obvious.

Jim let the sat phone drop to his side, wondering how long he would be here. *No way to know at this point.*

He punched in Heather's encrypted bag phone number,

wondering if she would be where she could hear it. She picked up on the second ring.

'Hi. How are my two favorite people?'

'Hi,' she said, with surprise. 'I've missed your voice.'

'Missed you, too.'

'Everything is fine here. Pedro, the little rascal, got into a fight at school. Don't ask me who won.'

'Is he okay?'

'Actually, he seemed happy about it. He's out checking the water with Shuskin and Ben. He seems to like talking to the old guy. Maybe Shuskin will fill me in about the disagreement. He wouldn't say much to his mom. Is that normal?'

'It will take me a while to remember back that far. How's Lola and Shuskin, Betty Lou… Ben?'

'All good. Ben, the old guy, and Pedro seem to be the happy trio.'

'You saw something in Shuskin I guess I missed. Hope you are right about it.'

'I have no doubt. He's almost a normal old man, around the boys anyway. Still hides from strangers. When are you coming home?'

'I don't know for sure. We were headed home today. Instead, we flew to Rio. There's a new confidential issue, an orthopox, possibly smallpox. If not, I'll likely be back tomorrow. I'll call and let you know in the next hour if it's smallpox.' He hesitated, his old avoidance taking hold for a second. Then, he overcame the reservation and said, 'If it is Variola, it will take longer as we need to find the source. Hopefully not bioterrorism. Maria and her team are here. Guessing it will take a day or two to track the cause. If it's from a lab that shouldn't have it, it probably won't take long. If it's a government or terrorist release, that makes it more complicated.'

'I want you here for Christmas.'

'Me too. Still possible it isn't smallpox and, if so, I'll be back as soon as.'

'You'll let me know when you know for sure if it's smallpox?'

'Less than an hour.'

'I'll get Pedro and keep him with me, so you can talk to him when you call back. He misses his dad. How did Nus behave in the Amazon? I wanted to go. Did he act stupid?'

'He was himself. Got wasted with the local shaman. Might take a while to get rid of his face tats, if he ever can. Collected a lot of samples.'

'Oh, wow. I wonder… I want to know what they are.'

'I thought you would. I'll call you as soon as Maria identifies the virus.'

'I love you, mister.'

'I know. Tell Pedro to keep out of trouble.'

'You can tell him yourself. When you do, tell him fighting is not good.'

***

Outside Mateo's room, there was a lot of talking. Finally, two officers—one the arrogant captain and General Ramos—walked into the room.

'Doctor Salvatore Pazano,' said General Ramos.

'General, it is a pleasure to see one of my patients looking so healthy and with several promotions, too.'

'Yes, Doctor. You took care of me and removed the bullet.'

'And no trouble with your leg?'

'Nothing but a reminder that the FARC, in battle, sometimes miss the heart.'

'I overheard the captain asking my aide about this man's identity. He mentioned you, not all that pleasantly I might add. It is my son's wedding reception. But still, a little escape and greeting you after all these years seemed a nice respite. I don't know this man. What is wrong with him?'

'I do not know. I'm not sure. I suspect a virus. Something that perhaps I have not seen previously. A virus expert should be here soon. The MPs called a couple of minutes ago to say they had passed him through. He is a Russian.'

'That would be Doctor Ivanov.'

'Yes. You know him?'

'Not personally, but his asylum issues from his home country are well-known. Many countries would not accept him.'

'An intriguing past, no?'

'I think you could say that.'

As the door opened, Viktor said, 'Not so intriguing, I fear. Just a scientist, by God's grace.'

'I thought Russians did not believe in God,' said General Ramos.

'That is not quite correct, many do. What I mean is, it is not my belief system. Rather, what part of my name means in Russian.'

'Thank you for coming on a Saturday night,' said Salvatore Pazano. 'I am sorry, are you a clinician, or…?'

Before he could finish the sentence, Viktor Ivanov answered that he held both a Ph.D. and M.D., specializing in virology.

'Please, then, tell us what you think.'

Doctor Ivanov asked for the patient's notes. He scanned them. Then, he peered at the patient. Looked at his eyes and arms. Opened Mateo's mouth just as Doctor Pazano had earlier. 'Doctor, please come here. You noted the blotches in his oral cavity. Look closely at his face and then at his hands and arms. What do you see?'

'I don't see anything. No, wait. There are some faint red blotches. They are new.'

'Do you have a diagnosis?'

'I think no. We need to see how the patient does overnight and see what the tests can tell us. If you have the time, General, let's the three of us go to your office. I'd like to hear how your rise to top general came about. Also, I would very much like a coffee. I have grown rather fond of your Colombian coffee.'

Chapter 37

Will Crystal sat on the sofa in his office, next to Bertrand Gupta. Sitting in chairs facing them across a wide, gleaming, mahogany coffee table were Deputy Director of Intelligence, Martin Pearson, and next to him, former head of National Clandestine Services and now Deputy Director, Eric Sands. Eileen Skinner sat in the third chair. She had replaced Eric Sands as the head of NCS.

'There is nothing positive to report from Rio yet,' said the general. 'Colonel Johnson just called, and they should have an ID in a few minutes. Clinical points to smallpox. This doesn't concern us unless it involves a hostile government. Have a look at our intel and see if there are any reports or mentions of smallpox, Variola, orthopox viruses, any viruses, or bioterror alerts.'

'I was involved with a Russian virologist's defection,' said Eileen. 'I remember him telling us about the extensive incubation devices and missile delivery systems they had developed. I recall that the Russian scientists did a lot of research on shortening the incubation time to make it harder to identify and inoculate for.'

'No one under twenty in the world has had a vaccination,' said General Crystal. 'With the average ten-day time frame from exposure to showing symptoms, it is easy to inoculate and prevent its spread. However, it's most efficacious in the first four days. Shorten that incubation period, and the chance of an uncontrollable epidemic increases exponentially.'

'I remember the Russian telling me that they researched how to splice it with other viruses, such as Ebola and Marburg. I don't believe they were successful.'

'Dig into your files and get me a summary of the Russian and, if he's still alive, where he's located.'

'I can tell you now. He's in Bogotá.'

***

Angélica placed the phone back in its cradle. 'They are expecting us next Tuesday. Mrs. Marsh says they will have all the largest organizations present, and she is looking forward to our arrival.'

'Do you know these groups?' asked President Noboa.

'I have heard of the World Wildlife Federation and Amazon Watch. I have never heard of Mrs. Marsh's association. It is, I hear, influential, and coordinates between the various groups. She says that it is an important step forward having the government of Ecuador supporting efforts to preserve the indigenous people and the environment. I am proud of you, Papá.'

Noboa looked fondly at his daughter. He felt an overwhelming love for her that bubbled into his consciousness. *How I have wasted my life with superfluous concerns,* he thought. 'You have matured, my dear, into a force to be reckoned with.'

Angel felt confident about her new-found ambitions. She now had a real purpose in her life. *I wonder where Jago is, what he is doing, if he is okay.* He was only one small reason for this change in her. Her new self had always been there, hiding below the silly schoolgirl antics and her thrusts and parries into the real world. Directionless. Seeing the Shuar people, the cruelty of the miners, and their blood spread on the ground, erased her childish thoughts. Slammed by reality, she had a revelation about her romantic notion of being a rebel—it was not one she could endure. Her personality solidified, finding its comfort zone between the romanticized jungle rebel and the potentially powerful position as the daughter of the president of Ecuador.

Jago and the colonel gave her the model of how to lead, how to act. Her father gave her the ability and connections. She would take the lead and give the Amazon a future, not of first world innovation and development, but rather of laissez-faire leadership. Largely left alone, these people were happy. Could as much be said for those in the cities?

***

Jago was pleased with the small clearing they had spotted. It was over a kilometer from the river, far enough not to be stumbled upon by accident. They dug a hole, filled it with bags of gold, covered it, scattered debris on the surface, and made notches on three trees that triangulated their treasure's position. He was pleased that they would bring wealth to the FARC, not only with the gold but with the helicopter. San had contributed to bringing that wealth. Jago was sad over his loss. He had cared for him, even though he recognized that San was not the best of their lot.

'It will take a long while to pick our way to the river,' said Lobo.

'We will find you after we finish camouflaging the helicopter.'

Three hours later, Jago's unique birdcall was answered by Cherry from up the river, and then by Lobo from the opposite direction. Jago, followed by Chico, León, and Carlos emerged onto the trail and turned north toward their home territory. The first drops of the afternoon deluge were starting to fall. They luxuriated in the warm cleansing.

'All signs of our passing soon gone,' said the short Chico, as he looked up at Lobo. They moved slowly until Cherry caught up with them. The heavy rain felt warm as it turned the path to mud and soaked through their clothes. Together now, the band picked up their pace. The rain would soon stop, and they would find a camp for the night, knowing their gold was safely buried, as was their lost companion, San.

Most of them only felt a small sense of loss for San. He had never been popular. Now, entombed in the miners' cave, he slipped into their memory, as had many of their friends and past companions. They were used to death and shifted back into the present, embracing life. What had started as a fight for survival with the Colombian army had turned into a golden fantasy.

They were all silently recalling the same thing, as Carlos said, 'Those norteamericanos were no bad men, I think.'

'They're okay,' said Chico.

'Maybe yes, maybe no,' said Lobo. 'This is a good place to leave the trail for the night.'

A small track led into the jungle. They followed it for several hundred meters to a small open area. The rain stopped as abruptly as it had begun. They settled in for the evening, comfortable, with a small fire heating a pot of water for coffee. They had food left that the Americans had given them.

'Yes, yes, I like them very much. Not what I would have expected,' said Chico.

'It is true,' added Jago. 'It is their government that is bad, just like ours.' As the sky darkened, they reminisced about their recent adventures. All, that is, except for Cherry whose thoughts were about the man she had met and would never have. Her thoughts were pleasant ones. Like Jim, she was a consummate realist. She now had Jago and would, for the first time, commit to him. Thoughts of Brush made her blush inside—a pleasant feeling. *The future will be what it will be,* a phrase she had liked when she heard one of the Americans saying it during the past few days.

Chapter 38

'Jim, meet Davi, our interpreter,' said Brush. Davi did not look happy.

'You ready, Davi? This is important. The people you are going to talk to will not want to talk to outsiders. You think you can convince them you are not a threat?'

'I will try, sir.'

'Do you know anything about the area near Rue Bambina?'

'No. But it is rua here, not rue.'

'How is your driving?'

Davi perked up a little, 'Very good.'

'You drive. Let's hit it.'

The look on Davi's face said he was unfamiliar with that Americanism.

Brush said, 'That means, let's start driving to Rua Bambina, not that you are going to hit something.'

As the Land Cruiser turned out of the hospital emergency entrance, Brush said, 'Let's check comms.' Glenda sat in front, navigating with a cigar box-sized, handheld GPS. Davi cruised at a respectable speed, but driving cautiously. 'Davi, don't kill anyone, but step it up. We need to get there pronto, pal,' said Brush.

'Sheilla,' said Jim. 'Are you tracking us?'

'Little red dot moving along.'

'See if you can find any missions, research labs, or hospitals near our destination.'

'On it, Jim. You look to be about twenty minutes to your

destination.'

'Jim,' said Maria, 'This is not a huge surprise. But Geoffrey says no doubt it is, and I quote, 'the big bad old dumbbell-shaped virus' that could only be VAR. The assay is positive too.'

'Okay. I'll let you know what the situation looks like where they picked up Pan. Epidemiology is probably the most important front to work on besides the patient.'

'We're starting containment procedures now at the hospital,' said Maria.

'Call the general; let him know. Then get the rest of our teams here. Tell him I also want Neilly's Spanish speakers here as soon as. The WHO rep is going to take over, so start getting ready for that. We'll assist until he gets organized. After, we focus on our main mission: finding the source.'

Not too happily, Jim dialed Heather. 'It's Variola major. If we can find the source, and it's not a terrorist operation, I'll still be home quick like. Is Pedro there?'

'Dad, Dad, where are you?'

'Brazil.'

'You take me to the jungle? We fly in a helicopter? When you come home?'

'Hum. Three questions in a row. You are learning from your mother.'

'Yes. Dad, you teach me to…'

Jim guessed he was going to say fight. He interrupted him before he could say it. 'We'll talk about fighting when I get back.'

'Promise?'

'Yes. I would like you and Heather to visit the Amazon. The people are very nice. Would you like that?'

'I like it.'

'I'll be home as soon as I can. See you soon. You be good. Pass the phone to your mother.'

Pedro did as he was told and passed the phone to Heather. Jim could hear him in the background, saying. 'Yes, you teach me.' He chuckled thinking it was good that he had not said, 'You teach me to fight'.

'Teach what?' asked Heather.

'Lots of things. Gotta go. Call you later.'

Heather understood that Jim would not say that unless he did have to hang up. 'Take care. No more firefights, please.'

'Bye. Talk soon, beautiful.'

The Land Cruiser turned down Rua Bambina. 'Glenda, Pan's pickup point?'

'Two blocks up on the right.'

'Stop here, Davi. Brush, take a look around.'

'Always wanted to stroll around the back alleys of Rio. Let you know if anything is interesting.'

The silver sports UTE continued down the street.

'Glenda, tell him where to turn, so we can do a grid search of the area. Maybe we'll spot something.'

'Jim,' said Sheilla. 'No labs or research facilities anywhere close. Several clinics and one hospital.'

'Tell me about the hospital. What's the name? Why wouldn't emergency services take our guy there?

'I'll see if I can figure that out.'

Glenda held her hand up. 'I got it. It's not a real hospital. Got to be our place. Three blocks away. Davi, turn right, then left back to Bambina.'

Over their radio, Brush said, 'Easy one, guys, and lady. I walked from Pan's alley about two blocks, and a small sign on the building said something that looks to me like infectious diseases.'

'You need to *brush* up on your romance languages, mister.'

'Very funny, honey.'

'The name I'm showing is the "Centro Nacional de Infecção,"' said Glenda.

'You got that, Sheilla?

'I do, Colonel.'

'Get everything you can on it and give us a summary. Then do a more in-depth workup. Who's your contact at CIA?'

'Martin Pearson.'

'See what they have on the place. Then I need to know who's in charge.'

'Late night wakeup call, eh?' said Brush.

'Seems like the thing to do. Let's go back to the alley and let Davi earn his keep.'

***

'Bertrand, explain to the oversight committee what we are dealing with, and give them my apologies. I'm going to coordinate our response until WHO takes over. Just shows it's not as easy as we thought to keep a killer locked away in a bottle.'

'Are you considering its release part of a bioterrorism plot?'

'We have to keep that in mind, but no, I doubt it. Colonel Johnson will have it tracked down soon enough. I want to keep on top of it with WHO and the CDC, so we don't run afoul of them, or their authority and procedures. If, on the off chance, it is bioterrorism, BWC will take the lead.'

***

'General Ramos, I apologize for misleading you. Some other time, I would be interested in hearing about your rise to lieutenant general, and I would appreciate that coffee I mentioned. Your patient has somehow contracted smallpox. Note the faint spots appearing on the face, arms and hands, and the more developed sores in his oral cavity. This man is highly contagious. Everyone exposed needs inoculation.'

'Doctor.'

'I prefer Viktor.'

'Viktor. What makes you certain? Do you not need tests to confirm this?'

'Yes, we need tests. However, I have a great deal of experience with the orthopox, both in the lab and in the field.'

There was a knock on the door. 'Yes, please enter,' said Pazano.

A nurse poked her head in. 'Doctor, the patient is awake and in a lot of pain. What should we do?'

'We are on our way.' The three men, led by Viktor Ivanov, who nearly bolted from his chair, followed the nurse out the door and into the corridor.

As they entered the patient's room, Doctor Pazano turned to the nurse, 'Keep everyone else outside. The only people to enter are myself, Ivanov, or as I request.'

Mateo was groaning, holding his head while shifting around in bed. 'Oh, mother of god, my back hurts. I'm burning up, and my head is throbbing. Where am I?'

'Nurse, five micrograms of morphine, quickly.'

'Doctor Pazano, I would suggest you increase that to thirty micrograms.'

Salvatore Pazano looked astonished at Viktor Ivanov.

'He is in incredible pain, and it will only get worse. You may have to increase further. For now, I would administer a continuous drip at a rate of twenty per hour, starting immediately after the initial dose.'

Doctor Pazano leaned over the patient and said gently, 'Cómo se llama?'

'Mateo. Who are you?'

'I am your doctor. Your full name, if you please?'

'Mateo Mareno Rojoz. Is this a hospital? Please give me a pain pill.'

General Ramos recognized the name. This was the brother of his son's bride. If the Russian was right, anyone Mateo had had contact with at the reception had been exposed to smallpox. He walked out of the room and to his aide. 'Captain, I want you to use discretion. Say nothing about this man being here. Nada, understood?'

'Yes, sir.'

'Go back to the party and make excuses for me. I will return later. Say it is an important matter of state. Mingle with the family of the bride. Be subtle. Make pleasant talk. Listen to see if they think anyone is missing and who he had close contact with.'

He walked back into Mateo's room. 'I have sent my aide to verify his identity. Doctor Ivanov, are you through here and can we speak? I would like to know more about this disease. Doctor Pazano, and Major, you, of course, appreciate this is a sensitive matter. Please say nothing to anyone about the possible diagnosis.' And then, he added, 'For the time being, I want to consult with the president about this matter. I'll make calls from your office.'

'Certainly, General.'

'Doctor Ivanov, Viktor. Please accompany me. We shall talk, and you can advise me when I discuss this with the president.'

The general did not call the president but instead started to ask Viktor Ivanov a series of questions. 'Viktor, I would like to understand your attitude. Even though you say it is dangerous, you do not seem worried about this disease.'

'Forgive me if I sound unconcerned. By way of explanation, I am a scientist who has spent a great deal of his life working with this disease. For starters, let's call it VAR. Much of my time has been in one lab or another, working to rid VAR from its natural human hosts. Truthfully, it is very exciting for me to see it again as a natural event when we all thought it was out of the human population. I don't mean to sound insensitive; however, I have missed seeing the greatest killer of all time, multiplying without treatment in humans. Before dying, I would like to see this magnificent virus progress unhindered and do what it has evolved to do.'

'Please explain to me, if it is such a great killer, why it has been exterminated?'

'It is a highly evolved entity. A superb killer. There is only one mistake in its cycle that renders it susceptible: the long incubation period. This man, however, did contract the virus many days ago, maybe nine or ten days, maybe fewer days depending on the strain and the individual. In another day, he will start to blister. It is highly contagious at this stage. But for those exposed, such as us, we have several days to inoculate ourselves. That is its downfall.'

'In Russia, did you work on using this as a bioweapon?'

Viktor did not answer the general.

'Come, Doctor. I am not your enemy here. I may have a use for you in this. I need more explanation and then perhaps, if you are willing, and if I judge you correctly, we will do something mutually beneficial. Will you trust me?'

Viktor looked long at the general. He did not trust politicians, religious zealots, military officers, Americans, or Russians. In fact, he trusted no one.

Chapter 39

'Jim, I've located the director of the Infectious Disease Center.'

'Did you question him?'

'It's a her, Professor Iglesias, and she was not very forthcoming. I think she wanted to see directly who she was dealing with. She will meet you there at nineteen hundred. The IDC seems to have several functions. One is supporting the university hospital with lab work. It's a large facility that has had its scope reduced several years ago when it functioned as a research center.'

'What about vaccines?'

'Barbara said we have enough stock to treat approximately 100,000 people. The CDC is said to have more than enough to inoculate every U.S. resident.'

'Depending, of course, on the situation, but with their stock added to WHO's, there should be more than enough. We won't need to disclose that we have more than a little for emergencies.'

'The CIA is providing us information and, as Martin phrased it, Bertrand is building a chronological account. Apparently, Mr. Gupta takes all the known facts and then puts them together into a comprehensible story. I'll pass a summary to you as soon as I have it. There should be something from them before you meet with Professor Zarita Iglesias.'

'The WHO rep from San Paulo has just confirmed the doctor's diagnosis. WHO is marshaling their response team. If you have the source located after talking to the professor, I think your mission is complete.'

'You're right. Not terrorism. It's no longer under our mandate.'

'Oh, Neilly is still on his way. He said that if JP and the others had to come off their downtime, the team stays together, and they all would come. I contacted him not long after their plane left. The general had already diverted them to Rio. He said something about his team taking their break there if they couldn't have one at their home base.'

***

The captain returned from the wedding and addressed Ramos. 'The family, sir, your new in-laws are worried about their son. He wandered off and was upset. However, they are not searching for him. They expect he will return to the reception soon.'

'Find me a conference room near the reception but out of sight. Here is a list of people. I want them there immediately. Get them to leave quietly. Then personally bring the Ecuador army commander fifteen minutes after the others are assembled. I want to talk to those on the list before he arrives.'

The captain was curious, but he knew better than to ask the general what was going on. He valued his position, even if it was no more than messenger boy. His nerves, however, were not doing that well. Stomach acid bubbled into his throat nearly every day.

There were seven names on the list, ranging from captains to colonels. The list included the type of men the general used in his never-ending war on the FARC and ELN. The worst was the Ecuadoran, Major General Juan Mancuso.

Mancuso never smiled. He had close-set black eyes and a black and gray brush mustache, resembling that of Hitler. He was reported to be very rich and had been a confidante of General Ramos since their early encounters with the rebels along the southern border of Ecuador. Rumors were that he was involved with the drug trade.

***

Mateo knew he was in a hospital and had been racked with pain. The pain in his head and back were now obscured by morphine. Likewise, the drugs had stopped his restless fingers from scratching and digging at his incessant itches. He felt fine, almost happy, as his mind drifted in and out of drug-induced dreams.

He saw himself return to the wedding. He moved past his mother's table, but she didn't see him. She sat like a statue; her once elegant face stretched hideously. He wanted to ask her what had happened to her face. Instead, he floated toward the dance floor where Camila was dancing. He couldn't see who with. As he approached her, several officers turned in unison toward him. Their gleaming sabers pointed up, extending six feet into the air. The closer he moved toward her, the further she danced away. No matter where he moved, the soldiers blocked him. Camila's dress barely covered her full breasts. She ignored him and coyly smiled at her uniformed dance partner. He couldn't see the man that was captivating her.

He circled, trying to get through the wall of army men and sabers. Camila's smile grew larger each time he was able to see through the diminishing slits that separated the men's plank-like shoulders. Around and around he went as she twirled ever faster. Camila's toothy smile grew into giant teeth, detached from her body.

Suddenly, everyone stopped. Frozen. All except his enemy, the man dancing with her. The man's head swiveled around, and Mateo felt fear course through his body. There was no flesh. Only the face of a skeleton. He moved straight to Mateo, put two bony hands on his shoulders, and started to shake him violently.

'Are you okay, señor? You are shaking. I am changing your bedding. Are you hungry?' asked the nurse.

Through blurry eyes, Mateo shook his head. He felt his body tilted this way and that before he drifted off into more fantasies.

The nurse knocked on Major Salvatore Pazano's door. 'Doctor, I think you should look at the patient. He woke for a few seconds while I changed his linen. I saw some red spots appearing on his face, and when he opened his mouth, I could see sore spots. I do not like it, Doctor.'

'Sí, sí. I come now.'

As they walked down the hall toward Mateo's room, three men pushing a gurney opened his patient's door.

'What is this?' asked Pazano.

'General's orders. Are you Doctor Pazano?'

'Yes.'

'Then you and your nurse are to come with us as we move the patient to isolation.'

'I can't leave. I'm on infirmary duty.'

'There is a replacement arriving in a few minutes. You will come with us, as directed. It is Lieutenant General Iván Tomar Ramos' wish for you to come now. It is not good to argue.'

Chapter 40

'We found the source, Will. A laboratory. Most likely a protocol error,' said Jim.

'Quick work. Fill me in.'

'The Infectious Disease Center, the full Portuguese name will be in the report. They had hundreds of old samples in minus sixty freezers in the basement. They assumed they were mostly plant samples and some bacteria. The director and her staff had not previously looked at the list that the two inventory takers compiled. They just scanned it. Variola isn't there.'

'If it was there.'

'We will know for certain when we find the inventory takers.'

'I wonder how many more smallpox samples are still in similar freezers around the world?'

'Our best estimate would probably be too low,' said Jim.

'Any others on the inventory list that we should be concerned about?'

'I don't know yet. If VAR is missing, maybe other samples are missing too.'

'Lots of lethal bugs that would bring a high price from terrorists. We'll won't have an answer until we find them.'

'One of them is apparently on family leave, and the other is here somewhere. Neither answered their phones. We don't know yet which is on leave and which is in town. Sheilla is checking airlines and rental cars for both names. No chance there will be a record of people using buses. Whoever is on family leave might still be in the area. The director didn't know and is trying to contact their immediate supervisor.'

'Ideas on how it moved to the patient?' asked Will Crystal.

'We have no hard evidence as to how Pan contracted it. Probably one of the inventory takers was contaminated and somehow spread it a few blocks to where the patient Pan hung out. Possibly ended up in the trash bin, or the inventory taker gave him food. We are going to locate both of them. Hopefully, we can have everything pinned down by tomorrow and head home. World Health can then do their job.'

'Politically, you are right. After we have the full story, we should stand down and let WHO track whoever else is exposed. Two good points in all this. So far no one has died, and this got me out of a Washington congressional meeting.'

'Lucky man.'

'I have to stay here in D.C. as Angélica Noboa is coming with her father to address a meeting. President Noboa wanted to thank me for sending a rescue team. Through her experience in the Amazon, our twenty-eight-year-old Angel has emerged as someone to be contended with. She has her father pressuring the VP to help them promote protections for the Indians.'

'It's the right thing to do.'

***

'Gentlemen, let me introduce Doctor Viktor Ivanov. We have also invited our compatriot from Ecuador, General Mancuso. Something extraordinary has occurred, and I see it as a great gift. It might be a way to clean out the infestation of rebels in Caqueta and Puntamayo provinces, with the small added benefit of strengthening our control of the cocaine production,' said General Ramos.

His last comment raised a small chorus of chuckles. 'Not too small, por favor.'

'I know all of you feel as I do about the peace efforts of our fine president.' More chuckles from the group. 'There will never be peace with these pigs. Never!' He slammed his fist on the table, causing a few to jump.

'No peace for those pendejos,' said a major wearing four rows of ribbons that attested to his battle experience. A five-inch scar extended from his lip through bristly black stubble to his left ear.

'The good doctor has enthusiastically agreed to support a plan we have developed. I'll let him explain the details in a few minutes. Without firing a single round, we are going to kill both the FARC leadership and their pitiful followers. How, you ask? With one of the world's greatest killers resurrected from its tomb. More deadly than the plague. More lethal than all the wars of mankind. Are you with me?'

There was a resounding chorus of 'Sí, General, Sí, Teniete General.' The general motioned for Doctor Ivanov to explain. Ivanov spent ten minutes going through his qualifications and a simplified version of their plan. There were still details to work out; however, he had convinced the general it would work. Ivanov would at long last get to see how this killer did its work in the real world.

'Thank you, Doctor. I need not tell you that this is confidential. Go back to the wedding reception party. We will return to Tolemaida tomorrow with our patient at zero-eight hundred.'

***

'It will be quite late when we get to Luiz' address. It is in Botafogo near the Batista Cemetery. Much further than Mateo's. With luck, we will find out more than we did at Mateo's apartment. He does not appear to have many friends, and no one knows of a girlfriend,' said Professor Iglesias. 'Colonel, will you please apologize for my rude behavior to the woman in, where was it— Washington State? I am afraid that I was a little surly with her.'

'I don't blame you, being called in without knowing us, on your weekend,' said Glenda. 'I'll pass it along.'

'Thank you. We have a thirty-minute drive. What more can you tell me?'

'Only that we have one man nicknamed Pan,' responded Jim. 'He lived on the street close to your facility. He was picked up by an ambulance yesterday and brought to the hospital. Our team has positively identified smallpox. We've sent samples now to the CDC in America. They will try to identify the strain.' He could not mention the BWC. He envisioned Nusmen excited about working with a new orthopox strain.

All outside inquiries to the BWC were made through a fictitious army medical disease laboratory, headquartered in the offices on the first floor. Which, as Heather had observed, provided a good cover.

'Professor, would you please tell us everything you know about the samples that were kept in your basement?' asked Jim.

'Several years ago, we were a fairly active research facility. An old professor ran the center until he died about three years ago. He was not very active at the end but had enough seniority to potter around where and when he wanted. The research activities were slowly transferred to the university. Our facility is now a medical lab. Someone at the university got wind of the large quantity of samples collected by the old professor, and they requested an inventory so they could review what was there. The rest you know.'

'Is there anyone that might know how the samples were obtained?'

'I imagine not. I'll ask my PA to research past employees.'

'Excuse me. What's up, Sheilla?'

'We've sent all the background we could find to Maria. That's about it. There are a few interesting items about a well-known professor that worked on lots of research projects and produced several publications. We found two that referred to smallpox. Oh, we have not found any travel records yet. The airlines down there do not seem to keep their passenger records as a priority. Nor are they being helpful to us. The message was, they might be able to find a record by next week. We could find no records with other types of transportation. Misa and Vidya should be able to get the information soon, I hope.'

'Okay. The samples we sent should arrive later tonight.'

'You know who is standing by with bated breath.'

'Not hard to guess. Professor Iglesias requested you be given an apology if she was rude when you talked to her.'

'Tell her thanks. I was sorry to disturb her weekend.'

Jim disconnected. Almost immediately, his sat phone chirped again.

'Jim, Neilly. Our ETA is two-four-zero-zero local time. From what I hear, you don't need my interpreters now?'

'Maybe. Maybe not. You're flying with your whole team?'

'No one objected to flying to Rio. And as you know, we prefer to stay together, except we left Gaston with his family. He'll join us if we need him. Otherwise, he flies down in five days. We have downtime coming, and the rest of us liked the sound of Rio. Call me if you need anything. Otherwise, let's meet up in the morning?'

'Call you around eight.'

The Land Cruiser pulled up in front of a massive gray apartment building.

'Brush stays with the car. We will get better results if Professor Iglesias and Davi ask questions.'

'It is number eleven-zero-two, eleventh floor,' said Zarita. 'Call me Zarita or Ms. Iglesias and, if you don't mind, you will be a Mister. Colonel and professor might intimidate them. I am glad to have you along, Glenda. Another woman will also make this easier.'

'We'll see if he is home, or if anyone else is there,' said Jim as they walked to an elevator. 'If not, we'll split up. Davi and I, and you and Glenda. Glenda and I have comm, so ask if you find out anything or need us.'

They found Luiz' apartment. Through a small window in the door, they could see it was dark inside. A neighbor poked his head out. 'He's not there.'

Zarita walked to the man. 'We have an urgent message for him. Can you tell us where we could find him?'

'The beach with friends, I think.'

'Which one?'

'Maybe Barra da Tijuca. I heard him mention learning to parasail.'

The man closed the door before Zarita could say thank you.

'What do you want to do, Colonel?'

'We go to the beach in the morning.'

When they were heading back in the car, Jim called Neilly.

'How do you feel about a trip to the beach in the morning?'

'What do you have in mind?'

'We need to find a guy. I'll fill you in tomorrow. Say zero seven-hundred.'

'Bright and early on our R & R. The U.S. consulate arranged quarters and transport for us. Wait a minute.' Jim could hear him say something in the background. 'The address is 248 President Wilson Avenue.'

'Subtle. Hang on. Glenda, 248 President Wilson Avenue?'

'I have it on GPS.'

'Zero-seven hundred. Adiós.'

'Professor, would you like to join us in the morning?'

'I was just getting to like your calling me Zarita, and I want to help. Pick me up in front of my offices at seven-twenty. It's only a little out of your way.'

Jim walked into the hospital and found Maria with Pan. A new metal door had been installed at the entrance, and a throbbing pump was connected with oversized tubing to a large metal rectangle. A small glass plate, caulked into the metal box, emitted a bluish light. Another large tube left the box and was inserted into a piece of plywood fitted in the window.

'Looks ingenious, Maria.'

'The hospital didn't have a negative pressure room or a better place to build one. My guys put this together.'

'How is the patient?'

'If he makes it, it will be a miracle.'

'What is your best guess?'

'I wish I had a good one. The poor guy is loaded with microorganisms and parasites. His immune system isn't worth beans. We've identified *Pseudomonas aeruginosa* and *Staph aureus* so far.'

'CRPA *Pseudomonas*, and the *Staph* is MRSA?'

'You guessed it. The carbapenem-resistant *Pseudomonas* and methicillin resistant *Staph aureus*.'

'From the hospital?'

'We have not bothered to check. Little doubt, though. I'll give you a full report.'

'We're almost out of the vaccine we brought with us. The hospital staff is inoculated. The police have attempted to get the street people into an auditorium. WHO workers are starting to filter in from local areas, and a large group is expected in the morning. They'll take over then. Their main rep from Sao Paulo is in an office near the nursing station if you want to talk to him.'

'Wouldn't accomplish anything. I think I'll get some shut-eye. We have an early start in the morning. Headed to a beach, looking for one of the people that likely started this.'

'Curious, Jim. So, don't keep me in suspense. How did it get started?'

'Hundreds of samples collected over forty years. Someone decided to inventory them before they were destroyed or sent to the university. Variola wasn't on the inventory, but it ended up in Pan's alley hangout a few blocks away.'

'On purpose or by accident?'

'Can't say yet, probably accidental.'

'Seems pretty straightforward. What's with the beach?'

'It's the weekend, and one of the two people doing the inventory is learning to parasail with friends at a beach. Neilly's team's arrived. They are going to help us search for the guy and then get some R & R.'

'I think I feel like joining them after I'm finished here. A day or two on the beach. You mentioned two people?'

'We haven't got a line on the other one yet.'

'Oh, I forgot to tell you. Pan has a real name—Bento.'

Chapter 41

Viktor was excited. He never understood, nor cared to consider, what drove him to see this killer work its magic in a human population. When he fled Soviet Russia, he had forced himself to desert his work and tried in vain to forget what they might have achieved: to weaponize a virus, to enhance its destructive ability by shortening the incubation period, to combine it with other viruses, to increase its resistance to temperature and humidity, and above all, to make it resilient enough to ride along on a long-range rocket to its target.

At first, they had made hundreds of pounds of Variola major by injecting embryo eggs and then harvesting the virus. With substantial stocks accumulated, they found ways to incubate the virus without the need of embryonic eggs.

Since General Ramos had presented him with both the opportunity and the challenge of his audacious plan, Viktor had spent most of the night reviving dormant information from deep within his mind.

The first order of business would be to move the patient to a location where they could contain the virus. The plan would have to be kept secret. The second order would be to inoculate the military personnel. The third, and most important, would be to infect thousands of people with only a limited supply of the virus. How to do it? They only had Mateo as the breeding incubator.

Viktor had not slept. He needed supplies from his university laboratories. He needed to check on Mateo's progress.

Unbeknownst to them, Major Pazano and his nurse were as much prisoners as was Mateo. The doctor had complained to the general's aide, Captain Sanchez, about their conditions. The captain appeared amused, assuring him there would be changes soon. The general wished only that he would do his duty as a doctor and try to save the patient who was now in his son's family. He assured the doctor that what he was doing was in the national interest. The general informed Doctor Pazano that for his service, he would shortly be promoted, to Lieutenant Colonel Pazano.

The pay raise that accompanied the promotion would mean a great deal to Salvatore's family. His patriotism, blended with the money, convinced him to trust the situation. Or, rather, to suppress his suspicions and to cover them over with the illusion everything would be fine. The general was an old acquaintance, and Salvatore had served him well in the past. The general would wish him no harm. After all, this was the best of all possible worlds, as he was fond of saying, quoting Voltaire. *Everything would work out fine in the end*, he said to himself.

Viktor, on the other hand, knew a bit more about politics and had often seen first-hand what loyalty achieved in Russia. It was unequivocally demanded, but without reciprocity when one's usefulness ended.

Strapped to a gurney, Mateo was loaded into a white helicopter emblazoned with a large red cross. Closely following were Doctor Pazano and his nurse, Viktor, and Captain Sanchez, who was now permanently assigned as Viktor's aide, as well as acting as a permanent information conduit to General Ramos. Two soldiers carrying automatic weapons nervously guarded Mateo. The white medevac chopper sat, with its blades carving the morning air. A Eurocopter, containing the general's aides and General Mancuso, waited a few meters away, setting off first into the brindled morning sky and lifting steadily into the tropical morning air. The white medevac rose next, followed by a larger Chinook, containing the rest of the military conspirators.

The three helicopters rose into the pink and blue dawn, tipped their noses languorously down, and headed to their home base at Tolemaida, fifty miles south of Bogotá,

Mateo had become lucid during the night. He said he wanted his family and his mother to nurse him. Viktor readily agreed and said they would join him in a specialized hospital where he would be cared for and nursed back to health.

Viktor understood all too well smallpox's incubation phases. There was often a short interlude when the host felt better, before developing a serious rash on face, hands, and arms. During this next phase of the disease, the patient would not feel fine. He would rot from within. His itching would drive him nearly insane.

It was an ugly disease, a smelly disease. The victim would either die in ten to fifteen days after the symptoms exhibited, or survive miserably scarred for the rest of their life. Mateo's desires that the beautiful Camila become his cherished wife were now an impossible dream.

Mateo's future was cast the moment he dropped the glass vial that contained a sample of the pox pus, collected long ago by an eccentric professor, a believer in saving every plant, microbe, fungus yeast, mold, and biological specimen. Unfortunately for Pan and Mateo, he added the deadly orthopoxvirus, Variola major to the collection.

***

Jim felt the warmth of the morning as the Land Cruiser stopped at the address given by Neilly. Marilyn leaned out the window of the lead Peugeot van and gave him a thumbs-up. The three vehicles headed south toward the brightening day and the white seaside foam. The hazy morning clouds had lifted, leaving a faint strip of azure-pink sky over creamy white sand and blue ocean. At the same moment, the helicopters were preparing to transport Mateo to a less uplifting destination: a military base colored in dull lime and greenish beige.

***

'Martin, please don't change the way you've become. It still amazes me to hear you knock on my door, and it's been ages since you called me Bertie.'

'If you really miss being called Bertie, it would be easy to rectify.'

'I know you are kidding. My first words were "please do not change back to your old self." I always liked you, but now I like you a lot better since you lost the joker part of you. What's up?'

'As you are aware, we have been monitoring the mission in Ecuador. Most of our contacts are in Colombia, not Ecuador. So, there isn't much useful information to be had.'

'I'm aware of that, Martin. I suspect you are going someplace with this?'

'Yes, sir. We heard a rumor that the Colombian army has got something big planned. This seems contraindicated when the government and the FARC are trying to engage in peace talks.'

Martin handed Bertrand a one-page, double-spaced report. 'Take a look. It is from one of our military sources.' Martin turned and started out the door, 'We're trying to see if this has any validity. Maybe we'll get some new pieces of the puzzle soon.'

Martin knew he'd caught Bertrand's attention with the word *puzzle*. Bertrand peered through his reading glasses, scanning the page, and then set about reading it methodically. *Why indeed would the Colombian army be planning something big against the FARC?* wondered Bertrand. It's only one source saying he overheard a rumor. But it made sense to Bertrand that the army might want to disrupt the peace talks, so he was curious.

He thought through the current situation. A peace process was once again starting between the Colombian government and the FARC. After they entered the drug trade, the rebel forces grew too powerful. The government realized they were too well-financed to defeat in a conventional war. Many of the FARC had had enough and wanted to resume a normal life. All they needed was an excuse. Not to mention that many of the army troops were also growing weary of the never-ending war. And above all, the citizens and peasants were sick and tired of both the army and the rebels. The time was ripe for peace. *Hmm,* he thought, *the army commanders never wanted a peace negotiation. If negotiations were successful, they would be downsized. Are they planning a coup? Or do they want to interrupt the peace talks? Or is it something else?*

***

'General, this is potentially interesting.' Bertrand handed him a copy of the double space report Martin had just provided him. 'Perhaps it caught my interest since your colonel was just working with the FARC rebels. Our drug war continues on front lines in Colombia. Peace there would possibly make it easier to slow down the drugs entering our country, something our president seems determined to put a halt to.'

'Do we know all the players in the drug business? Who gains, who loses?'

'My point exactly. The military stands to lose if there is peace.'

'Typical. Lots of bad blood in these long-running conflicts, and it would be a surprise if some in the army were not involved in drugs.'

'At this point, only a one source rumor; however, the source has a record of supplying reliable information. The thing that piques my interest is how it blends neatly into a situation I could see realistically developing.'

'Let me know if anything more concrete comes your way. Colonel Johnson does not see the smallpox release as a terrorist event. We've put a lot of resources down there, and it will likely amount to an accidental release of old samples. Still, World Health is pulling out all the stops, as they should. I expect our end will be wrapped up soon.'

'If we could, Director, let's explore the puzzle I alluded to. I find it strange, if the suggestions are to be believed, that the military would be planning something against the rebels on the eve of more peace negotiations, unless it is to thwart the government or the process.'

'Maybe. Continue.'

'Martin had worked up a profile on several of the military commanders, and one stood out: a three-star general by the name of Ramos. He has been at the forefront of the war with the FARC in the western areas of Colombia. Reputed to be a ruthless commander, he stands to lose the most if there is a peace accord. We also have him tagged as a possible player in the drug trade.'

'Connected with the politicians, or working outside them on his own?'

'No idea at this point. Eric Sands, Martin, and Eileen will be joining us in a few minutes for the intel briefing. I am concerned here that we don't have better answers. It's Eileen's area, so perhaps she can offer a better explanation.'

'Before they arrive, you know my choice is Eric Sands to succeed me as the next director. Do you still agree?'

Bertrand nodded.

'Good. I wanted to make sure. I am going to start planting that seed with the president, so I can make my escape before they get too used to me.'

'I'll support you and, yes. I do think Eric is the best possible choice. It doesn't mean that the White House won't nominate someone from outside the agency.'

'That's my main mission: the right person must get nominated this time. Not a political nominee, a company veteran. And that is either you or Eric. I know you do not want it any more than I do, so that leaves Eric.'

'You know that there is no one here, and that includes Eric, who would not like you to remain.'

'Thank you, Bertrand. I appreciate the thought. But CIA deserves someone who is here 100 percent of the time and provides stability for years to come. Strong leadership and stability with the right person are what the company needs.'

Chapter 42

'Pedro, quiet, please. I'm talking on the phone.'

'Is it Dad?'

'Shush, it's Nus.'

'Sorry about that. Jim said it was fine if I wanted to come to the lab. I want to see what you collected in Ecuador and hear all about your adventures.'

'Cool. There're some neat specimens. Come over anytime.'

'I'll have to work out something for Pedro, and Sharifa is due for her first baby. I really, really like her, and I want to make sure she gets special care. I can't wait to have our first baby camel.'

'Did you hear about the smallpox?'

'Jim called me. He didn't say much. I want to hear all about it. He might be home in a couple of days. I suppose it would be okay if I'm at the lab when he gets back. We could come back to the ranch together.'

'See you whenever.'

'Bye, Nus.'

***

'That was a hell of a good talk—persuasive, impassioned,' said the VP. 'Truthfully, Will, I have always liked her. Sweet girl, and not just because she was Gustavo's daughter. This sort of astonishes me. She has always been a bit on the—how do I say it—not exactly spoilt or childish, maybe opinionated without sufficient justification. Someone you might like but don't take seriously. Opinions based on a current fad or whim. She was persuasive in this speech and, I must say, logical.

What she pitched made sense. I'm astonished.'

'Maybe she just needed the right cause. Or, perhaps, we all have a turning point in our lives,' said Will Crystal.

'I noted another turning point—my old friend has become proud and supportive of his daughter. As unlikely as this sounds, he might be willing to take a back seat to her with this issue of the indigenous people. I'm thinking that it might be nice for their personal relationship, but it might be read as weakness with others in his government or the military.'

'The profiles we worked up when she went missing suggested that relationships with the military and Noboa were strained at best.'

'Keep an eye on it, Will. Advise me if anything starts to go sideways.'

***

'Lola, I'm leaving in the morning for three days. What do you need from the store? Will you be okay with Shuskin and Pedro?'

'I no like it when you gone. Pero, sí. Está bien. I okay… I still no trust that old man.'

'I think he likes you and what you cook.'

Lola swished her hand back and forth, rolled her eyes. 'I still no like him. Muy loco. Un niño in old, wrinkled body.'

'I trust him. He's had a hard life. Underneath, he is a good man. Look what he did, bringing Pipestone back, and he's bonded with Pedro.'

'What that mean, bounded?'

'Bonded. Sort of like glued. It means they like each other and are good friends.'

'I still no like him. He loco. He different from me. Maybe part him okay.'

'Pedro has you, and me, and Jim for a dad. After his family was killed, I think he likes having someone to act as a grandfather.'

'I take care of them. You no worry.'

'One more thing, Murray is going to come up every day when I'm gone to check on Sharifa. I'm worried about her first pregnancy, and I want to make sure she is okay. I love that camel. Sometimes I think she is my favorite of all the animals. I've asked Ben to check on her several times a day and to call Murray if there are any signs she is getting ready to deliver.'

'Llamas are favorite, no?'

'Yes, but Sharifa followed me around the field the other day and when I stopped walking, she came up right behind me and rested her head on my shoulder, with her big, sappy maternal look. Brought tears to my eyes. She is so special.'

'I watch Pedro. I can no watch animals.'

'I know, Lola. I'm just talking. You are the only one I can talk to like an equal.'

'What you mean equal? You boss.'

'Lola, even if I am bossy sometimes, you are part of our family. An equal part of the family.'

Lola turned away. Heather put a hand on Lola's shoulders and gently turned her, looking straight into Lola's moist eyes, 'You are part of our family, Lola. Even if you ever wanted to go back to Mexico, you will still be family.'

'I no want go to Mexico. I have nothing there but bad memories. I stay here.'

'Then, you shall. I want you here. Pedro and Jim want you here. And you want to be here. Shuskin likes you, and I know his eyes light up when you are cooking something for him. One family, Lola. All of us brought together.'

***

'Nusmen, please, I need you at the debriefing. It's important.'

'A waste of time, Sheilla. No way,' said an unshaved Nusmen, with one button done up in the wrong hole of his white lab coat, and his plaid shirttail protruding out through the gap.

'If you ever want to go in the field to collect anything again, come to the debriefing. I'll let you go first. It won't take long.'

'I have too many important projects,' said Nusmen as he walked away.

'Yeah, like getting the rest of that red stuff off your face.'

To think, I used to like him. What was wrong with my head? she thought to herself.

Sheilla walked to the small conference room, still feeling irritated with Nusmen. Everyone who had been involved in Angélica Perez's rescue sat chatting around the large oval walnut table. Katarina's light blond Scandinavian hair contrasted with Mark and Captain Kramer's darker skin. The shyer Bridgit and Fred sat next to Misa and Vidya. It was a rarity for the two computer experts to attend meetings.

Sheilla was still preoccupied with Nusmen. She was miffed that he somehow found a way to upset her. 'Mark, please briefly summarize the mission.' As Mark went over the mission, Sheilla kept thinking about Nusmen. *Why was I ever attracted to him? He's a beanpole, ungroomed with totally crazy-wild hair. He has no manners. He's an obsessive manic, eccentric to say the least, and brilliant. That's it—I'm a sucker for intelligence. His blinded me for a while.*

Mark's saying her name managed to penetrate her thoughts.

'Sheilla, you have anything to add?'

She looked around the group realizing she had tuned out and pulled her thoughts back into the present.

'No,' she managed to get out. 'Everyone, a great support job. Well done. The general asked us to keep track of the progress of Jago's group. Katarina has prepared a description for each member of the group. They've ditched the helicopter and are proceeding back toward the Colombian border. Mark, try to project their location from speed and probable direction, and then see if you can get anything on satellite.'

'What's the continued interest in them?' asked Kramer.

'CIA has heard a rumor about a large operation against the FARC. As we have learned, Colonel Johnson, Major McGuire, and Agent Glenda Rose, found Jago's group to be not bad people and formed a working relationship with them. They could be useful contacts.'

'The next issue is to monitor closely what is going on in the Ecuadoran government, especially the military or anyone plotting against president Noboa or his daughter Angélica. The daughter we helped rescue has apparently turned into a dynamo, pushing to help the Amazon Indians. What she is pushing will not likely be popular with some in the government, in the military, or with some influential corporations.'

'Am I missing something about why the BWC is interested in monitoring the Ecuadoran government? Besides the vice president's interest. I suppose that is sufficient reason but…' asked Kramer.

'Noboa is a democratically elected leader and, more importantly, as you so aptly put it, the friend of the VP.'

'Indeed, that is the political and personal reason. Is there more?'

'I don't know. General Crystal didn't say. Just that he wants Misa and Vidya to monitor their communications, and for you, Kramer, to assess the intel data.'

'It makes it harder to piece intel together without understanding what we are looking for. One last question, what happened to Nusmen's face?'

'Captain, you are probably the only one that doesn't know the answer to that. You need to get out of your cubbyhole and come to the lunchroom more often. We're finished here, I'd like some lunch. Join me, and I'll tell you about Nus' adventures in the jungle.'

Katarina looked at Misa who nodded. 'Us too. I want to hear this again. It gets better every time you tell it.'

Chapter 43

'It's a pretty beach, is it not?' said Zarita. 'I like this Barra da Tijuca better than the popular tourist beaches.'

'Very pretty,' said Glenda. She wanted to add that it would be much nicer without the nondescript architectural boxes that lined the street on the other side. She liked Zarita and her enthusiasm and decided not to take anything away from the obvious love she felt for her city and its seaside. She had turned out to be quite the tour guide as they drove through the city and along the famous Ipanema Beach.

Jim looked out on the beach that was just beginning to come alive. A few scattered groups of people were making their way to stake out spaces for the rest of the day. Two windsurfers skimmed over small waves in the light winds.

Two men stood outside an empty open-sided bar. A single skinny palm tree, lightly swaying in the breeze, separated the bar from a meandering cement walkway between the road and the beach. One lone bicyclist pedaled along the path.

'Early each day, the Avenida do Pepê, the avenue we are driving on, is famous for a long-distance run,' said Professor Iglesias to Jim, who sat next to her on the right in the back of the Land Cruiser. Neilly sat next to the window on her left. Glenda was riding shotgun and had turned as Zarita spoke to Jim. She detected an unmistakable look in the professor's face. *She's attracted to our colonel. Watch out, Jim.*

A gray windsock near a bar, tethered on a tall spindly pole, curved and straightened as small gusts filled it. 'Seven to eight knots,' said Jim.

'How can you tell?' asked Zarita.

'He's a pilot,' said Neilly. 'A full, straight-out windsock at airports signifies eight knots of wind or more.'

'Ah, direction and speed, vectors for pilots.'

Jim turned and looked at Zarita appreciatively. She was a beautiful woman in her mid-forties. Shiny, short black hair. Neatly cut. A slightly round face with dark almond-shaped eyes set against a clear creamy-beige skin. More than her comely looks, Jim was attracted by her obvious intelligence. That had always been the case for Jim.

'Pull over, Davi,' as Jim peered around Zarita out the window on Neilly's side. 'Gaston, spread some of the team out along the beach, especially by the kite surfing area. And put someone in that bar. Keep Abenaa central, so she can back up whoever needs her. Same for JP.'

'Interesting woman,' said Zarita.

'She's from Nigeria,' said Neilly.

'Another permanent addition to your team?' asked Jim.

'Maybe. She's fluent in Portuguese, Spanish, and French, has a master's from the University of Miami, in romance languages, and she can get by in one African dialect. Nothing like JP but good. We have a probable mission coming up. We'll decide after that.'

'I don't know anything about your team, as Jim referred to it. But a mission sounds military?'

'It's not something we advertise, but yes.'

'You don't look military, and I noticed three women. Is that usual?'

Neilly chuckled and looked up toward Glenda. Zarita followed his glance.

'She is military, too?'

'Unfortunately, no, she is not part of our team. She is capable enough. People are in our group are based on their abilities, not their gender. Just say the word, Glenda.'

'You're a charmer, Neilly.'

'Not a typical North American attitude, may I say,' said Zarita. 'I like it very much, though.'

'Let's get to work. Thanks, Professor, for getting us the pictures of Luiz,' said Jim as he put his hand on the door handle. 'Davi, stay with the car. We'll call you.' Before Jim could open the door, Brush walked up and stood grinning through the window. 'I was going to ask you, Glenda, to go with Neilly, and Zarita and I'll check out cafés and restaurants,' said Jim. 'But Glenda, you go with Brush, and we'll leave Neilly up to his own devices.'

'If he's here for kiting, it shouldn't take us long to find him,' said Neilly.

As Jim and Zarita walked to the far side of the street, Jim's cell phone rang. 'What's up, Maria?'

'Besides WHO people crawling all over the place, we're trying to find some foreigners who were at the site where our patient was picked up. We don't know anything about them. One medic thought they sounded European; the other said they were Portuguese. They will be hard to track down. Also, I don't think Pan is going to make it. That's it for now.'

Chapter 44

'I don't think there is anything to this rumor,' said Deputy Director of Operations for Latin America, Eileen Skinner, a petite Puerto Rican with short bleached blond hair that contrasted with her tan skin. 'At least nothing that will make much difference to us. The army is still against peace with the FARC, so they will always be trying to disrupt it. Pollas en vinagre.'

'Translation?' asked Martin.

'It basically means bullshit. And the drug wars will always be just that. You want the literal translation, Martin?'

'Why not?'

'Excuse me, General, Bertrand. To humor Martin the literal translation means—dicks in vinegar.'

'Glad I asked!'

The general liked the brash and sometimes rough edges of the DDO. She was never far off the mark in her analysis, and often her off-color humor made him laugh. In this case, he couldn't agree more. The government wasted far too much money on fighting drugs, with the effect that a few got extremely rich.

His opinion and Bertrand's coincided in that the money would be better spent educating Americans about the impact of drugs on their lives and on their rehabilitation. Americans were one of the largest users of both legal and illegal drugs. The war on drugs had never produced positive results and probably never would. It only increased the wealth of the cartels. The CIA's deep involvement with the drug trade often included profiting in order to run black ops. Fortunately, that was a thing of the past, at least while the general was the director.

'Still, the best we can do is to make sure the Colombian government succeeds,' said the general.

'Lots of issues in Venezuela, Argentina and, of course, all the usual Central American countries. Nothing worth our discussion, and all summarized in your reports,' responded Eileen.

'What about Ecuador?'

'Nothing significant.'

Watching her, the general picked up a slight change in her eyes and body. He was adept at reading body language; it disturbed him to sense something. 'Let's pay attention to them. The VP is worried, not only because the president is his old school chum, but also because he thinks Noboa is losing his resolve to lead. He is worried that his daughter is taking a more influential role, and that she does not have the experience. Make it a focus to monitor their military,' said General Crystal.

Play this smart, she thought. 'As we speak, the biggest potential threat to Noboa is a general, Juan Mancuso. He's out of the country and at a wedding with his counterpart in Colombia, General Ramos.'

'I want you to watch things closely. Meet up with Eric daily, and if you feel there is anything worthwhile, let Bertrand or myself know at once. Also, don't forget to keep tabs on the FARC group on their way back to Colombia.'

'Anything new on the pox?' asked Eileen.

'It appears the release of the virus was an accident. Colonel Johnson is still looking for the exact cause. They think they know who it was and where the virus came from, but they have not talked to them yet. WHO is now on-site and starting containment procedures. The BWC HazMat team was the first on the scene and are currently assisting Johnson, McGuire, and Stuart. The lab director where the virus was kept is cooperating. She requested an inventory of thousands of samples collected by an old professor who was mostly involved in plants and environmental bacteria. However, he was a packrat and collected everything he came across, whether in his field of expertise or not.'

'Two probable facts,' said Bertrand. 'One, a structural plan is in place to contain a spread of smallpox from a natural or terrorist attack, and, two, smallpox in its natural form and by its slow incubation period is not a serious threat.'

'Keyword you just said was in its natural form,' added Martin. 'So, as long as someone hasn't engineered its lethality and combined it with something fast-acting like Ebola, it can be controlled.'

'General, can it be genetically enhanced?'

'Not to my knowledge. The Russians tried and failed.'

Chapter 45

The few early morning beachgoers could easily have merged into Seurat's "L'île de la Grande Jatte," with one distinct difference: Seurat's painting depicted the upper crust of society, the French gentry of the 1880s, in which women carried frilly parasols to shield their pale skin, and the men wore tall black hats. At Barra da Tijuca beach, the scene differed dramatically: masses of Brazilians embraced the sun. The frocks from the famous painting gave way to mere threads, and the protected white skin turned to fully exposed shades of bronze. As the morning wore on, the crowds thickened. The ambiance was one of revelry, not of social restraint.

The searchers were dispersed along the street and the beach, scanning for Luiz. Parasails were unfolded on the beach, and the sky became dotted with color. Since they'd been told that Luiz was learning to kitesurf, each male was observed carefully as they launched their boards into the sea.

It was nearing noon when Glenda and Brush walked to a beach kiosk to order juice and spotted Luiz, along with a woman and another couple, unloading gear. Their sun-bleached blue Fiat stood in front of the hot pink and blue Classico beach bar. The team quickly converged.

Jim and Zarita made their way over to Luiz.

'Mr. Santoz,' said Zarita. 'I am Professor Zarita Iglesias, the director of the Centro Nacional de Infecção. I am sorry to interrupt your Sunday. May I have a word with you? Perhaps we could treat you to a coffee?'

Luiz looked stunned for a moment and then nervous. 'Ah…certainly, professor. I recognize you. How is it you know me?'

'We'll explain everything.'

'We?'

'I see a table available outside the café just over there.' She pointed. 'If you need a hand unloading your equipment, my driver would be happy to help. He would know where your friends are, and that will make it easier to find them after our discussion. Let me introduce an American friend of mine, Mr. Johnson.'

Neilly asked JP to help at the car. 'Abenaa, I want you to listen to the conversation and translate for the colonel.'

Seconds later, the five-foot eight-inch, curly-headed Jean-Paul walked to the group, nodded to Zarita and Jim, and in his fluent Portuguese, introduced himself to Luiz's friends, and asked if he could help carry their equipment. JP could be very engaging, and the group was in animated conversation as Jim, Zarita, and Luiz walked toward the cafe.

As they walked, Zarita explained that Jim specialized in microbiology and virology for the American government. 'There is no need to look worried, Mr. Santoz.'

'But, of course, I am very, ah, concerned, Professor.'

'Please sit. Let's order coffee, and I will explain.'

'How did you find me here?' he asked.

'A neighbor of yours said you might be here. So, we simply decided to check, and with luck, here you are. Now, let me tell you why we wanted to find you. There was a seriously ill man. Medics picked him up close to our facility. Do you have any idea how this might have happened?'

Abenaa, listening from a few feet away and looking out to sea, whispered in Jim's ear as she translated the conversation.

'Do you remember if there were any labeled Variola?' asked Zarita.

'I don't remember any with that name. It would be on the computer.'

'When you were cataloging samples in the basement, did any break?'

'No director. We did not break any.'

'Mateo and I worked together doing the inventory.' Then, Luiz hesitated.

'Mr. Santoz, Luiz, it is important that you tell us everything you might know,' said Jim. Zarita translated.

Luiz looked at Jim.

'I don't want to lose my job or cause Mateo to lose his.'

'We will have to see. For the moment, you have to be truthful,' said Zarita in Portuguese.

'Sim, professora. Compreendo.'

He continued in his Brazilian Portuguese, 'I do not recall seeing any samples labeled with the name you mention.' Then he looked down at the table and said, 'Mateo's sister was getting married, and he had leave to go to the wedding in Colombia. He worked on his own all weekend. I would not help him because I was here, learning to kitesurf with my friends.'

Jim looked at Zarita. 'Where is his sister's wedding?'

Luiz wondered how it was that Jim knew what he had just said.

Zarita translated for Luiz.

'I know very little, only that he is from Bogotá. He was flying there on Wednesday to attend the wedding.'

'Is there anything else you can tell us? His sister's name? Anything at all?'

'Nothing. Oh, I think he said his father was upset since his sister was marrying an army officer. He said he liked a girl, but I do not remember her name.'

'I am sorry to say I am not acquainted with all the people that work at my facility. What is Mateo's full name?'

'Mateo Rojoz.'

'Nothing else?'

'Possibly Mateo Mareno Rojoz.'

'Is there anything else you would like to know, Colonel?' she looked at Jim apologetically for saying colonel, especially since it was her idea not to.

Luiz's eyes showed his nervousness at the mention of Jim's title.

'Tell him that many people and doctors in my government have honorary military titles. He needn't be worried.'

'Sorry, Jim.' She looked into his gray-blue eyes. She slowly pulled her gaze away and explained to Luiz who seemed to accept the explanation.

'Jean-Paul, join us. I will ask Luiz whether he minds you staying with them in case we have any more questions later today.'

***

Sheilla sat listening as Jim explained to her what they had just found out from Luiz. 'I don't think that the one we just interviewed knows anything about how the virus ended up on the street. The other one worked alone over the weekend. We need to find him.'

Chapter 46

'Do you want us in Colombia?' asked Neilly.

'No reason, yet,' said Jim.

'You want to take a medic, either Fleur or Jeff? Or an interpreter?'

'My Spanish doesn't get me far, that's for sure.'

'Why don't you take Abenaa. I'd like your opinion of her. And she doesn't need R & R like the rest of us do.'

'What are her specialties?'

'Besides her native Nigerian, she is fluent in Spanish and Portuguese, and has an electronics engineering degree. She knows her stuff with booby-traps and anything with a charge set to it. Her official secondary, however, is comm.'

'Just her. Doctor Dakine is enough medical for now. Enjoy Rio. There are worse places for a little R & R. I'll call you if we need you.'

'I'll have her get her stuff and meet you at the airport.'

'Zarita, we are going to collect our gear and go to the airport. Thanks for your help. I'm afraid our car will be full, so we will get you a ride in the van. They can drop you off. They're nice people, so you are in good hands. Thanks for your help. Sorry if it took away from any plans you might have had.'

'I am glad to help. We caused the problem. I was hoping, however, that we might celebrate finding Luiz over dinner tonight. Some other time, perhaps? Here's my card.'

'Davi, another new Americanism for you—burn rubber? I want to get our belongings and get back to the airport pronto.'

***

'Maria, we are going to take a little jaunt to Bogotá. Are you about finished up here?'

'Yes and no. I'd like to stay and see how our patient does if that is an option. Otherwise, WHO has taken over locating any potentially exposed people and inoculating them.'

'Your team will be more use in Colombia. We should be at the airport and ready to fly in about ninety minutes. Meet us there.'

'Roger that, Colonel. I'll get everyone rounded up and get to the airport. Not sure if we can make it in ninety minutes. We'll do our best. What's in Colombia?'

'One of the two workers taking the inventory went there for a wedding.'

'You think he is infected? If he's symptomatic, it should have been reported. It's hard not to notice in the later stages. A good guess would be if it's not reported that he didn't contract it.'

'But you're not convinced?'

'Let's find out.'

***

'Look, Nusmen, you didn't see fit to take part in our debriefing.'

'But I want, need, to know about the orthopoxvirus.'

'It's always "I want" with you. We have work to do, and that does not mean humoring your curiosity.'

Then Nusmen shocked Sheilla. 'I'm sorry. I know I can be difficult. An outbreak of smallpox is a significant historical event. I received the samples from Doctor Dakine and am close to identifying the strain. I might have something useful to add.'

Sheilla wondered if this was just Nusmen trying to manipulate her, and then she realized it was his business. 'For the present, we are just trying to locate someone that might have been exposed. I'll let you know if anything happens that would be of interest to you.'

'You promise?'

'Jeez, Nus. I said so, didn't I? I've got to go. I have people waiting for me.'

'Okay, guys,' said Sheilla as she entered the employees' small lounge.

'Do I look like a guy?' said Misa. She gave Vidya a look that said, just don't.

'Is he still calling you Mike?'

'Fortunately he isn't, so don't give him any ideas about calling us guys.'

'Okay, people. I'll spit out a short version of the story once again of Nusmen's adventure in the jungle. Then down to business.'

'You tell it better than anyone else. Vidya needs to hear your telling of it.'

Misa and Vidya both laughed and clapped as Sheilla told them about Nus' antics in the jungle. Sheilla explained, as she had done before, how Nusmen came to have his face painted, possibly with a substance that could not be removed.

'What a crack-up,' said Misa. 'The guy is a treasure.'

'Hmm,' said Sheilla. 'He can also be a big pain in the ass.'

'He already looks bizarre with his hair, so the face designs will make him an even more distinguished resident nut,' added Vidya.

Sheilla was feeling tired. Maybe she was more relaxed as things were quieting down. Or were they? *I have a premonition that this operation is not yet over.*

'Here's the current issue. We are looking for a male named Mateo Moreno Rojoz who flew from Rio to Bogotá last Wednesday. We won't know anything else about him until a Professor Iglesias calls us with his personal details.'

'Where is she getting the information?' asked Vidya.

'She works, as does this Mateo at—let me look—at Centro Nacional de Infecção.'

'It's in Rio, right?' asked Misa.

'Yes, I should have said so.'

'I just wanted to make sure.'

'He apparently went to his sister's wedding in Bogotá. She is marrying a military officer. That's all I know so far.'

'Misa and I will get to work. We can probably hack the institute, or whatever it is, without hearing from the professor you mentioned. I doubt their security will be any good.'

'Okay, guys.' She smiled at Misa. 'All the correct spellings are on your briefing sheet. Call me with anything. Our team will be in the air shortly and will soon be in Colombia. Departing Rio just after noon, should be in Bogotá, two hour time difference six hour flight, she said to herself, ETA then just after four their time, or two our time. I want to have as much information as possible for them by the time they land. Mark, what is the status of the FARC rebels headed back to Colombia? The general, for some reason, does not want to lose track of them. Let's find them.'

'After they landed and went on foot, I don't know.'

'Get satellite and locate them.'

'Yes, ma'am. Should I have Fort Huachuca help?'

'The general wants to keep track of them, so use everything you can. So, yes. Ask them to assist.

***

The three helicopters churned the cool morning air, slipping over the green Colombian countryside and through the pastel morning sky. Viktor had no interest in nature and observed his subject. Mateo's brief lucid moment had lapsed into delirium.

The faith that General Ramos was placing in Viktor elated him. Viktor was known and respected as an expert in his field. Being held in high esteem by his peers, however, had never fully translated into self-assurance. It pleased him to know that someone so important believed in his work.

His daydream was interrupted as the helicopter flared and settled to the ground. An ambulance backed within a few feet of the white Huey with its over-sized red cross. To Salvatore and his nurse, he was a patient in need of care. To Viktor, a grand experiment. To the others, Mateo was nothing more than a rat in a lab, a means to an end, nothing more than a human incubator.

Viktor climbed into the ambulance with Mateo. But the doctor and his nurse were escorted to a car. The doors closed, and the ambulance sped from the field toward a building that had been specifically prepared for their human embryo. Mateo groaned weakly and tried to lift his hands, but he couldn't; the straps held him tightly on the stretcher.

He's itching, thought Viktor. He looked closely at Mateo and smiled at the red rash forming on his face and hands. He had been very certain of his opinion, but the increasing symptoms of Variola major nevertheless provided the reassurance he needed that his diagnosis was correct. *I should have no doubt, so why do I need reassurance?* he wondered.

Viktor looked out the window as the car carrying Major Salvatore Pazano and his assistant turned right rather than following the ambulance. He saw Salvatore move forward from the back seat to talk to the driver. Then, his thoughts returned to his only true friend, Variola major.

'Why are we leaving the ambulance and my patient?' demanded Salvatore.

'I am taking you to your quarters next to the medical facilities that have been set up for you. Soon, the ambulance will bring the patient.'

The car drove past a building with a pharmacy whose sign read Clínica Médica. 'Why are we not going to the base clinic?' asked Salvatore.

'It is a special facility, more private and better equipped.' The car finally stopped next to a small path. 'We will have to walk to the building. It is not many meters. Please, follow me.'

They walked for a couple of minutes and heard some talking ahead. As they rounded a corner, two men were resting on their shovels, over a shallow pit. Several scraggly cut roots hung from the side of the hole. Salvatore looked at his nurse, whose eyes grew large.

Suddenly, a red hole appeared on her right cheek. The driver was holding a small pistol with a round tube attached to its front. The good doctor realized he was about to die.

The driver nodded to the two men and casually walked back down the path toward the car, stopping to relieve himself. Then, he smiled. This was the only duty he had been given by Captain Sanchez. His reward: the rest of the day off.

Chapter 47

'Where are we landing?' asked Abenaa.

'A military airfield called CATAM next to El Dorado International,' said Jim.

Jim had been discussing plans with Brush, Glenda, and Abenaa, between phone calls with Sheilla, Captain Kramer, the general, and Eileen Skinner at CIA.

With mission planning out of the way, he called Heather and Pedro.

'It's a new baby, a boy,' Pedro said excitedly. 'Just like me.' Now Bobby Darin has a brother. Mom said I could train him to pack for me.'

'What's with the llama baby? You have llamas at home?' asked Abenaa, her dark complexion a stark contrast to Glenda's translucent skin.

'Lots.'

When Jim didn't expand on his answer, Abenaa decided it was best not to pry into his personal life. Jim looked at her oval eyes, separated from her dark skin only by the white surrounding the opaque pupils. She had short black curly hair, and her muscular arms were exposed below her T-shirt sleeves. She looked more military than the others in Neilly's unit.

'You have an interesting name,' said Doctor Dakine.

'Yes, many think so. An ordinary name in my home country. It means girls born on Tuesday. Lots of my people are named after the day of the week.'

'I didn't mean to…'

'I don't mind, Doctor,' interjected Abenaa, before Maria could say more.

The FAX machine was actively spitting out papers. Jim scanned them as they arrived. They had tracked Mateo to where the wedding reception had been held.

He pushed his comm switch. It was Sheilla. 'You should be met when you land. General Crystal has advised the base commander you are arriving on an unofficial state department mission.'

'Maria and I will see what we can find out from the military personnel that were at the reception. Brush, Glenda, and Abenaa will check out Mateo Rojoz's parents' home in Bogotá.'

'The drivers of the base commander have not been told you are looking for Mateo. You have two cars with drivers waiting. Misa and Vidya are checking everything they can to trace Mateo's location. So far, there is no clue. It shouldn't be a problem to find the honeymoon couple. Hopefully, you can get a complete guest list from the parents or the base. The groom's father, General Ramos, flew to his headquarters base earlier this morning.'

'We're about to touch down.'

Maria put down a set of earphones and sat down next to Jim. 'Geoffrey, Doctor Cahart, just let me know that our patient, Pan, or rather, Bento, died a few minutes ago. It's not a surprise. Thirty percent chance of dying for everyone, and he was in poor shape. Still, I was hoping to save him.'

'I'm sure you did everything you could for him.' Jim watched her, thinking she was a very caring woman with a big heart. He understood why Heather had remained close friends with her since their school days. Then, he added, 'With him gone, one piece of the puzzle—how he contracted the virus—dies, too.'

Abenaa looked out the window. 'Incongruous palette of concrete military, gray and verdant green,' she said softly.

Brush looked at Glenda and raised his eyebrows.

Abenaa turned from the window and saw the wondering look on

their faces, shrugged, and said. 'It is a foible. I mentally paint images.'

Brush and Glenda rode in the back of an Audi Q7. Abenaa rode shotgun, chatting with the army driver as they drove across central Bogotá to San Cristobal where Mateo's parents lived.

Abenaa turned around to the back seat and said, 'The driver says San Cristobal is not one of the better neighborhoods. I told him we were looking for the parents of a student friend of your daughter's.' She looked at her oversized, two-pound GPS. 'Left on Calle 27. They live across from a small park about two blocks ahead.'

'No windows on any of the first-floor houses,' said Glenda.

The houses were two-story boxes. 'Tells you something when all the doors also have steel bars on the upper floor windows.'

'There isn't much graffiti, and lots of them are painted in bright colors,' added Abenaa. 'An improvement over the endless red brick for the last couple of blocks. Stop here,' she directed the driver. 'Their house should be down about a hundred feet. Let's walk the rest of the way.'

***

Jim and Maria were met by an air force captain, who stepped out of a white Mercedes.

'Nice ride,' said Jim.

'Sí, it rides very nice.'

'It is an American expression. It means this is a nice car,' said Maria.

'Comprendo. It is General Fernandez' personal car, Mr. Johnson. I am his aide, Lieutenant Martinez.' He clicked his heels smartly and saluted, then opened the back door for Maria, motioning Jim to follow him to the other side.

The car slowed as they approached two guards with automatic weapons, standing at the entrance of an austere gray building. Inside the door, another guard was stationed at a metal detector. Jim was glad he had not brought a weapon from the plane.

While they were in the air, Sheilla had provided him with the layout of the building where the reception had been held, along with all the information they could find on the reception and the people attending. With Sheilla coordinating with the CIA and the BWC team, they were starting to sift through phone records, emails, and security cameras in the hopes of finding any information about Mateo.

***

Sheilla walked into Misa's and Vidya's private enclave for the second time in the last two weeks. Misa turned toward the door, irritated, until she saw who it was. Then, she smiled. She was always delighted to see Sheilla. Through the time they had known each other, Sheilla and Misa had become fast friends.

Sheilla knew she was one of the few who could enter without an invitation. Still, she always gave it consideration before she did. She understood their desire for space and privacy and respected it.

There were no phones in the cavern, as the others called it. Only dozens of glowing screens, large and small, taking up every square inch in the dimly lit room. Phone calls were screened by their PA and then directed under a strict protocol to a message on their computer screens. They could then decide if the call was worthwhile or not.

Only eight people could enter the cavern and talk to them directly: their two BWC PAs and Fred, who all knew better than to interrupt them unless it was urgent; the General, and Jim, of course, had official access: Sheilla was always graciously received; General Will Crystal used her as his intermediary, and had only entered once: Heather was now unofficially on the list: the two ex-black hat Fort Huachuca kids, Sergeant First Class Jason Lyle and Colonel Jake Montgomery, aka the Wolf Puppies, had a live message board tied to the cavern's computer screens.

They were as comfortable using their message board as they had been talking in person when they first worked together at Fort Huachuca. The four chatted throughout the day and night, and if the need or impulse arose, they changed to live video conferencing.

286

They bantered constantly; Misa Volkov was teased about her fifteen year senior age and British accent, Jason and Jake about their young age and that the U.S. government had caught them hacking. Jason and Jake referred to Misa and Vidya as senior citizens. Vidya Chaudhary was the quietest of the four. Occasionally, Vidya joined in the back and forth. More than often he was challenged to a hacking dual by Jason, which he usually won.

Misa was routinely challenged about whether she could compete with the young hackers. It was an empty dare. Just like Vidya, she routinely won the contests. She could give and take the mental back and forth with her sharp wit, except in one area. She had an interesting quirk—she wore eclectic clothes, sometimes based on movie space themes. Her fashion choice might have provided grist to their teasing, if they had not sensed something that restrained them. It wasn't her sharp wit. There was something fragile, something that said don't poke me here.

When the four had worked together at Fort Huachuca, they had picked up a nickname the "Wolf Pack." With only Jason and Jake remaining at the army base, they became known as the "Wolf Warriors," and jokingly the "Wolf Puppies" by the older Misa and Vidya. When reunited on a joint project, everyone called them by their original name.

The army were hoping to entice Sergeant Lyle and Colonel Montgomery with accelerated promotion, giving them extraordinary military ranks for their age, in order to retain them past their forced "get out of jail enlistment." The two had no intention of accepting the army plan. They planned to negotiate a much sweeter deal.

They liked what they were doing. The excitement was in having an open license to hack systems. It was fun for them as young ex black hat hackers with one important difference: they were now free from worries of incarceration. And as a bonus, they had access to the world's best hardware and software.

'What's up, Sheilla?'

'Nothing really. I just wanted to say hi.'

'It's nice to see you.' Misa genuinely meant it. She respected Sheilla, and both she and Vidya loved their new home and circumstances. Situated farther from Mexico left them feeling more at ease, even if it was only an illusion. They had been as safe at Fort Huachuca as here, but in their reality, the farther from Mexico they were, the more relaxed they felt. Their only real friends, besides their computers, were Jake, Jason, Heather, and Sheilla. They had both been gone so long from England that they had lost touch with friends there. They lived in a different world and had little in common with anyone other than Jason and Jake.

'What say we do something wild and crazy like getting a cup of coffee?' asked Misa. 'Whilst this is home, some, outside our cave, brighter lights and conversation with you sound just right.'

Misa had guessed Sheilla wanted to talk to her on her own. 'Vidya, beep me if you get into any trouble.'

Vidya pulled off earphones. 'Excuse me, I was talking with Jake.'

Misa reached over and clicked her keyboard. An image appeared of a wisp of a kid in his early twenties, stuffing Cheetos in his mouth.

'Better increase your rate of consumption, Jake, or you are going to lose weight. You're all skin and bone.'

'All the calories go to my finger tapping and, of course to superior digital brain cells.'

'We all have our alternate realities, Jake,' chided Misa. 'Say hello to Sheilla.'

'Hi, Sheilla.'

'Hi, Jake. When are you going to become General Jake Montgomery? You will go down in the history books as the first twenty-year-old general since Pennypacker of the Civil War.'

'You're a military historian too, wow?'

'Nope, just an information junky like you. Looked him up once.'

'Come on, Sheilla. Let the kid get back to work. They're way behind us hacking into the Sud America gov computers.'

As they talked, Sheilla could hear rapid-fire keyboard clicks. 'In your dreams, Grandma. Talk later.'

The two women linked arms and walked out of the dark into the fluorescent light of the BWC.

***

After knocking on a blue wooden door, they were about to give up when a woman caught their attention from across the street. The woman, wearing a vivid green and pink dress, leaned out of a first-floor window. Abenaa walked closer and, looking up, conversed with the lady in rapid Spanish. After a minute, she walked back to Brush and Glenda.

'She says they're not home. They went early this morning to mass and have not returned. It took a while to get the name of the church. She was reluctant to talk to me. I think she thought we were police at first.'

When they got back in their car, Abenaa gave the driver the name of the church, and directions from her GPS. A few minutes later, El-Carmen church towered tall and imposing, nestled below the steep, tree-covered mountain backdrop.

'Just like at the hospital in Rio, stripes are the preferred decoration in South America,' said Brush.

'It's similar colors to the hospital in Rio, but not much else is the same,' said Glenda.

'I love it,' said Abenaa. 'Absolutely magnificent.'

'It is a bit toy land for my taste,' commented Brush as he got out and started to walk toward the front entrance.

'A fun place to get married, I think,' said Glenda as she caught up with him.

Brush stopped and looked at her. Her strawberry hair contrasted dramatically with the green vines growing over the adjacent buildings. Her light skin, freckles, the nearly invisible strawberry blond eyebrows, barely noticeable above her golden eyes, captivated him as they always had. He looked at the church with its alternating rosy-red and white stripes. Small delicate spires sprouted in dozens of places.

'After you, beautiful. Let's find our guys first,' he said winking.

They walked up the steps to two oversized doors. An image of a priest hung above the doors. 'Someone thinks they're important,' said Brush.

'Knock it off, buster. It's probably a saint who's more important than we will ever be. Show some respect.'

Abenaa tried the door, and it opened. They walked inside.

'Jesus,' said Brush.

'Exactly,' said Glenda. 'But watch it. Your voice carries. Have you ever seen anything this ornate?'

'Hum, I like the way you talk, sweetie pie. More entertaining than Jim. It's as empty as it is ornate,' said Brush. 'Only a couple people in the pews.'

'There's a priest standing at the front,' said Abenaa, hurring forward.

Brush and Glenda decided to stay where they were. They took a seat and marveled at this unique gothic church. The pews were solid, maroon wood with lighter red inserts. The main wall was dark cobalt blue. The red and white banded pillars arched in all directions in front of the sky-blue walls.

The floors were covered in opulent tiles that resembled a Persian rug. Complementing the red pillar stripes, the floor tiles had two red bands that ran from the door to the altar. Scattered in the wall panels were large colonial paintings.

Abenaa walked back with the priest in tow. He was past middle age, thin and the same height as Glenda. 'He speaks little English but agreed to accompany me in case there are any further questions you might have.'

The black-robed priest nodded.

'He says he has known the Rojoz family for many years,' said Abenaa. 'They are not among his most faithful at mass or confession. He says they are nice gentle people, and the wedding was splendid and solemn. He was happy to have so many high-ranking officers present. He says the Rojoz' came to mass today and stayed for a while to pray. He briefly talked to them and learned they were worried about their son, Mateo. They do not know where he is. He disappeared from the wedding reception, and they are very worried.'

Brush raised an eyebrow, and Glenda leaned slightly closer to Abenaa as she relayed what the priest had said, 'The parents said Mateo was disturbed at the wedding reception, and this surprised his mother, as he had been happy sitting with her through the ceremony, here at the Iglesia del Carmen.' She looked at the priest, and he smiled at the mention of his church.

'That is all he knows. The last he saw of them, they were hurrying out of the church.'

***

'We're at a dead-end, buddy,' said Brush.

'Same here. The base commander confirmed nothing important. Said it was a grand affair. We are waiting to talk to the MPs that were on duty last night. The army side of the wedding party flew to their home base eighty klicks south.'

'Jim,' said Sheilla, 'there is still nothing from any hospitals that fit Mateo, or pox symptoms. The Ecuadoran army commander was at the reception, and he does not appear to have returned to Ecuador. Nothing certain yet, but it is starting to look like the two commanders are more deeply entrenched in the drug trade than we thought.'

Glenda, Brush, and Abenaa stood on the steps of El-Carmen.

'Let's walk around and chat up anyone that looks like they might have been here for a while. Like that street vendor over there.'

'Not likely,' said Brush. 'He's pushing that cart pretty fast. He was likely nowhere near here.'

'Which means there might be others that work the area, especially after mass.'

***

'Your Spanish and Portuguese seemed pretty good in Rio,' said Jim.

'My medical Spanish is passable,' said Maria. 'I'm pretty rusty.

My undergrad was Spanish with a minor in Portuguese, before I decided to go to med school. But that was ages ago.'

'When the interpreter shows up, the one base commander is so generously providing us, let's continue to not let on we understand any Spanish. Mine is nowhere as good as yours. I can pick up a couple of words here and there. That's all. You might pick up something useful.'

Jim had studied Spanish off and on for years, but his level of understanding remained mediocre at best. He had never been diligent, studying for brief interludes with long hiatuses. His strong suits were logic and critical thinking, effectively an innate understanding of complicated situations. Languages were not his forte.

For Jim, gaining some semblance of Spanish fluency now took on greater importance, both out of respect for Pedro's heritage and for the sake of communication with Lola. So that the youngster could bridge the two cultures, his dad encouraged Pedro to speak both English and Spanish.

Jim also had a loathing for some of his countrymen's disrespect for immigrants, especially Latin immigrants, a ludicrous attitude in a global world. However, he understood his Cherokee relatives' feelings about immigrants from the Old World, who had once come as conquerors. Today, the migrants from south of the border only arrived to work and find a better life.

The politics of eastern Washington were the opposite of the more 'liberal' coastal attitudes of Seattle. Xenophobia had been the cause of Pedro's disagreement and fight in his school. A teacher overheard the altercation before it had turned into a fight. The other boy had told Pedro that he had no right to be here. That he should go home where he belonged. The boy had only been regurgitating what he had heard his father say over their dinner table. 'My father says you spicks are nothing but animals. He says that your bitch mama is a tree hugger llama lady.'

Pedro could not contain himself, and he lunged at the bigger boy. His rash act ended with the bigger, white-skinned, short-haired boy pinning Pedro to the floor and punching him in the eye. Then the boy lifted his head, as he had seen in action movies, and head-butted Pedro's small dark face.

However, the boy, who liked to be called Butch, had missed something important from the movies. Instead of hitting Pedro with the front of his skull, he hit Pedro on the forehead with his nose. Butch yelped, blood ran down his nose, and he screamed that Pedro had hit him with his head.

Just like many school fights, figuring out who'd won was anyone's best guess. The boy's nose stopped bleeding, but Pedro's eyes slowly took on a dusky dark color, clear evidence to the school children that he was the loser.

Embarrassed at this outcome, Pedro was determined to have his dad teach him to fight. In his dad's absence, he'd asked Shuskin. But the old man looked down and said nothing. Then Pedro had asked Ben. The young man's life, just like Pedro's, had been filled with violence. Even at his tender age, Ben had killed a man: the cartel member who had murdered Duane, his adopted father. One on one fighting, however, was not something he had ever learned.

Pedro had witnessed first-hand that the world was a dangerous place. He'd watched the psycho Najma brutally kill and torture his family. Then later, he'd found out she'd wounded his new dad. Seeing Butch's massive head racing toward his own was comparatively minor in comparison to what had happened to his family. Nevertheless, Butch was the catalyst for Pedro's newfound resolve to become a defender of himself and of those he loved.

Ben looked at Pedro, not knowing what to say. Pedro looked

sheepishly up at Ben. *Will I ever grow that tall?* he wondered. Tall or small, they both shared the same desire to learn how to defend themselves.

'Besides your black eye, you have a bruise on your forehead. Maybe your dad, do you think?' said Ben. 'The colonel, would teach us both to fight?'

'I ask him.'

That was it. Together they walked off happily to feed the llamas. They were both content, thinking that in their future they were both sure to become skilled fighters.

***

A blue, open-sided jeep pulled up to Jim and Maria.

'Lieutenant Manuel Gomez, sir. It is a pleasure to meet you,' said the young, eager-looking officer in perfectly pressed army fatigues. 'The general said I am to assist you in any way you require.'

'Were you at the wedding reception last night?' asked Jim.

'Yes, sir.'

'You know who we are trying to find?'

'The general's aide told me, but I do not personally know him. The bride's brother. I might recognize him if I saw him. Why are you looking for him?'

'A personal matter,' said Jim.

Maria added, 'He's my daughter's friend. Mr. Johnson happened to be in Rio and said he would accompany me to search for him.' She hooked her arm in Jim's and gave him an adoring look.

Jim gave her a wink and said, 'First, let's find the base guards and see if they know anything about when he left.'

They drove around the airport and over a bridge. On the other side was a sliding chain-link gate with a small shack and two guards.

'They're not military,' said Jim.

'This is a service entrance. The one that was used for the reception guests to enter,' responded Lieutenant Gomez.

They walked up to the guard standing by the gate. Gomez spoke to him for a minute and then turned to Jim. 'He says there were many people that night.'

'Ask him if any males in their twenties left by themselves in the evening.'

'He says he did not see anyone, and he was on duty all night.'

'Okay, ask the other one.'

Lieutenant Gomez walked ahead, and Maria whispered, 'Something isn't right. It sounded like the answer was rehearsed.'

The second guard looked around nervously as Lieutenant Gomez asked him the same questions. He haltingly repeated the answer that the first guard gave in exactly the same words. Then, he nodded slightly as if to say he had correctly recited the words he had been given.

'Let's go to the main gate,' said Jim.

'Sir, that gate was not used that evening for the reception, and these two guards were the ones on duty.'

'Very well, Lieutenant. Take us back to our plane. It doesn't seem that there is anything else we can do.' Then he turned to Maria, 'I'm sorry, dear. I don't believe there is anything else we can do here. We should return to Rio.'

'Very good, sir.' The lieutenant smiled broadly with a sense of relief.

Jim turned to Maria and took her by the shoulders. 'Are you okay? We tried. We'll wait for our companions and then leave.'

Maria picked up on the subterfuge and asked, 'I have never been to Bogotá. Could we stay here for a couple of days and tour the city?'

'If it would make you happy. I have some vacation time, and we could ask General Fernández if we can leave the plane here for a day or two.'

'I will ask him, Mr. Johnson. It should not be a problem.'

They said thanks for the lieutenant's help and for the hospitality of the base commander. The lieutenant said he would send a car for them and take them to their hotel as soon as they called.

'We didn't find out anything,' said Maria.

'We found out lots. One thing I found out is that you are quick on the uptake, Doctor.'

Maria blushed at the compliment. 'When you said it was personal, I just thought I would expand on it a little and offer the young man a fantasy for his trouble.'

'They're holding back. They know where Mateo is. Or, at least, saw him. The question is why? You should get some rest while we wait for the others to return.'

'It's a bit early for sleep.'

'I think you've just been drafted into the military. Rest when you can. You never know when your next chance will be.'

Maria eventually drifted off while reading. Jim sat trying to mentally organize what he knew and what it might mean. *The lab technician, Mateo, had been here. The military at the highest level wanted it kept a secret. Assume he was exposed to the poxvirus, why would they want to keep it hidden? Could there be any other reason that a special effort was made to lie about what had happened?*

***

El Carmen was set back, one block away from the main street that buzzed with hundreds of people. A peaceful sanctuary in a bustling city. Abenaa, Brush, and Glenda walked into the crowds with Abenaa asking the occasional question about Mateo's parents.

'I think we are hindering Abenaa's getting answers,' said Glenda. 'My man, how about we eat something and let Abenaa work this on her own?'

'I have heard there is a great restaurant on top of the hill above the church. Incredible views. Very romantic if you two are ever back here,' said Abenaa.

'Another day, ch,' said Brush while looking up the steep hill to the top. *Romance and tepuis,* he thought.

'You want to try some street food?' asked Abenaa.

'Two birds with one stone. Buying something might get you some answers,' suggested Glenda.

'Let's try that one.' Abenaa pointed down the street. 'The tricycle with all the printing on the outside. I'll help you order.'

'It's tiny. How does anyone squeeze inside?' asked Glenda.

'Can't be more than five feet tall and three feet long. At least we know where the menu is. Plastered on the outside,' said Brush.

'What do you feel like?'

'Is it okay to eat salad?' asked Glenda.

'Gamble maybe. How about the Mazorca Desgranada? Shaved corn with several other things, almost a salad. I'll try to gauge if the veggie parts are sanitized. I'm going to grab something I can eat while I walk.'

'What do you want, Mr. Maguire?'

Brush knew she was playing it safe, not calling him major, so as not to alarm the vendor if she understood the word major. She was a woman who looked to be in her thirties with strands of gray mixing into her long black hair.

'Burger with the works.'

Abenaa smiled and relayed the order. 'What to drink?'

'Juice,' said Glenda, 'and he always drinks cola.'

'I'll get Brush a Colombiana. A very popular cola, and how about fizzy apple juice for you?'

'Sí, y una lata Manzana Postobón,' she said to the lady.

Abenaa smiled as she watched the lady heap cheese, fish, a relish, and another six things on the burger, making it about four inches thick. She set their food on the narrow shelf and pointed to the condiments.

Brush folded the paper back on his burger and looked at Abenaa.

'Jesus. What the hell is on this thing?'

It's a typical street vendor burger with fish, beans, and most everything else she has to add.'

'Fish on a burger, eh?'

'Try it.'

Abenaa pulled out several 1,000 peso bills while she rattled off some animated Spanish. The woman stuck her head out the opening and pointed at a man with a pushcart, several storefronts down.

'I asked her who works the street in front of El Carmen after mass. I'll check him out.'

'How much was that? I'm not up on the peso conversion,' asked Glenda.

'About 12,000 pesos. Maybe four bucks American.'

'I think I'll move here when I retire,' said Brush. 'We'll wait for you over there.' Brush pointed to several benches back toward the church.

Twenty minutes later, Abenaa walked rapidly toward Brush and Glenda and handed Glenda a Styrofoam box. 'Got something. Not much. But the Meregón vendor was outside the church and said he saw a couple getting into what looked like an army car. They were about the right age as Mateo's parents. I had to buy the Meregón. It's good, though. Try it. Strawberries, meringue, and whipped cream.'

Glenda rolled her eyes and said, 'On me, it will turn into fat. On you two, it will turn into muscle.' She passed hers to Brush.

'Why not?' said Brush.

***

Jim heard a vehicle approach. He stood up, stretched, and walked to the entry door after verifying who it was.

'Find out anything?' asked Jim.

'Other than the parents might have gotten picked up by an army car. Nada, partner,' said Brush.

'We're getting picked up in few minutes and going to a hotel. We got a song and dance at the base. Means they want to keep us in the dark about something.'

'What's the plan?'

'We play tourists. We will probably be watched. Both CIA and BWC are now focusing on Tolemaida, a military base south of here. Sheilla will work out a way to get Neilly to Panama. CIA will have a base somewhere. We'll all hook up there tomorrow and then come back into Colombia on the sly.'

'They never get any R & R.'

'That's the life.'

'Other way might be to fly back to Rio, and all of us come back to Ecuador together.'

'Considered it, but don't want to waste that much time. Easier for them to track us, too.'

'So, we'll file a flight plan to the U.S. and, as soon as Colombian air traffic control hands us off, we'll duck out in Panama.'

'Sounds like a little intrigue,' said Glenda as she walked up. 'What'd I miss?'

Chapter 48

'Is the BWC wired into the monitors?' asked the general.

'Yes, sir,' said his PA. 'Just click here when you want them on.'

Sheilla appeared on the screen. 'All set here.'

'Summarize our story,' said the general to Bertrand.

'Lab tech Rojoz somehow contaminates himself and unknown articles with smallpox. He passes it to street person dubbed Pan. He flies to Bogotá. He disappears from the wedding. His parents disappear. Why? The army takes them to keep them quiet. Conclusion, Mateo is no longer in Bogotá. He was taken to the army's forward headquarters base at Larandia.'

'It is still unconfirmed from our sources on the base,' said Eileen. Her short bleached-blonde hair kept her from looking like an upper-echelon government employee.

'Eileen, I haven't introduced you to Sheilla.'

'Nice to meet you officially, Sheilla. Of course, the director has spoken about you many times.'

Martin looked at his computer. 'We just intercepted a phone call. Your Colonel Johnson is the topic of a phone call from CATAM to Ramos' headquarters in Larandia. It doesn't sound like they know much about him other than the government jet and the call from the State Department to show him courtesy, but it proves the connection with Ramos.'

'Let's formulate a plan,' said Director Crystal.

'In the bigger picture, we have the scuttlebutt that the military might be planning something big against the FARC,' said Bertrand. 'We have to assume that there are multiple aspects of the whole.'

Sheilla added, 'We can add the apparent weakening relations between Noboa and his military. The Fort Huachuca group is monitoring Ecuador and there seems to be growing resentment about Noboa's daughter's sudden ascent. Also, Ecuador's commander, General Mancuso, has not returned from the Ecuador wedding. Assume he is with Ramos. Perhaps they are planning something together.'

'Yes, it all could be interrelated when you consider that drugs and money are part of our overall picture,' said Bertrand.

'And also,' said Eileen, 'graft from mining and oil companies.'

'What does all that have to do with the missing lab tech?' asked Sheilla.

'Let's see,' said General Crystal. 'If our assumption is that both militaries are working together, they might be looking to protect their interests by disrupting the peace process initiated by the Colombian government. The BWC's main mission was to look into smallpox, and that is still in play. We have to assume that Mateo Rojoz is infected. Sheilla, as a precaution, send more vaccine to Panama and get the rest of Dakine's team there to meet Neilly and Jim. Eileen, where can we insert our group?'

'We do have a small covert operation base near Larandia. We could cover them by flying the jet from Ecuador with a U.S. destination. Instead, we have them land in Panama. Fly back in a short takeoff and landing plane to our Colombia base.'

'How is the base staffed?'

'People come and go, but just two communication guys,' said Eileen.

The general thought for a minute. *Perfect location. Odd that they can leave two comm people unprotected so close to the army base.*

'Set it up. Martin, gather as much intel as you can. Coordinate with Colonel Johnson and DDO Skinner. Sheilla, keep the two computer whizzes at Fort Huachuca working on Ecuador. The White House won't take it well if we let something happen to Noboa or his daughter.'

'General,' said Sheilla, 'you asked us to keep track of the FARC band. We don't know their exact whereabouts at the moment. We're looking.'

'Keep looking. They might be useful.'

***

Jim remained silent throughout the discussion, agreeing with the connections they had made and projecting ahead. The only thing that made sense, or sort of, was a plan to use Mateo and smallpox against the FARC. *How,* he wondered. *How to infect more than a few people?* What did make sense is that the army disrupts the peace process, weakens the government's position, or distracts them and gains more control over the drug trade. *Money slash power.* He knew he was missing something, or a lot of somethings.

***

Like Jim, Viktor was also thinking. He tugged at the small, arched tufts of hair next to the glistening central crown of his head. The plan was simple enough. While simplicity should make it a success, the plan would fail the way Ramos envisioned it. Smallpox could be, as it had been decades ago, the world's greatest killer. *But not for long,* he thought. Its defect, as always, was the long incubation period during which a vaccine could easily halt its path to human destruction. Ramos planned to prevent the vaccine from getting to the FARC. He might keep news of the pox contained for a time, and thereby cause some devastation. Eventually, the vaccine would find its way to the people, attacking the virus, stopping its parasitic plunder, just as had happened in the past. Ramos' plan— not the rebels— would die.

Viktor, along with others, had spent years attempting without success to shorten this evolutionary incubation anomaly. What had served his love child so well in early history became its downfall with the advent of vaccinations, he thought to himself for the thousandth time. And with governments, there were millions of existing smallpox vaccine vials sitting on shelves, waiting for an opportunity such as this.

He confirmed to himself. *This will be my last chance to observe the virus work through its natural cycle.* Providing him, as one of the world's preeminent living orthopox experts, a front-row seat. Ramos' plan would fail on the big scale. The world would rally and once again subdue his virus. *But my plan, my wish, won't fail,* he thought—a last chance to see my virus run its full course in at least a few humans.

Variola major would ravage a few thousand people before a horde from the World Health Organization, protected by UN troops, rushed in to stem its spread. Still, he felt privileged to be able to observe the damage. In Russia, they had planned to do something similar. This time would be different, he hoped. It would be several days or so before the world discovered that the killer disease had reappeared among the rebels.

Then, perhaps, another week before the onslaught of doctors. General Ramos thought he could control the communication to the outside, allowing Viktor time to see an exponential expansion of his exquisite killer. He doubted it would go much further.

The general wanted to destroy many, or most, of the FARC; weaken them beyond repair. Viktor wondered about the general, usually a rational thinker, this time he seemed different. Inhabiting an alternate reality, a delusion probably born of a last hope.

Viktor walked to the locked room within the prison where, as Mateo's luck would have it, he was either sentenced to death or to a life of disfigurement. Even if he survived, would General Ramos let him live? He was using him as a human incubator. His purpose served, Mateo would be of no further use to the general.

The ventilation equipment hummed loudly. Ramos' engineers had built a system for spreading Mateo's virus throughout the prison. Viktor had helped them design it, ensuring that the virus would survive as it moved through the ducts to its human hosts. The pox virus had an advantage, a protective coating. Viruses were simple entities, just strands of DNA or RNA. Some were encapsulated like the poxviruses. Others were not. They all had one thing in common: their need for a living cell in which to multiply. Millions of these parasites were being released into the ventilation system, transported through shafts to the prison holding areas, and inhaled by hundreds of FARC prisoners waiting for their release.

Sitting quietly beside Mateo were his parents, Luciana and Juan. They were terrified by their son's condition. However, they were trusting people, and they were well pleased by Mateo's care. Ramos' aide, Captain Sanchez, had graciously transported them to the army base where, he assured them, specialized care would be provided.

The Rojoz did not know what disease their son had. They were told it was serious, but not to worry. With the good care he was getting, he would be fine. They had been treated well, and grew increasingly grateful to the funny little man, the famous professor—Viktor.

***

'Change of plans,' said Jim. 'We head back to the plane on the double. We're heading out at twenty-one hundred.'

***

'Jim, more info,' said Sheilla. 'Misa's new word association program tumbled to the Russian slash smallpox guy. She has been going into his background, and it's pretty interesting. It turns out we have extensive files on him and his old organization. We are getting what the CIA has also, as they were involved in helping him get out of Russia. Here's the short version.'

'How's Russia involved?' asked Jim.

304

'You'll see. He was either the head of the Biopreparat, or in charge of the bioweapons program that worked on developing weaponized smallpox. He's currently working in Colombia. And here is the more interesting part: he was a no show at the university in Bogotá today.'

'What's his position?'

'Research and some teaching. Maybe some sort of recombinant DNA research. Vidya is looking into it and will get a summary.'

'I have a feeling we know where to find him.'

'Before you ask… Your supplies are on the way to Panama City and you have transport back into Colombia to a CIA base. You will have twenty-one people in all. Neilly's full team and four of Dakine's group. Supplies are arriving in Panama City ETA zero-four hundred. You should be back on the ground in Colombia by zero-five-forty-five.'

'Good work, Sheilla.'

'Two more things. As you requested, the CATAM controllers have a flight plan filed through to D.C. As soon as you are handed off to Panama air control, they will assume you're headed there. Second, the CIA has a contact who seems to have access to both the rebel and the army base. I'll send you his bio. His name is Roberto Campo. A med doc. By the way, they apologized about not getting an operative inserted with the miners.'

'Didn't matter. Good work Sheilla.'

Chapter 49

'You look a little pale, Doctor Dakine. Motion sickness?' asked Abenaa.

'More like claustrophobia. Bouncing around in this thing with only itty-bitty windows doesn't help.'

'There's enough room if you want to stretch out on the floor?'

'No room for your feet then,' said Maria.

Neilly sat across the five-foot-plus-wide interior of the Sherpa transport plane and overheard Abenaa. 'JP, off the cargo pallet. The doc isn't feeling well.'

JP sat up, spun around, and stepped to the floor. 'Come on, Doc. I'll help you up.'

'No, please. Go back. You were sleeping.'

'Come on. Up you go. Lie down, and you'll feel better.'

Neilly shouted back, 'ETA thirty-eight minutes. Our ride might get a little smoother, Doc, after we pass the shoreline.'

'There're lights all over the hills,' said Marilyn looking out one of the small windows.

'I hear they're for adding light to the coca plants in their first weeks after planting. Supposed to make them grow better.'

'Right out in the open like that. Go figure.'

'Nothing to figure; this is Cali.'

'Cartels?'

'Everyone has a finger in, from the military to the politicians. And of course, the cartels. I'd call it a national pastime.'

The twin-engine Sherpa, with its twenty-nine-foot-long interior, was at full capacity with twenty-one people, their gear, and two equipment pallets. The pilot had skirted Larandia and was coming in from the southeast to a short dirt strip.

'Our new home down there,' said Marilyn.

'Yeah, they all look the same, don't they? I'd rather look from up here. No bugs. Unlike the zillion mosquitoes down there. Q one, Zepher two from the east.' The plane touched down and slowed near the end of the short field, did a 180 turn, and headed back toward where several helicopters sat off to the side.

The big back door and the side door opened to the cool morning temperature. Jim, Neilly, and Mac were immediately taken to the communication hut.

'Pretty fancy comm set-up,' said Mac.

Specialist Martinez said, 'I'm pleased to meet you.' Martinez knew they were looking at better equipment than they'd expected to see and said, 'Most of the drug interdiction is coordinated through here, so we have the latest and greatest.'

'Mac, you okay operating this equipment?'

'No problem. Looks like a blast.'

Neilly looked at Martinez. 'Sergeant Smith will take over. You assist. Take a break, or eat some chow, and be back in thirty minutes.'

'Mac will give you a shout if he needs anything sooner,' said Neilly. 'Let's get us hooked up to live comm first.'

'Okay. Colonel gets wired up first. Then everyone else.'

After Martinez left, Jim said, 'Let's get me dialed into BWC and CIA. I want to see what they have that's new before we finalize a plan. Neilly, we online?'

'Loud and clear. I'll get the equipment sorted and see you in a bit. Call me if I'm not back and you're ready to talk.'

Jim heard the sound of a branch scraping on the metal building. He went out the door. Neilly was still outside about ten meters away, but not looking in Jim's direction. Jim walked behind the building. Moments later, he led Specialist Martinez out to the front.

'Jasper. Come back to the comm shack.'

Neilly walked up. 'My best guess is he was going to do a little snooping,' said Jim.

'That right, Martinez. What were you doing back there?'

Martinez tried desperately to think of something to say. *I was taking a leak… a smoke break… neat birds sometimes back there.* In the end, he said nothing. Most of the excuses that came to mind seemed lame.

'Put him someplace secure. We'll find out who he is reporting to when we have time.'

'If ops have been going upside down here, information is getting passed out to the wrong people,' said Neilly. 'You work for the cartel?' he asked Martinez

'No, no. I would never do that, sir.'

Jim stared at the young specialist. Martinez could not hold his piercing blue gaze and looked down. 'Do some thinking, specialist. We'll talk later. You give me the truth, or I'll make it my mission to put you in deeper shit than you ever thought possible.'

'Believe him. He can do it.'

Martinez walked off with Neilly behind him. His first thought was maybe he should try to run into the jungle. Immediately, he realized he shouldn't mess with these guys. Underestimating them could prove fatal. Besides, he worked for the government, after all, for the CIA. Everything would be all right. *So just be cool,* he said to himself.

Jim watched him walk away, wondering who he worked for. The cartel? The Company? The Colombian army? Who?

'What's up, Sheilla?'

'We sent you multiple scenarios, contacts near the base, diagrams, and anything that might help. Katarina has worked up bios on the military commanders. Vidya has sent you a full bio on the Russian prof. It's extensive. We'll keep looking for his whereabouts. CIA has contacts in Bogotá, checking his house. He's a loner. I'll let you know if we find out anything, but I would be surprised if he is not somewhere close to Ramos. Too coincidental.'

'You find our friends?'

'No. We have probable location trajectories; we've been looking with satellites. General Crystal thinks it's important enough that he wants drones back in your area.'

'Okay. Mac will be on comms here. I want you to coordinate this as usual. I'll call when we have a plan.'

She assumed that would be the case. Nevertheless, she was pleased that, rather than the CIA, the colonel wanted her as his base controller. She had fallen in love with this job and with the feelings of respect she now received. *The way things are supposed to be.* Not like her old days with a narcissistic FBI boss and the misogynistic attitudes that permeated their local office culture.

'I'll be here when you need me.'

Jim had gained enormous respect for Sheilla, and he was grateful that the general had scooped her away from the FBI. She was levelheaded and good at what she was doing. That had first become obvious with her handling of the Seattle terrorist attack.

Jim would now give slightly more consideration to what the CIA had to say than he had previously. Things were different with the general in charge. The CIA would not throw them to the wolves, that is, if General Crystal could help it. Still, the one reason he and Brush had survived so many missions was because they had never relied on anyone besides themselves. Especially the other government agency, as they often referred to the CIA. *Listen to them. But don't trust them.*

***

'Vidya found out something about the Russian smallpox expert,' said Misa.

'Let me guess. From the company's computers?'

'A treasure trove of data.'

'Your guys seem to enjoy snooping around in their computers,' said Sheilla.

'Yeah, I know it's odd, with the general there and all. Look at it as an insurance policy for him. It's a big place with lots of, um, working groups. And, as far as we know, they've never detected us poking around.'

'The more time goes by without you being detected, the better I sleep. Still, it worries me.'

'I have to admit Vidya did some pretty ingenious work. Still, you never know who is on the other side.'

'I hope he's as good as we think.'

'He is. Here's the latest. He found a Russian defector named Sasha. An informant for the CIA and a smallpox expert. He was working on enhancing the virus, genetically recombining it, weaponizing it. A lead scientist in the Russian program.'

'Oh, really.'

'There's more. He disappeared when he was in charge of an expedition to recover Variola from frozen bodies in the Arctic.' She paused, waiting for Sheilla to make the connection.

'This Russian is our missing virologist in Bogotá!'

'You got it. Sasha is a nickname for Alexsandr. The scientist's name was Minkin Alexsandr Danilovich. Now known as Viktor Ivanov.'

'He's a CIA agent?'

'Possibly. But why would the Russians not be able to track him to Colombia?'

'Wouldn't the CIA hide him better? He knew about the Soviets' bio programs.'

'You're right. Defectors have a habit of dying, unless...'

'Double agent?'

'He could be. There's a plethora of explanations.'

'Phew. The general would know about this, wouldn't he?'

'This is where it gets interesting. Vidya connected him to DDO Eileen Skinner's group. He thinks that her group is connected to the drug trade. After the Vietnam war, the CIA started to lose a big source of black op funds from Asia. Skinner appears to have people that moved from the Asia drug running to her operations in South America.'

'So, how is this Sasha connected to drugs?'

'If he is, it's still a mystery.'

'I'd better call the general.'

'Just to be certain, I'll connect you to him using our encryption program and ask Vidya to monitor. Can't be too careful.'

***

Viktor lifted the top off a large stainless-steel jug. The escaping liquid nitrogen vapor made swirls of condensation as it touched Viktor's warm breath. He peered through the vapor cloud at a temperature gauge attached to the apparatus holding other vials of his beloved virus. Satisfied, he lowered the apparatus attached to the lid, screwing the cap back on.

***

'General, hold on to your hat. It's about the Russian professor who didn't show up for his job at the National Bogotá University. It seemed coincidental that he was a smallpox expert and disappeared, but we've found out much more about him. And this is the interesting part. It was from the CIA's computers.'

The general sat silent for a minute, wondering what hell he would have to pay if his team got caught hacking CIA computers. He quickly decided that he would have a discussion with Bertrand, Martin, Eileen, and Eric about the plausibility of having outsiders test the security of their computers. The Wolf Pack would be the obvious choice, safer from a security risk than an outsider. That might cover BWC, but he hated the deception. His thoughts circled back to Sheilla and their conversation.

'What did they find?'

'CIA had the Russian, Viktor, under their control for several years after he disappeared on an Artic mission to collect smallpox from frozen Eskimos. Just for the record, his real name is Minkin Alexsandr Danilovich. Known as Sasha.'

'Connect this up for me. What's new?'

'Eileen Skinner was in charge of Clandestine Ops.'

'Keep going.'

'I think she would have mentioned it to you.'

'Old business. Maybe not.'

'Here's what bothers me, sir. The Russians aren't known for letting anyone get away after going against them. Why is he alive? They could have easily traced him to Bogotá. With the current operation going on, she should have informed you.'

'It might simply be that his information is historical, of no current value.'

'Maybe. So, possibly old news, but there might be other explanations.'

'Anything else?'

'Not concrete. Vidya, you there?'

'I'm here. Tenuous, but my gut tells me there are still connections to the drug trade in CIA.'

'Oh crap,' said the general. 'Not what is needed. Okay, you have more details?'

'Give me another couple of hours.'

'Keep digging.'

'We will.'

'This is not good news. But it is what it is.'

'I'm getting rather fond of that outlook.'

'I'll never regret the day that I pinched you from the FBI. That, and got Vidya and Misa to move in with us. You all make me proud of what the BWC has become.'

'That makes two of us, sir.'

'But I would appreciate you knocking off the sir when it's just the two of us. Otherwise, I'll have to revert to calling you Ms. MacCarrick.

***

Viktor unzipped a duffel bag. The chirping phone inside was black and oversized. *Befitting black ops,* he mused. He clicked the answer button and heard a male voice on the other end say, 'Sasha.'

'Yeah.'

A female voice came on. 'Any trouble?'

'All is well.'

'Proceed with the plan.'

'And my laboratory?'

'Well-funded.'

'It's about time.'

'We have funded you all along,' said Eileen.

'No more than you had to. You've made the current deposits?'

'They are in your university research accounts now. Call and check if you don't trust me. By the way, company will be arriving. A special operations unit. If you are wise, you will be finished by the time they arrive.'

***

'New information, Jim,' said Sheilla. 'The Russian is, as we expected, up to his nose in this. Misa and Vidya are trying to find out more, but the short story is the man is somehow connected to the CIA. We don't know what the full story is yet. He disappeared from Russia, and the CIA got him. Get this! Eileen Skinner, Deputy Director of Operations, headed the operation.'

'You inform the general yet?'

'First thing.'

'Good. What else?'

'Nothing. Smallpox expert. Otherwise, we don't know who he works for.'

'Keep the general informed. We're vulnerable here, so this is a priority. We'll need satellite coverage of our base. Drone coverage. I need to know if we are going to have visitors.'

***

'Clear,' said Jim.

'Comms are up for the full group,' said Mac.

313

'Where do you want to meet, Neilly?' asked Jim.

'Hut C has enough room and coffee. I'll bring our topo maps.'

'You, Marilyn, Brush, Glenda, and Gaston, meet there in five. Everyone else, we'll be mobile shortly, so let's gear up.'

Just as Jim walked into the hut, his phone chirped.

'We found Jago,' said Sheilla.

'How far from our location?'

'A little over 200 kilometers.'

'Marilyn could fly there in ninety minutes. Two hours with prep time. Pass the coordinates to her GPS. I'll get her in the air.'

Jim looked at the group. 'The Russian professor is connected to the CIA somehow, and we don't know who else he is working with. The comm guys here were in a good position to pass on information to cartels, CIA maybe, even the army? We can't assume the CIA is on our side, especially not until we find out what's going on with the DDO Skinner. In short, this base and operation might be compromised. As usual, our best advantage is being out of sight and mind. We need to move. Besides our plane, what else do we have here, Marilyn?'

'Three choppers, all Hueys. If we need to fly them, who pilots? Gaston, first, and then...'

'Brush or I will back up if needed.'

'Any idea why the CIA would just leave three choppers sitting here unguarded? Unless you count the two comm guys as guards. Something isn't right. In fact, it's way off,' said Neilly.

Mac walked in, holding his finger to his lips and passed a sheet to Neilly, who passed it to Jim. It said, "Room bugged." Jim passed the note around the table, looked at Neilly and the others, clueing them that what he was about to say was a pretense. 'I think we should get out of here until we figure out what's going on. We take the choppers and the plane to Panama. Let's head out in thirty minutes. Everyone agree?'

Mac searched the room and found the bug.

'Let's mount up.' They filed out the door. Jim stopped

everyone outside. 'What made you suspicious we were bugged?'

'I was diddling with the equipment, and suddenly you were all coming in loud and clear.'

'Mac, take Marilyn and check out the choppers to make sure they don't have tracking devices. Then, make sure we have secure comm we can take with us. What I said was mainly for any snoopers but, unless you all have a better idea, I think we boogie out and find a better place.'

'I agree,' said Neilly. We're too obvious here. Someone might have already passed our location to the army or the cartel. Let's disappear somewhere close.'

'We leave the plane here?' asked Glenda.

'Secure Specialist Martinez and his pal on the plane. Sheilla will clear the pilot to a Panama base.'

'We'll be tight on space in the choppers,' said Neilly.

'We'll leave nonessentials with the plane.'

Jim walked off and found a spot where he couldn't be overheard. 'Sheilla, we are going to move. Short-term, we need you to locate a spot where we can land without anyone spotting us. Somewhere close to here.'

'I'll get Fred on it pronto.'

'We'll get airborne.'

'Okay. Back to you.'

The three Hueys lifted, heading south-southwest. Fred found what appeared to be an overgrown grass strip with no sign of people nearby. Sheilla sent Marilyn the coordinates and asked Jim what else he needed.

'Put Misa, Vidya, and our two Fort Huachuca friends on this. With the four of them focusing, they should be able to find out if the Colombian Army can track our air movement. Or if they know anything about us, or about our mission. Then I want Jason and Jake to go back to watching over Angélica and Noboa. And Misa to help Vidya with the CIA.'

'The comm guy could have alerted someone before we secured

him,' said Jim.

The first focus for Neilly and Jim was to ensure the safety of the team. Neilly's special forces—Jim, Brush, and Glenda—were all capable fighters. If they stayed at the CIA base, and if the army found out and attacked in force, it would be overwhelming odds. No cavalry arriving. It would end the same as the Alamo—a valiant fight with them all ending up dead.

Fifteen minutes later, the three overloaded choppers set down in the long-abandoned drug cartel runway. 'Jim, we see a large rusting metal Quonset hut on satellite. Can you get the choppers in it and out of view?'

'Saw it. We'll scout it out, Sheilla. What's your confidence level about this location?'

'Looks good to us. So far, no sign of any communication about your movement or your presence in the country.'

Neilly posted guards. He sent Fleur and Jean-Paul patrolling to the south. Jeff and Joe to the north. Aleski and Roberta found a position near the perimeter. García stayed near the choppers, scanning with his sniper scope. 'Gaston, check the Q hut. See if we can use it.'

'Let's talk,' said Jim.'

Mac sat down next to the chopper, getting his comm gear in order. He was using an encrypted connection to BWC, another to the CIA. Misa had set up a relay from Jim to Sheilla and to the general.

Brush sat back and crossed his legs, a long blade of grass protruding from his lips.

'Our purpose was to find the lab guy, Mateo. My guess is the army general nabbed him with the intent of using smallpox as a weapon somehow with the Russian's help. The only people they could use it against would be the FARC, since many of them will be symptomatic at the same time.

Glenda tapped Brush's foot with hers, 'What do you think?'

He shook his head. 'The same, as far as I can see.'

Jim looked at Glenda.

'I think,' she said, 'All your reasoning, so far, has been sound. As was the move here. So, what's next?'

'Neilly, any comments?' asked Jim.

'Your operation, Colonel.'

'Rojoz is probably on Ramos' forward base. We have no one we can trust there to help us. Probably could infiltrate it. But a big gamble, not knowing where to find him. If he contracted Variola in Rio, it's too late for vaccination. The mission is now figuring out what they have planned. Two ways: one we surveil the base; two, Sheilla, Misa, and Vidya figure out what's going on by monitoring their comms.'

Marilyn and Maria walked over and sat down.

'Stretch us pretty thin to surveil the army base and keep this site secure,' said Neilly.

'And pick up the FARC,' added Marilyn, 'if that's your plan?'

Brush pulled out a new round blade of wheatgrass and said, 'And Jago isn't just going to let you swoop in and give him a lift. He won't know who you are.'

'I can work out an intercept LZ with BWC.'

'Why not use a loudspeaker if you know where they are, and there's no one else around?' suggested Glenda.

'Could work. Figure out a short message that lets him know it's you.'

'Shorter the better,' said Glenda.

Jim sat for a few seconds, tugging on his lower lip. 'If we decide this place is secure, Brush, myself, and two others will go to Larandia to recon. Marilyn, you take who you think you need and pick up Jago. The general was right; we are going to need more people. We hide the other choppers,' Jim looked at Neilly, '…in the Q hut?'

'Gaston should have it checked out in a few minutes. It's tall enough and structurally okay. We can fly in and out. If we do, they'll be out of sight from the air. We are going to have to find some fuel.'

'You, Mac, and Glenda work with Sheilla and the general. We are going to need another med reaction team somewhere close with an ample supply of vaccine.'

'Panama?'

'Probably the best place.'

Chapter 50

'Doesn't look like they're worried about intruders. No security that I can see,' said Brush.

'Almost too quiet. Let's work our way in, take a closer look.'

'Crocs lounging along the edge.'

'Yep, no need for fences with all this swamp and critters on their perimeter,' added Jim.

'And the skeeters, biting every patch of my exposed skin; I think it's best to skirt the swamp and its inhabitants. The river is narrower there, and we can approach the airfield from the far end.'

'No guard towers, which seems odd for a headquarters base and as close as it is to the rebels' main encampment. All the buildings are on the opposite end of the runway.'

'I prefer less swamp, but we'll be more exposed. Not much cover down that way.'

'Better than providing food for the critters.'

'Seneca, your location,' said Roberta.

'Moving toward your side,' said Jim. 'Can you cover us from your position?'

'Marginal. It took most of the night to get to this spot. It's not that great, either.'

They worked their way toward Roberta in a drainage ditch alongside the runway.

'Gold, status?'

'Clear.'

'Base?'

'Nada,' said Mac.

'Update on the pickup.'

'Bird is near its rendezvous,' said Sheilla.

'Moving.'

Sheilla watched two red blimps along the edge of the runway. Jim's and Brush's were stationary, and then the dots started to move. 'I like these new GPS trackers,' said Fred.

***

Marilyn flipped the loudspeaker switch.

'Hey down there, boys and girl. Want to do some gold panning with us? Give you a ride,' she said into her mic, while she hovered close to Jago's coordinates.

Joe sat by the door and looked through his binoculars. 'Feel like they could hear us back in Quito.'

'Base said no warm bodies close to here, other than your package.'

'Someone moved into a small open area at your seven,' said Joe.

Marilyn turned the chopper around and drifted toward the meadow. 'I'm going to set down in that meadow when you have a positive ID. Stay close to that gun, in case it's not them.'

She nudged the cyclic forward with a little left rudder and drifted toward the small clearing. 'Is that one of Jago's men? He looks more like a boy. I don't remember anyone that small, but I didn't get to interact with them much.'

'I remember him, young Cuban kid. Chico's his name, and he hung out with the big guy named Lobo. The rest of them will be in the trees.'

Marilyn turned the nose toward Chico and set the chopper down. As the skids worked their way in the grasses, a man that dwarfed Chico moved out of the heavy foliage.

'That's his big buddy.'

Jago walked out about twenty feet from where Lobo had emerged and walked directly toward Marilyn. Joe motioned them into the chopper. His Spanish was good enough, and, with Jago's English, they just managed to communicate.

'I'm not going to ask you how you located us. It leaves me feeling, how you say?'

'Vulnerable,' said Marilyn.

'Why have you come to us?'

'Besides us being so nice and maybe giving you a ride, we would like your advice.'

Jago waived the rest over to the helicopter. 'I see, information for a ride.'

'We would like to know how secure a site is?'

'Where is the camp?' asked Jago.

'Not far from Larandia.'

'Señora, you speak of my neighborhood. El Diamante is not far.'

'What is El Diamante?'

'It is the main FARC base not so far from Larandia.'

'Oh.'

'Where you camped, I think, has no name?'

'No. An abandoned grass airfield, south and east of Larandia approximately ten klicks. You know it?'

'Is there a building?'

'A very large metal building.'

'Sí. Yo sé. I know it well. How you come to that place?'

'It was isolated with no people around. We needed to leave an exposed position. We're low on fuel. Sit up here. Put your headset on and I'll explain.'

Jago moved to the co-pilot seat while the rest settled in the back. Cherry moved behind Jago's seat in order to watch the woman fly the helicopter. *I like this,* she thought. Then she glanced at Jago. She detected no attraction. Pleased, she turned back and watched Marilyn. Cherry was used to women in the FARC having roles the same as men. However, while they carried guns and died, they were not leaders. Nor did they fly helicopters. She liked what she saw.

'Why you come here, señorita?'

'Call me Marilyn. Colonel Johnson wants…ah, we need your help. I will explain to you on the way.'

She pushed her talk button. 'Base, we have the package. ETA eighty minutes. Marilyn did her best to explain about smallpox and why they were after Mateo. Jago listened and asked a few questions. Then, he added, 'Larandia was a very bad place and difficult to attack, surrounded by swamps and with many experienced army fighters. Many of our people are imprisoned there.'

***

'Jim, we've been analyzing Larandia. There are linear formations all around it except for the airfield. We thought they were water barriers or dikes at first. They're extensive. We are now certain that they are a network of connected bunkers. We also found information that the army has a large force there. Larandia has never been successfully attacked.'

Roberta trained her scope on another mound. 'Somethings not right. Too symmetrical. Shit, we can see small openings on the side. It's manmade.'

'You and García secure your position,' said Jim. Too many unknowns. The mound is likely a pillbox observation post. Possibly sensors too. They likely know we are here. Heads up.'

'New problem. Helicopters headed in and boats on the river,' said Sheilla

'Roger, we're moving back,' said Jim.

'Mortars,' yelled Jim, a fraction of a second after hearing the telltale whistle that had become ingrained in their minds in Vietnam. He and Brush hit the ground at the same time and immediately bounded up after the shell exploded a hundred feet in front of them. Another burst behind them.

'Bracketed,' said Brush. They both knew what to do as they sprinted to the left. They had gone about forty feet when there was an explosion where they had just been.

'Veer right,' shouted Jim.

They moved, seconds before a mortar round exploded behind them.

'Thought my days as a sprinter were over, eh?'

They ran and dodged, guessing through experience where the mortar men would place rounds, ducking one way and then the other until they ran into a small stream bed. Both ran left into the ditch, remaining visible for a few seconds and then angled down into it. As soon as they were out of sight, they turned in the opposite direction. Keeping low, they moved as fast as they could. The mortar rounds followed in the other direction. They stopped after a hundred meters.

'Base. What do you see?'

'Troops are out of the helicopters, moving in your direction. The boats are downriver from the direction you first took. Gold is moving slowly, and no one is close to her. The helicopters are now moving toward you. Wait, they are moving to where you changed direction. No one in front of you toward point bravo.'

Jim and Brush picked their way through the streambed. It gradually widened, and they were able to pick up speed.

'Pretty quick like, they're going to realize we switched directions,' said Brush.

'Yep, we need to get across the river before they move back this way.'

'Choppers will spot us if the crocs don't eat us.'

Jim picked up two river worn rocks about ten centimeters across. After putting them in the front pockets of his BDUs, he eased into the river, took some deep breaths, and disappeared.

Brush sighed and followed Jim, thinking, *If we don't thrash about swimming on the surface, maybe the crocs will give us a pass.*

'We'll hole up,' said Roberta. 'Dark soon and base can direct us.'

No answer. 'Base, you read?'

'They're underwater.'

Roberta watched the river. Two minutes later, a head rose to the surface and then disappeared. Another minute, and a body crawled out on the far side of the river. Roberta watched as several crocodiles raised their heads and then scurried into the water. *Jesus, they can move fast,* she said to herself.

'Who moves fast?' asked Sheilla.

'The crocs. There're dozens of them.'

A few seconds later, she saw Brush's head break the surface. *Man, this is going to be close.*

'Seneca, the boats can't connect with the river you just crossed. The ground troops are fanning out along the swamp. Helicopters still searching, moving your way now.'

No answer.

'Troops have moved back into boats, and they are heading south. They can turn north on another river that joins yours and be on the other side of you in about thirty minutes.'

Still no answer.

Chapter 51

Bertrand sat listening to General Crystal while thinking about his beloved agency. He held it up on a pedestal but did not overlook that agency people had gone astray before, and it would happen again.

'It's impossible, with what we ask of people, not to have some lose their moral compass,' said Bertrand.

'It can happen in the army too,' said General Crystal.

'We ask people to be undercover for years and then wonder why it is difficult for them to keep their loyalty straight. Someone like Eileen has long tentacles into the CIA. I'm going to ask Martin to gather a small group and find out what she is doing. I want to believe it's nothing, but the information suggests we need to make sure.'

'We have to keep her involved in our discussions until we have answers. I'll have my computer group and the two from Huachuca dig into this. They already have their hands full watching Ecuador and Colombia, but this is a part of the story we need to figure out. They're better equipped to figure out the Eileen story than we can here. Let's switch things around and turn monitoring Ecuador, as much as we can, over to some of Martin's people.'

'Splendid idea,' said Bertrand. 'One question. How would your computer team be better equipped to find out about Eileen?' Bertrand passed his hand through his hair. 'Forget I asked.'

***

'Okay guys, we just came this close'—Sheilla held up her thumb and index figure separated by an eighth inch— 'to losing Colonel Johnson and Major McGuire. Fred, I want you to do everything you can, with everyone you can bring on board, to help back up Misa and Vidya. Whatever they ask, do it.'

'Sure, but they never need us for anything.'

'They have their hands full and will appreciate your help, I promise. Mark, we almost lost our guys, and they are not out of trouble yet. We need to step up the sat surveillance of their operation area. We should have picked up Larandia's hidden defenses sooner. I don't want any more surprises. We're operating twenty-four seven. Plan on being here until this mission is over.'

'I'm coordinating drones with Glenda,' said Mark. 'Three more are on their way to a base in Panama. We'll move them closer when we have a secure place.'

'Risky bet choosing the rebels over the CIA,' said Kramer, who had been silent until now. 'We'll need the FARC's assistance if we can't trust the CIA. But the CIA will quickly learn what we are doing, as they certainly will have contacts in the FARC, just like they probably do in the Colombian army.'

'I don't like this,' said Sheilla. 'A simple mission to track down one guy has now turned into something else. We don't have necessary intel. We don't know exactly who the enemy is. We can't trust the CIA. We are outnumbered 1,000 to one on the ground.'

'Too many players,' added Mark. 'I don't like the odds, either.'

'Most of you are the finest people I have ever worked with. We have the general, and not all of the CIA is against us. Our ground teams are without peer, and we have the best computer skills, as we've shown many times. Let's make sure we stay ahead of this game before it bites us. We can and will,' said Sheilla.

***

Fred tapped some keys, and a satellite image appeared on the large screen in the conference room. 'Check this out.'

'There are hundreds of them,' said Sheilla. 'Give me a total count on how many people those buses can hold.'

As they watched the screen, Fred worked on his laptop. 'I'd estimate that the buses can hold over 2,000. There are fifty of them. The people are still loading. I can refine that estimate in a few minutes. I have a simple program we use for crowd size stats.'

'I counted those entering one bus, thirty-nine. Your estimate is close.

'Kramer, find out if what we are seeing is in any news announcements.'

'It's right here, just posted. Associated Press has a story. The government of Colombia announced that the army will be freeing hundreds of FARC prisoners from its army base at Larandia. They have arranged transport for them to their home territories. Many are going to the large FARC base at El Diamante only a few kilometers away. A goodwill gesture by the government troops and the army to help the peace process.'

Fred kept looking at the sat images. 'Here's another count. There are over 200 army vehicles, stationing themselves along the road out of Larandia.'

'What do you think, Kramer?'

'Transport guards for the buses.'

'Maybe, but why so many?' asked Sheilla.

Mark almost jumped out of his chair. 'They're going to kill them and bury them in mass graves away from the base.'

***

General Iván Tovar Ramos stood to the side, watching as the prisoners loaded into the buses. He couldn't help grinning. The prisoners that looked his way saw something different than they were used to in their most hated and cruel enemy. A man they blamed for killing many of their members, leaders, and friends. Was he happy to be releasing them?

Some, who could overcome their anger for the man, felt that maybe the peace process was real. That they would be able to rejoin society, and that Colombia would become a different place. A better place. Others were confused by his happy expression. Why would this butcher be happy about their release? Had they misjudged him?

***

Sasha, alias Viktor, used the release of the prisoners to execute the plan he had worked out with his CIA controller. He didn't know why they wanted the general and his top officers dead. He didn't care. He cared that he would get the funding for his research. If this was what it took, so be it.

The CIA black ops group run by Eileen was simply eliminating competition from their drug trade. Without the general involved, she felt confident they could take control. Her goal was to eliminate Ramos and then have the FARC and the cartels weaken each other, putting her ground operatives in control of the drug trade.

Sasha unscrewed the cap of the oversized jug and lifted it off. Liquid nitrogen swirled around the opening. He plucked one small plastic capsule from its holder and placed it in a small atomizer. As the substance in the capsule thawed, its contents would be dispersed into the air. He pushed a button on the front. He moved close; he could hear a faint whirring sound. He quickly left Ramos' office and went to the officers' club where he repeated the process. He then did the same in several of the officers' quarters.

He took the insulated jug to his quarters and locked it in a closet. He removed another Styrofoam box that he had sealed earlier. It contained several vials with pus from Mateo's sores. He walked outside and found General Juan Mancuso sitting in a jeep.

He handed him the small white, feather-weight box that contained a capsule from the jug. 'You have the blankets and now also this?' The Styrofoam container's lightness betrayed the gravity of its contents.

'Yes, thank you, Doctor.'

Viktor nodded graciously as the jeep drove toward the airfield.

***

'Seems planes do land at the airfield,' said Jim.

'Not what the place seemed to be. Not deserted,' said Brush, shaking his head, thinking about mortars.

'Lots of activity at the army base,' said Sheilla. 'It looked deserted one minute. Now lines of buses have driven in, and people are streaming out. Wait! A news flash says the army is releasing prisoners as a goodwill gesture.'

'Gold, are you in a position to see what is happening on the base?'

'Negative. A small plane just landed. Other than that, we don't have the elevation to observe much.'

'Find a position to observe for the night. We'll see you mañana.'

Roberta rolled her eyes. 'I love the army. We get to camp out again.'

'No hot grub for us tonight.'

'Crocs almost had some. Rations will be fine with me. I'd rather stay here,' said García.

***

'I want this kept completely confidential,' said Bertrand. 'So far, you, me, and the general are the only ones who know. Nevertheless, stay alert. We can never be certain what is known within these walls.'

'I am on the edge of my seat, Bertrand.'

'Pick a small group to assist you. If you think appropriate, someone from the IG staff to investigate Deputy Director Eileen Skinner. Use caution. She might have some traps set.'

Martin couldn't respond; he just sat dumbfounded.

'The Russian in Colombia was in her area of interest years ago. We need to know if that interest stopped when we thought it did, or if it is ongoing. In short, does the Russian still report to her? Or does he report to someone else? If so, who? If it is to her or someone in her group, then what is their interest in Colombia? One more rather large question: What black ops are we running in Colombia? Any connected with the drug trade?'

'More to the point, what ops is she running, right?' said Martin as a statement more than a question.

'If she or they are, then connections to whom? Cartels, government, army?'

'Bertrand, I need to say this. I know a long time ago, we clashed a little when I called you Bertie...'

'Don't, Martin. It's history.'

'I know it is. After Mexico, I gained a new lease on life and work. And I want you to know, I appreciate your confidence now. I always have, but I never said it before.'

'I always had confidence in you. To quote my philosopher namesake, "The good life is one guided by knowledge." Now go find us some.'

Martin raised the stub that was left after Najma amputated it at the knuckle. 'And guided by missing body parts.'

Martin started for the door. 'Martin, again...careful.'

'Okay, got it.'

***

It was well after dark when Jim and Brush strolled back into their camp. They had radioed ahead. Glenda was waiting near the south edge of the overgrown runway.

'Hey, babe.'

'Good thing you didn't get yourself killed, mister.'

'Doing my best to avoid it.'

'Welcome home. We're calling the place Squito Meadow.'

'Sounds about right. Just what I need. More mossies after the swamp.'

'We're holed up in the Q hut. We had extra mosquito nets, so we rigged some of them together to make a bug-proof enclosure. Then, we sprayed the outside with some OD army cans of bug spray.'

'As good as home. Better than wading with the snakes. Right,

Jim?'

***

'Welcome back,' said Neilly. Sounds like you've been having all the fun.'

'Could call a live explosive obstacle course fun if you apply some imagination,' said Brush.

'Nothing for us docs to attend to?' said Maria.

'Haven't looked. If we don't have some leeches, I'd be very surprised,' said Jim. 'If you have some antiseptic ointment or iodine we can borrow, we'll go change into something dry and remove any hitchhikers.'

Maria reached into a bag and tossed Jim a tube of antiseptic ointment along with a squeeze bottle of seven percent iodine.

Neilly turned to Maria. 'Not your usual hotel?'

'I always liked camping,' said Maria.

'You might convince me to like it,' said Sunita, 'if there wasn't something crawling on me every few seconds.'

'You can say that again,' said Trisha.

'Just ignore them,' said Abenaa. 'As soon as you get in your hammock, you will be fine. Just try mental control.'

'Hammock. Good idea. I'm off,' said Sunita.

'Not without me, you're not,' said Trisha, jumping up.

'Make sure you sit in the hammock and brush yourself off. Take the pills I gave you, rub the lotion on yourself, and spray your clothes,' said Doctor Dakine.

Jim and Brush walked over.

'Any leeches?' asked Maria.

'Just a couple of cute little babies,' said Brush.

'The reason we are here,' said Jim, 'is the lab tech, Mateo. We've lost control of that with all the side shows.' Jim stopped. The distinctive thump of a Huey grew louder.

Standing outside the Quonset hut, Jeff waved the chopper in. Marilyn took the helicopter forward until he gave the signal to stop.

Fourteen people jumped out.

Jago walked to Jim. 'This is one part of my unit. We go back and pick up the other ten and two barrels of fuel. This chopper will return nearly full in one hour. They will make camp a short way from here. We have been to this place many times.'

'You were loaded to the gills.'

'No entiendo.'

'It is just a saying that means full. I'm surprised that the chopper could fly with that many people.'

'Sí, many.'

Glad to have the extra bodies and fuel,' said Jim. 'My worry is who the CIA or the army have people embedded at your camp.'

'I trust my unit members. Maybe it could be true. You worry, Colonel, that spies will pass our location to our enemies and we could be attacked? We did not say anything to anyone about coming here.'

Jim nodded, hoping Jago was correct.

'Let's get a move on,' said Marilyn as she walked up. 'I overheard, and Jago told everyone what we decided earlier, that they had stolen the chopper in Ecuador, and he needed the rest of his unit to pick up supplies they had taken from the Ecuador army. No one saw me. I stayed in the Huey with my helmet and visor down.'

Sí, Colonel. No one asked about her.'

'Might work. Have Mac set up a radio jammer and collect all cell phones.'

Jago disliked that the colonel did not trust his men and women. On the other hand, he understood his caution.

***

'I see no other story that works for me, General,' said Bertrand.

'Sheilla, your thoughts?'

'The same. They took Mateo Rojoz and his parents. The only explanation is that he has smallpox, and they've found a way to pass it to the FARC prisoners. It's the only thing that adds up.'

'I don't know if our colonel is one step ahead but, on his request,

I've sent the backup HazMat med team to Panama. They have all the vaccine we have left in our stores—enough for about 5,000 people. Not enough if the FARC rebels have hundreds infected and are spreading the pox as we speak. Worse, they were likely exposed all at the same time. All the prisoners went in different directions. It is impossible to find them all before symptoms manifest.'

'If it wasn't diabolical, it would be ingenious,' said Sheilla. 'What about more vaccine?'

'WHO is prepared to send it. They don't know the whole story yet and are clamoring to be informed. They should be the first to know, but we need to hold them off for a little longer. They were told we are being cautious and are investigating.'

'Not much to be done now,' added Bertrand. 'If we are correct, the FARC is going to need a lot of vaccine.'

'One question. Fred says that army escort had hundreds of soldiers. A large contingent moved to the FARC's largest camp in the south of El Diamante. They have bivouacked a mile away and have put up guard stations at the exit roads. What's that mean?'

'That supports the story we've constructed,' said Bertrand. 'They are staying close. It will take several days for those infected to show signs. To stop the spread, the vaccine has to be given before the symptoms. They are going to try and prevent anyone getting into the FARC compound and anyone from getting out.'

'Mr. Gupta, that does not make sense. Why would they think anyone might supply the vaccine to them?' asked Sheilla.

'For the same reason that we are discussing it. We know, or suppose we do, that plans always fail because of the inherent flaws,' said General Will Crystal.

'Ah, insurance,' said Sheilla.

'Jim, with the help of the FARC, is going to have to bring the vaccine we have into the main camp. Then we must trace where all the other prisoners went. Without a doubt, we are going to miss many, despite our best efforts. WHO has the resources to track them. Eventually it will be contained. But I fear many will be infected and did,' said Will.

'Here's the problem,' said Bertrand. 'The rebels find out the army is behind the outbreak. The army reports to the politicians. The peace process blossoms into a war. Who are the beneficiaries?'

'The only player that wants to keep the war going is the army.'

'Why don't we use Eileen's contacts to get the vaccine to the FARC? She's the one with the contacts down there. If we don't bring her into this, she'll start wondering why we aren't,' said Martin.

The general caressed his chin. 'We keep it between us for a day and then bring her in. We'll get her to start using her contacts to deliver WHO's vaccine to the FARC. We keep her out of what Jim is doing. Jim will get our vaccine supplies to the rebels in the camp. Jago will be able to assist him.'

***

Sasha had always been a loner. He didn't care for people. Even as a child, his interests were not the same as the other children's. As an adult, he had little respect for or interest in anyone outside his field, especially the military or politicians. It still offended him that he sometimes overheard jokes about the funny little man, and the way his dark hair uncontrollably curled up on the sides of his mostly hairless skull.

The only thing that interested him was his research. He was not a speed maniac like Nusmen. He plodded along, slow and steady. He rarely ever wavered from his task. Twenty-four-hour focus. Besides his passion for orthopoxes, he was drawn to any lethal virus. He didn't know why, nor did he care. Perhaps knowledge of something that lethal, with an ability to destroy humans, gave him a feeling of power. Or perhaps the attraction was inexplicable. In Nusmen's words, the killer viruses were *neat*.

After the discussions with Bertrand, Martin, and Sheilla, General Crystal decided to phone Nusmen. 'Nusmen, we have a developing situation in Colombia. We are probably going to need more vaccine for the poxvirus than can be sent from Rio.'

'Wow, what situation?'

'We think smallpox is being used to attack the FARC by the Colombian Army.'

'We're out of vaccine.'

'We need more, which is one of the reasons I'm calling. The other, let me know as soon as you figure out the Variola strain.'

'I'm sequencing it now. It will be finished in three hours. We started replenishing the vaccine as soon as we shipped the stocks to Panama. I need to get back to work, sir.'

The general chuckled. 'Keep me updated. Understood?'

'Yes, sir. I understand.'

***

'Let's finish up here. Get this in the gel.'

'What was that about smallpox and the FARC? Is Jim in danger? Why do they need more vaccine?' asked Heather.

'I don't know. Some plot or other. Your boyfriend will be fine. He always is.'

'I wanted to ask the general about Jim.'

'Don't let him know we are working Variola together. He might not like it.'

Nusmen continued to pipette samples into a gel electrophoresis unit.

'You never liked Jim much, did you?'

'Huh, we have to work together now. I thought he was okay the last time we talked. Check the electrodes on the others while I finish this one.'

'Answer the question, Nus.'

'I think I like him fine. Maybe I haven't so much before. He's pretty scary and in charge, you know. He's my boss.'

***

'Typical,' said Neilly. 'A mission never turns out the way we expect it will.'

'Keeps life interesting,' said Brush.

'Assumption is the prisoners will pass on smallpox to a lot of their people. It can be stopped if we or WHO can distribute enough of the vaccine,' said Jim.

'Besides the army creating havoc with their enemy, what's their end game?' asked Mac.

'It means they zonk a lot of FARC and families,' said JP.

'The death rate is close to thirty percent. That's pretty devastating. Sheilla just told me that, from their research on Sasha, the Russians never thought of using Variola as an ultimate weapon. Rather they would use the virus to cause confusion and disarray,' said Glenda.

'The army,' said Mac, 'causes disruption, then when they are weakened, they go in and clean house.'

'Good guess. With one proviso—when the FARC figure out what the army did, they might attack them outside their camp. Then, Ramos retaliates sending the rest of his forces from Larandia.

'Ramos' troops will get smallpox unless he can vaccinate them,' said Mac.

'Plenty of time to vaccinate after, except for the soldiers involved in shuttling the FARC onto the buses. Unless he wants them to get sick, he would have to vaccinate them before,' said Jim.

'If he vaccinates the soldiers working with the FARC prisoners, an investigation would show he had advance knowledge. So he has to sacrifice them,' offered Glenda.

'Spect so,' said Jim.

'This plan could only have been hatched after Mateo fell into their lap,' said Neilly.

'They would be sitting ducks. Bunched up in their camp, weakened by the virus,' said Glenda.

'How do they explain how the FARC gets the virus?' asked JP.

'Ramos could say he tried to help his infected relative. They had no idea what he was sick from. The virus spread, and the FARC prisoners got it,' said Mac.

'That's it. And along with some of Ramos' troops,' said JP.

'So, now that we know the plan, we take vaccine to the FARC with Jago's help,' said Brush. 'Game over.'

'Except for the infected soldiers and prisoners that went back to their villages,' said Glenda.

'Eventually the pox will be contained,' said Jim. 'But Ramos might still get what he wants: a renewed war with the FARC, BWC, CIA, and in a few days, WHO, will need to start tracking down where the prisoners went. Either that, or start a massive inoculation program.'

'What mass inoculation program?' asked Maria as she pulled the netting aside. 'I can't seem to get to sleep.'

'We're just rehashing the situation,' said Brush.

'It's insidious, but also with a little diabolical genius mixed in. The way Ramos had it planned, they would look like the good guys and still get rid of many of the rebels,' said Glenda.

'And still keep their war going,' said Brush.

'It is going to be a long time before this is over,' said Maria.

'She's right. An impossible notion. We'll never find them all,' said Glenda. 'From what you say, it will be eradicated like it was before, but lots of people will pay for this with suffering.'

'WHO will bring in hundreds of people. They will try to isolate those that become symptomatic and inoculate whoever they were in contact with,' said Jim. 'We do what we can first. Sheilla will have to try to back-track using satellite. The FARC will have to give the vaccine to everyone that can be found.'

'Some goodwill gesture by the army,' said Neilly sarcastically. 'You think the FARC will let a government organization come in? They might blame this on the government, not the army.'

'Doubtful. We need to convince them. Jago might be able to help,' said Jim.

'And they could be right. Maybe the government or someone in the government is in cahoots with Ramos,' added Brush.

'Finding the lab tech, Mateo, is no longer the primary concern,' said Jim, 'other than they might still try to use him to infect more people or we might be able to help him.'

'One thing I know,' added Neilly, 'we are okay here as long as no one knows. Otherwise our position is crap. Not defensible.'

'I agree. Let's bring Roberta and García back now. Marilyn and the rest of Jago's company should be here soon. Then what?'

'We reverse course. The better place to be is in El Diamante with the FARC. We start vaccinating and training them to vaccinate. We talk to Jago as soon as he's back,' said Jim. 'I'll call the general and get his thoughts.'

***

'The CIA has only one asset that can get in and out of Larandia. A med doc, a Roberto Corpus. Finding Mateo might be useful, but your immediate mission, as I am sure you already figured out, is changed to stopping the spread of the pox to the larger group and also prevent the resumption of the war, which is likely the goal of General Ramos. Weaken them. Kill as many as possible. Peace process goes up in smoke,' said the general.

'I agree,' responded Jim. 'I don't know how much influence Jago has with the commanders, or even whether he would want to prevent more fighting. Some of the rebels are probably used to their current life and will be content, just like the army, to keep the war going.'

'The word we hear is most are weary of the fighting,' said Will, 'all of them government, rebels, and many of the army troops, Ramos is the exception. My job is to find out if the government is involved and to find out Eileen's history and her current involvement with the Russian. I need to know how deep this runs in the CIA. One last thing. Angélica Perez wants to talk to Jago.'

Chapter 52

The general sat in the leather director's chair, waiting for Eileen. Martin had provided him with an extensive history of her involvement with Viktor, aka Sasha. He felt anger that someone so high up would betray the organization. Bertrand and Martin had not seemed as upset. Bertrand had said, 'In truth, it is nothing short of a miracle that it doesn't happen more often.'

With the ops and black ops, and people buried for years undercover, he's right, thought the general. *We ask too much of our people.* He looked up as the door opened, and Eileen stood quietly. Her petite body was overshadowed by the large door frame.

'You wanted to see me, General?'

'Yes,' he said as he motioned her to take a chair.

Her defensive instincts pitched in. No coffee or tea. Not a casual talk on the sofa or easy chairs by the gas fireplace.

As she sat, she said, 'Our man on the ground, Roberto, Doctor Corpus, is entering the base as we speak. He is reliable.'

General Will Crystal held her gaze and said, 'Is the Russian reliable?'

Her eyes never left his as her mind raced, puzzling out what he meant by the question. 'Please explain, sir.'

'Precisely what I would like is an explanation of your dealings, past and present, with Viktor Ivanov.'

'Past dealings were a long time ago. If you will allow me, I'll go through the old files and prepare a report.'

She felt a sense of relief. He didn't know much.

His booming voice shook her, as he said, 'Minkin Alexsandr Danilovich, known to you as Sasha.' He glared at her, despising her betrayal of the agency and of her country.

The relief she had felt drained from her. If her bronze-toned skin could turn pale and reflect her feelings, she would be a ghostly white. She couldn't answer as his eyes continued to bore into hers. How did he find out? How did he learn Viktor's real name, and more importantly, the nickname she used for him?

'Ms. Skinner,' he said in a voice that enveloped her head, swirling with anxious thoughts.

Maybe he doesn't know much, just still fishing. Don't give him anything, she thought.

He continued, 'I have men and women on the ground. People I care a great deal about. Enlighten me.'

'He's an old contact, nothing…' Before she could say more, the general pushed a button, and the door opened. Martin and Eric walked in, followed by two military police and a dark-suited individual who proclaimed he was FBI.

'Sure, wait, General. I'd like to…'

'I want the truth. All of it. When you understand that, we talk.'

Bertrand, Eric, and Martin watched her being escorted away. The general motioned for them to sit down. 'Anything new, gentlemen?'

'A lot. A helluva lot, but not from us,' said Martin. 'We dug up the things I already apprised you of. It doesn't amount to anything compared to what your IT guys came up with. I have no idea how they found out so much, and Sheilla wasn't telling me how they did it. I'd like to know.'

Despite the general wanting separation between the BWC and the CIA, it was not possible. Still, he planned to keep the sharing as limited as he could.

'Martin, perhaps you'd be so good as to tell us what you learned rather than ask questions.'

'Sure, but I'm still curious.'

'Martin,' said Bertrand, with a voice that immediately encouraged Martin to comply.

'Eileen first came into contact with the Russian when he defected from the Russian Biopreparat. They spent two years interrogating him. They then sent him to Colombia and helped him get his current position with the university. That is where the story stops in our records. I'm comfortable that he is not a double agent or in contact with the Russians.'

'Curious that the Soviets just let him talk, and then skip off to Colombia for a new life,' commented Bertrand.

'It only makes sense when you factor in that his projects were discontinued, and the Russians had little further interest. Our knowledge stops with him going to Colombia. I talked with Sheilla only minutes ago. She adds a great deal to the story. It appears that Eileen has kept in close contact with Viktor, and she supplies him with funding grants.'

'That makes no sense,' said General Crystal.

'It doesn't. Except it now seems Eileen and her group are also involved in several black ops in Colombia.'

Bertrand furrowed his brows. 'I don't like the sound of where this is going.'

'Guaranteed you won't like it,' added Martin. 'To continue. She and a small group are directly involved in the drug trade.'

'Shit,' said the general. 'I thought all that ended in Asia a long time ago.'

Bertrand looked at Martin. 'The general gave Ms. McCarrick permission to share information with you. We want you to officially start liaising with her and her team. Get to the bottom of this. Please keep in mind this is the first time the general has ever allowed anyone from the company to work directly with BWC.'

'The connection with the Russian is still not clear?' said General Crystal.

'All I can say right now is that Eileen is connected to Colombia, drugs, and the Russian. They are related somehow, and we'll figure it out.'

***

The unmistakable thump of a Huey stirred the night air. 'Rock, Crusader is approaching.'

'Secure. Park outside,' said Neilly.

Marilyn set her chopper down a hundred feet from the rusty Quonset Hut.

'Hey, Mister Brush,' said Cherry, sauntering over. 'I no think I see you again.'

Brush couldn't help but grin at the dark-haired woman wearing a small purple tassel on her olive drab shirt collar. 'Your little jungle walk seems to have suited you, Cherry.'

'Are you flirting with me, señor?'

'No, but you do surprise me. The jungle is not always the friendliest place for our bodies.'

'It is my place, Major. It is part of me. Next to Jago, it is what I love.'

Brush looked closely at her. 'I think those things that you love would be foolish not to love you back.'

She touched his cheek. It was obvious to them both there was something special between them, something that made them feel good, even though they both knew it would remain out of their reach.

'We agree, señor.'

He nodded, knowing that his ability to keep this woman at a distance was yet more evidence of his caring for Glenda. 'Yes, we agree. Where is Jago?'

'He will be here soon. He understood I wanted to talk to you alone for a short time.'

***

'How many of my men are dead?' demanded General Ramos.

'Over one hundred,' answered Capitán Romero Ramos. 'You were meant to be one of them. I was meant to be one of them.'

342

'What has the Russian said?'

'We have just started to ask. It will not be long.'

'I want to know now. The cartels, the government... the FARC... who did this? They have killed many of my top officers. It was only luck that you, my son, were not at the Larandia and dead too. Do not kill him without finding who, why, and how we cure this poison.'

'Sí, Papá. I do not think you are safe here at the hacienda, either.'

'The soon to be dead FARC can't get out of their encampment, and they are celebrating. They are no danger. Did General Mancuso die?'

'I do not know, but I think not. I think he left in a plane. It was not at the airport.'

'What more can you tell me?'

'Very little. The men I sent to investigate looked sick. We killed them before they could get close to us.'

'After you finish with the Russian, join the rest of the men outside El Diamante. It is too dangerous to stay at the base.'

'It is easier to defend. My men can camp at the airfield. Whatever this sickness is, it does not seem to travel far.'

'No, this must be the FARC and the Russian. They did this. They learned our plan from him. I do not want our forces split. We will watch them die at their home base and kill the rest when they are weak. It is as the norteamericanos say, tit for tat, eh?' Then he laughed.

'You will join them or stay here?'

'We both stay until you find the answers from the Russian, then you join our men.'

'But, father, we will not be safe here without the army close by. The FARC will know. Why not return to Tolemaida? Take the troops. The FARC will die, no matter.'

'We have plenty of men to protect the hacienda, and as I said, most of the FARC are contained in their compound. Stick with the plan. The drug shipment needs to leave. It is a very important one. Find out who betrayed us from the little man. Then, you are to make sure that whoever our enemies are, they all die.'

'I'll be back with what the Russian says shortly.' Capitán Romero Ramos inherited one thing from his father—a complete lack of civility and empathy for human or animal life. He did not inherit his father's size or commanding manner. He was short, thin, and often appeared effeminate. Some thought his cruelty was to compensate for his feminine appearance.

'Do not be long, and do me a favor. I hate the sight of that little man's hair. Do as the Indians do in the movies.' Ramos laughed at the thought of removing the Russian's scalp. 'It will help persuade him to talk as well, I think. Yes?'

***

'Colonel Johnson, something is not right at Larandia. The army has left, and sat images show dead bodies outside the buildings. And another thing, our Huachuca Wolf Warriors have just picked up communications that General Mancuso has left for the Shuar village. Comm intercepts say he is meeting a company of soldiers there.'

'Where are the president and his daughter?'

'With the Shuar.'

'Protection for the president?'

'It doesn't feel right, sir. The president and Angélica left and communicated they wanted to go on their own. I don't like the sound of it, and no one has heard from them since they left.'

'I trust your instincts, but possibly the army with Mancuso is going to protect them, whether they want it or not.'

Sheilla didn't say anything.

A few seconds later, 'Okay, no choice. It could be a cluster fuck in the making if we lost Angel and the president now. Apprise the general. We will have to go back to the land of the Shuar.'

***

'Jago, we have some things to discuss. We're going to split up. That means you will have to split your company. Bring your squad leaders.'

'In the FARC, it is known as a guerrilla unit. Two of your

companies.'

Jim said nothing and looked at Jago, conveying that this was not the time for education.

Jago realized how serious the colonel was. 'Ten minutes for me to gather them.'

It was a large group that sat in the old hangar, including Doctor Dakine's HazMat team and Jago with his five subordinates.

'We have to split up,' said Jim. 'Neilly, I want four of your team to go with Brush and myself back to the Shuar. We'll need to take JP to translate, and one watcher. Jago, if you would send four of your group, ones that were with us before, that the Shuar know.'

All nodded. 'Doctor, you and your team, the rest of Neilly's and Jago's guerrilla unit, will go to Larandia.' Doctor Dakine started to say something. Jim stopped her and said, 'We think there is no one left there. No one alive anyway. Comm intercepts suggest a biological weapon. You'll have to suit up and investigate. Then coordinate with Sheilla and General Crystal about what you find. Let the general deal with WHO.'

'Yes, Colonel.'

'Neilly's and Jago's unit will act as protection. When you've wrapped up at Larandia, return to El Diamante and start training as many of the FARC as possible to inoculate those in the camp. Jago, work out with the doctor and Neilly how you will get the vaccine distributed and administered. You are going to have to inoculate everyone, including yourselves. Eventually, when there is enough vaccine, you will have to decide if you will let either your government or outsiders assist you.'

'It will be our leader's choice, not mine,' said Jago.

'Where do you want me?' asked Glenda.

'You're the best we have at coordinating the logistics with Sheilla, Maria, and the general until we get back from checking out the situation with the Shuar.'

'No way! I'm going with you. Mac can coordinate as well as I can.'

Jim looked at her for a long couple of seconds. Cherry looked expectantly at Jim with a slight smile. Brush looked at him like, what are you going to do about this, buddy?

'You're right, Glenda. Mac can coordinate with Sheilla. It's your time to visit the Shuar. Neilly, turn Roberta around. We want eyes on Larandia.'

Glenda felt embarrassed that she had challenged Jim, her boss, in front of the others. She immediately realized that he was not protecting her, but that she was probably the best with logistics and coordinating. She still wasn't used to being treated as a person, a team member. She decided to give him a chance to change his mind back to her handling the logistics.

She said, 'If you…' Jim cut her off. 'Decision made. Let's go forward.'

He doesn't look upset, she thought. However, she would not allow it to happen again. *Well, unless he's wrong about something,* she said to herself.

***

'Marilyn,' Jim said over the intercom, 'Larandia looks abandoned. Do a flyover, drop us off, and give us some protection. If it's clear, then we'll shuttle the rest of Neilly's team in, then the HazMat, and then Jago's group. We leave in ten hundred.'

Marilyn looked at Lobo and then at the diminutive Chico. She moved her head back and forth, weighing the cargo. *Full bird with the door gunner and supplies,* she thought. 'Sheilla, a bigger bird in Cuenca, if you can, and a Blackhawk fully armed.'

'You copy, Sheilla?' asked Jim.

'Yes, sir.'

'We need fast transport from Larandia to Cuenca as soon as possible after we arrive at Larandia. ETA thirty minutes.'

'On it, Colonel.'

Chapter 53

'Looks deserted, Colonel.'

'They have hidden bunkers surrounding the buildings. Might not be as empty as it looks. Gold, you have us?'

'In sight. No activity.'

'Fly over the buildings. Stay at 500 feet.'

'There are three bodies outside the green building.'

'Advise, birds picking at the bodies. Some birds are dead. Use caution. Keep me updated.'

'Will do,' replied Maria Dakine. 'Ah, is it always like this around you?'

'Maybe gas?' asked Marilyn.

Something lethal, airborne, chemical—not biological—too fast-acting, mused Jim. 'Don't rule anything out. Chemical is a good guess.'

As they circled the desolate base, a jet roared past and landed on the runway, just as a vehicle drove onto the base and up to where the dead men lay.

'Uh oh,' said Marilyn.

'Visitor,' said Jim. 'He's out of the car.'

'Probably the CIA contact that was asked to go in.'

'Try to call him off.'

Marilyn quickly spoke to Martin, who was now liaising and connected to the operations live comm. 'Martin, can you contact your man?'

Martin had obtained the CIA's Larandia contact information from Eileen Skinner's computer. He dialed Roberto's contact number.'

'Doctor, leave the area immediately. A biohazard team is close by.'

'There may be someone alive.'

Roberto hesitated. He craned his wide brown head and stood on his tiptoes to try to see better the people on the ground. They couldn't be alive with the birds pecking at them. Then he saw a bird fall on its side. He became frightened and backed away.

His eyes started to tear up, and he started to salivate. He became confused and stumbled back toward his car. It was apparent from the Huey that the man was in trouble.

'Marilyn, hover about a hundred meters upwind. After I'm out, gain altitude and stay upwind.'

Brush immediately grabbed for the atropine from his leg harness.

'You might need two.'

Marilyn maneuvered the chopper as Jim had asked, and he jumped out and ran to the man who was now lying next to his car. Doctor Roberto Corpus writhed in pain, holding his throat. He foamed at the mouth, and Jim, if he had not been certain before, was now from the wet trousers and the fecal smell. *Nerve gas? Fast-acting. Maybe VX,* he thought.

He pulled out the atropine canister and banged it into Roberto's thigh. Then, he moved farther away and stayed upwind, knowing he could not touch him. He waited for his symptoms to stop. *Any second now*, he thought.

Doctor Corpus started to breathe a little easier. Jim knew he couldn't do anything else. The best they could do was to get the chopper back and the medical team on site. Jim ran upwind and pointed for Marilyn to retrieve him.

No one said anything as he jumped on board. Marilyn put the nose down just feet above the ground and moved Jim to the plane that had just landed. The fastest plane he could have hoped for, a Globemaster III.

'I could give Sheilla a kiss,' said Brush. 'That certainly qualifies as a fast mover.'

'Not a chance, buster.'

'It's a fast flier, sweetie.'

'Not that, the kiss. I'll do it for you.'

Brush raised his eyebrows, and Glenda Rose Stuart smiled at him.

'I don't believe what I just saw,' said Glenda. 'He risked his life for someone he didn't even know.'

'It's what he does, and you would do the same. Wouldn't you?'

'I guess that makes three of us,' said Glenda, knowing that, like Jim's, Brush's heart was in the right place.

Marilyn set down close to the jet. Jeff was the first out of the chopper. It was a competent group: JP to interpret, Gaston if there was a need for explosive rigging, Aleski, Jeff, and of course, Jim, Brush, Glenda who, as an undercover FBI agent, had acquired a diverse skill set. And four of the most capable FARC fighters: Cherry, Lobo, Chico, and Carlos.

'I won't tell you how careful you need to be if it's VX,' said Jim.

'Watch yourself, Maria. I want to get to know you better when we get home,' added Glenda.

'Guess this is what we signed up for,' said Maria.

***

All through his life, Sasha had been fleeing. He never thought he would escape his mother Russia. Then the Americans came along. He had no reason to believe that the CIA was any different from the KGB, other than through rumors and stories that America was slightly better. He was still not so sure after experiencing both. He had escaped Russia and left the United States behind; he finally had come to believe that he would die in Colombia of natural causes. Something he had not expected in either Russia or the United States.

He had been wrong on all counts. He'd never considered that he would have a reason to free the capsule fitted under a back crown. It had given him a perverse comfort to know that he would never allow himself to be tortured. He had a low pain threshold, and the idea of torture appalled him.

Here I am, an old man, still living. I surprise myself.

He could sense that Captain Ramos would hurt him; that he was cruel. Even if he provided all the information they asked, the captain had the look of a man that enjoyed hurting people. *My lab has funding and will carry on,* he thought, and he felt pleased with that.

The door opened, and the young captain walked in with a slight smile. Then, he smiled more broadly but did not show his teeth. He walked to a side bench and picked up a hunting knife. Then, he picked up a knife sharpener and started to draw the blade across it, once, twice, three times.

'I am sure it was very sharp before, but now I am certain.' He nodded to a big man. 'Hold his head very still. I think one usually removes a scalp after someone is dead. That is what I have seen in the movies of the wild American West. Is that not so, Doctor?'

Sasha knew it was finally time. He tried to restrain his shaking. Still, he was not unhappy, as he thought of Mateo. He'd had the privilege of one last glimpse of his virus at work. He only wished he had had time to find out the strain. Perhaps it had been something rare.

The man put his beefy hands around Viktor's paunchy neck.

'I will tell you what you want to know, Captain.'

'I knew you would, but there will be time for you to say all you want after I remove the flesh atop your head with its silly little curls. My father said he hated those little tufts curving up on the sides. How to start? This will be an education for us both.'

He moved the knife to his left hand and, with his right, flicked his fingers at the tuft. 'Not even gray yet.' He nodded at the big man, telling him without words to hold their prisoner firmly.

As Capitán Romero Ramos was sharpening the knife, Viktor had pushed the loosened crown off with his tongue. It would have been impossible to get the crown off with only his tongue, but the moment he knew he was being captured, he had loosened it with his fingers. The thought of what might happen would have made Viktor quite ill, but now he knew it would never happen.

He spoke softly, and Romero moved closer to hear, relishing the little man's terror. Viktor moved the capsule between his teeth. It was brittle and designed to break. He bit it. The white powder was free. He moved it quickly to his tongue, mixed it with saliva, and spat directly at the young captain's face. The big man slapped Viktor's head. As he let go of his grip to slap him, Sasha turned and spat at the big man's pocked-marked face. Both men looked disgusted as they wiped the spit away. Then Romero grinned and spat back at Viktor. He was surprised that he had so much spit. Then his eyes started to water. He felt dizzy.

The Russian was foaming at the mouth and breathing hard while the would-be scalper watched as a wet space appeared at the front of his pants. He fell to the floor. He couldn't breathe. Pain coursed through his body. He writhed on the floor.

Three soldiers rushed into the room after hearing the banging that the young captain made as he kicked the floor. One looked at Captain Ramos and the other at the big pocked-faced man, known to them only as the "Interrogator."

Within minutes the three men were dead. The general's aide, Captain Sanchez, was called. He had no idea what was going on as he looked into the room. He held his breath and backed away, moving the other soldiers back with him.

***

Marilyn returned as fast as she could from Larandia to pick up the rest of the HazMat team and the SF. Neilly said he wanted the rest of his team here for on-site protection. That left room for only three HazMat members. Doctor Dakine chose Trisha Marshall, her disease specialist, and Jeremy Longridge, the virologist, for their initial investigation. There were six Special Forces: Neilly, Fleur, Mac, Joe, García, and Abenaa, not counting Tom and Roberta who were already on-site.

'García, we'll drop you on the way in, on the opposite side from Roberta and Teckie Tom. Take Joe. We'll leave you in a depression in a running insert. We'll move to the edge of their bunker areas and clear them.'

Marilyn flew just a few feet above the ground. She timed a down move in a depression. Neilly tossed out a canvas bag of supplies and ammunition. García jumped out with his sniper rifle, with Joe just seconds behind him.

'Do a flyover. I want to see Roberta's exact location. Then, drop us at the end of the bunkers nearest the buildings on the upwind side.' Spotting Roberta and Tom's position, Marilyn touched down as Neilly had ordered. They formed a protective perimeter, and then the three HazMat, in their bright yellow space-like protective suits, carefully stepped to the ground. They walked slowly toward Doctor Corpus' car. Dazed, he slumped against the tire.

'How are you doing, Doctor?' asked Maria.

'I've felt better. Thankful to be alive.'

Maria introduced herself and was about to ask him to stay put until they could get him help. She noticed a slight change in the wind direction.

'Let's move him farther away. Put him in the car.'

Trisha and Jeremy helped him up and into his car. Jeremy drove him another 200 feet beyond where the dead soldiers lay.

'Do you want to stay in the car or out, Doctor?'

'Inside. I will keep the window down.' Jeremy gave him a bottle of water and assured him they would be back as soon as possible. Then he walked back to where Trisha and Maria were looking at the dead soldiers and buildings.

'Jeremy, after you help me get the clothes off one of the soldiers, I want you and Trisha to take a quick look inside the buildings. I'll do an examination, collect samples, and maybe necropsy one of the dead birds. Any ideas on how to keep the living birds from leaving?'

'They certainly could spread whatever this is if they fly off to who knows where,' said Trisha. 'I don't see anything we can do to stop them.'

'Me either,' added Jeremy, 'the only thing we can do is try to keep more from flying here. But they don't seem to live long after pecking at the bodies. I don't think they're going anywhere.'

'I thought they were crows, but they have a whitish underbelly, a different type of bird.'

'Let's get started,' said Maria. 'Both of you, remove this man's clothes while I check in with the BWC and then take a quick look inside the closest building.'

'Base, you have our resident biochemist standing by?'

She wanted to say crazy, wild-haired, nuts, geeky—something, anything that described Nusmen. She reframed as it was not in her nature to say negative things about people, and the impulse to do so surprised her.

'We do,' answered Sheilla.

'Put him on, please.'

'Why are we using call signs?' asked Nusmen. You said this is a secure connection.'

'Just pretend it's a game,' said Sheilla.

Nusmen sighed… 'I don't have time for games.' Then he said, 'Oh… describe what you see.'

Doctor Dakine quickly but methodically described the state of the body and the birds.

Trisha and Jeremy walked up and waited patiently in their fully self-contained bright yellow HazMat suits. Dakine looked at them, knowing they were sweltering, and said, 'Describe what you saw inside the buildings.'

'A lot of dead soldiers, all with remnants of saliva, urination, and defecation,' said Trisha.

'Take a look at the others outside. Let me know if you see anything new or different. Don't go inside again until we have the rest of the team. It will be a few minutes before the helicopter gets back. Then split everyone into teams and check all the other buildings.'

'Now, Nusmen, I want to know exactly what you think caused this?'

'It's a nerve gas,' said Nusmen. 'It couldn't be anything else.'

'The operative word there was *exactly*. I think we figured it for nerve gas—what kind do you reckon?'

'Later-generation organophosphorus. VX is a good guess.'

Fred said, 'From what you described, the medical programs we have predict just what Nusmen has said.'

Nusmen turned toward Fred with a look that seemed to say, 'Of course, it would be what I just said.' Then, he turned back to the mic as Maria said, 'I'm going to do swabs, take clothing samples, and several tissue samples. Anything else we need to do to verify the diagnosis? While you are thinking about that, we have an exposed patient we need to attend to. Doctor Cahart, Geoffrey, are you listening?'

'Absolutely. You should use call signs.'

'Yes, well, forgot… We have oxime in our kits. We'll get the exposed doctor injected ASAP. Not much else we can do now.'

'If it's something other than VX or a VX derivative, it is probably too late. The aging time before the AChE bond becomes irreversible is quite rapid.'

'The atropine probably stopped the bonding,' said Trisha.

'Hopefully,' said Doctor Dakine.

'Your samples will be picked up in forty minutes,' said Sheilla. 'We have a DOD neurotoxicology expert that will be here when the samples arrive.'

Nusmen looked at Sheilla with a big grin. 'Exciting.' Then the grin faded. 'What do we need some expert for?'

'The general said so, to speed things up. How can you smile about people dying, Nusmen?'

'Well, I, ah wasn't thinking about them. It's the nerve gas that's exciting.'

***

'Jesus,' said Geoff. 'We just found a male in a jail cell, serious pustules on his face, arms, and upper body, along with an older man and woman, tied and gagged with no rash or pustules visible. There're a lot of air ducts. Noisy ones, running full force.'

'They must be the Rojoz. The missing parents and their son. Don't do anything until I get there with someone fluent in Spanish,' said Maria.

'Corporal, get to Geoff's position. Check on the ducts he is talking about. Tell me what you think they're for.'

'I think it is obvious what the vents are for.'

'Turn the system off, if you are sure,' said Maria.

'Yes, Doctor.'

'Geoff, look around for a key to the cell.'

It did not take Corporal Mendez long to find the electrical panel. Several wires were jury-rigged into the wiring. He flipped the circuits. 'Are they off?'

'Yes. Look for the jail cell keys. We can't find them.'

'Maybe it's electric. Not keys,' said Mendez.

'It isn't. Old-fashioned keyhole.'

'I can come in and blow it,' said Neilly.

'Give us a minute. They're probably here.'

'I found keys,' said Trisha. 'And what looks like an atomizer in the commander's office.'

There was only one oversized iron key. Trisha put it into the lock and turned it. The cell door opened.

'Looks more like a cheap motel room than a cell,' said Trisha.

'Corporal, keep talking to them. Reassure them we will take good care of them and their son. Tell them to be calm. I'm going to give them a shot before you untie them. I don't want them to get all freaky. Geoff, get a stretcher and one of our medkits. Trisha, keep looking around. Be careful to check in with me with one click every few seconds. If you get into any trouble, say so. Or give me an SOS by three rapid clicks, pause, three clicks.'

'Got it.'

The Rojoz couple looked terrified, even as Mendez tried to comfort them. Doctor Dakine administered the smallpox vaccine after noting there were no telltale vaccine marks on their arms, nor any visible signs of a rash. 'Tell them what I am doing, Mendez. Then tell them we are bringing equipment in to treat their son and ask them to stay back and not to touch our suits.'

While Mendez continued to talk to Luciana and Juan Rojoz, Maria turned her attention to Mateo. As she examined Mateo, she talked out loud, so everyone could hear. 'Mateo Rojoz has tightly packed pustules covering about ninety-percent of his face and arms and approximately seventy-percent on his upper torso. He appears unconscious. Corporal, tell his parents that we will do our best to cure him. Don't tell them that, with this manifestation, the survival rate is low. The odds are in his favor. Still, it might scare them to know he might die.'

Geoff came back in with the stretcher. 'Get him hooked up to an IV and saline. We'll take all three outside. I don't want to take a chance of the nerve gas drifting in here. For the record, Corporal Mendez says the venting went into a prison. It looks like all this venting has been rigged up to spread Variola to the prison areas. I think we can assume they spread the pox to the other prisoners before releasing them.'

'Diabolical,' said Sheilla. 'Any idea what the nerve gas is all about?'

'No,' said Maria.

'General Ramos wouldn't have done this to his soldiers and officers,' said Sheilla.

'Unless… maybe he wants to blame it on the FARC,' added Kramer.

'I have no idea at this point. Most importantly, we identify it; we won't know how long-lived it will be in the environment until we do. They're quite variable. If it's VX, it could be one hell of a long time, weeks to months, before it dissipates.'

***

The Globe Master was making short work of getting them to Cuenca. Jim relaxed and closed his eyes for a minute. He was wondering why Angélica had exposed herself and her father to danger by going unaccompanied back to the Shuar. But his thoughts were interrupted by Sheilla's voice.

'The doc you saved is still doing fine.'

'What's the latest?'

Sheilla then filled Jim in about the situation at Larandia. 'We've recovered the lab tech and his parents.'

'His situation?'

'Late stages of smallpox.'

'Prognosis is less than thirty percent survival?'

'Iffy, but Maria says he is healthy. He has a good chance.'

'The base is deserted unless you count the dead soldiers. We found several dozen soldiers four miles away, around a house. A big house. The only others we can find are outside the FARC encampment.'

'Sounds like officer housing,' said Jim.

'We're checking. At Larandia, the army rigged the ventilation system to suck air only a few feet from above the patient. Doctor Dakine reports that Mateo has joined pustules on his face, arms, and chest. Many are ruptured. The parents said that a woman spent many hours rupturing the blisters, mixing them with something, and then placing them in a small device that she turned on in the ventilation system. It is, or was, an atomizer.'

'Where did the ventilation system empty?'

'Into a large prison holding area.'

'What else?'

'The family is outside now, and Mateo Rojoz is in critical condition, but stable. They clearly used him to infect the FARC prisoners.'

Jim's mind raced, fully envisioning what the military had planned.

'We have a DOD toxicologist standing by at the BWC to analyze what killed the soldiers and what almost killed the doctor you saved.'

Chapter 54

It was not long after sunrise when Jim spotted President Noboa's helicopter sitting in a clearing over a mile away from the Shuar village.

As they approached the grassy meadow, Jim ordered, Gaston and Aleski to secure their perimeter.

The helicopter touched down. Both the FARC and SF forces were out by the time it settled into the grass. 'Let's take a look at the president's chopper,' said Jim.

There appeared to be nothing wrong with the chopper on the outside. 'I'll look inside.' Jim climbed in and said back to Brush, 'Do a walk around.'

Moments later, Brush opened the door. 'See anything inside?'

'Radio wire's cut. Starter wires and the ELT are disconnected.'

'Someone wants them off the grid, eh?'

'JP, you and Cherry scout the area toward the village,' said Jim. 'Chico, Lobo, load into our chopper with Brush. Scout the area, stay high, then fly north out of hearing range about ten minutes. Find a place to land and wait.'

'Smart, no?' said Chico.

'Why?' said Lobo, as Brush ran the blade rpm up.

'If someone hear us land, they hear us go. They see us leave and go north. Gone from area.'

'You guys have ears on back there?' asked Brush as he started to pull in power.

'Sí. Sí,' they both said.

'Watch out both sides.'

***

'We're close to the Shuar camp. We can smell smoke and hear chatter,' said JP.

'Take it slow. Get a close look, and see if you can locate our objective.'

'Will do.'

'Ghost, what do you see?'

'The military camp is about five klicks west northwest,' said Brush. 'The village looked normal, as best I could see from high up. I'll let you know when we find a parking spot.'

'How's your fuel?'

'Enough to give you air cover if you need it. Getting home, probably not. While we are enjoying the scenery, I'll make sure that our two new buddies understand the finer points of the seven-point-six-twos on this bird. Not much ammo. With the over-sized engine and stripped down, we can carry more people, but fuel efficiency is not so good. Keep it in mind.'

'Observing the village. Nothing abnormal,' said JP.

Jim thought for a few seconds. 'Use your judgment. Go into the village or scout around more. Maybe penetrate near the huts of Pwanchir and Pempeyo. We need our targets' location.'

JP and Cherry observed the village for another thirty minutes. JP used his monocular scope. They were looking west. With the sun still behind him, he was not worried about reflections. Still, like the rest of his unit, he was rarely incautious.

'What do you think, Cherry?' JP asked softly in his fluent Spanish.

'You have very good Spanish, Mr. JP.'

JP smiled at her. 'Okay. Let's move around to the far end where our two Shuar friends live.'

They backed up and moved south. They found one well-used trail and moved across it. As they moved closer to the village, they heard a faint crackle of a radio and a man talking in Spanish.

JP motioned to Cherry to move back. 'Seneca, Spanish speaker just outside the village on a radio.'

'See if there are any others, and then come back,' said Jim.

They spent the next two hours checking the village perimeter. They found a second military observation post.

'Two observation posts, south and north end, with two soldiers at each. Returning now.'

***

JP held the topo map. 'Aleski, the soldiers would probably approach the village from this direction. About the only place I see that you can view at least part of the village and have eyes on the army approach is here.' He pointed to a small rise on the map.

'I doubt there will be a line of sight through the undergrowth. Put someone else closer to the army camp, and I'll find a way to cover as much of the village as best I can.'

'Comm check?' Everyone nodded. Jim looked at Cherry and Carlos. 'We're possibly going to get caught up in an outnumbered fight. I need one of you to move outside the army's camp and let us know if they approach the village.'

'I go,' said Carlos.

'We move in at zero-four hundred. Cherry and JP, you know the position of the army observers. Eliminate them at zero-three-thirty. We secure a position near Pempeyo's hut and see what we can learn from them. Any questions?'

'I'll leave now and find a position,' said Aleski. 'I'll take Carlos. We'll make our way around the north side of the village, and then he can go on toward the army camp.'

'The wild card here is the army. We need the recon of their camp.'

Carlos had paid attention, but JP went into more detail with him in Spanish to ensure he understood that it was important and so that there was no confusion in Jim's orders.

'Cherry, any questions?' asked Jim.

'No, señor. Nada.'

'Jeff, Glenda, and Gaston, we'll approach from here.' His long finger traced positions on the topo map. After everyone knew the plan and their positions, Jim said, 'Let's spread out. Keep radio contact. We rendezvous here.'

Jim turned to Glenda. 'Let's move to the east side of the clearing. Gaston, you too.'

They settled down just outside the clearing and watched the others disappear in different directions.

'Base, do you read?'

Sheilla answered within seconds, as Jim knew she would. *When did she sleep?* he wondered.

'Affirmative,' she answered.

'Anything new?'

'Fred assures me we are on secure comm. Otherwise I couldn't say much.'

'Go ahead.'

'Mancuso has returned to Bogotá.'

'No word if he took any of the army company back with him?'

'None, so we assume they haven't left.'

'Okay, our plan,' said Jim. 'We stay stationary until zero-four hundred. Then, we enter the village. We're observing the army camp but have limited resources. Sat info or drone would help.'

'Understood,' said Sheilla. 'There is a drone now at Larandia, and another arrives at Cuenca in less than thirty minutes. I'll get them on site.'

'Good. We are shy of intel, and we want to avoid engaging the army. I'll check back with you at zero-one-twenty, unless you get anything on the army company's deployment sooner.'

'Shut-eye time,' said Gaston.

'I'll give it a shot, too,' said Glenda, as she propped herself up against a tree.

I wonder what Heather and Pedro are doing? I should be able to call tomorrow. Jim sat for some time, thinking first about them, then about the army, and finally about Angel and her father. *If we can figure out where they are holding them, and they're not dead,* he thought. *No use speculating.*

His thoughts were interrupted by a voice. 'Some new information,' said Sheilla. 'First, the house I mentioned with some army outside. It's Ramos'. It is where he stays when he's at Larandia. It's well fortified, but he has much less of the army guarding it than usual.'

'The general is thinking about taking him out?'

'The consensus seems to be that we cut off the head of the snake. He's not been a very good citizen. The general says you're on the ground. It's your call. The president felt he had to notify the Colombian president about the army's actions. The Colombian president is ticked that General Ramos has interfered with the peace process. He wants him removed. The general said he didn't specify what that meant.'

'Feasible?'

Neilly jumped into the conversation, 'We put eyes on the compound two hours ago. With Jago and air support, it should be doable. It is not being guarded well. Guessing that they think the FARC are contained at their base by their main force.'

'You okay with this?' asked Jim.

'I have a feeling that it's either now or later. Without Ramos and his officers, the army will have lost, and the government might be able to talk the rest of them down,' said Sheilla.

'I concur. It will probably save lives in the long run. Capture as a first option. Good luck,' said Jim.

'We'll keep you informed.'

'Okay, Sheilla. What else?'

'The young pups, Jake and Jason, have been bored silly monitoring Ecuador. They intercepted this, though. A takeover by General Mancuso is in the works. He is trying to rally other commanders and a few politicians. No one apparently knows where the president is. That is, except us and Mancuso. I'm assuming Mancuso is having them held.'

Jim didn't answer for a minute. 'Degree certainty on a coup?'

'High.'

'When?'

'Our best guess is tomorrow. There's more.'

'Mateo's parents said that the army put blankets on him every hour over the two days they were there. A little background research reveals it's something the English did to the American Indians. The gift of a free blanket infected with the pox. A goodwill gesture that nearly wiped out the Indians.'

'I remember reading about that once.'

'Mateo's parents also said they were colorful blankets. Too few of them to do much damage to the rebel forces.'

'You think they brought the blankets here?'

'I do. And it jibes with the intercepts. We think they are going to try and do as much damage to the Shuar as they can and blame it on the pox. We think they want to get rid of interference in giving mining concessions after they have control. Makes sense. It's the same basic plan the army is using with the FARC. They've decided to eliminate the problem after Angélica's push to save the indigenous tribes and their land. Our guess is they were going to subject the president and daughter to the same pox fate.'

'If they're not already dead.'

'Yes, Colonel. Hard to say at this point.'

'Get me info from the drones as soon as. Then, get some vaccine on the way for the Shuar.'

***

Jim looked at his watch. Nineteen-fifteen. He called everyone over. Jim made sure Brush, Lobo, and Chico were listening. He explained the new situation.

'New plan, then?' asked JP.

'We head to the village just after dark. Cherry, Glenda, and JP head in first and take out the two army outposts. After we enter, we do a quick look around, just to make certain the pres and Angel are not there. Then, we move on to the army camp and retrieve them. We assume they are alive until they aren't. Carlos should be able to give us something on the army camp before we move there.'

'Minus the four at the village, that'll leave about three dozen?' said Brush. 'Not bad odds, eh?'

'Typical. We've had worse. Gopher, forget the village. Move north around it, and find a spot above the army camp. Better terrain there, and we will need your eyes on the army. Advise location when you're settled in.'

'Affirmative,' responded Aleski.

'As soon as the village is secure, Jeff, Gaston, Glenda, and Cherry, join Carlos at the army camp and recon.'

'I like the way plans always sound simple,' said Gaston. 'What about the chopper?'

'Stays in reserve.'

Visible under the subdued red glow of the headlamps, Jim lounged back, his lanky body against a tree. He stretched out with a long blade of grass caught at one end in his teeth and the other end pinched between his thumb and index finger.

'That's about it. Soon we'll have some recon from you four, Aleski, Carlos, and the drone. Our advantage is surprise. The chopper only has limited ammo, but we will have Aleski watching over us.

'A few tranquilizing darts might not hurt,' said JP.

'Suggestions?' asked Jim.

No one said anything.

Jim thought about the oversized Lobo and the pint-sized Chico in the chopper. Then he looked at Cherry. 'You might like to know that your favorite general, Ramos, may not survive the night.'

Cherry smiled, her eyes crinkling, 'It has been our wish for many years. How you do this?'

Chapter 55

Neilly looked at his partial team. 'We're cleared to go. The numbers are on our side with the help of the FARC, who are going to carry the fight with a frontal assault. I feel comfortable with the plan. Ramos' men are experienced fighters. Let's not get careless. We're going to go in from the near side. The FARC on the opposite side. We move in as close as we can get to the general's house. The FARC launch a frontal attack, and Marilyn backs them up from the air. The mission is to capture Ramos and any officers, if possible. We sit back and see if he moves out of the house after the FARC launch. If not, we go in after him.'

'García and Roberta will position here and here.' He pointed to vantage points on opposite sides of the house on the sat image Sheilla had sent.

'Call signs are: Roberta, Gold. García is Mosquito. Mine is Rock. Marilyn is Crusader. Our target, Ramos, has not ingratiated himself with anyone in the government lately. If grabbing him gets too complicated, we terminate him. I'll make the call. Understood?'

'Understood, boss,' answered Roberta. García nodded.

'Marilyn, you shuttle the med team to the FARC camp. Dakine's team is organizing inoculation procedures. Jago says there is a low area and a depression on the far side from the army. They shouldn't hear you from their encampment on the front side. Jago will send someone with you to liaise. You'll bring back warm bodies for the operation. Wait in Larandia until I signal you, and then support the FARC assault. Any questions?'

'I've got a minigun and an M-60. Who are going to be my door gunners?'

'Fleur can handle the minigun. See if Jago has anyone experienced for the M-60.'

'I don't like anyone I don't know on a gun.'

'Your decision. Advise when you decide.'

Jim watched her go and turned to Roberta.

'What about their choppers?' asked Roberta. 'Ramos has three.'

'Jago will blow them. Marilyn's first backup if they start to get off the ground. I don't want to give either yours or García's position away unless we have to, but if they start to get off the ground and past Marilyn… Roberta, you'll be in the best position to take them out. García is back up.'

'Those three UH-1H will be toast at that range. I doubt you'll need us with Fleur on the minigun,' said García.

'Shit happens,' said Roberta.

'Every day.'

'The general's troops could reinforce in about an hour,' said Roberta.

'If Jago gets stalled outside the compound, reinforcements will have him sandwiched,' added García.

'That brings me to you, Tom. Coordinate with Sheilla. Jam their comms. Sheilla and the computer geeks can monitor and block their radio communication. Any cell calls they make will go through the cell tower here.' Neilly pointed at the location on the map. 'Jago will leave two people to destroy it before they launch their assault. No comm equals no reinforcements. However, if they get an SOS past us, our safety net is still that we have an hour.'

***

'Bravo in position,' said Neilly.

'Comms neutralized,' reported Teckie Tom.

'Alpha in position,' said Jago.

'Gold and Mosquito, change of plan. Assist B with guards at gate and fence, and then, take out the choppers.'

'Wilco,' said Roberta and García.

Fire erupted near the front gate and along the fence. Roberta and García took out targets near the fence. Immediately, three soldiers ran for the choppers. Roberta and García each took out one. The other pilot made it to the leftmost chopper and started to spool up the blades. The cockpit was not visible to either watcher. The chopper started to lift as Roberta found the tail rotor hub with her second shot. The chopper at first started to slowly rotate to its left, and then picked up speed before touching the ground with its skids. The left skid caught on a cement curb, tipping it over. The main blade churned the dirt, before breaking apart. A broken piece found the fuel tank, and the chopper erupted in flames.

The two watchers turned their attention to the general's house when several of Ramos' guards moved to the porch and started firing at Jago's rebels. The guards were experienced fighters. They moved rapidly from left to right, taking cover and moving with a precision that impressed Neilly. Nevertheless, they dropped one by one as his two snipers found their targets.

The attack ended quickly as Jago's soldiers moved to the house. Jago had stopped momentarily beside a fallen rebel. He bent over and then rose, walking toward the house. A door opened on the house, and the general turned toward the advancing rebels. With hands raised, he walked onto the veranda. He stood for what seemed like a long time as Roberta and García watched him through their scopes, their fingers touching triggers, waiting. Before Neilly's orders to hold fire came, they watched as the general's back erupted, misting the air with flesh, blood, and bone.

Jago had no intention of letting their prize survive another moment. General Ramos had been the cause of death for far too many of their comrades for them to allow anything besides his execution. Being part of the general's elimination would become a major source of pride for the attacking rebels. Jago knew he would not be able to restrain them and made no effort to prevent what seemed to them all the final battle for their freedom and the taking back of their country. Partly as payback for the years his people had suffered under this man, and partly to secure his place in the future of the FARC, Jago had made sure that he was positioned to execute the general. Normally, he disdained politics. Every once in a while, the situation allowed an exception.

The small battle today had not been thought of by Jim or Neilly as the end of a long war. Jago's men and women, however, knew that this battle, coupled with their government's talk, held the promise of the struggle's end.

The general's troops never received a call to reinforce their commander's compound. The block worked, but the rebels received a call. The soldiers outside the FARC's base were perplexed by a sudden rupture of shooting and cheering. Guns shooting into the heavens, the cheering and celebrating spread across the compound like a ripple in a pond at the news of the General Ramos' death.

***

Nusmen paced back and forth in the large empty hangar, waiting impatiently for the arrival of the samples from Doctor Dakine's team. She had collected and sealed two of the atomizers, samples of blood and tissue from the bodies and the two dead birds. In another container, she had sealed pus from Mateo's blisters and blood samples from both him and his parents, all cushioned in oversized containers.

His impatience was suddenly broken by the sound of a jet, taxiing to the front of the hangar. He rushed to the door.

Nusmen was excited as he rushed to the elevator with the samples. He debated what to work on first. Both sample types enthralled him—the first pox collected in the environment since its eradication and an exotic nerve gas. Both would be moved to the level four security where he would not rest until they were fully analyzed.

His mind raced. He wanted to perform every analysis himself. He didn't want the so-called government toxicology expert involved, but he had no choice. Not only because of General Crystal's specific orders but because even he could not be in all places at the same time.

The general knew Nusmen well enough to anticipate that his biochemist lab rat would want to do everything himself. He gave stern orders to Nusmen. Further, he asked Sheilla and Doctor Milton to instruct all staff to immediately report to Barbara or Sheilla if Nusmen caused any trouble.

Barbara looked at Nusmen and smiled. 'Well, Nus. It looks as though every eventuality has been anticipated, and you will have to be a good boy.'

Nusmen looked back sulkily. 'I'll be in level four working on the pox.' Nusmen soon forgot the general's order. He started working on the virus, injecting it into egg embryos. He had brought a laptop and researched different nerve agents while he worked. *Fascinating what the Russians did. They worked for years to make a more potent VX gas, and they succeeded.*

As he acquired knowledge about the gases and their chemistry, he became more and more exhilarated. The orthopox would have to incubate. There was no harm in looking in on what the toxicologist's so-called expert was doing. He might even be able to help.

Chapter 56

The light dimmed to shades of opal. The jungle was still. There was no wind. The sounds began their transition from day to night. The jungle cacophony intensified as darkness closed in.

Jim had sat patiently, waiting for the progression from gray to charcoal to the inky-black darkness that only the jungle can produce. No starlight. No moon creeping through the interwoven canopy of leaves and plants to the understory.

His thoughts turned back to Heather and Pedro, his family. *I have become a family man, but what else am I?* To some, he was an efficient killer. To others, a compassionate savior. In his mind, he was neither. He did what he did because the situations gave him no choice.

I've never shared my thoughts with anyone about who I am, he mused. Not even Brush, although Brush intuitively knows. Jim thought of himself as a social outcast, a rebel. *Who was it that said, 'Resist much. Obey little?'* After a moment, he remembered that he'd read it in an Edward Abbey book. The quote was from Walt Whitman, and Edward Abbey had adopted it. *What was the book?*

It was a good title, not normal. Then it popped into his mind—The Monkey Wrench Gang. Jim admired the book and its author for many reasons. The anarchist, Abbey. A true rebel. Abbey's love of the desert mirrored Jim's own. However, Jim was vastly different from Edward Abbey, who despised all government in Washington. Jim most often had little respect for elected politicians and their perception of truth, but his life was inextricably intertwined with the U.S. government. And there were those he respected.

He, Brush, and the general had survived by not trusting bureaucrats. *How many are corrupt?* he wondered. Many were out of touch with the people they pretended to represent. But what were they like underneath? It was a stupid question. Vietnam had taught him that many people fell to the ends of the moral spectrum. There he learned that when people were not held accountable, some had no compunction about harming the weak, raping children, killing those that could not protect themselves, and torturing the helpless for fun.

At the other end of the spectrum were the kind, loving people. As dramatic as the differences were, when there were few rules such as in Nam, the dichotomies of human nature were on full display. Back in the "world," in society, most evil people buried their true nature. The evil ones blended in and assumed a normal moral appearance, only occasionally allowing their true nature to burst into public view.

In society, Jim was an observer, not a participant. He was often detached from people, especially when they employed groupthink, which he despised. Sometimes, he felt himself floating through, or above a crowded sidewalk or gathering.

Normalcy could not prevent an occasional bubbling through the fabric of obscured personalities. If they showed him evil, he had no remorse in removing them. If they fell to the other side of the equation, the kind side, he did what he could to help and protect them. On reflection, he understood that it was almost impossible for Heather to understand who he was.

Jim stood.

'Let's execute,' he said. 'Firecracker,' the call sign for Cherry, Glenda, and JP. 'Advise when targets are down. Gopher, report.'

'In position. Not many soldiers visible. Lots of tents and fires. It's very quiet. Could be sleeping. Or a better guess, they're not here.'

'Jim,' said Sheilla. 'The drone shows a few heat signatures other than fires in camp. Something feels off. We do not show them leaving. They should be there. The airwaves are silent. You won't see much on the drone images. It's armed and active. Fuel left for three more hours. Refuel now or stay?'

'Keep it on-site. Expand the recon area from the soldiers' camp to the Shuar village.'

Jim was the last to leave the meadow. He looked up one last time before entering the darkness. Silhouetted against the night sky, treetops reached for the stars. Long slender vines hung from branches, making their way to the ground. Other vines, thick as elephant trunks, spiraled up the larger trees.

He followed the path with his night vision turned off. In the darkness, it was nothing more than a figment of his imagination. Slow stepping, he turned his head back and forth to get an image of the path that the others had walked moments before him.

Ahead, a small red light blinked twice. He stopped instantly. If the army taught you anything, it was that a signal to stop meant now. The same light blinked three times. JP was walking in front of Jim and being cautious. Instead of walking forward, Jim placed his GPS under his shirt and switched on the night illumination. They were just outside the village.

They stood waiting for Cherry, JP, and Glenda to report the elimination of the two army listening posts. Minutes later, Cherry said, 'Clear.'

'Firecracker, move to positions. No delay.'

'Sí,' said Cherry as she moved out of the village to the north.

'Ready, Ghost,' said Jim.

'Ten minutes out,' said Brush. He turned to Lobo and Chico. 'Careful where you aim.'

'No delay to rendezvous,' said Jim.

JP and Glenda walked fast to Pempeyo's and Pwanchir's hut. Jim, Jeff, and Gaston were already talking to the two men.

'Army's here somewhere,' said Jim.

'JP, ask if they know anything about the president or Angel?'

'They say they left with the military. The military is camped just outside the village.'

The two Shuars stood pointing.

'How far and how many?' demanded Jim.

'Not far and many. They gave us blankets and acted friendly, but Pempeyo did not see sincerity in their faces.'

'You have lots of movement less than a couple of hundred yards from the village, to your west and northwest,' said Sheilla sounding nervous.

'JP tell the Shuar to stay put and not to follow us.'

'Ghost, fly as close as you can to the north side of the meadow but stay out of hearing range.'

'On my way.'

'Base, I need visual both to the east of the village and the meadow. Drone stays on the meadow side.'

Gaston, you're in the rear, at the meadow, take the north. Jeff, you're point. At the meadow take the south side. Glenda with me, NVGs on.

Jim was moving fast with JP, as Jeff jogged ahead. Gaston let Jim, Glenda, and JP move forward ten meters before following.

'Colonel, soldiers are in the village.'

Shots erupted from the village.

Jim raised his pistol and fired two shots in the air, followed by three more. He did not want to have a firefight in the village He needed to draw them away.

'They're taking the bait and moving our way' said Gaston.

Random shots were fired behind them as they retreated. They were wild shots and it told Jim that whoever had fired was not well disciplined.

'Base, you have all positions?'

'Yes. Sorry, we…'

'Save it. Constant updates on positions. Let them pass well outside the village, then use the drones to light 'em up. Start firing from the village side. Herd them toward us. Ghost, stay north of Meadow and out of hearing.'

Brush had formed a visual of the battle scene. Jim would lure the army back to the meadow with a little encouragement from the drone firing rockets at their rear. Jim would signal when he was ready, and Brush would sweep in from the north to the meadow, strafing the army. *They're badly outnumbered,* Brush said to himself. He tried to keep Glenda from his thoughts.

Appreciating the improved depth perception in the ghostly illumination, Jim was slow jogging, concentrating on the path and what was ahead. He dearly hoped that the army had not left men in the jungle on the far side of the meadow.

'Base, update Ghost's location, Firecracker, and Gopher positions.'

They hadn't discussed contingency plans simply because they didn't know where the president and his daughter were being held. Jim was almost certain that, if Angel and her father were alive, they would be in the military camp.

The army had been expecting a rescue mission by soldiers loyal to the president, not by U.S. Special Forces. It had been well-planned, and they had evaded detection except for the two listening posts. *Good plan, not well executed,* thought Jim. *Their inexperience is the one thing on our side.*

Jim's response was to set up an ambush, using the drone to eliminate as many as they could before they got to the meadow. The drone would be hampered by the dense foliage and would only be able to target the soldiers when they hit a clear spot. It was too risky to use the drone in the meadow. Too close to their positions. Jim would let them advance into the meadow, and the chopper would attack from their flank. Jim, JP, Glenda, and Gaston would take on the ones that had made it through the ambush.

'You're outnumbered. Best estimate ten to one,' said Sheilla.

'Base, monitor their comms. The prisoners are still our objective.'

'On it.'

Brad was listening to the communication exchanges. Sheilla did not have to pass on what the colonel had said. Nevertheless, she confirmed he had heard.

All five made it to the meadow and then across as multiple explosions lit up the darkness behind them. Without a clear line of sight, the drone could not effectively direct its Hellfire missiles. Still, some of the soldiers would be eliminated. They would soon know how many. *As a minimum, the unexpected missile attack would disrupt them, and then push them into the ambush. If their commander is seasoned, he will be concerned about the source of the explosions before engaging,* Jim reasoned. A drone attack would never be considered as they were still in the experimental stages, and few had even heard of them.

Jeff was the first to the meadow and rushed to the south side. Jim, Glenda, and JP moved straight across. Gaston stopped with a claymore and, within seconds had it set with a tripwire strung across the trail.

'Ghost advised friendlies north, south, and east.'

Gaston nodded, as if to say good booby-trap. Then he moved to the north side. He was second in charge, and Jim had put him in the safest position, whereas the colonel had placed himself in the most dangerous position.

'Firecracker, Gopher, hold position. Give it a minute to see if Base can locate the objective.'

'I think we might have them,' said Sheilla. 'Six blips on my screen moving from west of the village toward the army camp. I wouldn't expect the army to move away from you.'

'Is there an intercept point for Firecracker?'

'They're moving on a trail. Approximately 300 meters ahead of them is a small opening. Firecracker one can make it if they hustle. Gopher is further away.

'Guide us. Nos vamos rápido,' said Cherry.

'Gopher,' said Jim, 'have Base position you. I'm about to be busy.'

***

Sheilla didn't feel comfortable making tactical decisions. However, she was proud of the trust that Colonel Johnson placed in her. In this case, it was a necessity. *No mistakes now, girl,* she said to herself.

A loud blast from the far side of the meadow. The claymore. Several minutes passed. Slowly, individual soldiers emerged into the faintly lit meadow.

Despite losing men, their commander was still moving them in pursuit of Jim's earlier shots.

'Main body still moving toward you,' said Sheilla.

A good ground commander would probably choose to move several of his men to the flanks and sacrifice a few charging the middle. The flankers would have his enemy in a crossfire. As it was, Jim and Glenda would pull back, leaving their two flankers to either ambush those entering the meadow or prevent the soldiers from flanking Jim and Glenda.

Jim needed to understand the opposing commander to be able to counter his or her moves. Everything he was seeing and hearing told him the commander was not a strategist. A word that Jago had mentioned to him perfectly described what he was doing with the opposing commander. "Chesswits." *Nice word,* thought Jim.

'Base, numbers and location approaching the meadow?'

'The cover is too dense to say for sure. The drone targeted several groups that were bunched up. I think it was effective. Best guess is thirty remaining.'

'No calls for backup?'

'None.'

Several soldiers had moved into the clearing. Three were moving toward the abandoned chopper. Jim let them advance toward his position. He searched for targets in the night vision scope. Behind the front soldier, a radio antenna waved in the air. He selected the soldier next to the radioman.

Jim sighted on who he thought was the leader and squeezed the trigger. Then, a fraction of a second later, he shot the radioman, both with a single shot. He flipped the selector for automatic as he ducked and dove to his right. The foliage, where he had just been, erupted in fragments of wood and leaves. Then, he rose and swept left to right across the closest group who, foolishly, were still upright in the meadow. He eliminated, or wounded, four. The remaining soldiers dove to the ground. Jim alligator crawled behind a log he had spotted fifteen feet from his original position.

A small group of soldiers moved to Jim's right flank. Glenda fired on full auto, ducked, and shifted her position. While she had been well trained in the FBI, her training had not included jungle warfare. When she was recovering from gunshot wounds in the hospital over a year ago, she and Brush had spent many hours discussing various tactics, both hers and his. Putting those discussions into practice for the first time now had saved her life. The undergrowth where she had fired from, and immediately left, exploded in a torrent of bullets.

As outnumbered as they were, it was skills learned through long experience, and to a lesser degree, those Glenda and Brush had discussed in her long hospital convalescence that equalized the firefight.

The soldiers nearest the disabled chopper ran towards Jim's left flank. JP lobbed a grenade at the three tightly grouped soldiers.

Gaston and Jeff knew to stay in reserve as long as possible. Their job was to prevent the attackers from making an end sweep, or from getting behind Jim, JP, and Glenda.

'Hold fire,' said Jim.

'Ghost, you're up.'

The soldiers on the far side of the meadow continued to fire on Jim's old position. With no return fire, he hoped they would gain confidence and attack across the meadow. Once again, their inexperience played into Jim's hands. One, two and then nearly a dozen soldiers moved cautiously across the meadow. No one needed to hear anything from Jim. The second he opened fire, JP and Glenda fired on the exposed soldiers nearest them. Between the drone, Gaston's quickly rigged claymore, one grenade, and Jim's NATO MP-5, and the well-placed rounds from Glenda and JP, the Ecuadoran army company had been reduced to just over a dozen.

'Pull back,' ordered Jim. 'Hunker down.'

Just as he said that, the remaining force emerged into the meadow, charging their positions. Jim slowed their charge by taking out the two in the lead. The others dropped to the ground and continued to fire as Jim low crawled away toward his rear.

'Base, move the drone to cover Firecracker.'

Just as the army soldiers rose, a reassuring thump, thump beat the evening air. The sound was like a sedative to Jim, slowing his heart rate and countering adrenaline.

The soldiers stopped advancing as they looked toward the sound.

Brush turned the chopper sideways, 'Lobo, try not to hit our guys. Halogen going on. Watch those baby blues.'

Brush clicked off his NVG just as he switched the powerful light on. The meadow scene jumped into view, green plants, the president's helicopter, ten soldiers blinded by the light.

Lobo caressed the M-60's trigger. Shell casings spit out as he swept the machine guns' bullets through the soldiers. The soldiers fired blindly at the searchlight. Their shots were wild, as Lobo continued to strafe them.

'Hold tight, turning,' said Brush.

Brush floated above the meadow for a few seconds, then sharply banked to his left, doused the light, and dropped down. Within seconds, he had maneuvered to the other side of the meadow, turned the searchlight on again, giving Chico his chance at those still standing.

This time, Brush moved his position after only a few seconds. Two soldiers survived and retreated toward cover. Gaston fired two short bursts, dropping both. Only one soldier remained, a battle-hardened sergeant. He had sensed that his company was outclassed. He was still on the other side of the meadow, shielded by tree trunks, and when Gaston fired, the sergeant saw his muzzle flash. He fired half a magazine in Gaston's direction and then quickly, just as Jim, Glenda, and JP had done, crawled away from where he had fired from. Shielded by the trees, he got up and ran.

'NVGs on. Report,' said Jim. 'Then we get back to our objective.'

One by one, each reported in.

As Brush banked away from the meadow, he was relieved to hear Glenda report in. Then she yelled. Brush tensed.

'I'm on an anthill. They're all over me.' She whacked and brushed madly at them. Brush, feeling relieved said, 'I wish I was there with you. Watch it. Some ants have a pretty nasty bite.'

Jim moved to Glenda and flicked an ant off her neck. 'Brush is right. These are bullet ants. You don't want to get stung.'

'Jesus, bullets, and bullet ants. All in a night's work,' said Glenda. 'Thank God for not much exposed skin. Except I got something that stings like crazy on my hand. Man, oh man, this is freaking painful.'

'Just looked them up,' said Sheilla. 'Very nasty sting. It's a neurotoxin. Hmm, one of the worst according to what I'm looking at. Nothing you can do. It's painful but not dangerous.

'You got that right. I think I would rather be gut shot again.'

'The toxin is supposed to give you a real high as it wears off.'

'Soon, I hope.'

'Jeff, circle around and make sure we're clear. Gaston, same for your side. Let's see if any are still alive,' said Jim.

'No can do,' said Gaston. 'I have a small first aid issue to deal with.'

'How bad?'

There was no answer.

'Jeff, correction. You go straight to Gaston. Jean-Paul check for survivors. He's only a few meters away from me.'

Gaston was not moving when Jim got to him. 'Jeff, head to the village pronto. Careful on the way. The Shuar might need some medical attention,' said Jim.

'His status?' asked Jeff, gritting his teeth. *Let him have a slight wound that Jim can handle.*

There was a long pause.

'He's gone.'

'Oh, man,' said Jeff.

No one else commented. They all wanted to. They had all lost comrades, friends in the past. Gaston had been a favorite of everyone. They liked his family. They liked it because he had a family. They steeled themselves to the reality. They needed to finish the job at hand. The team members were not prone to getting angry at their opponents when they lost someone. They took the loss personally, but it wasn't their enemies' fault for doing their job.

Jim sighed. It was always in the cards to lose someone. That didn't make it feel any better. His mind drifted back to Seattle when he had first encountered Neilly's team and his XO, Gaston. 'Base, notify the general. Notify Neilly if you or he thinks it's best. But, I'd rather talk to him personally after we're airborne. He should hear it from me.'

***

'Nusmen, let me do my job. I don't need any help. I thought you had orders to keep away from me.'

'I can help. I read up on nerve agent chemistry last night.'

'I've been studying this my whole life, and you're an expert after a one-night stand?'

'Yes. Let's get these into the mass spec. And I know the equipment here. Then, I want to do UV, IR, and then NMR. We can do them at the same time. It'll verify the result with multiple tests, and it won't take any longer.'

'It's my analysis. Agreed?'

'I don't care about that. I want to see what it is.'

'It's a V agent. I assume VX.'

'I was reading up on all the derivatives that the Russians were developing.'

'It could be dozens of different ones. Who would have access to the more exotic fluorinated organophosphates? It's going to be one of those, I'll bet.'

'To answer your 'who' question, the Russians, of course.'

***

'Base, status of the group you are tracking?' asked Jim, trying to shake the feeling of losing the unit's executive officer, the only married man with kids, and someone he had grown to like and respect.

'If our objectives are in the group, they are nearing a fifteen-meter open spot. Firecracker and Gopher are positioned for an ambush.'

Cherry and Carlos quietly moved behind the two rearmost men as they passed their position, quietly knifing them. Aleski watched with admiration through his scope.

'Objective confirmed. Two in front and another two in back,' said Aleski.

One of the soldiers turned and saw the two men on the ground in front of Carlos and Cherry. He lifted his rifle. Aleski squeezed his trigger just before the soldier could fire; the man's head exploded from the large .50-caliber bullet. Cherry and Carlos could not shoot the other man standing between them, as the president and his daughter were in the line of fire. They leaped sideways and hit the ground. The man opened up in their direction, on automatic, expending his clip. Even with the wild shooting, the soldier had the advantage of his targets not being more than a few meters away. Several of his rounds found the soft tissue of a human body.

Aleski took out one of the front soldiers. If he started shooting toward the rear, he might kill Angel or her father. He considered the soldiers' orders. Could they have been told to eliminate the president?

'Stupid man,' Cherry said as she jumped up and ran forward. The soldier was not experienced and fumbled with his empty clip. Cherry moved at an angle. With the two captives out of her line of sight, she shot the young man, then spit on him.

The one remaining soldier appeared in Aleski's scope. The oversized bullet, meant for long-range, traced a path to the man's head in a fraction of a second. It was much easier to hit a target's central torso. It was a point of pride for some snipers, but in this case, a body shot would have continued through the soldier and might have hit Angélica or the president.

The president and Angel stood, turning from left to right, wondering what had just taken place in only seconds.

'Ready for extraction,' said Aleski as the drone unleashed the remaining two missiles on the soldiers' camp as there still might have been soldiers there. The camp had been designed as a ruse, manned with only a skeleton group, left to make it appear as though it were active. The mission had morphed from a rescue to ensuring no communication traversed its way back to Mancuso.

Knowing the president was alive might cause Mancuso to perpetrate a coup before the president could return home and take control.

Sheilla had sent Brush the GPS coordinates of an area just large enough to land in. Aleski hustled to the opening and turned on his flashlight. Brush flared, shearing off leaves and branches as he forced the chopper into the pint-sized clearing.

Angel and her father covered their heads from the blowing debris. Aleski grabbed them and moved them toward the door. Cherry joined them, but Carlos was not there.

She ran back. Carlos' young body lay in the dirt, covered in blood. The young army soldier had gotten lucky with his thirty-round burst.

'Madre Dios, amigo.'

Aleski ran back. 'Let's load him.'

'No, no, señor. He belongs in the jungle, the only home he knows.'

Aleski nodded. He approved. He had no use for burials and all their trappings. He often thought about what he would do to avoid it when his time came.

They moved back to the chopper. President Noboa started to reach down to give Cherry a hand in, but Angel quickly got there first, clutching her past antagonist's hand.

'Por favor, Cherry. Allow me.'

Chapter 57

‘You be good, and take care of both Lola and Grankin,’ said Heather, as she held Pedro's shoulders in each of her hands.

Pedro had really taken to old man Shuskin, just as the old man had accepted, willingly and with pleasure, his new role as protector, friend, and companion to the young boy. At some point, Pedro had started to call the old man Grandpa Shuskin, then Grandkin, and later he shortened it to Grankin. Heather liked the nickname, as she had always felt it was a bit derogatory to call him "Old Man" or by his surname "Shuskin."

The old phantom of the woods, the ghost many never saw, who mumbled and refused to talk or associate with people, had been transformed. At first through a simple act of kindness—seeing something good in Nusmen that no one else saw—then with a good scrubbing in a cold mountain lake, and at last finding refuge in a homesteader's cabin on Wolf Canyon Ranch. His days were now filled with chores he liked doing, Lola's food, animals, and a small brown child whom he had grown to love.

‘I take care of her and Grankin. We take care of each other.’

They were a family. She stifled the emotion she felt and managed to smile at her son.

‘When I come home, I hope it will be with your dad.’

‘You come back in helicopter?’

‘The helicopter, please. You know it is correct to say the helicopter. It needs an adjective.’

'Yes, yes, the chopper.'

She looked steadily into Pedro's earnest eyes. 'Okay, we'll try. While I'm gone, you are responsible for many things besides Grankin and Lola. You have your llama baby, Sharifa, and many of the mothers to watch out for. Ben will be here every day. He'll take you to school and will pick you up. And Roy is going to come up to help with the horses.'

'He is teaching me to ride.'

'I know he is.' *Pedro's English is improving,* she thought, *at least some of the time.* 'Roy is a very good teacher. You be careful and do what he says. The horses are nice, but never forget they're very big.'

'Yes, Mama. I be careful.'

Heather laughed and shook her head. He had spent his first years of life solely speaking Spanish. It might be a long time before his English overcame the ingrained Spanish from his early childhood.

***

Two security guards escorted Eileen to the sofa.

'Remove the cuffs. Wait outside,' ordered the general.

When they had stepped outside and closed the door, the general said, 'Your choice, Eileen. I've been told you have been helpful, at least so far. I want to hear the story from you. Start at the beginning. Stay with the big picture. If you omit anything important, distort anything, leave anything out intentionally or unintentionally, you will never see the light of day again.'

'Will I ever, anyway?'

'Maybe not,' said Martin, 'at least in the conventional sense. But it could be worse.' Martin held up his thumbless hand. 'You still have your thumbs. At least, for the time being.'

'You told Martin and Bertrand your story. So, let's say you are telling the truth.'

'What more can I add?' She held both palms up.

'We have thirty minutes. Use it wisely. Start from the beginning, keep it short, and then I want to hear the full story about your operations in Ecuador.'

'You already have it.'

'Eileen, I warn you.'

She sat passively.

'What can you offer me?'

'Enough,' he boomed.

She closed her eyes and massaged her forehead with her fingers. She looked at the general and let out a breath.

'Let me say first, I went off the farm. Things, shall I say, got complicated. I can still help.'

She spent the next twenty minutes doing as the general had ordered her, adding several parts that she had not previously disclosed. They all sat silent for a minute, digesting the extent of the black ops that had been run right under their noses.

'What are the missing pieces?' asked Bertrand from the chair to the right of the general.

Eileen nervously chewed her thumbnail. She nodded as she made her choice. This time she wouldn't hold back. *What choice is there?* she conceded to herself.

***

Nusmen said excitedly, 'It's not VX gas. It's a derivative. It has alkyl substituents on its nitrogen and oxygen atoms.'

'Nus,' said Sheilla as sternly as she was capable, wiping her hand over her forehead and then pushing some long red strands of hair back over her shoulder. 'We're not biochemists. Keep it simple.'

She almost slipped out with "keep it simple, stupid" in exasperation. Nusmen was totally ignorant in his understanding of people, but his understanding of biochemistry, and more broadly science, was on the opposite end of the spectrum. A veritable fountain of knowledge.

'What is it? In plain English.'

Nusmen looked flustered. 'I just said. It's a phosphoramidateor, fluorinated…'

The toxicologist, who had learned firsthand that Nusmen was as brilliant as he was socially inept, held up his hand. With a slight smile, he said, 'Novichok. An extremely lethal VX derivative, and as Nusmen was probably about to add, with a long environmental life span. Dispensed as a powder or aerosol. Developed by the Russians in 1980. This derivative is known as Novichok A-232/9.'

'Yeah, like I was saying,' added Nusmen.

'Maria, you get that?'

'I heard, Doctor Thomas. I'll get everything from our computer. I want to thank you. You too, Nusmen. Any quick suggestions that might help us on the ground here until I have a full understanding?'

'It's an organophosphate acetylcholinesterase inhibitor,' interjected Nusmen earnestly.

Barbara started to laugh, then everyone laughed except Nusmen who pivoted his long neck and looked from one to the other. He didn't have a clue what could be so funny. After a moment of sitting there watching with his mouth hanging open, it was contagious and, he started to laugh too.

'There are several things you can do,' said Doctor Thomas. You no doubt have the military atropine self-injectors?'

'And biperiden.'

'Both effective. The problem is that this Novichok has a long half-life in the environment and has not adequately been studied. Some say as short as four months and others longer. So, I am afraid that you first need to quarantine the site. I suggest a wide radius. You need barriers to contain it from running off in rainwater. Get the site covered with anything you can. First tarps, and then maybe cover those with sand. You will need to build a more permanent cover if possible.'

'Excuse me,' said Sheilla. 'Doctor, could you please excuse me while you and Doctor Dakine continue to talk?'

***

'The toxicologist is talking with Maria, general.' Then she sighed.

'We've had two losses during the rescue.'

'Spit it out. Suspense is not my forte.'

'We lost one of Neilly's men. His second in command, Master Sergeant Gaston, and one of the FARC.'

The general maintained a close tie to his men. He was not happy to hear this. However, he felt a small sense of relief that it was not Jim, Brush, Glenda, the president, or Angel.

'They are still in the village. Jim requested not notifying Neilly until they left. He wants to be the one to tell him.'

'His call. It is no one's favorite task, but his responsibility. He owes it to Neilly. Damn it, anyway.'

Sheilla wanted to tell him that maybe they had been lucky. Outnumbered forty to one. She decided it wasn't the right thing to say.

'I want you to get on the phone with Martin Pearson. He has a story to tell you. Get the details from him. Get our computer team on it, and verify every detail of the story. I want to know the specifics with absolute certainty. Then I want Martin and you to continue to liaise. It's time we find out what the hell is going on in this agency.'

***

Brush set the chopper down in the meadow with a thud. He quickly shut the engines off and climbed out. 'Let me see your hand.'

'Is that the way you always land?' Glenda raised her eyebrows.

Brush shrugged. 'I should fly more. Does your hand still sting?'

'Not so much.'

'Aleski, where's Carlos' body?' asked Jim.

'Cherry said to leave him. She said he was always part of the jungle.' Then he sighed and looked over at Gaston, lying by the side of the meadow.

'President Noboa, please remain here with your daughter. Aleski, Cherry, keep them safe until we get back from the village.'

'No, no, Colonel,' said Angel. 'I'll go with you. It is also better to stay together.'

'Then I will go as well,' said President Noboa.

***

Eileen sighed. She was not going to be able to trade information for her freedom. She was caught in their net. Fighting would be futile. With complete and open cooperation, she could hope for compassion. Despite everything, she still loved the agency. The company had been her life, her home. The decision was now made.

'I have more to add to the Ecuador part of the story. I warn you, though, this will not be to your liking.'

After she started, General Crystal, Martin, and Bertrand exchanged looks. They all recognized that Eileen had decided to cooperate. They wouldn't know for certain, however, until the story had been verified and cross-checked. While they listened, her demeanor, animation, and pace, convinced them she had finally given in.

'Wait, stop. You said President Noboa,' said Martin.

Bertrand shook his head. 'This is not the story I want to hear.'

'You want the whole story; he comes with it.'

'Proceed,' said General Crystal.

'It goes back more than fifteen years. We were part of the group investigating the Russians. That is where we first encountered Viktor, aka Sasha, as I said. His social skills were zilch, similar to those of your biochemist. His bioscience, however, was superb. We wanted to know what the Russians were working on in virology and what this guy knew about making lethal viruses. After we had extracted what we believed was all the information he had, we realized his capabilities—he could continue to make new discoveries. We wanted them.'

'Why don't I know about this at BWC?' asked General Crystal with a slightly louder and irritated voice.

'Good question, sir,' said Eileen with a slight smile.

'You said Noboa. What's he got to do with this?' asked Martin.

'I'll get there. After the original debriefings, we went dark. His discoveries would not be sanctioned here. So, we set him up in Bogotá at the university.'

'But you needed money, right?' stated Martin.

'Yes.'

'That's when you went into the drug business?' asked Bertrand.

'Sort of. Rather, we shifted it from Asia.'

'And you say Noboa is involved?' persisted Bertrand.

'The business started with some of our local contacts. It grew to include cartels, and eventually the payoffs got bigger and higher up until they reached near the top.'

'Besides Noboa, who?' asked General Crystal.

'Sir, he is the only head of state. The others mainly were military. Mancuso at the top in Ecuador and Ramos in Colombia.'

'You are saying that the head of the Colombian government is clean?'

'Squeaky, but there are lots of mid-levels involved.'

'You can identify them?' asked Bertrand.

'Yes, of course,' she said with some pride.

'You orchestrated the whole operation including bribing a head of state? I have a feeling you are going to tell us several DEA and customs are involved. How high up in our government?' asked Martin.

'Let's break for a minute. Eileen, step outside,' said the general.

'Martin, have your team debrief her. Every detail. Get it transcribed, and have her sign it. I think we all agree that the probability is she is giving us the straight story for the first time, but triple check everything. Colonel Johnson, Major McGuire, Agent Stuart and others are with the president and his daughter in the Amazon as we speak.'

'So, what do we do with him?' asked Martin.

Bertrand rubbed his chin and said, 'We have to notify the VP.'

'Unless he disappears,' said Martin, 'and avoids the pain and embarrassment of having the story come to light. A failed rescue. Blame it on Mancuso.'

***

Jim listened silently to the general as they walked toward the Shuar village.

'I'll get back to you as soon as we clear the village, sir.'

He let out a deep breath. No good solutions popped into his head. Two men killed, rescuing Noboa. To be fair, rescuing them. Now, he understood that General Mancuso had another reason for wanting Noboa dead. The weak link in their operation. A costly one at that. He'd been paid off for years to keep the wolves off the trade and to let the army enrich themselves. But lately, he was growing soft and listening to his daughter. Noboa's elimination wasn't only about a coup; it was also about the money they would not have to pay him.

'What's up, buddy?'

'Hang back with me.'

Both slowed, drifting toward the rear and out of hearing range. Still, they talked softly.

'The general just called. Noboa's dirty. Mixed up in the drug trade.'

'Surprise, eh? What does he want us to do?'

'I don't think he knows yet. Looking for suggestions from us. We bring him back, he'll be an embarrassment to the White House.'

'Leave him in place, and run him, eh?'

'Doubt it would work. Angel would never go along. I think she deserves better, too. Then there's the coup.'

Brush shrugged. 'You think she has a future?'

'Don't know. She has spunk. Not sure yet if she is savvy enough to play in that arena.'

'Your area, partner, not mine. Politics mystify me. Glenda might have some ideas.'

'It's a tough call. Let's give it a few minutes. I want to be out of here, back to Ecuador, and then…'

'And then, home?'

'Home for the holidays.' They both extended a closed fist and touched knuckles. 'This mission took on a life and timeline of its own. Heather and I were just starting to understand each other. I don't want that to change. I want to get back.'

'No argument from me. A little home time with Glenda sounds good.'

Jim nodded slowly with a closed lip smile.

Brush looked at him, waiting for what he had to say.

'Sorry, buddy. Just thinking about you back when you entertained dozens of women. You never had a place that could be called home.'

'Couldn't complain then, and I can't complain now. Glenda's worth the lot.'

'We're both lucky.'

Chapter 58

Except for a large group sitting around a campfire near Pempeyo's and Pwanchir's hut, the Shuar village had returned to its usual late-night rhythms. Jean-Paul was sitting next to Angélica and her father, chatting animatedly through JP with the two Indians. Tshui jumped up and down when she saw Jim, then ran to him smiling.

Jim scooped her up and swung her around in a circle while she laughed. He looked at her. 'Shouldn't you be sleeping?'

Jean-Paul looked at Jim. 'Those rules don't apply outside of our civilized world. This little girl is here for one reason, and that is to see you. You have made quite an impression.'

Angel looked over and said, 'It seems that he has that effect on many of the women of Ecuador.'

JP raised an eyebrow and looked back and forth between Angélica and Jim.

Then she said in Spanish, 'The effect does not appear to go both ways.'

'You want me to translate that?'

Angel didn't reply, and Jim was not paying any attention to anyone besides Tshui. 'JP, can you tell her that I have a son just about her age, and I would like to bring him here to meet her. Would she like that?'

'I'll ask her. But remember time and distance are something quite different for you and her. If I tell her, she will be expecting you tomorrow.'

'I think perhaps I can manage it in a month or so. Can you convey that? I would like to bring Heather and Pedro here. Heather would love the botany, and I want Pedro to know that other cultures may be different, but that the people are just as important here as anywhere.'

Angélica turned to Jim and studied him for a long time. *Are there other men such as this one out there. One for me?*

JP talked for some time to Tshui. The little girl grinned, showing the small gap between her front teeth, and started to jump up and down. She wore the same blue dress she had worn before. This time, however, there was a yellow feather headband holding back sleek black hair from her round face. A face that bore the same red Chiote plant face markings as Nusmen's.

'I did the best I could. I think she understands. I hope you don't have to disappoint her. You can see how excited she is.'

***

President Gustavo Noboa didn't contribute to the questions, but one could tell from the looks he gave his daughter that he had become proud of her. He looked less czar-like with his goatee untrimmed, several days of stubble, and crumpled, dirty clothes.

He patted Angel's back and stood. 'I'll return in a few minutes, daughter.' JP handed him a headlamp. He nodded his thanks and, looking left and right, chose the jungle to his right. He walked for a few minutes until he got to a brushy area, pulled his pants down, and squatted.

A second later, he yelped and fell forward. *Estúpido, squatting on a thorn,* he said to himself, shaking his head. He finished his business and walked back. The nearer he got to the camp, the more distorted his vision became. He stumbled back to the group.

'What's the matter, Papá?' asked Angélica.

'I do not know. I thought I sat on a thorn bush. Perhaps it is a poison plant.'

JP said into his mic, 'Jeff, come over to Pempeyo's hut on the double.'

'Roger that.'

'Just sit, sir, and Jeff will take a look.'

Gustavo Noboa had never felt worse. He tried to sit and fell on his back.

'I do not feel at all well, daughter.'

'Can we move him inside?' asked Jeff as he pointed at Noboa and then the door to the hut.

Pempeyo nodded that it was okay. JP and Pwanchir tried to get him up, but they couldn't. Instead, they carried him into the hut. They put him down on one of the new brightly colored blankets.

Jeff stooped through the door and turned his headlamp on high.

'He said he received a puncture wound as he was taking a dump.'

'Okay, flip him over on his stomach, and get his pants down. Angel, you want to leave?'

'No.'

They got his pants down. His right cheek was red and inflamed with two distinct holes centered in the redness. 'Those holes are from a bite. My best guess is a snake, and from how far apart the holes are, something pretty bleeding big,' said Jeff. 'Severe edema. The fang holes are starting to ooze. Lymph nodes already enlarged.'

'We need BWC to research, urgently.'

Jeff probed Noboa's neck, and looked into his eyes, and then saw that his gums were starting to bleed. 'I've nothing to give him other than anti-inflammatories and morphine. Until I know what the venom is, anything else might cause more harm than good. I'll set up a saline drip after I check his blood pressure. Nothing else I can do without more information.' For all his medical training, he felt impotent.

Jim got Sheilla on the sat phone.

JP turned to Jim, Jeff, and Angel and said, 'Pwanchir said it was Sally. I'm not quite sure what that means. He's getting the shaman. Maybe he'll have another magic remedy.'

Jeff quickly inserted an IV and hooked up a drip. He turned to Angel. 'It would be a good idea for you to talk to him. I don't want to scare you.' He let out a puff of air through his nose. 'The truth is, he does not look good. His blood pressure is dropping, and he is starting to have trouble breathing.'

Tears rolled down Angel's cheeks. She dropped to her knees beside her father. 'You'll be fine, Papá.'

He made a pretense at a smile. 'Listen to me, daughter.'

'I can't hear you, Papá.' She leaned in closer.

'I have not been a good father. Forgive me,' he rasped.

'Stop, don't talk nonsense. I love you. Just rest.'

'I love you too, daughter. You have always been special. Listen to me. I have been weak and greedy. I tried my best for the people.' He hesitated. 'I have taken money from General Mancuso. I became his puppet. I am ashamed.'

'Never mind, Papá.'

'No, listen. Talk to Señor Zambrano. BVBA Bank of Uruguay. It is for the family. For you to use to help the Indians here. They deserve it.'

'Never mind, Papá. Don't talk, please.'

'Daughter, Angel. I can hardly see you. Promise me to use the money wisely. It is much money. Many millions.'

'What? How could it be so much? What have you done?'

'I have been a bad person.' His voice trailed off. 'You do the right thing.'

Angel leaned closer, sobbing. She looked up at Jeff. 'Do something.'

'I'm sorry. There is nothing more I can do. If I knew more about the venom, maybe.'

'Sheilla says from the distance between the fang marks, it is probably a Lachesis muta, a Bushmaster. They are researching it to see if there is anything you can do. She says its venom is not as strong as some of the other snakes here. But it can inject huge volumes, several hundred milligrams, and its bite is fatal in many cases. It's a haemotoxin. Nusmen is looking for a plant antidote. He says his friend the shaman will know.'

The shaman walked in with Pwanchir. He moved up close and peered at the bite marks. He took some powder from a pouch and sprinkled it on the president's red swollen buttock. Then, he stood and walked out after saying a few words to Pwanchir.

'What did he do or say?' asked Jeff.

JP looked at Angel and paused. 'He said there is nothing to be done. It is the snake spirit of a bad missionary, called Sally, who disappeared a long time ago. She haunts the forest around their village. He says they must now move the village and try to escape her. She is evil.'

Angel bent over her father and clutched him in a tight hug, heaving as she sobbed. Jim didn't say anything. There was nothing to say. After a moment, he turned her face up, looked deep into her eyes, then pushed some wet hair back.

She looked back at Jim, the second strong man who had entered her life in the last few weeks. She turned to her father, clasped his hand, and talked to him softly.

Moments later, Jeff took his other hand and felt for a pulse. He closed President Noboa's staring eyes. Then, he covered him with the army's brightly colored, pox-infected blanket.

Chapter 59

Like ripples on a still pond, word spread through the rebel camp. Their main foe for many years, General Ramos and his top officers were dead. Little by little their commander's and officer's death leaked out of the camp and to the army troops outside.

As the story spread, many of the soldiers laid down their weapons and walked away. A few close to the compound were even embraced by the FARC. Many of the soldiers were tired of Ramos' relentless war on the rebels. Some were even sympathetic to the FARC cause but too afraid to not do as they were ordered. Like their FARC peers, they longed for their homes, families, farms, villages, and most of all, freedom from the fighting.

None knew that a different kind of battle for survival would start in earnest as the virus doubled and tripled inside many of their bodies. It would be several days before the first signs appeared. During their time of rejoicing, singing and dancing, each virus turned into a thousand more, and by morning, millions, infecting one human cell after another.

***

'I must take my father home.'

'I'm sorry that things worked out this way.' He looked into her dark, sad, red-rimmed eyes. 'We'll help you any way we can. I would have liked it if I could accompany you. I can't. I need to return to Colombia.'

'Comprendo, my tall norteamericano friend.' She stood on toes and kissed Jim on the cheek, while giving him a hug, her thoughts a mirror image of Cherry's for Brush. Something that could never be, other than a wish from deep inside. *Cherry has Jago. I have no one,* she thought, as tears for her father once again turned to sobs.

'Sheilla, I'm here with Ms. Perez. We'll take her father back to Cuenca. Please arrange transport for them back to Quito.' Jim looked at Angel as he said, 'Patch her through to whoever she wants to talk to when she's ready.'

Angel nodded as Jim disconnected and said, 'Give me a few minutes,' and she walked back to her father.

'Sure,' he said, giving Angel some time to decide what she would say and to whom.

Then he lifted the sat phone again and called Neilly. 'We've run into a problem. The president's dead. A snake bite. A bushmaster.'

'Go figure. How'd that happen?'

'He was doing his business, bare butt to the wind.'

'Hmm.'

'We're arranging smallpox inoculations for the Shuar. JP and one or two others will have to accompany them to the village. I don't think there's much chance of any more soldiers popping up. Still, they'll need security. Also, there is little chance they will allow anyone to give them inoculations without JP present to explain, unless we can find someone outside that is in the Shuar community. I hope they'll trust him. See you as soon as we get back.'

'I heard that,' said Jean-Paul, 'you get the girl Tshui to do it, and others will follow. The key, though, is the medicine man. He's going to be tough to persuade.'

Angélica walked up. 'Tell Sheilla who you would like to talk to, and she'll get them on the sat phone and get you set with a secure connection.'

'Jim,' said Sheilla, 'Hold on for a sec. Before you pass the phone. I have someone standing next to me that you need to talk to first.'

'Colonel Johnson, Martin Pearson.'

Jim was surprised, but he let Martin talk without saying anything.

'We have substantial information about the president's involvement in the drug trade, along with several in the army, specifically General Mancuso.'

'President Noboa mentioned that to Angel a few minutes ago.' Jim didn't mention that the general had also told him as much.

'All right, it's not shocking news then. This might be, though. Noboa, Ramos, Mancuso, and our DDO at CIA have been partnering with each other and the various cartels, both growing and distributing drugs.'

'Hum.'

'Guess you knew some of that too.'

Jim looked at Angélica as he responded. 'Any more talk of a military coup?'

Angélica's mouth dropped open, and her eyes grew wide. 'You mean Mancuso was going to overthrow my father?'

'I heard what she just said. That's what it looks like,' said Martin. 'We don't know yet how deep it runs. Ms. Perez and her family are in danger. With the vice president involved, it makes it a special issue, not to mention some of the State Department's higher-ups' concern for stability in the region.'

'What does General Crystal want?'

'He wants your thoughts.'

'I want to head to Cuenca. I'll call you from there.'

'I'll be here,' said Martin.

Angel looked at Jim and said, 'Let's talk on the way to Cuenca and discuss this before I say anything about Papá to anyone.'

Jim watched her walk away, wiping tears from her face. 'You hear, Sheilla?'

'I did.'

Martin took the phone and said, 'It would be prudent to not let anyone know. It might alter the dynamics of her dad's enemies.'

'I'll talk to her about it, although she seemed pretty quick on the uptake about the implications.'

Martin smiled at Sheilla and passed the headset back to her.

'Anything else, Colonel?'

'We'll talk later.'

Martin watched Sheilla as she talked and disconnected the call. Then he said, 'You have beautiful hair, Sheilla. I know it is a strange thing to say.'

'I don't see it as strange, Mr. Pearson.'

'Will it be Mr. Pearson and Ms. McCarrick?'

God, where did he come from? wondered Sheilla. Neither of them could hide their attraction.

'I think Martin and Sheilla will be very satisfactory.' Then, with the confidence she had acquired in her job, 'I have some work to do.' She handed him a pager. 'I'll let you know when I'm finished. We could get a bite to eat in our lunchroom?'

She called Mark, 'Get someone to my office. Mr. Pearson needs a tour guide for an hour or so.'

***

'How many medics do you have in your encampment?' asked Doctor Dakine.

'Many very capable' answered Jago. 'Most are not schooled. There are a few with some university training.'

'Will your people let the World Health Organization give them inoculations?'

'I think not. Many will think it is a plot to make them sick.'

'That's a political problem for us. We are required to notify them. There are large shipments of vaccine and syringes on the way here.'

'That problem is not ours. We'll take care of our own, and these WHO people can do what they want. Just not in our camp.'

Maria sighed. 'I understand. At least I think I do. Why would you trust them. Will they let my team help?'

'I will see to that. I trust you and your colonel. My people will too.'

'Supplies will start to arrive tomorrow. I'll see what Colonel Johnson has to say.'

***

Jim was running scenario after scenario in his mind. Suddenly the SF training base was in sight. He and Angel had sat next to each other, without a word between them, each buried in thoughts.

Angel reached out and touched his arm. 'I wish to thank you for all your help. I need to handle this myself, and I think I have a way.'

This was the new Angélica Perez, thought Jim. He nodded. 'You know where to contact me if we can help. I would hate to see something happen to you now.'

'And I would like you to succeed in inoculating the Shuar. You have to make it work. In many ways, they are the last bastion of humanity in our so-called civilized world.'

'We'll do our best,' he said, as he mulled over what she had just said.

'My plan has its risks,' said Angélica. 'There is no time to explain. Wish me luck,' she said as the helicopter settled to the ground. 'No, wait. I want to talk to you in private for a minute.'

Chapter 60

'Nusmen, I need you in my office. Now! I asked you thirty minutes ago,' Sheilla said, sounding as irritated as she felt.

The nuances in her voice were lost on Nusmen. It was something that was simply out of his understanding.

'I can't.'

'You rethink that right now and get in here. The team wants to know what the strain is. They're curious after spending all this time with it. Where did it come from? They want an explanation. They have better things to do than sit there waiting for you. And even more important, they need to know everything they can about the nerve gas.'

'I'll call you back.'

'Nus, you listen to me. You get here in less than five minutes or I'll send someone to get you and lock you up for the rest of the day after we're finished hearing your pearls of information. You got that? Now,' she said in way that let Nusmen know she was serious.

'Okay, ten minutes.'

'Now. It's in less than four minutes. I'm calling security and sending them to you, in case you are dumb enough to not get here in three minutes fifty seconds.'

Sheilla pushed her chair with her feet and started to spin. Every circle, she glimpsed the clock. *I will lock him up. The general and Barbara will back me up. How could I ever have thought I liked him? Stupid me. Two minutes. I didn't know the depth of his problems,* she thought. *That's why. He's going to start to be a team player no matter what his problems are.*

Then a smile appeared on her face as the clock said twenty-nine after. One minute to go. Martin would be back after his tour with Barbara in fifteen minutes. Why she had ever found Nusmen attractive was a mystery. It had probably been something to do with having low self-esteem from her FBI job. Or, being lonely at the time and suddenly liking any male that seemed smart and docile.

In her new position, she not only felt respected, but appreciated. She regained the confidence she had had before she had signed on as a tech with the FBI. After getting to know the large staff at the BWC, and finding no one that she was attracted to, she dove into her job, forgetting about men. Her whole life was here. She accepted her fate and decided that she was comfortable controlling her own space, both here and at home. A place she hardly recognized anymore. *My real home is here.*

Like an unexpected thunderclap, Martin Pearson had shown up. This wasn't need or loneliness. This was a physical attraction she'd never felt so strongly before. Her chair spun. She watched her office door pass by. A slight feeling of disgust for Nusmen entered her thoughts, dislodging what she was feeling for Martin.

'You're late!'

Nusmen said sulkily, 'Only a minute.'

'I suppose I should be glad you could make it at all. Let's go.'

Sheilla called Misa as they walked to the conference room.

'Misa, do you have Maria and her team standing by?'

'They're ready and waiting with both video and sound.'

'Like all of us.' Sheilla gave a Nusmen a look that should have said everything to him. Instead, he was thinking about his phages and missed her look of displeasure.

They sat down, facing the conference room computer screens.

'Nusmen,' said Maria. 'What I am mostly interested in is what else you and the DOD learned about the VR gas. Second, we would like to know the pox strain. Who is going to research it? You or CDC? That's not as important as it might have been since we can make the assumption it was collected from a patient in Rio or close by. Still curious, and we all want to know. Tell us about the VR gas.'

'It's a fluorinated phosphoramidateour phosphonate.' Nusmen sat up straight, tangles of hair making him appear taller than he was. His face lit up in happy animation. 'What's really cool are the variety of organic groups. This one is phosgene oxime. It's a nettle agent,' he almost shouted in his excitement. 'It's a potent agent all by itself. It's totally cool.'

Nusmen waited for someone to see how awesome this was. He expected to hear cool and wows coming from the HazMat team. Instead, everyone sat in stunned silence, not so much from what he said or his enthusiasm, but just from the man himself. His bobbing Adam's apple, his twisted, uncombed hair, and his cheeks covered in drawings of what appeared to be animals. When he raised his hand, he had tattoos circling both wrists.

The staff, including Sheilla, thought they were used to Nusmen. Sometimes they found him to be almost normal. With the tattoos added to his other oddities, however, they realized they could never become completely accustomed to him. The truth was they were thinking they had never seen or known a person like Nusmen. Maria broke the silence.

'Thank you, Nusmen. Sheilla sent us the DOD's report. What I want to know now are some specifics of the cross-linking you mentioned in the report. How does this change the longevity and its potency in its current environment? We are building barriers around the contaminated site. What should we do with the soil under the agent?'

Nusmen stared at Maria and then at Trisha and Geoffrey, sitting on either side. 'You have to draw it up through the soil, to the top.'

'Explain what you mean.'

'Seal it in and run dehumidifiers to make it really dry. It will be like a desert, and the moisture in the soil will be drawn up, bringing the agent with it.'

Sunita, who understood the physics of the environment better than the rest said, 'Transpiration sounds interesting. Why not just dig it up and treat it with something that will neutralize it?'

'Draw it up first, like I said. No people involved. No contamination to worry about. Gotta go.'

'What if it hits a water source below. The ground is very saturated here.'

'Drill some boreholes or get a hydrologist to do a computer scenario on the water table.'

Nusmen got up and started to leave.

'Wait, wait,' said Maria. 'You didn't say anything about the origin or strain of the orthopox?'

'I don't know yet, African, I think.'

'So, you, not CDC are working on it?' asked Maria.

'Yeah,' said Nusmen.

Nusmen started for the door and then turned back, 'Oh, why do you guys call yourself HazMat anyway? Shouldn't you be whatever that other abbreviation is, ah *Chemical Biological, Radiation,* something or other?'

'Hazardous Materials is less scary than CBRN when we tell people what we do. Especially the Nuclear part.'

'Oh, well. Later then.'

Nusmen started for the door again, 'Nus, what are you going to do with your face?' asked Sheilla.

'Huh?'

'Those drawings on your face.'

Nusmen lifted his fingers to his face, touching his cheeks and chin where the red drawings had been applied by the Shuar woman. Thinking about the women, he could only remember them as they appeared to him at the time, through blurry intoxicated eyes. He saw the circle of women laughing as the one old lady turned his head from side to side and etched his face.

'I sort of like them now.'

'Do you ever look in the mirror?'

'Why?'

'You look a little odd, that's why.'

'So?'

'Never mind. Go back to work. Wait, you have them on your wrists, too. They're different-looking.'

Nusmen looked down at his wrists. 'My friend the shaman did them himself. He said they'll keep my soul from getting lost. I like them.'

***

Heather sat looking at her special notebook. Feeling good about the progress with Jim freed her mind. She had started to think about writing poetry again. She didn't care whether it was good, bad, or mediocre. When she felt good, it just came out of her mind and into her private notebook.

She had written one for Jim's birthday, but she wasn't sure if she would show it to him. That was not true, even if it was a pretty silly poem. She knew she would. She wouldn't be able help it. He knew, and she knew, that when she was happy, she wrote poems, and writing a comic one still said volumes.

Even if you are a Big Mac
If you're made of fat and sugar substitutes
Even if you are a Coca Cola,
This is the real thing.
This does not exist only when the passion is hot;
It is not a place of warmth when it's freezing.
This is not a relationship for a reason
Or a season.
This is for life.
A water lily has its roots in the mud;
A perfect rose has thorns.
We need a flaw in the carpet.
I take you as you are
And in that entirety lies perfection.

You're the one I want.
I'm glad you were born.

Happy birthday, darling. We missed having your birthday together, but I know you will be here for Christmas. The warmth she felt melted away. She scrunched up her nose. Pretty silly poem. Then she laughed. *What more could I ask of life: a perfect man, an adorable son, this scenery, and writing my corny poems.*

Chapter 61

Jim led Angel to one of the sheds. He opened the door. It was empty.

Once inside, Angel turned to Jim and said, 'I'll need your help after all.'

Jim didn't say anything, wondering what she would ask.

'I want to get General Mancuso to the U.S. and detain him. I think your vice president, my family friend, would maybe do so. Do you think he would?'

'What is your idea?'

'Here is the argument. Mancuso is involved in a coup d'état against a democratically elected government. He is involved in the drug trade. A drug war your country fights. I want to find out who in my government is involved with Mancuso. I need a plan to get him to the U.S. I need your help with that.'

Interesting. Tactical thinking. She doesn't know about our CIA's involvement with Mancuso.

'What is your opinion?' she asked.

'It's possible. I'll make a call. Follow me.'

Jim walked to the comm room. 'Mac, the general again.'

'No prob. Here's your sat phone. Ready to go, but I can connect you.'

After a couple of minutes, Mac passed Jim a headset. 'He's on.'

'Angel, let's get a cup of coffee while he talks?'

'Okay, sure.'

'What's up, Jim?'

'I just received an interesting proposal from Angélica Perez. Mancuso, as you know, is involved in the first stage of a takeover. He's also involved in the drug trade, and I assume that the others in the government that are involved in the drug business are implicated in the coup. She suggests getting Mancuso to the U.S., detaining him, and getting answers as to who they are.'

'As long as Eileen has told us everything, then we already know who they are, except there might be more lower level people.'

'If that is correct, then it should be easy to interrogate Mancuso and confirm his and her answers. There might be others Eileen doesn't know about. I think Angélica has a good idea. She doesn't know why Mancuso would go to the U.S. Eileen should be able to get him there on some pretense or other.'

'We take him in custody and then what?'

'A drug charge. Have him give you names and compare them to Eileen's. Check them both out at the same time. Angel gets the loyal military to arrest the bad guys. Mancuso gets some sort of limited immunity for his cooperation. Then turn him over to the new Ecuadoran government if they succeed in stopping the coup.'

'It's not a bad plan—democracy saved and drugs eliminated—simple on our end. But it sounds risky on hers. The VP would be on board. Do you think she can pull it off on her end?'

'She's changed and matured. That's for sure. Still, a pretty limited experience at twenty-eight years old. No idea what the military would think of her.'

'Talk to her. I'll stand by.'

When Jim walked back into the food shed, Mac stood fidgeting with the coffee maker while Angel sat deep in thought.

'Let's say he could be detained. How do you prevent his army buddies from taking over?'

'When I find out who they are, I'll also know the ones not involved. Then with the loyal army officers, we jail Mancuso's cohorts.'

'What makes you think the others would do that?'

'I understand that you think I am young and inexperienced. True, but my father had one close ally in the military who knows me well. Someone he wanted me to trust. When I get back, I'll talk to him.'

'Your father could be wrong. He might not be a friendly.'

'Again true. That is why, with a confession from Mancuso, I would know for certain that he is trustworthy. If he is, then he would assist me, no? How to persuade Mancuso to go to the United States. That is what I do not know.'

'Let's say it's a plan. Let's say we can help with Mancuso. You still have a problem. With your father gone, the coup could go forward rapidly.'

'Yes, time is of the essence. It is critical to get Mancuso out of the way as soon as possible.'

***

'Thank you for all being here,' said Maria.

Jago had assembled as many rebels with medical experience as he could. Abenaa translated for Doctor Dakine. Maria had decided that, other than greeting the group in Spanish, someone with better language skills would pass along what she said more convincingly. *I have forgotten so much since college,* she thought. *This will be a good place to learn again.*

'I am sure most of you have heard of smallpox, the scourge that was eliminated many years ago.'

There were only a couple of nods in the group of nearly ninety people. Maria marveled that the group had slightly more women than men. Earlier, Jago had told her that there would be many women, not because they were inclined to learn medical issues, but because the FARC had a large percentage of women. Maria looked at the assembled group.

Some women were wearing berets, some cradling automatic weapons in their laps, and others wearing various colored headbands. Some were pregnant. Some had tassels that dangled from hats and clothes. Many wore small, personalized items. This was not the military dress she was used to seeing. These were fighters with personalities.

The men wore more traditional olive drab or camouflaged fatigues. Some held their weapons while some wore red and yellow armbands.

None looked like typical medical personnel.

'Have any of you seen smallpox victims?'

One older man nodded his head.

'Could you explain to your compatriots what you have seen?' asked Doctor Dakine.

The man proceeded to give a graphic description. He concluded by rolling up his sleeve and saying he was protected by the shot given to many of his friends. 'Mostly dead, sadly,' he lamented. Then, he added, 'Not from this shot—from the government.'

'Thank you,' said Maria.

The old man said, 'I have heard a story.'

Maria nodded.

'Many years ago, a slave ship brought the pox to Mexico. In one year, many died. The pox spread to our country and killed many more.'

Maria had been avidly researching the history of Variola. 'He is correct. When the Spanish arrived in Mexico, there were twenty-two million Indians. Years later, there were only two million left.'

She had their attention. She had stretched the facts a little. In 1520, an infected slave on the Spanish ship had indeed brought the pox to Mexico. At the time the ship made port, there were an estimated twenty-two million Indians in the country. The pox killed eight million by the end of the year. Over the next sixty years, the virus, along with many other diseases introduced by westerners, reduced the population to two million, an astounding ninety percent reduction in the population.

'It is true,' said Maria. 'The shot will protect you from the virus. It does not do so after many years.' She looked at the old man. 'A dozen years, and then it will not protect you any longer. To be clear, sir, you are no longer protected. You need a new shot. If you will allow me, I will give it to you now.' She opened up her medical case and extracted a needle.

Someone in the back said, 'We catch you if you faint, Mr. Gonzales.'

The old man pulled his left arm out of his shirt and said, 'Por favor, Doctor. I no want this sickness. It is very bad.'

'Thank you. Now you will not contract this terrible disease,' said Dakine, trying to emphasize how much the inoculation would help.

'Muchísimas gracias,' said Alfredo Gonzales. He stood tall and held out his arm.

Doctor Dakine gently lowered his arm to his side and administered the inoculation for all to see.

'Once you contract the virus, and you may all have it now, it will be about ten days before you know. If the shot, the vaccine, is given before ten days, you will not get sick. But once you have the illness symptoms, the shot will do no good. Then it will be too late. It is a serious killer, especially of children.'

A young woman, wearing a red headband, stood up, 'Why you tell us this, Doctor? What you mean we have it now?'

'Because many of you might have been infected.'

'How this happen?' asked another man.

Jago stood. He thought now was a good time to tell them about the dead general and his officers' plot. He concluded by saying that, to protect us all, everyone had to receive a vaccination.

Maria added, 'We have some slight advantages. The virus survives better in the environment when there is low humidity. This, fortunately, is not the case here. The dampness helps us slow its spread. I must tell you that the vaccine is safe, but there are exceptions for old people who are weak, and there are risks for pregnant women.' She glanced over at a woman in the last trimester of pregnancy. 'If you don't have the vaccine, the risks are far greater for both you and your unborn child.'

'Abenaa, can you help give some inoculations, and also show them how to do them?'

'Can do.'

'Mr. Gonzales, would you give the inoculation?'

'Sí.'

'Volunteers?'

Little by little, everyone stood, and soon all were giving and being given the inoculations. Maria was pleased. It was a start.

Chapter 62

Neilly, Jago, and Doctor Dakine stood together near the runway at Larandia as the Globe Master III settled on the runway and taxied to the hangar. The door opened, and the steps were lowered. Jim appeared in the door, wearing solid olive drab army fatigues, and walked down and over to Neilly. Following close behind him were Brush, Marilyn, Glenda Rose, Aleski, Jeff, Cherry, Lobo, and Chico.

Neilly exhaled. 'Shit, Jim. What am I going to say to Jenny and his three kids? We've been together for ten years, both as friends and running this team together.'

'I'm sorry. It was bad luck. It shouldn't have happened.'

'Yeah, luck. We all survive with luck and die without it. It's a rule we live with, isn't it? Smaller transport will arrive in a few minutes. Let's get him loaded and on his way home. Aleski and Jeff will accompany him back. With Fleur and Doctor Dakine here, we can spare Jeff. I want the two team members who were on the operation to be there for Jenny. Maybe it will make it seem worthwhile if she wants details. Jeff knows her well and is good with his kids. I should be the one to tell her in person.' He looked at the ground. 'I'll have to talk to her later.'

A small jet approached the field, touched down, and taxied over to them. 'Let's get him on the plane.' They opened the cargo door. Lobo took one end of the body bag and Brush the other. They carefully placed Gaston's body in the cargo hold. Jeff walked up the steps, followed by Aleski, cradling his sniper rifle. They both turned, gave a quick salute, and pulled up the steps.

'Why they put him down there, not inside?' asked Chico.

'It's a long journey home. High up in the air, the cargo hold will stay cold,' said Jago.

***

General Mancuso sat in the presidential jet en route to Miami. *This will be my plane now,* he thought as he smiled. *I will fly many times to North America to visit my investments.*

After General Crystal gave her no choice, Eileen easily persuaded Mancuso to agree to a meeting to discuss plans after Ramos' and Noboa's deaths. The meeting would delay his takeover of the government by only a few days. He smiled again. He would see his latest investment project, a condominium hotel named after, and managed by, a famous American. With such men, it was not hard to invest drug cash.

The jet landed and taxied to a private area. He was pleased to see that, with his new position, the government had sent many people to welcome him. They had not done so before. He stepped off the plane and saluted the group below. Along the side of the steps were several men dressed in expensive dark suits and sunglasses. They escorted him a few feet from the steps.

'General Juan Mancuso, you're under arrest. Place your hands behind your back.'

He tried to turn back to the plane but was held and handcuffed.

'I have diplomatic immunity…,' he pleaded.

'What you have is the right to remain silent. That means shut up,' said one of the men in dark glasses. Three black Suburbans pulled up, and he was none too gently pushed into the back seat of one. An FBI agent sat on each side. They pulled a short distance away, and took him out, and turned him over to a different group of armed men who loaded him onto a small turboprop plane.

'Where do you take me?'

'A man leaned close, hooked Mancuso's cuffs to the sides of a steel chair, and said, 'A very famous island hotel that will be your new home.' The man nodded, signaling another man to place a black cloth bag over Mancuso's head. Then, his feet were secured.

Someone held his head as a needle first pricked and then pushed into his neck, injecting a strong sedative. *They're going to torture and kill me. His last thoughts* as he drifted off.

***

Oversized blue-white lace snowflakes shifted from side to side as they softly settled into the canyon. Yesterday, the weather had turned the ranch into a crystalline forest. Pedro, Shuskin, and Heather stood looking at the glass apples on the old homesteader's tree.

'Where they come from, Mama?'

'Beautiful, aren't they? Do you remember that we left old apples on the tree?

'They had wormholes.'

'Yes.'

'We talked about the mule deer eating them as they fell off. Some of them refuse to drop to the ground. They get old and soft, and when we have a freezing rain like we did yesterday, they become coated with ice. In the cold, the apples turn mushy, and slip away, leaving only the delicate ice covering that we call glass or ghost apples. It's very rare.'

Shuskin reached up to one and touched it gingerly. The touch caused it to shatter.

'You broke it, Grankin.'

'There are more, Pedro. They will soon disappear. He just wanted to feel how fragile they are.'

'Lift me up, so I can feel one.'

'You, señor, are getting very heavy for me. Just for a few seconds.'

Pedro looked closely as the refracted light shimmered from the surface. He reached up to touch it. Before his finger got to the crystalline surface, it fell, disconnected from its tenuous holding.

'Uh-oh. It's gone.'

'We are lucky to see them. You have them in your mind. You can see them whenever you wish. I don't think your father has ever seen one. You will have to tell him about them.'

'Dad missed his birthday and didn't see our surprise.'

'Truthfully, I can't remember when he was ever here for his birthday. Good thing he doesn't put much stock in them.'

'He put sock in Christmas,' wondering exactly what it was he was saying.

'Stock not your Christmas sock, my little...' She stopped and corrected herself. 'Yes, my big boy. He promised he would be back for Christmas. Maybe there will be more glass apples.'

***

Pedro sat inside the big barn, his back against a large stack of bales, on a bed of loose straw, remembering the glass apples. He had been fascinated by the shiny, cool, prisms of light. Mama had been right. They were in his mind; he could still see them. *Was it the same as having one to keep to look at again and again?* Heather had explained to him that was what memories were. *Maybe it is true. I close my eyes. I will always have them.*

Rosie moved her big coarse-coated head onto his lap. Pedro stroked her neck. She rolled her head and looked at him with amber-brown eyes. Then, he reached past her front leg and petted the curled-up Agatha. She rarely left Rosie's side. They slept together and, when they were outside, the cat walked underneath her huge body. Agatha would not leave the barn without her companion.

The cat was lucky to be alive. She had lived for two years in the wild until one day Jim had heard her meow at the main gate. She was emaciated; patches of hair were missing. Somehow, she had survived the coyotes, and the ravages of parasites, eagles, and owls.

Jim had always wondered why she had meowed that day. Was it that she had had enough of living free? Or something inside her had told her she was at the end and would not survive much longer.

Agatha purred softly. 'You can remember things in your mind, too. Outside was bad for you. Inside with Rosie, you are safe.'

It was an odd sight watching the cat, nearly the same tawny color as Rosie, walk, staying just out of the way of the Irish Wolfhound's feet. Rosie's large body shielded her from the winged dangers from above. There were no worries for Agatha with Rosie, as coyotes gave the Irish Wolfhound a wide berth. One look, and it was obvious to anyone that Rosie understood the relationship with Agatha, and willingly accepted her role as companion and guardian.

As Rosie's head lulled on his lap, Pedro was happy; he felt as safe as Agatha did. *Tomorrow will be fun*, he giggled. Heather had promised that they could go riding with Roy in Pipestone Canyon. She had said it was too slippery for the horses in the hilly upper ranch.

'As we walk down to meet Roy, we'll see if we can spot the cougar that Ben said he saw in the canyon.'

'Is it a big one that will try to eat us?'

'No, sweetheart. Cougars don't eat people. There are very few incidents documented over the last hundred years of cougars' bothering people. It's a myth born out of fear and ignorance. They eat deer and other small game.'

'It eat my baby llama?' Pedro asked with worry in his voice. 'What incidents mean?' He was starting to add more than one question in a string like his adopted mother was known to do.

'It means something that happened in the past, or in this case, didn't happen.'

'I no understand.'

'It just means that the cougars have never bothered the llamas.'

'But you always worried when we go to the mountains about them.'

'We still have to be prudent.'

'Pruent.'

'With a 'D', Pru…D…ent. It means to be careful. Maybe it would be fun for us to camp in the barn tonight. But you have to be careful not to handle the llama baby too much. It is not good if they imprint on you during their first few days.'

'Daddy said the same thing. I be careful,' while he wondered what it meant to imprint. Then, Pedro looked at Heather proudly and said, with a slight pause between each word, 'I… will… be… prudent.'

****

'Colonel, I want to stay here and help with the vaccinations,' said Maria.

'If that's what you want, I have no objection. If there's a HazMat emergency, we can fly you from here, if need be. How long do you think?'

'I don't know. As long as it takes. I expect several months to chase everyone down. WHO will be more concerned with the total population, and I want to pay special attention to the FARC.'

'What about your affairs at home?'

'I have a couple of friends and my PA, so I think they can manage for a while.'

'Fine with me. Let Sheilla know whether you need anything, and we'll do what we can. I think our FARC friends will benefit. Tomorrow is my flight back to the ranch.'

'Just in time for Christmas. Heather will appreciate that. Not to mention Pedro.'

Jim captured her eyes and held them for several seconds before saying, 'We've known each other a long time. You did a great job here. We're lucky to have you.'

'It's now my home away from home,' she said laughing as she put her arms around Jim and hugged him.

'I'm thinking about taking Pedro and Heather on a holiday in a month or so, to visit the Amazon. We'll stop by here, make it a fuel stop, and we can see how you are coming along. I'd like Pedro and Heather to meet Jago and the others.'

'I imagine that I'll still be here, boss. If you need a doc along, let me know. It will be great to see her and Pedro. I'd like to get to know him better. And if you decided it was okay, I really would love to see the Amazon and spending the time there with Heather would be great.'

****

Jago trotted up to Jim. 'I need your help, amigo.'

Jim nodded, wondering why Jago would be in such a hurry. He had never seen him this way.

'I have no way to get forty kilometers southwest. Our men are under attack. Your helicopters could get us there?'

'Who is attacking?'

'A cartel and perhaps others.'

Jim needed to be sure who they would be fighting. He could not risk fighting troops that had been sanctioned by the Ecuadoran government.

Jago sensed his reluctance and perhaps the reasons. 'There are no government troops, but perhaps maybe people from your CIA.'

Jim held up his finger as he dialed the general. 'Jago says the CIA and cartel are attacking his men.'

'I'll call you back,' said General Crystal.

Jim disconnected and made a decision. He called Marilyn. 'Get the birds ready. We may have a mission in a few minutes.' Then he called Sheilla.

Jago nodded. 'Thank you, my friend. We must hurry.'

***

Sheilla and Martin were sitting in the small cafeteria drinking coffee, both lost in their new-found attraction for each other and wondering where it would lead. All the while realizing they hardly knew each other. Sheilla remembered that Martin had been tortured by Najma in Mexico. They had talked professionally on the phone for the past year with neither once thinking more than that the other had an attractive voice.

Sheilla's phone buzzed. She sat up a little straighter, tensing, and flicked her dark red hair back. 'Yes, Colonel. Immediately. He's still here. I'll call you back.'

'That sounds ominous,' said Martin.

'Let's go.' She then called Mark as they walked and gave him a list of the people she wanted in the mission room. 'Jago has just asked Jim to help him. His men are being attacked, possibly by CIA personnel teamed up with cartel members.'

'Buggers. Eileen's rogue operatives? It couldn't be Eileen herself. She is locked down tight. Colonel Johnson has talked to the general and Bertrand, I presume?'

'He mentioned the General Crystal, no one else. He needs information. Whatever we can provide from satellite. The drones are too far away,' she said as they opened the door to the mission control room. Sheilla saw Fred walking toward them. No one else was inside the room yet.

***

'General Mancuso has been arrested in the United States,' said Angélica, which caused Colonel Sanchez to freeze.

After a minute, he said, 'I have always been your father's friend and, if you will allow me, I'll be yours.'

It was true that Sanchez had always seemed to be loyal to her father and their family. He was in charge of their protection detail and, on more than one occasion, had saved members of her family. Angélica thought she could trust him. She desperately needed him.

'What is your relationship to General Mancuso?'

'Why do you ask?' sounding apprehensive. He was aware of Angélica's father's having some involvement with Mancuso, and while he had a long history with Angélica since her childhood, he didn't know for certain where she stood.

'I arranged for his arrest in the United States.'

'I see.' His face hardened, 'I am disgusted by people like Mancuso and what he does to our people.'

'My father was being paid by him.'

'I suspected that perhaps he was. It was not my business.'

Angélica shook her head, still finding it hard to believe.

Sanchez continued, 'Your father was intelligent, but not smart in the ways of people such as Mancuso. Mancuso was for himself, not the people of Ecuador, and he is greedy. Your father was far from perfect.

However, he did do many good things. I think he was not greedy or bad, but it is hard to believe that he took money.'

'I have to decide who to trust.' They stood silent for several seconds, waiting. Each trying to decide if they could trust the other.

Then, when she said nothing. 'There are some you can trust, señorita.'

'Tell me then, who are our enemies, and who are our friends?'

Colonel Sanchez had always liked Angélica. He was now pleased that, by her using *our* that she had chosen to trust him. He spent nearly an hour outlining what he knew, and what he thought he knew, about the politicians and the military.

'Do you think there will be a power grab within the government?' asked Angélica, using this as a final test of his loyalty and knowledge.

'There was talk of a coup before your father died. Many will become bold with your father dead. Mancuso was feared and hated. His officers are the same. Sí, they will try to grab power. Zambrano is to be watched.'

'I have never liked him.'

'With good reason, señorita Noboa. He became head of the security forces not because he was liked. He is very effective, and I fear could be even more ruthless than General Mancuso. An enemy not to be taken lightly.'

'We have a job to do then.'

Chapter 63

J im didn't have the information he required to charge into a fight, no matter how much he liked Jago. He trusted him in many ways, but in this case, he didn't understand what was going on, or why. *You know the why, Arthur Conan Doyle,* he said to himself. Whenever there was a mystery that seemed unsolvable, Sherlock Holmes entered his thoughts. He needed to know who the enemy was.

'We go, my friend?' asked Jago.

Jim decided to back his new friend, at least for the moment. They would head toward Jago's men and whoever was attacking them. Before they arrived, Sheilla or the general would provide the information he needed to commit, or not.

Jim trotted along with Jago toward the two helicopters. Marilyn was in one, getting it ready.

'I will fly the other, no?' said Jago.

'No,' said Jim. 'We need you focused on your men, not on flying.'

Jago's men and women stood a few meters away, waiting for his orders.

Jim answered his phone.

'No satellite for several minutes, and the one drone is at least two hours away,' said Sheilla. 'We're trying to find out anything we can, communication intercepts. I'll call as soon as we have something.'

'Try to make it in the next thirty minutes,' Jim said as he

disconnected.

'Thoughts on this?' said Neilly who had walked up behind Jim.

'Fate and luck,' answered Jim.

'Good plan. So, we get in the air and, with a little luck, someone will call us with what we need to know before we arrive.'

'I like the way you think Neilly.' Jim looked at Jago, pointed at the helicopter that Brush was walking toward, and twirled his finger.

***

They were headed into another mission, if you could call it that, with no planning. Sheilla needed to get them information. Everyone was working on trying to find out anything they could, but they were all coming up empty. She needed to think, and went to her office where she sat twirling, her long dark red hair lifting slightly from her shoulders while her body spun. Her brain cells churned; neurons came up empty. There was nothing to do but look for the impossible. Time was short. She had given up, lost in herself, when her phone rang.

'Sheilla, we might have something,' said Misa. 'It's not much.'

Sheilla sat up straighter in her chair.

'Vidya got this from the agency's phone call monitoring archives. Someone named Fernando said that they were going to take advantage of the situation and solidify their control with the cartel. He said there is only a small rebel contingent at the distribution center. They are going in, and have enough men to take it easily.'

'It is something, Misa.'

'This was routed to Director Skinner. No record of her contacting them back.'

'Anything is helpful. How many men?'

'A good question. We'll keep digging.'

'Thanks.'

Sheilla knew she only had a few minutes to call Colonel Johnson. Sometimes in this job, a few minutes could seem like hours. She dialed General Crystal.

He answered on the first ring.

'General, a message to Eileen Skinner. A man called Fernando said they had not heard from her and that they were going to take advantage of Ramos' death to take a distribution center from the FARC. They said they did not need many men as it wasn't heavily guarded. I have to let the colonel know ASAP.'

'He's on the ground. He decides. Give him whatever support you can. We are going to try to contact Eileen's CIA operatives and call them off, but it is probably too late.' When time was short, Sheilla really appreciated his abrupt manner.

She quickly dialed the colonel and passed on what they had found out, and that the general said it was his decision. After she hung up, she thought for minute. *Why should we be interested in this? They could fight over their drugs. We're not there for this.*

***

'Bring her in,' said General Crystal.

'Sit, Eileen.' He motioned with his hand to one of the chairs facing his desk.

'Thank you, Director.'

The general rolled her greeting through his brain, wondering if there was anything behind her calling him Director, rather than General Crystal. Seconds later, he decided that she was making an attempt to show her respect to him as the head of the agency, her agency.

The general, as usual, came straight to the point.

Eileen noted that there was no coffee offered, which she would have dearly liked.

'Why are your Colombian operatives attacking a FARC drug distribution center with the help of a local cartel? Have you had contact with them?'

'No, sir. I'm incommunicado. No way of talking to anyone.'

The general was certain that was the case but wanted to ask as she might have found a way to communicate. She gave no sign she was lying. In addition, the BWC's message intercept, or rather the hacking of the CIA's computers, supported her answer.

'I suppose the answer is pretty obvious. The army and the FARC have had more power over drugs than anyone. With Ramos out of the way and the possibility of the FARC either weakened or cutting a deal with the government, it probably seemed like an opportune time to take advantage of the situation. Strengthen our control.'

That answer paralleled his thoughts and was further supported by Mancuso's being out of the picture. He was not about to give Eileen any extra information, and he was pleased she had not referenced Mancuso's arrest. She gave no indication that that information had gotten to her. He was starting to feel comfortable with her cooperation.

'Thank you.' He hit the intercom button and was about to ask that she be returned. Instead, he said, 'Two coffees?'

'Thank you, sir. Before I leave… You know, of course, that I recognize where I went off the reservation,' she said, using the cliché for screwing around outside her mandate. 'I say again. I love this agency. If you believe nothing else, please believe that,' she said with eyes welling toward tears, but not producing any. 'What are your plans for me?' She took a sip of coffee, peering over the top at the general.

'Unknown at this point.'

Shit, she thought. *He's a hardass. Also, a straight shooter. I'm royally fucked. No more than I deserve.* She finished her coffee, nodded slightly, and rose.

'Thank you for the coffee. Good day, sir.'

***

Angélica sat passively in an office, waiting. Everything was in motion. It would not be long before the result, or the consequences, of their plan would be determined. The weak link was needing many of the army personnel on their side to arrest those that they presumed would be against them. If they selected just one wrong person, or word was passed back to the opposition, they would lose. If they did, she could soon be dead or in prison.

Her thoughts roamed from her father to the Shuar, and once or twice to Colonel Johnson. Previously, she could not come to terms about who he was. A mixture of protector, tactician, and killer. After being rescued twice, going into a battle with him, hearing he had executed the red-haired Canadian miner and, in so doing, saved a young woman—her opinion was no longer confused. *I am accepting some of those traits in myself. I do not think I am the ruthless sort… I see now where sometimes one has to protect those in need.* Nice people were often weak in their resistance to tyrants. Perhaps, they could not understand how others could be evil.

Thinking kept her from dwelling on her fate. It would either be a new beginning or an end. *We overlay our understanding of the world and expect that others can be reasoned with, as we would have them reason with us. I have learned that is not so. Each must be treated in their own way. Mancuso one way. The Shuar another.* Soon Zambrano would either be standing in front of her in handcuffs, or he would be pointing a gun at her.

Angélica Noboa Perez had become not only a woman, but a woman of purpose, with a growing understanding of people and politics. *I accept my fate,* she concluded.

***

Jim clicked his mic and asked if Jago could hear him.

'Sí, very well.'

'What is the current situation with your men on the ground?'

'Nada. I have heard nothing.'

'Tell me what you know. How many attackers, how many defenders, their positions, everything.'

'We had twenty people, possibly. Half were guards and the other half merchandise processing workers. Most of the guards were killed. A well-planned attack, I think. There were only four guards left when I received the call for help. I heard nothing about the attackers. I do not know how many, or their positions, or if they have taken over.'

'Are there any signals you use with your men?'

'No.'

Jim looked at Neilly and frowned.

***

'Look in that tree.' Heather pointed to a large Aspen near the creek, 200 feet from where they were standing.

'It's the big owl,' said Pedro.

'It is a special one, a great horned owl. It's nice to see it. We usually only hear it in the evening.'

'I remember.'

'I can't see horns. Are they small?'

'They are feathers and yes, they are small. The tufts of feathers resemble horns.'

'Will we see the cougar?'

'Maybe, but the aspen trees are too small for them. We have to look in the rocks or the big ponderosa pines. Ones with large low branches. Keep searching. When we come back after riding, we could walk on the old road on the other side of the aspen grove. More pine trees on that side. No, that is too dangerous.'

'Why are there more pine trees on that side? Why dangerous?'

'Can you think of a reason there are more pine trees on that side?'

'The pine trees grow on the north side of the ridge. It is not so hot.'

'You are becoming very knowledgeable, young man.'

Pedro beamed. 'Why dangerous? Cougars won't harm us.'

'Do you have any ideas why I said that?'

Pedro thought for several seconds and then said, 'We are being prudent.'

'Excellent. That is very, very, good. I am proud of you.'

Heather looked at her watch.

'We need to walk a little faster. I don't want to make Roy wait. He wants me to ride Dawn.'

'That's Daddy's horse.'

'Roy said she needs to be ridden. Your father has not ridden her for over a month. Roy is going to ride her sister, QT.'

'She is a loco horse.'

'She is a handful and quite skittish. Roy is a very good rider. I think he sometimes likes a challenge.'

'Maybe she become my horse. He teach me.'

'I don't think she is a good horse for you. Your horse, Miss Blacky, is very good.'

'I like her. But she is very small. I want a big horse like Chief.'

'Chief is way too big for most of us. He is a nice boy, though.'

The road curved to the left. They crossed the small wooden bridge over the creek and passed another old homesteader's apple tree. There were no glass apples as it was too warm. Heather looked up the creek to where their secret meadow was hidden. Wistfully, she thought that maybe she and Jim could go there for the picnic she had wanted earlier in the year. I miss him, and I miss the way we once were. She bit her lip. We will be again. I will make it so.

As he opens up to me about who he is and what he does, we are getting to a better place. *I love that man. Now we have a different life, full of wonderful people: Pedro, Lola, Shuskin, Ben, and Roy.*

Happy in her thoughts, Heather undid the chain at the main gate. They walked out onto Beaver Creek Road and down to their right, and then left down Balky Hill Road, crossing the larger Beaver Creek. As they neared the driveway to the lower ranch house, they could see Roy, standing with the horses, outside the barn at the end of the drive. Pedro waved.

We'll all be together soon, she thought, as she watched Pedro run ahead to Roy and the horses.

***

The main entry gate to Wolf Canyon Ranch was in a cut at the base of Wolf Canyon. It had been carved over hundreds of years by a small above ground stream that went dry in the heat of summer. A well that could endlessly pump 200 gallons per minute provided an indication of the underground river's volume. Besides supplying all the ranch water, it supplied water to a grove of giant cottonwoods and the largest aspen grove in the Pacific Northwest. It was a grove that meandered down the canyon for well over a mile. There, the water apparently pooled in underground lakes, allowing the giant cottonwoods to grow. The huge trees were an uncommon sight in similar mountain canyons.

The land rose on both sides of the main gate. To one side were sandhills, laid down ages ago as a river cut the valley floor. On the opposite side, the more easterly slope and exposed to the west sun, were treeless hills covered with rabbit brush and sagebrush.

The steep areas above the sandhills were rarely visited by Heather, Jim, or any of the ranch people. Even the cows did not venture there as there was more grass on the sunny eastern side. It was the perfect choice to observe the ranch road and Balky Hill Road where Heather and Pedro were walking. Heather looked up, thinking one day she would see what it was like to be perched up there.

***

'Ghost, stay out of sight and hearing until I do a high flyover.'

'Watch it. Never know what exotic weapons the spooks might have,' replied Brush seriously.

Jim had Marilyn take their chopper up to 2,000 feet. It was late afternoon, and the sun rippled across the green trees below.

'Fly a straight-line northeast to southwest, half a klick out.'

Jim hoped that flying on the side and straight might keep whoever was on the ground from being concerned about them. Just another helicopter, buried in the afternoon sun, on its way to somewhere.

'If there was a fight, we missed it,' said Neilly.

'Smoldering car on the road and a heavy machine gun on a jeep in the ditch. I can see several vehicles parked inside,' observed Jim.

'Whoever was inside put up a fight.'

'I count three bodies on the road and another four inside the fenced area,' said Jim.

'I can now count seven armed men inside the gate,' Neilly said, looking through binoculars. 'I assume they are the raiders.'

'Whippet,' said Jim, Jago's call sign, after he switched his radio from intercom to their comm frequency. 'We do not see any hostages.'

'When they call me, they say there only four left, and they were under heavy machine gun fire. I think maybe it is too late.'

'Ghost, there is a small knoll about a klick northeast. Fast drop Gopher on the knoll, then insert Whippet east of the compound. We'll insert on the other side up the road and have them occupied while you are making your drops.'

'Roger that,' said Brush.

Jim scanned the area and then directed Marilyn. 'Set us down on the road just past that large palm, and then move back into the sun. Watch the heavy auto on the vehicle inside. We don't want to walk home.'

Marilyn first flew west and then came in toward the drop, with the sun behind her. Then she flew just over treetops to the insertion point, hovering just above the ground for no more than ten seconds before turning and heading into the sun.

***

Heather led, with Pedro in the middle, and Roy following. As Pedro's instructor, he wanted to watch how his young pupil was handling himself. Roy was happy anytime he was on horseback. Even happier than Pedro.

They went across Balky Hill Road, the horse's steel shoes slipping on the hard-packed patches of snow and ice. They rode across a field toward Pipestone Canyon. Heather liked riding on days like today. It was more an excuse to be out in nature than just for the love of riding like it was for Roy. As they approached the steep-sided canyon, she paid no attention to anything other than the beauty of the black basalt rocks, shiny with ice and icicles, kept cool in the shade of the canyon.

Meltwater dripped from the pointy tips of the icicles in a soft melody. The bottom of Pipestone Canyon meandered, curving this way and that between its steep sides on a narrow flat floor of snow-covered dirt.

In the summer it was home to one of the largest families of rattlesnakes in the Methow Valley. Heather visualized the lethargic snakes in their dens, just feet below where their horses clumped through the shallow snow. Hundreds of snakes intertwined, nearly motionless from the cold. As the weather turned warm, they would slither in all directions, never ranging very far from their den. Only once did she see a rattlesnake on the other side of Balky Hill Road. She had never seen a serpent on the other side of Beaver Creek Road or on the upper ranch.

What had taken them minutes to ride was an impossibly long journey to the snakes. There were plenty of field mice and the occasional bird for them to dine on, and sunshine to bask in. As is the way of the natural hierarchy, they were occasionally plucked from their sunny rock perches by an eagle, owl, or hawk. Heather had observed the birds of prey dropping the snakes to their death onto the rocks. Dead, they posed no danger while the birds ate their fill. It seemed a smart thing to do.

She had seen it many times. When she told the story to friends or anyone that would listen, she concluded that either she had a vivid imagination or that no one else in the west had seen what she had. Of course, she knew what she had observed to be true. It wasn't her imagination, and eventually she would hear confirmation from someone who had observed the same thing.

Like Jim, Heather loved the canyon. Their favorite llama was, after all, named after it. The baby llama, when christened, was not, however, named after the color that she now observed: the white snow, the dark rocks sometimes rusty red, even though they were the colors of his wooly coat. Jim had named the baby Pipestone because he had felt the same affinity for him that he felt for the canyon.

As they disappeared into the shadowed canyon, Heather's phone would have chirped if it could have received a signal. Jim called to tell her they were getting ready to leave, and he would soon be there.

They rode further into the canyon, the curved walls blocking the entrance and exit, and it became a tunnel capped by a narrow band of cerulean sky. Eyes followed their entrance into the canyon. Eyes focused only on their prey, sitting motionlessly watching the unconcerned riders. The prey, oblivious to the killer's presence, lived contentedly in the moment and without knowledge that a strike was imminent; the riders immersed in winter's beauty—mother, child, and faithful friend.

***

Jim on one side of the road and Neilly on the other, moved rapidly toward the compound's gate. On the opposite side, Jago and his group moved as fast as they could toward the flimsy barb wire that ineffectively fenced the other edge of the drug distribution center. It might keep a stray cow out, but mostly the fence defined a boundary. Jago and Lobo easily stepped over the loose wire, while a diminutive young new member of their guerrilla unit ducked under the spikey wire. *Carlos was gone, and now we rotate another little one into our band,* thought Cherry as she watched him catch his shirt on the wire. She shook her head, stepped towards him, and freed him. Then, she adeptly pushed the wire down with her hand, held it on the ground with her boot, and stepped over it into the compound.

Just as they entered, gunfire erupted on the other side. A dozen men moved toward the western side and opened fire on Jim and Neilly. 'Crusader,' Marilyn's call sign, 'a little cover fire, if you please.' The Huey drifted over the compound's entrance, and the novice door gunner strafed the area, causing the combined CIA and cartel to dive for cover.

Jim and Neilly advanced several yards and dropped to the ground. Marilyn backed off into the sun.

'Ghost, move in to cover Whippet. Let's show them more of what we have, and see if they want to give it up.'

Marilyn's door gunner had killed three of the men. The nine left took the opportunity to resume firing up the road. Both Neilly and Jim, however, were safely in the shallow ditch along the side of the road. A moment later, Jago moved up behind the cartel and the CIA. Jago fired just above their heads, while Brush moved overhead a hundred yards above and behind them. Glenda decided she liked being a door gunner and was hoping to be able to let loose more rounds. While the raiders were firing toward the road, they had not heard either Jago or the helicopter approach. They turned toward Jago. The CIA men immediately recognized they were in a trap and outnumbered, not to mention covered by two helicopters.

One of the cartel men foolishly raised his rifle. The young man, with more bravado than sense, was unable to bring his rifle level before Cherry fired a short burst into his chest. Before he fell to the ground, his head exploded courtesy of Gopher.

'I advise you to put down your weapons,' said Colonel Johnson who was now standing at the back of the eight men who, in the sudden silence, could hear Marilyn approaching. With men on both sides, two helicopters supporting, and at least one sniper in the hills, even the cartel realized it was time to surrender, or die. They still hesitated until the CIA, in unison, laid their weapons down. The cartel men, not necessarily by reason, but more from herd instinct, also laid their weapons on the ground.

While Jago's small band covered them, the SF quickly separated the CIA from the cartel. Jim watched Jago, wondering if, in anger, he might exact revenge by killing the cartel. He didn't. This was different from killing General Ramos. There he had a purpose. Jim's admiration grew another notch. Jago was skilled and experienced. He controlled his temper. He was growing old and staying alive because he used good judgment. Emotions did not cloud the tall, droopy mustached leader's actions.

Brush settled his helicopter inside the compound, causing a minor dust storm, while Marilyn set her helicopter down on the road outside the main gate. The engagement had lasted no more than ten minutes. Jago, Cherry, Carlos, Lobo and six others searched the compound.

They found only the dead bodies of their compatriots.

One of the Americans turned toward Neilly. 'We're on the same side, you know.'

'Do I?'

'You're American military,' said as a statement, not a question.

'You, my friend, are a spook, which means we are not on the same side of anything.'

'Call this number,' said the man who was the leader.

Neilly handed the card with the number to Jim who dialed the general and gave him the number. A few seconds later, Will Crystal called back, 'Eileen's group.'

Jim looked at the man. 'Guess that means that I shoot them, General?'

'Much of what they deserve; secure them and bring them back.'

Jim smiled at the man and said, 'Your orders, General.'

Colonel Johnson motioned with his MP5 to the man and the other CIA men to move toward the center of the compound.

'You can't just shoot us.'

'Why not?' asked Neilly as he leveled his rifle and said, 'Move it.'

The man still protested, 'We're all American. On the same team, aren't we?'

'Doesn't seem to be the case for either you or your ex-boss, DDO Skinner.'

The man stopped and looked back with a blank expression. 'What are you going to do?'

No one answered his question as they were ushered into Brush's helicopter. Neilly and JP followed them in. Lobo marched the cartel men down the road and told them, if they were wise, they would keep walking toward the sunset.

As Jim climbed into Marilyn's helicopter, he turned and looked toward Jago. Neither waved nor made any motion. But, the two men had arrived at an understanding, as battle compatriots often do; they had become friends who would remain so, in each other's thoughts, even though they might never see each other again.

I think now we can go home for Christmas, Jim thought to himself.

'It turned out to be an interesting vacation,' said Neilly on the radio. 'If only,' then he stopped. Neilly's way of dealing with the death was not saying the XO's name. By doing so, it would only make it more real. *I liked Gaston too,* Jim said to himself. Jim and Neilly were alike in so many ways that Jim was surprised when they didn't see things the same way. Jim, the ultra-realist, faced what he found to be the truth head-on. Neilly was still struggling to find reasons for his friend's death.

*****

'Nusmen, are you pouting?' asked Sheilla.

'Just thinking.'

'It's a hangdog look if I ever saw one,' said Martin.

'Who are you? Oh yeah. The CIA guy,' said Nusmen.

Barbara walked up and gave Nusmen a sympathetic look.

'He's down about his phage experiment. It didn't work.'

'It'll work. I just need to think. Why are you all looking at me like that?'

'Like what?' asked Sheilla.

'Like I need sympathy, or something.'

'It's your face, Nusmen. I'm glad to be able to see it again before I leave,' said Martin.

Sheilla frowned, 'Martin heads back to D.C. on the red-eye tonight.'

'I'm sure I'll be back soon,' said Martin, turning toward Sheilla. Then he returned his gaze to Nusmen's face.

'He's going to get it removed with a laser,' said Barbara.

Nusmen's mouth drooped a little as he looked at Barbara.

'I don't have time. I changed my mind.'

'You're going to leave them?' asked Sheilla.

'Until I can go back to my friend in the Amazon. He'll know what to do.'

Nusmen barely finished the sentence before he returned to his *I'm thinking* look.

'Okay. All right, Nus. We'll leave you to your thoughts.' Then Sheilla looked at Martin.

'Do you want to go for a walk? I heard the weather is nice outside.'

Barbara looked first at Sheilla, in astonishment, and then at Martin. *Sheilla hardly ever ventures outside,* she thought. Then that part of her that was a woman, not the director of the lab, hit her full force.

'I'll leave you two then. Enjoy your walk.'

She watched them head toward the elevator that would take them from the underground into the light. 'Love roars in when we least expect it,' she said softly.

'What'd you say,' asked Nusmen.

'Never mind. Let's get to our duties.' She started down the hall and then turned back. 'You've got other things to do, Mr. Co-Director, besides fretting over your phages.'

***

The morning light streaked across the FARC camp as half of a golden ball loomed large on the horizon. The warmth started to creep into Jim's skin. He had lots to do before leaving for home. Soon, he would feel the warmth of Heather and the heat from a blazing log fire at their ranch. *I'll gladly swap the tropic weather for home,* he thought.

He spotted Maria Dakine walking toward a large tent. She disappeared inside as he walked the dirt path toward the tent to say goodbye. A generator hummed not far away. Inside the tent, the doctor talked to several men and women. They started to open boxes, distributing their contents into shoulder bags with WHO emblazoned on the outside. As he walked over to her, the group started to open refrigerators.

'Maria.'

'Hey, Jim. Did you get some sleep?'

'Enough.'

'I like it here. And I'm glad I am staying for a while, but home is where the heart is, isn't it?'

'Keep in contact. Advise me of your progress and anything you need. Sheilla is sending someone to coordinate with WHO outside the camp. WHO reluctantly agreed to stay off El Diamante. They'll work the villages. The FARC's medics will try to track down their members. They won't divulge their members to WHO.'

'Suits me. I have my hands full here without dealing with WHO's bureaucracy. They're good, but just not a family like us.'

She turned and looked at the group who stood waiting for her orders.

'Everyone, you know where to start today. Vamos! I'll be along in a minute.'

Jim looked at her and, as always, felt a warm spot for some of the truly special people he worked with. The job was important, but as time went on, the association with the general, Sheilla, Brush, Glenda, and Maria grew in importance.

'Take care, Doctor. See you here in a month, I hope.'

'Jim, wait. We'll send Mateo and his parents home in a few days. Horrible scars are starting to show on his face. He is understandably not very happy. His parents, though, are overjoyed. We told them much of the truth. They now realize what danger he and they were in. And how lucky he is to be alive.'

'Life will never be the same for him now,' said Jim.

'No, but still, I'm glad he survived. Safe flight, Colonel. Say hi to Heather for me. Oh, and one more thing: the Rojoz family is four again. The daughter that was married to Ramos' son is with them. They found her in the house after General Ramos was killed. The general's son, her new husband, is also dead.'

***

Wearing a green David Clarke headset, Jim listened intently. In the end, all he said was, 'Good news. Thank you, General.'

'What's the good news?' asked Glenda.

'It seems the once immature Angel has gone from wondering what life is all about to successfully purging a coup.'

'She's grown up since we found her, hasn't she? I liked her. I wish

I had had more time to talk to her,' said Glenda Rose. 'I think she will become a strong woman.'

'You'll probably have a chance to see her in Ecuador or D.C. Maybe call her. She would probably like to hear from you. She likely won't have much time to make new friends.'

'I might do that.'

Brush walked over and joined in.

'I'd guess she liked us,' said Brush. 'It would be hard not to have a special affinity after our escapades together. And I'm sure she respects the heck out of accomplished women after seeing you, my strawberry-headed beauty, and Marilyn and Cherry, too, eh?'

Glenda nodded, her eyes twinkling. 'And accomplished men. I think I noticed the way Angel looked at you, Colonel.' Then, she narrowed her eyes at Brush, thinking about Cherry. He just grinned at her until she puckered her lips and puffed him a kiss.

Jim stood for a second, thinking about Angel, the professor in Rio, and Maria. *Yes, all attractive and accomplished women.* Then his thoughts turned to Heather. He felt good inside. There had never been anyone else for him. He suddenly felt an overwhelming desire to return home.

'I'm definitely ready.' said Jim.

'Let's get our butts on the plane then,' said Brush. 'It's time to go home for Christmas.'

Chapter 64

Heather marveled at the contrasting beauty of the steep black wall, whose tufts of white snow crowned anything horizontal. A stunted pine tried to nourish itself, working roots through rock cracks as its small trunk curved upward, craving contact with the sun.

Suddenly, Heather made a fist and held it in the air. Something she had learned from Jim. She turned and put her finger to her lips. Then she pointed down the canyon and slightly to her right.

Pedro and Roy inched their horses forward until they could see the deer with her small fawn. Suddenly the neck of the doe stiffened and grew longer, and her head froze as she looked at the intruders. The horses stood uncharacteristically still. No one moved.

The mule deer must have reasoned they were not a threat as she, followed closely by her fawn, walked further down the canyon. She stopped and looked back. Then she pawed at the snow to expose the grasses beneath. She moved a few more feet, then nervously nibbled a bush, with her youngster imitating her.

'I've never seen a baby that small this time of year,' Roy whispered.

'Yeah, it's lucky to be alive. It doesn't look to be more than two months old,' said Heather.

'Must've been born in that bit of Indian summer we had in late October.'

As they watched the mother and her little charge, the mule deer's body stiffened. She sensed the cold eyes above. Her rear legs kicked the snow as she tried to push herself into a run. It was too late. The tan cat landed on her back and dug its claws in. She went down as the powerful mouth closed on her neck. The fawn sprinted a few feet away and then back toward her mother.

'Oh my God,' said Heather.

'Help it, Mama. Don't let it die.'

Heather could only shake her head.

Roy said, 'It's not our place to interfere even if we could.'

Pedro kicked his heels in to move to the rescue, but his horse wanted only to go away from the life and death scene, not toward it. Roy's horse, QT, was a nervous horse by nature. She was stamping her feet and trying to turn. Fortunately Pedro's horse, unwilling to go forward, and Roy's horse, moving sideways into Pedro's, allowed Roy to grab Blacky's reins.

Heather watched, stunned, as she tried to keep Dawn from bolting. Dawn reared and tried to turn. Heather held tight, not letting her have her way. Within seconds, the deer yielded to the cougar's superior strength. There was a mechanism they had all observed. They called it the fright factor. It was as if the prey's mind removed itself, became anesthetized, succumbing to its eventual death without further struggle. The fawn was still unsure what to do and jumped back and forth. It didn't know enough to run further from the predator. Fortunately for the fawn, the big tawny brown cat lifted the mother's neck clenched tight in her teeth, shoulder muscles rippling, and pulled the lifeless body a few feet closer to the canyon's wall. She had no interest in the fawn. She had a much larger meal to give her the energy she needed.

'What can we do, Mama?' asked Pedro with tears streaming down his cheeks.

'There is nothing.'

'Can't we take the fawn home?'

'No way to catch it.'

'It'll still be able to eat without its mama. Won't it?

'No, sweetie. It needs its mother to survive.'

'Please, Mama. Do something. Look, it is walking toward us.'

Heather looked at Roy.

'I can try. Maybe it will come close enough.'

'Try what?' asked Pedro.

'Roy is going to try to rope it. Don't get your hopes up, but because it is so narrow in here, the fawn might get close enough. Roy might be able to do it.'

'Please, Roy, please.'

'Stay quiet, so it won't be frightened.'

The small, late-born fawn stumbled on toward the riders.

'It's in shock,' said Heather.

The lasso that Roy always carried on his saddle went 'round and 'round as he spun it, waiting for just the right coincidence of events to occur between him, the rope's motion, and the target. Roping was an art, not a science. Intuition and long practice would tell him when to let the lasso fly.

Pedro watched transfixed as the lasso flew through the air. The fawn seemed to notice it coming closer and lifted its head. It was too dazed to move away. The rope, with luck, went over its head. One part landed on the baby's rump; the other slid down the fawn's front legs. The rope was stiff and intended for cows, not tiny fawns.

Roy quickly pulled it toward him. QT was skittish but had been well trained in a feed lot. She backed up as Roy squeezed her sides with both heels. The fawn jumped forward, and the back part of the lasso slipped completely over its rump. Heather bit her lip. The baby was going to walk out of it. *A perfect throw,* she thought. *A sad ending. It will starve or freeze to death.*

Roy knew before the rope slipped over the little fawn's rear what would happen. His only chance would be to pull it tight before it slipped to the ground. Partly because of the slow motions of the shocked fawn, and partly because of Roy's skill, the rope tightened around the fawn's legs. The youngster fell on to its side, with the rope holding all four legs.

Pedro jumped down from his horse. Without him, Miss Blacky turned and ran back out the canyon toward the safety of home.

'No. Pedro! The cougar. Stop. Please stop.'

The cougar lifted its head and tensed. Its snarl sent shivers down Heather's spine. Roy didn't want to drag the little deer, but he did a few feet, getting it further from the cougar and closer to Pedro, who raced to the fawn, and dropped down beside it.

Heather tossed her reins toward Roy, not knowing if he would catch them or not. She jumped to the ground and ran after Pedro. Roy secured the rope and managed to grab Heather's reins. The cougar snarled, tensed, and then went back to tearing at the warm flesh.

As small as it was, the fawn was too large for Pedro to carry. Heather put Pedro's hand on the fawn's shoulder as she nervously watched the cougar.

'It's a little boy. Hold him down while I loosen the rope. She then surrounded its legs with her arms and lifted the small fawn. She glanced toward the cougar.

The captive fawn lay still, and then it suddenly thrashed with its legs before going still again.

'Walk easy, no quick movements, back toward Roy,' she said.

As they approached, Roy lowered the 30-30 Winchester from his shoulder and put it back into the scabbard.

Heather looked up at Roy as if to say, I don't believe this.

'We were lucky,' said Roy.

'If it wasn't for the doe, we might have been dinner.'

'That's not what I just told Pedro on the way down.'

'Ain't no way to know now anyhow.'

Pedro kept rubbing the fawn's neck and head.

'Will it be okay, Mama?'

Heather lifted it to Roy. The fawn kicked weakly, with no real motivation. Heather walked around and took the reins from Roy as he pushed the tiny fawn inside his heavy coat.

They had entered the canyon as three horse riders, and left as two with Pedro sitting behind Heather. He never took his eyes off Roy and the small bundle under his coat.

'I don't believe you got your rope around that small of a target,

Roy.'

'It was lucky. All that can be said about it.'

'You teach me to rope?' asked Pedro.

'Sure, we can practice when it warms up. The fawn's settled down some.'

'Mama, where are we going to keep him?'

'We'll talk about it tomorrow, sweetie.'

'Now.' Then more softly, 'Now, please.'

'Roy, you okay with him for tonight?' She turned her head back toward Pedro, 'Roy will take good care of him, and we'll pick him up in the morning.'

'Mama, please.'

"It's too far to carry him, and it's too cold. We're going to try to spot that hoot owl again.'

Heather gave Roy a look that said, 'Don't you dare say you'll drive us tonight.' Then she said, 'You have enough to do with the fawn and taking care of the horses. You have to catch Miss Blacky.'

'She ain't no problem. She'll be standing by the barn, waiting to get her saddle off.'

Heather wanted to walk up in the twilight, then a shiver went through her body as she thought about the cougar. No one said anything more about it. They were all in shock that this could happen right in front of them. Heather desperately wanted to know how Pedro was accepting what he had witnessed. She was afraid to say anything. This is what children learned on a ranch or farm—death, breeding, and babies were a part of their everyday lives.

Pedro pushed it from his mind. It was complete denial. As the cougar brutally killed the doe, his mind flashed to scenes of the evil lady killing his family. It was too much for him to deal with. Too many parallels. He survived; the little boy deer survived. He didn't yet comprehend the difference; the cougar followed its natural course and needed to eat; Najma killed his family for pleasure. One day, he would understand.

'You should get a going up the road before it gets completely dark.'

'Good idea.'

Pedro's spirits were lifted by the thought of having the fawn to take care of. He didn't want to walk, though. He didn't like the night. It scared him.

'Thanks, Roy. We'll be fine. It's never dark with all this white stuff reflecting the stars. The moon will be up soon, too.'

Yes, thought Roy. *All true. Maybe if I can get everyone settled in, secure this little guy in the shower stall, and then trail along behind them. The night can be dangerous as we just saw.*

Heather put her arm around Pedro and nudged him. They both waved at Roy, walked down the drive to Balky Hill Road, turned right, gaining a few feet elevation as the road rose above Beaver Creek and met its namesake—Beaver Creek Road.

Heather felt comforted by the oversized sat phone in her rucksack. She had no way of knowing that she had missed one call from Jim just as they had entered Pipestone Canyon, and another just after his plane took off from Colombia. She knew he would not break his promise to be home soon.

After they had locked the main gate and walked past the large, scraggly, old homesteader's apple tree, she stopped before the wooden plank bridge and looked up the old road. There was only a hint that it had ever been a road. Bushes and branches intruded through the white snow swath. Only a few feet away was the Secret Meadow. She smiled, remembering the special times there and the less than joyous last visit when she had prepared the special picnic welcome for Jim.

Her expectations for that day months ago had been dashed. With their newfound understanding, she realized that she had been wrong to expect Jim, dead tired, after a mission, to feel the same way she did about their reunion. He needed rest and understanding. *I should have realized. Later, I could have had what I needed.*

A nearly full moon rose over her right shoulder. With the snow, the moon, and the Milky Way, it would be a spectacular walk.

A flashing memory of the cougar caused her to pull Pedro in close.

The trees rustled in a slight breeze. The cool night air settled as the sun-warmed air molecules slipped into the atmosphere. She felt a chill as a shadow passed. A slight crunch of snow.

Before she could turn, a voice said, 'Walk straight ahead.' Then she felt the tip of cold steel pressed against her neck.

Heather recognized the voice. Spasms uncontrollably consumed her body. Her body became weak and started to shake. Her mind went blank.

'Boy, walk with this woman who thinks she is your mother.'

Pedro gasped.

'Mama,' as he looked up at Heather.

'Shut up, boy. She is not your mama.'

'She is my,' but before he could say mama again, Najma back-handed him hard on his left ear.

Pedro started to cry.

'That's right, baby boy. Cry, one last time. You will soon learn to be a man and have no use for whimpering and crying. Move it, woman. I said walk. Up the unused road I saw from above.'

Heather wanted to say that with the crusty snow it would take hours to get home on that road. That small part of her rational mind stayed silent, as she shuffled forward in a state of shock, pushing her feet through the crust-topped snow of the unused road. Her muscles seemed not to exist. Her legs felt powerless. Nevertheless, she managed to move. Pedro's hand gripped the bottom of her coat. After twenty feet, her heart calmed a little as she saw the entrance to the secret glade.

'Move in there,' said the venomous voice from behind her. The knifepoint never left her neck. A trickle of warm blood, cooled by the night air, found her collar. Heather's momentary elation at seeing one of her favorite places on earth abruptly vanished. *Not here,* she said to herself as she realized what made it special: hers and Jim's secret hideaway. A place of love and happiness, not death.

'Lay down, woman.'

Heather dropped to her knees and hands.

'No, woman. On your back. You, boy. Move over there.' She

pointed a few feet away.

'Don't hurt him,' pleaded Heather.

Heather did as she was told. The serpent, the devil lady, straddled her with the knife pointed at her throat. Full of fear, Heather lost control of her bladder.

Najma saw the expanding wet area and smiled. The power she had to cause fear was one of the few things in life that brought her pleasure.

Pedro saw the tears running down his mother's cheeks. He lunged at Najma.

Calmly, barely looking, Najma said, 'He is brave, no?'

Pedro neared the woman, now sitting on his mother's chest. As if in slow motion, she again backhanded him, this time on his mouth just below his nose.

Pedro had never felt such pain. He stumbled backward and fell, hitting his head against an aspen tree. He lay there in a daze, eyes locked with his mother's, neither moving.

The small double-edged knife pressed forward. Pedro's eyes widened, and then he could bear no more: oxygen drained from his brain.

Heather started to scream, but no sound came out as the knife cut into her larynx.

Her eyes blurred. Her head fell to the side. In her mind she saw the watermelon snow. She smiled inside knowing, remembering. Jim had saved her again. Just as she knew he had always loved her, he had saved her. Then, her mind cleared, and her heart turned dark as she realized it was not her favorite pink algae tinted snow, her watermelon snow, but her blood snow.